Praise for
JOHN

"Dazzling."
Andrew M. Greeley

"Maxim knows how to pull his readers in."
Chicago Tribune

"No one does better characterization or
plotting than Maxim."
Linda Howard

"Maxim, who's been writing top-grade thrillers for
more than two decades, continues to be one
of the form's best-kept secrets."
Publishers Weekly

"Just [a] few pages are enough to establish
Maxim's credentials as a pro."
Los Angeles Times

Books by
John R. Maxim

Novels
PLATFORMS
ABEL BAKER CHARLEY
TIME OUT OF MIND
THE BANNERMAN SOLUTION
THE BANNERMAN EFFECT
BANNERMAN'S LAW
BANNERMAN'S PROMISE
(previously published as A MATTER OF HONOR)
THE SHADOW BOX
HAVEN
MOSAIC

Nonfiction
DARK STAR

JOHN R. MAXIM

WHISTLER'S ANGEL

AVON BOOKS

An Imprint of HarperCollinsPublishers

AVON BOOKS
An Imprint of HarperCollins*Publishers*
10 East 53rd Street
New York, New York 10022-5299

First Avon Books paperback printing: February 2002
First William Morrow hardcover printing: March 2001

Avon Trademark Reg. U.S. Pat. Off. and in Other Countries,
Marca Registrada, Hecho en U.S.A.
HarperCollins ® is a trademark of HarperCollins Publishers Inc.

Printed in the U.S.A.

10 9 8 7 6 5 4 3 2 1

For John Griffin and Phil Henry
and . . . always . . . for Christine

WHISTLER'S
ANGEL

1

A year ago, Whistler would not have imagined that he could get used to such a life. Living on a yacht. Island-hopping as he pleased. No problem more serious than the odd balky instrument. No threat more worrisome than approaching bad weather.

It would have seemed more like the waste of a life for a man only in his mid-thirties. And for him, in particular, it would have seemed near suicidal. Yachts move, but not quickly. They are nakedly vulnerable. Whistler, himself, had once sunk, with all hands, a yacht twice the size of his own.

But that time, that whole world, now seemed very far away. That life no longer existed for him because Claudia had given him a new one. She was young, she was warm, she was lovely, she was wonderful. Finding Claudia had made all the difference.

On this morning she was still sound asleep. He had risen early, taking care not to wake her. He liked to go up on deck before dawn and sit, enjoying the sunrise. That was another thing he'd almost never done before Claudia came into his life. He had, of course, seen many a sunrise, but he'd seldom actually *watched* one. Before Claudia, all that a rising sun meant was that the darkness was no longer his ally.

He now saw the dawn as a time of utter peace. The only sounds at that hour were the lapping of waves and the soft, rhythmic hum that the morning breeze made as it passed through the rigging above him. No birds were yet aloft. There were few lights on shore. There were none on any of the neighboring yachts. In a while, though, the little grocery would open. He would walk up the dock and buy some fruit and a couple of fresh-baked croissants.

He would go unarmed, as he'd done for some time now. Claudia might chide him for going without her. She preferred to be with him as a second pair of eyes in case she was wrong about the danger being past. Or rather, in case her friend the pelican was wrong.

Yes, Claudia spoke to birds. And to dogs. And to the wind. More to the point, they spoke to Claudia. But Whistler had managed to get her to agree to try not to let others see her doing so. Claudia, as it was, was hard enough to forget without him having to try to explain . . . well . . . why she's different.

He heard movement down below. She'd gotten up after all. He could hear her in the galley making coffee. In his mind, he could see her in her short terry robe, yawning and stretching and smiling to herself, brushing her wheat-colored hair from her face, revealing those amazing brown eyes. Very soon, she'd be coming up to join him on deck. She'd be carrying two steaming mugs. Her eyes would find him and she'd greet him with a smile. It was a smile that no sunrise could match.

And she would remind him that today was the day. He had promised her that, beginning this morning, they would take the first step toward reclaiming their identities. No more counterfeit papers. No more assumed names. He'd prefer to have waited for a full year to have passed, but Claudia was probably right. It was time. A few weeks shouldn't make any difference.

Claudia was, by most standards, a beautiful young woman, even more so on the inside where it mattered the most. She was easily the kindest human being he'd met. The most loving, the most loyal, and the most generous. She was bright, quick and funny, good at everything she tried.

She was also, by most standards, certifiably crazy.

But he didn't care. He adored her.

2

They'd sailed north from Barbados to the island of Antigua.
If all went well, they would stay for a month, passing the last
weeks of winter. A month would be the longest that they'd
stayed in one place. On that morning he would rent a per-
manent slip. It would also be the first time in almost a year
that he'd used his real name, Adam Whistler.

Claudia knew that he still had some serious misgivings.
But she said he needn't worry. She would be at his side. She
would always be there to protect him. And so she stood with
him, holding his hand, as the dockmaster entered the name,
Adam Whistler, into the marina's computer. They both
watched the dockmaster's eyes. The marina's computer was
certainly linked to both Customs and the local police. And
although Antigua was British, not American, it was probably
linked to several worldwide systems that tracked people
whose names and locations were of interest to other law-
enforcement authorities.

He wasn't a fugitive in the ordinary sense. His where-
abouts, however, were surely of interest to any number of
people. But he saw no reaction on the dockmaster's face. He
maneuvered to where he could see the screen. His name
wasn't blinking. It hadn't been flagged. As far as the marina's computer was concerned, he was just another boater
passing through.

Claudia nudged him after they had left the office.

"I thought so," she said. "No one cares anymore."

"Believe me. They care. I'm not sure that was smart."

"Well, it's done. And you'll see. We'll be fine."

Claudia, apparently, was at least partly right. In the days

that followed, no police came to question him, nor did anyone seem to have them under surveillance while they were exploring the island on bikes. No one had searched the boat in their absence; he had rigged it so that he would have known.

He did not fear arrest. No one wanted him arrested. He knew that nobody wanted a trial that would have made headlines and ruined careers. Ideally, they wanted him quietly dead. Not just him, but his father as well. They had reason to hate and fear his father even more. But they were fully aware that if they made the attempt, there would never again be talk of a truce. And especially if they should hurt Claudia again; not even their families would be safe.

They had very nearly killed her the first time.

She'd been shot through the neck, which should have been fatal. And it was, in a manner of speaking. It was during a drug raid on her mother's place of business. Drugs were found, but they had been planted.

They were planted by people with whom he had worked until, as they saw it, he betrayed them. He had taken something from them. An incriminating ledger. They wanted it back at all costs. They wanted, in addition, some form of insurance that he would never speak of its contents. Killing him would have done them no good. They would still have his father to deal with. They chose instead to take something in return that both he and his father valued greatly. Their hope was for a standoff, one that neutralized them both.

The drug raid went badly. Two policemen, both corrupt, who took part in the raid, had been startled by Claudia's sudden appearance. It was dark. She had surprised them. They had fired at her shape. Whistler never knew which one of them had hit her. It would not have made any difference.

Left to him, he would have finished everyone who was involved. It was one thing he knew how to do, and do well. But he hadn't because a deal had been struck and Whistler had been forced to accept it. The other side had chosen to cut its losses and negotiate a détente. The deal was not everything that Whistler would have wanted, but he had promised his father to abide by it. The other side appeared to have kept its end as well, but only, perhaps, because he'd been hard to find. As he'd tried to tell Claudia, some wounds never heal, but he'd chosen not to go into detail with her as to the nature of those wounds. He had chosen not to tell her of the price they had paid. Aside from the dead, there were two other men who would live with disfigurement for the rest of their lives. One of these had been shamed, made to scream, made to beg, as he lost control of his bowels. It wasn't Whistler who cut him; someone else had got to him, but the thing had been done in his name.

He'd told Claudia only that they had been punished and that some resentment may have lingered. And he'd told her that these were not all by any means. There were others from his past who might be tempted to try him if only they knew what he looked like.

But she wasn't concerned. She said that he needn't worry. She reminded him that no harm could befall him as long as she was there to watch over him.

In Claudia's mind, this was not a conceit. It was neither wishful thinking nor hubris. She was sure, without a doubt, that she could keep him from harm because she was his guardian angel.

To be clear, she didn't mean this in a metaphoric sense or as a stand-by-your-man sort of thing. She meant it as a literal truth. She'd been given the job by a spirit that she met while she was clinically dead. Her heart had stopped before the ambulance reached her and again on the operating table. The doctors got it beating again, but even they didn't think that it would matter. She'd flat-lined for more than eight minutes the first time and another six minutes the next.

After dying for the second time, or rather, after reviving, she'd sent word that she wanted to see him. She was in a Denver hospital, recovering from surgery. It was four days after the shooting.

He almost didn't go, not because he feared a trap. By then he was not the one being hunted. One reason behind his re-

luctance was guilt. She'd been shot and almost died because
of things he had done, but of which she'd known nothing up
until the week before. Another was because the last time he
saw her she'd told him that she wanted him out of her life.
She had called him a liar and worse.

Two men in dark suits had come to the house where Claudia was then staying with her mother. They identified themselves as government agents and asked to speak to both of them
in confidence. They proceeded to tell Claudia that the man
she'd been involved with was not at all what he seemed. Until
recently, they said, he'd been in their employ. No, Whistler was
not a federal agent himself. He'd had a background and training that they'd hoped to employ in the service of his country's
vital interests. Regrettably, however, they'd been forced to release him. He had proved to be mentally unstable.

They produced a report by a government psychiatrist,
which they read from rather than showing. It said that although he might seem almost normal, he suffered from para-
noid delusions. He saw enemies and conspiracies wherever
he looked, especially within his own government. He was
also a thief. He had stolen certain documents. They wanted
to know what sort of things he might have told her. Had he
asked her, perhaps, to hold anything for him? A package or
an envelope, for example?

She asked them what he did while he was "in their employ." Their response was, "We're asking the questions."

That didn't sit well with either Claudia or her mother. Her
mother asked to see their photo IDs so that she could write
down their names. She also asked them for a closer look at
the psychiatrist's report they were quoting. They ignored
both requests. She asked them to leave. The big one replied,
"We can help you or hurt you. I would do what I'm told if I
was you."

"Well, *if I was you*"— her mother mimicked his gram-
mar—"I would get the hell out of this house."

The interview had gone downhill very quickly. The big
one looked as if he might slap her. The other one, the bald
one, waved the bigger one off and pulled a file from his

briefcase. He said, "We tried to do this without scaring you too badly. Now I'll show you what a psycho Whistler is."

The file, or the parts that he allowed her to read, said that he, Adam Whistler, was a cold-blooded killer who was wanted in a half-dozen countries. "He's not just a killer. He's worse. He's a butcher. You think he wouldn't kill you? Two women? Let me show you."

He produced several photographs of the scene of a massacre. It appeared to be a family. They all looked Hispanic. Men, women and children, grandparents as well.

"And this is just one. It's not even the worst. Now look close at the kids. See their throats have been cut? He did the kids first so their parents could watch. You want someone taking pictures like these of you two? Help us, we'll help you. It's that simple."

According to Claudia, this was followed by a rant against him and his "expatriate father." His father, they said, was, if anything, worse. A renegade, a traitor who'd turned his back on his country. An extortionist, an employer of killers for hire. A man who had taught his own son how to kill. And a man not above using innocent women as a cover for his criminal designs.

Most of this wasn't true, but enough of it was. However, Claudia was in no mood to sort fact from fiction. What she knew was that he had lied from the start. Claudia had confronted him. She caught him off guard. She asked him, "Just tell me. What are you?"

He said, "Wait a minute. You say one of them was bald? And the second man, the bigger one— thin lips and no neck? His eyes look like nobody's home?"

"And he stank of cigars. So you know them."

"Claudia, look . . . there are things I haven't told you . . ."

"Oh, really? No shit." She threw up her hands. "And this stuff about your father. He's actually worse? Who was your grandfather, Hitler?"

She knew his father. So did her mother. They'd met in Aspen four months before this happened, when his father had flown over from Europe. His father and her mother had since become friends, corresponding by telephone and fax.

"Claudia, none of this is at all what you think. If you'll let me, I'll try to explain."

"Do you kill people, Adam?"

"People who? You mean that dead family they showed you?"

"Them or anyone, Adam. That's a yes or no question."

"No, I don't. I mean . . . not people like you. I would never . . ."

"Oh, Adam, shut up and get out."

"Those men, what exactly did they ask you to do?"

"It no longer matters. I told them to stuff it. They were even more repulsive than you are."

Whistler was sure that he knew who they were. Two men, dark suits, and that heavy-handed could only be Lockwood and Briggs. They weren't trained agents. They were little more than goons. The one with dead eyes, the one who'd almost slapped her mother, was Lockwood, a man with a near-lizard brain who had once attempted to intimidate Whistler by actually twirling his gun. And Claudia was right; he did stink of cigars; he had one between his teeth at the time. It had apparently never crossed the man's mind that a pistol being twirled is nonfunctional.

Whistler dropped him with a kick to the crotch. Briggs was there at the time, but chose not to intercede, although Whistler had invited him to do so if he wished. Briggs was marginally brighter than Lockwood, but, as evidenced by the presentation he'd made, had failed to grasp the concept of overkill. They both worked for a man named Felix Aubrey, and the ledger Whistler took belonged to Aubrey. But he couldn't imagine what they'd hoped to gain by approaching Claudia in that way. One does not tell a woman, "See? He cuts children's throats" and then expect her to carry on as before except that she'd now be an informant.

The worst of it was, there was nothing to inform on. Neither Claudia nor her mother was being "used" in any way.

Neither he nor his father had any "designs." He had thought that they'd reached an understanding with Aubrey. All he'd wanted from them was to be left alone. They would be left alone in return.

He was sorely tempted to find her two visitors and throw them both out of a window. But as angry as he was, he decided to do nothing. It wouldn't help Claudia's opinion of him if she learned of their deaths on the six-o'clock news. He would simply go away, stay away for a while. In a week or so he would try calling Claudia. She might hang up on him the first time or two, but he wouldn't give up. He would get her to listen. After hearing the truth she might still despise him, but at least she would hate him for things he had done and not for what those clowns had told her.

Doing nothing turned out to be a mistake. He'd allowed himself to hope that if he took no action, they wouldn't bother Claudia or her mother again, having realized that they were in no way involved. In that respect, he'd been stupidly naive. Having shown their hand with that clumsy approach, they decided that they had better play it out, and quickly, before he or his father could respond. He should have foreseen that, but he hadn't.

Either way, there he stood, outside her hospital room, his heart breaking at the sight of her lying there. They had moved her that morning from Intensive Care, but her care seemed no less intense. There were tubes in both arms and one ran to her nose. Apparently she needed help breathing. Her throat was thickly bandaged and two drains had been implanted. She looked so very small, so very frail in that bed. But she seemed to be asleep and not in pain.

Her mother was with her. She looked up and saw him. She started to speak but she could only shake her head. She got up and left the room without a word.

He had spoken to her doctor about her condition. The bullet had hit her just over the collarbone. It had grazed both her trachea and her spine, but in the doctor's view, she'd been lucky. He said the shock and the swelling had caused some paralysis, but he thought that she'd recover full use of

her limbs. On that morning she'd been able to raise her left
arm. She could move and even flex all her fingers. She was
still quite weak and it hurt her to talk. The doctor said that
he could see her, but for only a few minutes. The doctor's
real concern was the loss of brain function. He said, "Well,
you'll see for yourself."

Whistler, reluctantly, entered the room. He tried to
make no sound, but she must have sensed his presence.
She took a deep breath and her eyes fluttered open. It took
them a moment to focus on him. When they did, he'd expected to see blame, condemnation. Their expression,
however, was gentle, serene. There was even a trace of a
smile.

She moistened her lips and asked him to come closer. Her
voice was raspy, not much more than a whisper. She told
him that she was glad that he'd come. She had needed to see
him so that she could explain why the light had told her to
go back.

"Um . . . the light?"

"The white light. You've heard of it. It's really there,
Adam. You really do see it when you die."

"Yes, I'm sure."

"No, you're not." She paused to swallow. She tried to
clear her throat. "But it's there. And it spoke to me. It sent
me back to you."

"Claudia, listen . . . you should not try to talk now."

"Wait, I'm jumping ahead. The white light comes later.
The first thing you know, you're out of your body. You're
just kind of floating above it. I saw myself lying in the dirt
where I fell. And I saw when the doctors were working on
me. But you never get upset. You almost don't mind. Then
you sort of remember that you have to go someplace and
suddenly you're in this long tunnel."

"And the light is at the end of the tunnel?"

"Actually, it comes toward you like it wants you to stop.
I slowed down, but I wanted to see past it. There were people there, Adam. Way off in the distance. They were on the
other side of a beautiful meadow. I could only see shapes,

but they were definitely people. They were waving at me, Adam. They were waiting to greet me. I bet one of them was my father. You think?"

Whistler shrugged. Or nodded. Or did something in between. He had known that her father was long deceased. He had broken his neck in a rock-climbing accident when Claudia was five years of age.

"And they had a dog with them. It was wagging its tail. It was good to see that dogs go there, too."

The whisper, he realized, wasn't all from her injury. It was as much a sound of wonderment, of awe. It did hurt her to speak, but she didn't seem to care. She narrowed her eyes as another thought struck her.

"I didn't see a cat, but there were birds in the meadow. If they have dogs and birds, they'd have cats, don't you think? Not that the cats would go after the birds. Nothing bad happens there. It's all love."

He said, "You need your rest. We'll talk later."

"Adam, sit."

"Claudia, I'm so sorry. This whole thing is my fault. I never dreamed that they'd try a stunt like that. And you were right about me . . . well, some of it, anyway. I just wish—"

"Adam, hush. Get a chair."

"I should go."

"You're staying, Adam. Now go get a chair. You're going to want to hear this sitting down."

A nurse stopped at the door. She tapped a finger on her watch, reminding him not to overstay. He nodded, but he did take a seat.

"Now hold my hand and listen," she said, and he obeyed. He was glad to feel some strength in her fingers.

"Believe me," she told him, "I know how this will sound. But you haven't been there. I have."

"I'm listening."

"And don't argue with me, Adam. You'll be wasting your breath. You don't have a choice. I don't either."

He thought he was about to hear some sort of prophecy. That some biblical catastrophe was about to occur if mankind did not change its ways. Or else that, although it was well after Christmas, three spirits were going to visit him that night and give him a chance at redemption. This last turned out to be the closest.

She proceeded to tell him she'd been given a mission. Her task, the light told her, was to go back and save him. She would teach him how to live, how to love, and love freely. She would be his friend, his companion, and his protector, so that he needn't fear those who still lived in darkness. And when he's become the man he can be, they would start to build a family, have children.

"Um . . . children?"

"I'm pretty sure, yeah. I think that's part of the plan."

"I see. Would this be anytime soon?"

"That's long-term, I think. No big hurry. First things first. Unless you'd rather . . ."

"I can wait."

She looked at him, squinting. "You think I'm nuts, don't you."

"Claudia, *no,* I do not think you're crazy. But I think you need time to get well."

"Adam, I told you. I know how this sounds."

"And that it wasn't your idea. I believe you."

"Do you really?"

"As you've said, you were there and I wasn't."

"Good. Now here's a question. Do you think I have powers? Wouldn't you think an angel would have powers?"

"Um . . . hold on a minute. This guy, this white light . . ."

"Who said it was a guy?"

"Okay, her."

"It's a spirit, Adam. So it could be an it."

"The thing is, I *have* read about the white light and the floating and the tunnel and all that. From what I've read . . . well, let me ask another way. Are you sure that this spirit turned you into an angel? Or did it just say it isn't your time yet?"

"Whistler's guardian angel. Exact words. Loud and clear. It knew all about you, Adam. It knew stuff I didn't know."

"Like what?"

"Like how *you* happened. How you got caught up in this. Then we talked about us and how I can help you, but I never asked about powers."

"I'm . . . sure that you have some. I would think that's a given."

"Whistler, watch it. Don't patronize me."

"Okay, say you might. But like what, in particular?"

"I don't know. Not miracles or anything like that."

"And flying, I assume, is out of the question as long as you're stuck with a body."

"Except that would convince you."

"It would, but don't try."

"What about heightened senses? Mine all seem so clear."

That was common, he knew, after any near miss. The aftermath of an adrenaline rush. It's been known to last for days, even weeks, before it fades.

"Maybe healing?" she asked. "No, scratch that. No miracles."

"Healing sounds about right. But start with yourself. I want you to try to get some sleep now."

She squeezed his fingers. "Stay with me."

He'd hoped that this was only the sedatives talking. Or the short-term mischief of an oxygen-starved brain. He sat and held her hand until she drifted off to sleep.

He didn't want to leave her for a number of reasons. Not least was that, when he did leave her room, he would have to face Claudia's mother.

3

Her mother, Kate Geller, had raised Claudia alone while running a business that she'd started. She'd begun by opening a small flower shop that grew into a good-sized garden

supply center in the town of Silver Ridge, outside Denver.
Knowing him had almost cost her that business.

Lockwood and Briggs, as he'd said, were both goons.
Goons always seem to want to prove that they're smart.
Their boss, Felix Aubrey, had ordered them to see what they
could dig up on Claudia and her mother that might help in-
duce them to cooperate. Lockwood and Briggs, being
strangers to subtlety, decided to approach them directly, on
their own, to bully them into assisting.

Aubrey must have been horrified when he learned of that
meeting. He'd assumed that he, Whistler, would respond
with a vengeance as soon as he learned of it himself. The fat
was in the fire. Aubrey's hand had been forced. He decided
that he had no time to lose if he was to regain the advantage.
If he couldn't use Claudia and her mother in one way, he
would use them as bargaining chips.

There were two greenhouses at Kate Geller's garden center,
in addition to the main display area and shop. The Geller
home was on a hill just beyond. One night after closing, he
had Lockwood and Briggs break into one of the greenhouses. They brought with them a dozen cannabis plants and
stashed them amid a group of ferns. They had already lined
up the local police and a judge to sign off on a warrant. The
police—at least some of them—and certainly the judge had
been in Aubrey's pocket before this.

The thing that galled Whistler was that he'd long known
it. Silver Ridge, however, was just one of many towns whose
officials had profited through their dealings with Aubrey.
Even so, as long as he caused them no trouble, he'd expected
no trouble from the local police. The most that they would
do was keep an eye on him for Aubrey and report that his activities seemed innocent. It was a mistake. He'd been very
foolish. Now, with the help of Lockwood and Briggs, the
local SWAT team was planning a drug raid on the Gellers. It
would take place just before dawn.

Claudia and her mother were already up. They'd had a
rush order for some funeral arrangements for a service to be

held that same morning. They were in the other greenhouse, the smaller of the two, when they saw the flashing lights of police cars. They heard breaking glass. They didn't know what was happening. They stepped outside, the mother ran toward the cars. Claudia, however, had pulled up short. She'd seen movement inside the larger greenhouse.

She entered through a door at its opposite end, where the greenhouse was in almost total darkness. She saw the two policemen ripping out ferns. She saw, in the beams of the flashlights they held, several plants that had not been there earlier. She also recognized one of the suits who had come to her house two days before. Briggs, the bald one, the one who had threatened her, had gone in with the two black-clad policemen.

The cops said she shouted, "I'll kill you, you bastards." She did not. She would not have. Not Claudia. All her mother heard her say was, "Hey, stop it." In that instant, several muzzle blasts lit up the greenhouse. The next thing Kate knew, she'd been thrown to the ground and the other suit, Lockwood, was cuffing her. He wouldn't let her up. He held her down with his foot. She kept calling out, calling Claudia's name. There was no answer from Claudia. Minutes later, she heard another gunshot.

The story was that Claudia had burst into the greenhouse, a small chromed revolver in her hand. The officers identified themselves as police, but that was when she cursed them, then she raised her gun and fired. They were forced to shoot back in self-defense. Seven shots were fired in all. Most hit plants or glass. One struck her in the throat.

She might or might not have had something in her hand. Shears or a trowel, perhaps, not that it mattered. The call for an ambulance was delayed for twenty minutes while Briggs was sanitizing the scene. While Claudia was probably still writhing on the floor, Briggs had produced that small chromed revolver and pressed it into her hand. He raised her arm and squeezed off a single shot. That was the later shot heard by her mother. She was no longer writhing when the ambulance arrived. That was the first time her heart stopped.

The government, meanwhile, seized everything they owned. The seizure was instant, automatic by law. That law took their home and the family business, calling them drug-related assets. It took their cars, their bank accounts, their IRA investments, and even the cash in their wallets.

As the law stood, all this would be forfeit. As the law stood, it would not be returned, not even if the government should decide not to bother taking the charges to trial. The local authorities would keep eighty percent of the revenue from the sale of the property. That was why the authorities of such towns as Silver Ridge were usually eager to participate. That was why some authorities, Silver Ridge's in particular, were not above making sure in advance that illegal drugs would be found.

The police charged Kate Geller with growing marijuana for the purpose of distribution and sale. Claudia, being in residence at the time, was charged with aiding and abetting. These were the only charges that had been intended when the idea of the drug raid was conceived. They might, or might not, have gone to trial. But the charges were to be held over their heads in order to ensure that the Whistlers would behave. The shooting, however, had complicated matters. Claudia was charged with attempted murder during the commission of a felony.

Whistler was in Arlington, Virginia, when this happened. It was where he was living at the time. He'd flown back there the day after Claudia told him that she wanted nothing further to do with him. On the day of the shooting, that afternoon, he got a call from Kate Geller's attorney. Before he could ask why she needed a lawyer, the lawyer put Kate on the phone.

She was very upset; he could hardly understand her. When she spoke of Claudia being "terribly hurt," he thought she was talking about feelings. It was only when her mother said, "She might never wake up," that he realized that something more serious had occurred. He managed to calm her down just enough to tell him what had happened that morning. She was calling from the Silver Ridge jail. The judge had refused to release her on bond. He would not let her be at Claudia's side, not even under guard and wearing manacles.

Whistler's first reaction was stunned disbelief. The next was a murderous rage. He had wanted to hurt someone—anyone involved. But the first thing he did was get out of his apartment and use a safe phone to call his father in Geneva. His father took the news with a maddening calm. He wanted to know everything, including what led to it. Whistler told him about Lockwood and Briggs and the call they'd made on Claudia and her mother. He said that he'd be flying out to Denver at once. He would contact him again when he got there.

"Do *not* fly to Denver," his father said firmly. "You stay where you are. I'm sending help."

"I'm not waiting for help. They can meet me."

"That's your anger talking, Adam. You know better than that. And why didn't you tell me they'd gone to Kate's house and told them all that crap about us?"

"I guess I hoped that was the end of it."

"Why would you have thought so? Because Kate threw them out? They made a stupid move; they guessed wrong about the Gellers. They assumed that you would go after them for that. But you didn't. Why not? Why did you keep it to yourself?"

"I don't know."

"Yes, you do, and you weren't using your head. All you could think about was you being dumped, I'm sorry, but you should have seen this coming."

"Seen what? Planted drugs? That they'd try to kill Claudia?"

"They never meant to shoot her. You do know that, don't you? All they wanted was something to trade."

"Dad, they shot her. I don't care what they meant."

"And, damn it, stop thinking this is all about you. They defied me as well when they went to that house. They knew they had to move before I found out. I didn't because you didn't tell me."

He was right, of course. Whistler hadn't been thinking. All he'd had on his mind were Claudia's words and the look on her face when she told him to get out. And his father was right about them wanting to trade. That would have been the point of the property seizure. "*You have something we want. We have something you want. Let's calm down and discuss this like gentlemen.*"

Whistler took a breath. "What help are you sending?"

"The twins. Then we'll see. Let me make a few calls. You are not to make a move until they get there."

"Could you . . . try to remember that I'm a grown man?"

"Then act the part, Adam. In the meanwhile, stay put."

The twins were the Beasley twins, Dennis and Donald. They had been with his father since Whistler was a boy. They were now in their fifties—heavyset, thinning hair, and had always been a little bit strange. The Beasley twins arrived and they came separately, as always. No one ever seemed to give them a second glance as long as they weren't seen together. He met one in Baltimore, the other in Newark. Having had to go through Customs, they arrived unarmed. Whistler offered to supply them with weapons. Dennis said, "Not here. We'll get fixed up out there."

Donald said, "We got friends there. They'll have what we need."

"Friends where? In Denver?" Whistler asked him. "Who are they?"

"Not from there. They flew in. Bunch of lawyers and such. They already got the lady out of jail, by the way. Your father put up half a million."

"Yeah, but—wait a second. We were talking about weapons. My father has lawyers who do guns?"

"Nah. Not them," said Donald. "Different friends who flew in."

"Yeah, but who?"

"Never mind who. You don't need to know. They flew in; they'll fly out when this is done."

He was glad to hear that Kate Geller had been freed, but: "Why won't you tell me who they are?"

"It's how they want it. No big deal. Just go with it."

"But they're already out there? They're in Silver Ridge now?"

Donald rocked a hand. "Thereabouts."

"Well, they couldn't have gotten there from Europe this soon. So these friends of my father are local?"

"I guess."

"You don't guess. You know. Why can't I?"

"Adam, will you stop? Just be thankful you got friends."

"Yeah, well, I'm getting tired of being treated like a kid. You'll recall that I'm not exactly new at this."

"No, you're not, but mostly it was never this personal. Being mad's a good way to get dead. Your father's right."

Dennis said, "Let's just get there and do this."

Whistler and the twins made their way to Silver Ridge, each getting there by a different route. Donald Beasley was the first to arrive. By the time they regrouped, Donald had the names of the two SWAT team cops who'd shot at Claudia.

"Want to know what these guys drive? One's got a Jaguar," said Donald. "The other one has a Corvette. You surprised?"

Dennis said, "Life's been good to the cops in this town."

Whistler didn't bother asking where Donald got their names. All he wanted to know was where they were.

"See that?" said Donald. "You're still much too hot. That's why those two cops weren't left up to you."

Whistler heard the past tense. "They're both dead?"

"One would assume."

"Don't worry about those two no more," Dennis told him. "Me and Donald, we'll go see that judge these guys used. You go get those two guys you know."

Lockwood and Briggs. "Do we know where they are?"

"Check the airport. They came in on the Aubrey guy's jet. It's a Hawker 700. Nice plane," said Donald. He told Whistler where the aircraft had been parked.

Nor did Whistler bother asking how he knew all this. He asked, "And the plane is still there?"

"Last we heard. Check it out."

Whistler went, although he doubted that he'd find Briggs and Lockwood. The twins, he suspected, knew that they

were long gone or else they would not have let him go by
himself. All the same, he did go on the chance of catching
up to them. Especially Briggs, who could have tried to help
Claudia. He hadn't; he'd just watched her bleed.

The Hawker they'd flown in on had been there, all right.
Whistler knew that plane. He'd used it himself. As he'd
guessed, it had departed several hours before. They had
probably fled back east in a hurry when they learned that
their two cops had vanished. Very well, thought Whistler. He
would track them down later. After them would come
Aubrey. He would find Felix Aubrey. He would see every
one of them dead.

The twins, it turned out, didn't just "go see the judge"
who had issued the warrant that had legalized the raid. They
already had him in the trunk of a car. Tossed in with the
judge was a road-kill raccoon that Donald had picked up
along the way. "It's good to give a man time to think," he
told Whistler. "We'll all have a little talk when he's ripe."

The judge had been "thinking" for more than two days
when Kate Geller called Whistler again. She had reached
him on his cell phone, said that Claudia was conscious.

"I've a feeling that you're someplace nearby, am I right?"
She must have been watching breaking stories on the news.

"Get over here, Adam. She's asking for you."

"I'm not sure that's a very good idea, Mrs. Geller. I think
it would be better—"

"Get your butt over here."

"I'll be there as soon as I can."

4

He'd seen her. They'd talked. Then he watched her fall
asleep. He sat with her until the nurse came in again and said
it was enough for one day. If her room hadn't been on the

hospital's third floor, he might have considered slipping out through a window. But he didn't. He went back to the waiting room where her mother was sitting. She looked up at him and again shook her head.

"You know, the damnedest thing is . . . you have such a nice face."

"Mrs. Geller—"

"And an honest face, Adam. Soft voice. Easy manner. And your eyes . . . those gentle gray eyes."

"Mrs. Geller, I'll be leaving. You should have no more trouble."

"I mean, who'd have known? Who would look at you and know?"

"Almost everything you think you know is false, Mrs. Geller. Not that it matters any longer."

"Why is that?"

"As I said, I'm leaving, and this time for good. I will never come near Claudia again."

"She knew you'd say that. Her white light said you would. That light must know you better than we did."

"She . . . um, told you all that? That she thinks she's an angel?"

"I think maybe you'd better stick around for a while."

"Mrs. Geller—"

"Don't get me wrong, Adam. I'd be glad to see you go, but I sure don't want her chasing after you. And it's not that I blame you for her being shot. It's just that you're not every mother's dream . . ." She stopped herself. She sucked in a breath. "Well, you seemed to be. For a while there, you were."

"Mrs. Geller, I'm sorry. And I do blame myself. I brought all this on you. I'm so sorry."

"Can you make this right, Adam?"

"There's a little more to do."

"You know that she's been charged with attempted murder?"

"There will be no testimony against her, Mrs. Geller. That charge and the drug charge should be dropped within the week."

"Those policemen who shot her . . . I hear they've gone missing. Just missing, or shouldn't I ask?"

Whistler looked away. He said nothing.

"And that other man. The one they brought in all cut up . . ."

"Um . . . what man is that, Mrs. Geller?"

"The bald one. Name of Briggs. They brought him in yesterday morning."

"Brought him here? He's here now?"

"Intensive Care. You didn't know? I guess I'm glad to hear that this is news to you, Adam. I was down there with Claudia when they wheeled him in. There's not much left of his face."

Whistler's eyes narrowed. She misunderstood the look.

"That man's hurt enough. You leave him be, Adam. He's scared and he's sorry. He said so."

"You spoke to him?"

She nodded. "I held his hand for a minute. He's not ever going to be the same again, Adam. No need to hurt him any more."

"Mrs. Geller, where was he found? Do you know?"

"Out at the airport. Seems his plane took off without him. They found him stumbling around where the plane had been. He was trying to keep his cheek from falling off."

"Any sign of the other one? Lockwood?"

"I don't know. But Adam, enough is enough. I hate that you know people who can do things like this."

"The truth is, I'm not sure I do."

He'd been thinking the twins, but this didn't sound like them. The twins would not merely have marked him. It must have been one of their mysterious friends. He assured Mrs. Geller that he had no intention of harming Briggs any further. Lockwood was another matter, but Lockwood would keep. That's assuming that he got out alive. He told her again that he'd be leaving that day. His only other business was to deal with the judge who was still, at that moment, with the twins.

He said, "This should soon be over. Or at least where

you're concerned. I think the judge will void the warrant that led to the seizure. You'll be getting your property back, Mrs. Geller. They won't try to hurt you again."

"Or you?"

"They might try. But not here. And not right away."

She got up. She started pacing. She did not like that answer. "You're saying they'll wait. They'll pick the time and place."

"And you're concerned that your daughter might be with me. Put that out of your mind. She will not be."

"Adam, tell me. Are you a good man?"

"Not the way you'd think. No."

"You worked for those people?"

"I worked *with* them for a time."

Her eyes narrowed. "That's not much of a distinction."

"Not to you. I know that. But in any case, it's finished."

"And just so I'm clear—you're all government people? You're telling me *my* government does this kind of crap?"

"No. Well, not exactly. It's not what you think."

"But you do frame people. And you take away their homes. And if they give you any trouble, you kill them. Am I close?"

"Mrs. Geller . . ."

"What ever happened to the good old days, Adam, when we only had the IRS after us?"

He answered, "Mrs. Geller, I will tell you this much. At the outset, the people this unit went after were people with a great deal of blood on their hands. They were people who deserved to be dead or in prison, but who couldn't be touched by legal means."

She stared. "A death squad?"

"A punitive unit."

"Death is pretty damned punitive, Adam."

"Mrs. Geller, many governments have units such as this one. For the most part, what they do is track laundered money and identify its source and destination."

"Now you're saying you're accountants."

"Accountants and attorneys do go after that money. One of their weapons is financial ruin through seizures and endless litigation. The search itself can be dangerous work. There are people, high up, who will readily commit murder to avoid exposure and the loss of position. That leads, now and then, to the need for stronger action beyond what accountants and attorneys are trained for. Now and then, there's a case of an eye for eye, but . . . no, not a death squad. That was not the idea."

"It was not? Past tense?"

He rubbed his chin. "These . . . things sometimes get out of hand."

He could hear his father saying, "*No, Adam. Not sometimes. It almost never fails. Any antidrug unit that's run off the books becomes corrupt sooner or later. Any punitive unit that gets into killing tends to solve all its problems by killing.*"

Whistler chewed his lip. He waved off the subject. He said, "As for Claudia, let's give her time. She'll realize that her white light was only a dream. She'll be glad I left quietly. You'll see."

A sad little smile. A shake of the head. "Did you talk to her doctor about the white light?"

"He never mentioned that part of it."

"He's had other patients who've had near-death experiences. Not a one could be convinced that what they went through wasn't real. He thinks this might not go away."

"All the same . . ."

"She's so very young, Adam. She's only twenty-four."

"Agreed. I'm too old for her. I know that."

"That's not what I meant. A little older is okay. But you're older in a different way, aren't you?"

He said nothing.

"And your father—he's full of surprises himself. A criminal? A renegade? He taught you how to kill?"

"Not a word of that is true, Mrs. Geller."

"Not a word? Or not exactly? Look me in the eye."

"Mrs. Geller, my father is the best man I know. If you liked him, you should try to trust your instincts."

She nodded. "Fair enough. I'll wait and hear it from him. In the meantime, Adam, you speak for yourself. I want to hear your side of the story."

"It's not much of a story. One thing leading to another."

She folded her arms. "I think you owe me that much. I think the both of you do."

"Mrs. Geller—"

"Try not to get her shot again, Adam. Okay?"

"Mrs. Geller, you're not listening. It's over between us."

She was still pacing. She gritted her teeth. "I want to despise you. But I can't and I don't. I wish Claudia did, but she doesn't."

Again, he was silent. He looked at his shoes.

"On the contrary, Adam, she thinks she's supposed to love you. Do you want to know something? She was almost there already. I think she could have handled the truth."

Still nothing.

"She's very special, Adam. She was special before this. And you . . . no matter what you think of yourself . . . have a decency about you that keeps showing through. Maybe she can really save you. You think?"

"I have to go."

"Adam, I can't tell you how I hate saying this. Do you know what I'd tell you if I weren't her mother?"

Whistler let out a sigh. He waited.

"I'd tell you pretty much what she asked me to say. That you shouldn't look a gift horse in the mouth."

5

He did leave that day, intending never to return. He tried to put Claudia out of his mind. For what he meant to do, there was every chance that he might not live to see her again anyway.

But Whistler couldn't make her face go away. The way she looked up at him. Those wonderful eyes. Explaining with total and absolute certainty that she was his guardian angel.

And then her mother. Another surprise. Her mother should have said, "Get out of here, Adam. Come near her again and I'll clobber you. She isn't an angel; she's not going to save you. She's not even going to save you from me, so get lost while you still have the chance."

But she didn't. What she said was, in essence, "Don't blow this."

The odd thing was, he could almost believe it. There was Claudia's survival. A miracle in itself. She should have been a vegetable at best. And if there really were such things as angels, he'd expect them to look very much like Claudia. They would, like Claudia, have an inner glow about them. A radiance that sets them apart. The first time he'd ever laid eyes on Claudia, he could have believed it right then.

He'd first met her four months before any of this happened. He did not then, however, think in terms of the celestial. He thought in terms of a warm and friendly girl of the sort he wished he'd met ten years before. A girl who, because of what he had become, seemed hopelessly out of his reach. He first saw her on a ski slope at Aspen.

He'd gone to Aspen to meet with his father. His father had flown over from Europe, where he'd lived for almost all of Whistler's life. Whistler first had called him, not to meet, just to talk. He said he'd tried to believe in what he'd been doing, to believe that it was making a difference. But the cure, he'd come to realize, was worse than the disease. The war on drugs, as fought, was unwinnable. It ruined more lives than it saved. And that war, for some, was as profitable as dealing. He'd known traffickers whom he would sooner have trusted than some of the people who opposed them.

"You'll forgive me for saying I told you so, Adam."

"I know. I just didn't want to see it."

"The first casualty of war is always the truth. What has happened that opened your eyes? Are you in trouble?"

"I might be. You know Felix Aubrey?"

"Know him? I warned you about him, remember?"

"Yes, you did and I heard you. Will you listen?"

"Go ahead."

"Aubrey keeps a set of records. Or he did. I have them now. And he's probably guessed that I took them."

"What's in them? How hot?"

"They could put him in prison. He would have lots of company."

The line went silent for a moment. Then, "Get over here, Adam. Get on the first flight you can."

"If I disappeared, he would know that I'm the one. I'm not sure that Aubrey knows who you are, but that might be the first place he'd look."

"Your point?"

"I don't want to cause trouble for you."

"Um . . . Adam, not to sound as if I'm full of myself, but I think I can probably deal with it."

"Even so, it's my problem. Could you meet me over here?"

"Name the place. But be careful. Don't say it straight out."

"Last Dollar. You remember? I can be there tonight."

"Last Dollar. I got you. So can we. I'll buy a ticket."

His use of "we" meant he'd bring the Beasley twins. He seldom traveled without them. The "I'll buy a ticket," meant that he'd fly commercial. He had his own plane and had access to others, but a private jet's movements were too easily monitored. Sometimes it was better to get lost in the crowd. "Last Dollar" was the name of a ski trail at Aspen. He'd skied that trail with his father many times, beginning when Whistler started college in the States. Before that, they'd skied all over Europe. He and his father had often gone skiing whenever there were problems that needed thinking out. Either skiing the Alps or going for a sail on the boat his father kept on Lake Geneva. There was something about a big stretch of open water, and especially the mountains with their clean air and vast snowfields, that helped put the rest of the world in perspective.

Whistler got to Aspen first. He waited at the airport through several arrivals before spotting one of the twins disembarking from one of the last incoming flights. The twin must have seen him but did not acknowledge him. About ten people back, his father appeared. Or rather, he loomed. A big man, he was wearing a brown Stetson hat and a three-quarter-length shearling coat. Shaggy hair and a beard made him look even bigger. He seemed a bit tired, but no less alert after spending twelve hours on airplanes. He was walking stiffly, however. Bad back. It had seemed to get worse in the past year or two. Although Whistler had found it hard to envision, he claimed he'd injured it doing the tango.

His father did not acknowledge him either. He proceeded down the concourse to the baggage-claim area. Whistler never saw the second twin get off. That meant that he was probably already there and was someplace in the terminal, watching.

The Beasley twins were bodyguards, among other things, but they weren't the kind who stayed close. One would be here, the other would be there. That way no one would take special notice of them, or even necessarily know that there were two until, one presumed, it was too late.

Whistler left the terminal and walked to the parking lot. There, he got into the car he had rented and waited for his father to come out with his bag. He left the lot and pulled up near his father. His father waited until one or both twins were in a position to follow. Only then did he throw his bag in the back and climb into the passenger seat. Only then did he reach, again stiffly, to embrace him.

"Your back hurting you?" asked Whistler.

"Comes and goes. It's nothing. I'll pop a pill later."

"I got us a suite that has a Jacuzzi. A good soak . . ."

His father waved off the subject. He said, "Those records you mentioned. I want to have a look at them for starters."

"There's an envelope under your seat. Photocopies."

"You still have the original?"

"Airport locker." Whistler gestured over his shoulder. "In a package addressed to you, just in case."

"I take that to mean that he can't kill you yet."

"Not until he can be sure he'd get it back."

His father opened the glove compartment. Its small bulb would give him enough light to read by, but not enough light to silhouette him. He felt for the envelope beneath his seat and started reading the copies.

"This is a ledger," said his father, surprised. "I'd assumed that you meant computer records."

"An actual ledger. Green cloth. Yellow pages."

"And in Aubrey's own hand? Not even in code. Why would anyone keep something like this?"

"Well, I know that Aubrey won't use a computer. He thinks they're too easily hacked and he's right. But I don't think he's dumb. Wait until you see some of the names in the ledger. He knows that if the law ever got its hands on that, the evidence would probably be suppressed."

"Give me a few minutes. Let me read."

Each sheet was a spread of two ledger pages. Each page listed names, sometimes only initials, in some sixty cities and towns nationwide. Under each name were what appeared to be disbursements. Some were cash, but most of them were property. There were buildings and vehicles of every description. There were computers, furniture, works of art, coin collections. There were several boats and airplanes, antique swords and chandeliers. They read like a list of auction items.

His father asked, "This is all seized property?"

"Apparently, yes."

"Seized, but not accounted for. Is that what you think? Otherwise, why keep a private record?"

"Exactly."

"I recognize the names of five or six congressmen. Political contributions?"

"All illegal."

"And a number of entries marked 'Recon-JC.' What is Recon-JC? Do you know?"

"No idea."

"Reconnaissance, perhaps? Scouting out seizure prospects?"

"I don't think so. They don't look like estimates to me. They're all in round numbers. Must be actual disbursements."

His father took a moment to leaf through several pages. "Then whatever it is, it has profited nicely. All cash in this case. Over three million dollars. But our friend, Mr. Aubrey, seems not to approve. He scrawled the word 'idiotic' next to one of these entries and he wrote 'an utter waste' by another."

His father muttered "Recon-JC" to himself, as if rolling the notation over his tongue would help him to parse out its meaning.

He shrugged and gave up. "How'd you get this, by the way?"

"I found it in Aubrey's house. I broke in."

"So, you already knew what was in it?"

"Not really. I'd seen him take it out of his briefcase once or twice. I just thought it might be worth a look."

"You're telling me that's it? That's all you had to go on?"

"No, I'm telling you that I was paying attention when you warned me that Aubrey was a snake. He seems to live on what the government pays him, but he has any number of relatives and friends who've improved their lifestyles considerably."

"So he's stashing and he's spreading it around."

"And within the Center, he has his own payroll. They're people whose names don't appear on the roster. They only answer to Aubrey."

"The Center?"

"New name. It's called the Center for Policy Analysis. The idea is to make it sound like a think tank so that nobody pays much attention."

"Do you answer to Aubrey?"

"I did. Now I don't. I told him I'd only take orders in writing. That pretty much left me with nothing to do."

"Except snoop around. And make Aubrey not like you."

"It's fair to say that we're not friendly."

"So, when Aubrey saw that his ledger was gone, I would think you'd make the short list of suspects."

"My apartment's been searched at least twice that I know of. My phone is tapped, but it's always been tapped. And of course he's had me under surveillance."

"Which you've shaken, I trust."

"Two plane changes back."

"If you didn't, the twins will have spotted them by now. Drive around a while. Let me get through the rest."

He read for ten more minutes, squinting to see. He grunted a few times, took a few weary breaths. At last he tamped the sheets back together and slid them into the envelope.

"This says they've been skimming. Big-time, but so what?"

"So what? They're all thieves, is so what."

"Where there's money, there's greed. Does this come as a surprise? You didn't join a Boy Scout troop, Adam."

"Don't start."

"And name me a single federal program that hasn't been scammed one way or another. The more money there is, the more fraud it engenders. Look at Medicaid, billions for treatments never given. Look at school lunch programs. They hemorrhage money. But, you're right. Don't get me started. I might offer my services."

"Could we stick to this one situation for the moment?"

"Yeah, let's. Aubrey's boss—what's his name again?"

"Delbert Poole. He's the director."

"But a figurehead, correct? He's no expert on drugs."

"Expert? Far from it. He's totally clueless. His only qualification is a moral certainty that all drugs, including alcohol, are evil. I watched him testify before a Senate committee on the subject of decriminalizing marijuana possession. He said that marijuana—citing this as a fact—causes teenage boys to be three times more likely to yield to homosexual advances."

"You're saying he panders to the Christian Right."

"It goes beyond pandering. More like total immersion."

"He's sincere in his beliefs?"

"Hard to tell with those people."

His father tapped the envelope lying on his lap. "I did not see his name or initials in the ledger. Could that mean he's honest?"

"I don't know."

"Or might it mean that Aubrey's not cutting him in?"

Whistler shrugged. "I'm not sure that Poole cares about money. All Poole seems to care about is stamping out evil and punishing the morally deficient. That includes, by the way, anyone who's pro-choice and certainly the gay population. Poole sees himself as the instrument of God. He sees everyone as morally deficient."

"Including Aubrey?"

"And me."

"Well, trust me on one thing. Poole cares about money. The only question is how he would put it to use. As for you and Aubrey, you both being so *unsaved,* why does he tolerate having you around? I can guess, but let's hear what you think."

"To fight fire with fire. That's the premise of the unit. I'm sure that Delbert Poole thinks we're going to hell anyway. In the meantime, we might as well be useful."

"Could he possibly not know what Aubrey is doing?"

Whistler wasn't sure whether Poole knew or not. He did, however, remember one meeting. Aubrey had pulled the ledger from his briefcase and had started to make a notation. Poole had cleared his throat until Aubrey looked up at him. Poole then looked away, but as he did, he made a little flicking motion with his finger. Aubrey glared at the finger and then at Poole, but he did stick it back in his briefcase.

"He picks and chooses what he wants to know. Aside from that, and this is just a feeling, I think Aubrey might have something on Poole."

"Of course he does, Adam. That's what Aubrey's all about. He did not advance in life through his charm." Harry Whistler took a breath and shook his head in dismay. "You sure know how to pick winners."

"I didn't pick them. They picked me. They requested me."

"And I urged you to tell them to stuff it."

Whistler drew an irritated breath of his own. "Are you going to make me say it again? Okay. I know. I should have stayed where I was."

"No, Adam," said his father, "you should not have done that either. If you'd listened to me—"

"Dad—"

"Okay, past is past. Are you listening to me now?"

"I could do with some advice."

"Here it is. Walk away."

"Just forget it?"

"The alternative is what? Blow the whistle? Come forward? You, of all people, are going to stand up and say, 'Gee, this is wrong. We should stop it'?"

"Me of all people? What is that supposed to mean?"

"You're the shooter for this unit, are you not?"

Whistler darkened. He said, "I am not just a shooter. I have not ever been just a shooter."

His father raised his hands. "Let's not get into that now. But we both know why they requested you."

"By the way, that's something else. I haven't done any shooting. But a couple of people have turned up dead, and I keep hearing that it's me who took them out."

A grunt from his father. "No surprise there either."

"I'm not being set up, if that's what you're thinking. There's no way to tie me in with those killings."

"Not set up, maybe, but you're clearly being used. You came to these people with a reputation, Adam. In my work, I hire reputations all the time. Most times, all they do is sit in on a meeting. They stare across the table at the opposition's people as if they can't wait to be let loose on them. Reputations, by their nature, intimidate, Adam. I suspect that's been your primary function."

"The twins don't just stare."

"No, they do what is needed. But like you, they've done less than they're thought to have done. The difference is that I'll never let them take a fall. Walk away from this, Adam, while you can."

"And do nothing?"

"What they do is almost legal. What you do's not even close. You can't win this one, Adam. Give it up."

"Dad, I can't. I can't just walk away."

"You can and you will, as you should have at the start. That ledger will be your insurance. I'll take it back with me, then I'll let them know I have it. You're out of this as of right now."

The argument didn't end there, of course. It continued through dinner and resumed in the morning. Whistler knew very well that his father was right. In the short term he might cause a few resignations, perhaps even a congressional inquiry. Longer term, however, very little would change. New names, new faces, same game. In the meantime, his own face would be in the papers. That was bad because there were plenty of others who might want to settle old scores. He knew that his father was right about that. Some would want vengeance for things that he'd done, and others for things that he hadn't done but ended up being credited for. And now they would know what he looked like.

His father said, "We had fresh snow last night. Let's forget this for now and go skiing."

Later that morning they were up on the mountain. They'd skied Little Nell and had paused at Last Dollar. His father's back was still giving him trouble. He would need to stop every few hundred yards, but quitting was out of the question.

He couldn't recall how the subject arose, but they found themselves talking about trust. He trusted his father. That trust was absolute. He remarked that he couldn't think of anyone else that he was able to talk to this way.

"No, Adam," said his father, "there's more to it than that. The truth is that you have no one else."

And he was right.

Here he was, a month shy of his thirty-fourth birthday and his personal life was nonexistent. He'd known a few women. Here and there. Now and then. But nothing that could have been called an involvement. And those that he'd met in his line of work all carried as much baggage as he did.

He and his father had been having this discussion as they

watched other skiers coming up on the chairlift. Most were couples; they were chatting and grinning. Seeing how much they were enjoying each other made Whistler feel lonelier than ever.

His father asked, "Have you tried to meet someone?"

"You mean someone like these? Someone normal?"

"Why not?"

"I get tired of lying when they ask what I do. I've been lying to people since I was ten, except then it was when someone asked me about you."

His father pretended that his feelings were hurt. "Well, I wish you could have grown up on Sesame Street, Adam. I'm sorry I was such an embarrassment."

"You know that's not what I mean. Cut it out."

"Then you're saying what? That you're doomed to be a loner?"

"I . . . meet lots of people who I'd like to know better. But it's over before it begins."

"We're talking dating, Adam. We're not talking confessionals. The lady, I assure you, won't bare her soul either. And, by the way, no one is 'normal.' "

"Yeah, well . . ."

"I do know how you feel. I might have felt the same way, but I had the good luck to meet your mother."

"Yeah, but Mom knew who you were from the start."

"I still kept things from her. Only things that would worry her. In all else, however, we were open with each other. We were partners in every sense of the word. My God, she was wonderful, wasn't she?"

Whistler's mother had died of ovarian cancer. Too young. She was only forty-six at the time. She could out-ski either one of them, out-sail almost anyone, but she carried herself with such grace and good humor that they both enjoyed being outdone by her in these and a hundred other ways.

"I still talk to her, Adam. Did you know that?"

"I've heard you. I've done that myself from time to time."

"That's okay, but get your own. Find another woman like her."

"There aren't any women like her."

"I'll ask you again. Have you looked?"

"I guess not really."

"You'll find someone, Adam, but you've got to let it happen. If you think it can't happen, it won't."

"I suppose."

"Now's a good time to start. Want to meet one? Are you ready?"

"Um . . . who?"

"That pretty young lady right there."

He was pointing at Claudia. It was totally at random. She was coming up on the lift at that moment and she had the chair to herself. She saw them looking at her and returned a little smile. She got off, did her boots, and was about to go on when his father called out to her. He asked her to wait. To Whistler's dismay, his father pulled him forward. He proceeded to make an introduction.

"My name," he announced, "is Harry Whistler, and this is my bashful son, Adam. He's an adequate skier and not so bad-looking except when he's rolling his eyes. Is he doing that?"

Her smile became a grin. "He's trying not to."

"Have you ever skied Europe? Ever skied the French Alps?"

"Only in my dreams. Maybe someday."

"Not to push it, but I'd love to have you both come to visit. I have a chalet there. You'd have your own room."

She looked at Adam. "Not to push it?"

"Please ignore him."

"Is there really a chalet?"

"In Chamonix, yes. But don't listen to this."

He didn't remember regarding her then as being exceptionally beautiful. What struck him most was her warmth. She had a glow about her that was purely her own long before she ever met that white light.

Her ski suit, come to think of it, was a solid white as well. That heightened the effect of the glow. Her body seemed lean, long-muscled, athletic. Bronze skin, nose lightly freckled, her hair golden brown. She wore it shoulder-length, curled under her chin, held in place by a white woolen headband. Her eyes were brown as well and had little gold flecks. Her mouth seemed almost too wide for her face, but the grin it produced was just dazzling.

She took off her glove and held out her hand. She said, "My name's Claudia. Hi."

Whistler took it, still trying to stammer an apology. His father, he said, was, well, his father.

A knowing nod said that she understood. "My mother does this to me all the time. No harm done. Nice meeting you, Adam."

With that, she waved and started down the hill. He watched her go. She was a marvelous skier. His father smacked his arm. "Why are you still here?" But he'd waited too long and he'd lost sight of her.

6

He saw her in the village early that evening. He'd gone out hoping that he would. His father, happily, had remained at their hotel, opting for a soak in that Jacuzzi. Whistler spotted her standing outside a ski shop, looking over a rack of jackets and sweaters on sale at fifty-percent off. She had unzipped her ski suit down to her breastbone. She wore a white turtleneck underneath. He could see that her body was considerably more shapely than the ski suit had previously revealed.

And she also looked younger than she had on the hill. Too young. This was crazy. He had started to turn, deciding not to approach her, but she glanced up and saw him. He was caught.

She said, "Hi, Adam." She'd remembered his name. He could feel the color rising on his cheeks.

"Claudia, look, that business on the mountain . . ."

"It was sweet if that was really your father."

"Oh, it was."

"You seemed more like good friends than a father and son. I like that. Is your mom here as well?"

"She's . . . no. We lost her. Some years ago."

"I'm sorry. Me, too. My dad, I mean."

He said, "Claudia, if I asked you . . . to have dinner with me . . ."

"You mean here or in France?"

"Well, I thought here for starters."

"Rats, I was ready to be swept off my feet. Are you terribly rich and successful?"

"Not terribly."

"Well, at least are you nice? You seem pretty nice."

"I could go and get a note from my father. Would that help?"

She laughed. "Maybe I'll take your word."

"Does . . . that mean you'll have dinner?"

"How about a cup of tea? Would you settle for that?"

"If I have to. Sure. Name the place."

"Help me pick out a sweater, then we'll walk to the Jerome. I'm meeting my mother there in ten minutes. Call your father, see if he'd care to join us."

"He's . . . taking a bath. I don't think he'd . . ."

"It's your chance to get even. Fix him up with my mom. Anyway, he's fun. Why don't you call him?"

"Sure, why not?"

Actually, he knew, there was almost no need. His father, very soon, would know where he'd be because, out of nowhere, looking over those sale racks, was one of the Beasley twins, Donald.

It might have been Dennis, but he thought it was Donald. Donald had always been the paunchier of the two. He had on a blue parka and a dumb-looking ski hat, the kind with the little red pom-pom on top. But Dennis, of course, would be dressed the same way and Dennis had a gut of his own. It could just as easily have been Dennis.

A double date with parents wasn't what he'd had in

mind, but he thought that it might grease the flow of conversation. He did call his father and his father came down. His father showed up at the Hotel Jerome sporting his Stetson and that big shearling coat. The tea did lead to dinner after all.

Mrs. Geller—Kate—was a handsome woman who almost could have been an older sister. Same coloring, same smile, and almost the same figure, give or take some matured redistribution. She wore a black turtleneck and a Harris Tweed jacket with a sprig of holly pinned to the lapel. She had the same easy warmth that had attracted him to Claudia. And his father had always had an effortless charm that Whistler had never quite managed. The two parents hit it off right away.

The fact that his father lived over in Europe—where he said that he was an investment consultant—seemed to add to the comfort level between them. A pleasant encounter, but ships in the night. He'd be flying back in another two days. She knew that they would probably not meet again, but she told him that she hoped he'd send a postcard. That allowed Whistler's father to give her his card and ask Kate for her home address. She reached into her purse for a card of her own and placed it on the table before him.

Whistler's father caught his eye and showed him the address. Whistler must have frowned when he saw it.

"Is something wrong, Adam?" Mrs. Geller had asked him.

"Wrong? Oh, no. Nothing at all."

"It's Claudia's address, too, if that's what you're wondering. She's moved back in for a while."

"You've . . . read my mind, Mrs. Geller."

What had caused his reaction was the name of the town. Silver Ridge was on the long list of affluent communities that were mentioned in Felix Aubrey's ledger. If a town was listed, someone there was in his pocket. It might be a police chief or a county prosecutor, a tax assessor or a judge. Whistler couldn't recall what names were listed or how many property seizures had occurred there. But the fact that

Aubrey had connections in that town seemed reason enough
to avoid it.

Not that he'd been invited. Whistler pushed it from his
mind. The future was one thing, the present was another, and
he was enjoying the evening. During dinner he began hearing all about Claudia. Not from Claudia herself, who kept
trying to change the subject, but from her intensely proud
mother.

"She's a wonderful dancer. She studied ballet."

He said, "I'm not surprised. I've seen her ski. Good
skiers always seem to be good dancers."

"She didn't stick with it. She keeps trying new things.
Did you know that she's a triathlete?"

"No, I didn't," Whistler answered. "I'm surprised and impressed."

"She's competed in two triathlons so far. Races mountain
bikes, too, and she ice skates like a dream. In college, she
was a star pitcher."

"Women's softball?"

"Men's baseball. She was pretty hot stuff. Claudia was
the only girl in the state to play on a varsity team. She was
featured once on ESPN. Scholar-athlete, too. Straight As
right through school."

"Mom, quit it," said Claudia. She was drumming her fingers. "Besides, most of that isn't true."

"It isn't?" Whistler asked.

"Well, it's way overstated. To begin with, I did not have
straight As."

"Okay, dean's list," said her mother. "Same thing."

"No, it's not. As for pitching, my best season was five
wins, eight losses, so don't sign me up with the Yankees just
yet. As for mountain-bike racing, lots of starts, zero wins. As
for those two triathlons, I only finished one, and in that one I
barely staggered across. And as for ballet—"

"Boobs too big," said her mother.

"Sure, and whose fault is that? Look at yours."

"I'm . . . ah, still impressed," said Whistler, almost blush-
ing. "I'm not that good at anything I've tried."

"Not true," said his father.

"Didn't think so," said Claudia. "Let's talk about you for a change."

That was where the lies started, mixed in with the truth. Grew up in Europe, went to French and Swiss schools, then came over here to go to college. All true.

"By here, you mean the States?"

"Here in Colorado. Boulder. I went to UC, but . . . well, I didn't finish. I dropped out in my senior year."

"Flunking? Girl trouble? What made you leave?"

"Nothing like that. I just needed a change. I joined the army. Finished school in the service. After that, I got into consulting." Partly true.

"What kind of consulting?"

"Right now I'm with the Department of Commerce. Trade agreements, import quotas—that kind of thing. Dry stuff, on the whole, but I do enjoy the travel." This part was entirely false.

But Claudia and her mother had no reason to doubt them. And his father, as long as they were being inventive, proceeded to fill in the blanks. He told a few stories about his boyhood, young manhood, all intended to make him seem wholesome, unthreatening, and at least a passable athlete.

"So he's an only child? No brothers or sisters?"

His father answered, "One of him is enough."

Neither Claudia nor her mother seemed to catch the evasion. In fact, there had been a younger sister. His father said to Claudia, "Adam lives outside Washington. Do you ever have occasion to go east?"

"Not to Washington. I've never been there."

"I'm sure Adam would be happy to show you around."

She grinned. "Not to push it, though, right?"

"Yes, he is," said Whistler, "but he's going to stop."

"Not on my account. I'm enjoying it."

She later told him how he'd stammered and blushed as he tried to ask his next question. "Sometimes I have business out here—well, in Denver. If I were to call you . . ."

"I'd like that. Please do."

"Really?"

"Yes, really."

"I mean . . . look . . . I know I'm putting you on the spot . . ."

The grin spread wider. "Did your father just kick you?"

Yes, he had. "No, I want to. What I mean to say is . . ."

"Do I have to kick you myself?"

"No, you don't."

"Then call me the next time you're coming."

7

Too young, too nice, and maybe too bright. Add to that the fact that she lived in Silver Ridge, where Aubrey must have eyes and ears. On the other hand, as his father said later, the question was more like "Where doesn't he?" Even so, it seemed a better idea not to venture where there might be dragons.

He would not call Claudia.

Well . . . maybe he would.

Maybe she would agree to meet him in Denver. Neutral ground. More to do. Better restaurants.

He did call. He suggested it, but she wouldn't hear of it.

She said, "You're invited to come out to the house. Your father says you need some home cooking."

"My father? When was this?"

"Mom and your father have been faxing each other. You know, just stuff about skiing and such, but your name came up once or twice."

"Once or twice?"

"Yeah, I know. He's still trying to push us together. But so what? Let's see if we click."

"Um . . . there's no boyfriend? No one else in your life?"

"Tom Cruise, Richard Gere, and a few Saudi princes. But I'll dump them if you're coming out."

"Start dumping. I'll be there next Friday night."

"You'll stay at the house?"

"Sure, I'd love to."

He flew out for the weekend. They spent two full days together. He came back almost every two weeks after that. He'd heard from Aubrey once. A request for a meeting. Whistler refused. After that, only silence from Aubrey.

Even knowing that he was probably still under surveillance, Whistler went about his days normally. He and Claudia would do all the usual things. Go to movies, go to dinner, take long walks or long drives. He would often ask her mother to join them. She did on occasion but would usually decline. Other times, he'd help out at the garden center. It was just down the hill from their house. Spring was approaching and both greenhouses were filled with trays of spring flowers grown from seed. Whistler's knowledge of plants had been almost nil if one didn't count poppies and hemp. But he found that he rather liked working with plants of the gentler and decorative sort. Trays that he'd prepared would have burst into life between one visit and the next. It was not a big thing; it was done every day, but it still seemed a minor miracle to him. He could almost see himself doing this with his own life. It seemed such a peaceful occupation.

His father, early on, had phoned Delbert Poole.

"Do you know who I am?"

"Some relation to young Adam?"

"I'm his father, yes, but I'm something more than that." He suggested that Poole make a call of his own. He gave him the name of one Roger Clew, a senior State Department official. He suggested that Poole telephone Clew at once and ask him about Harry Whistler.

"It is in your interest to know who I am and who my associates are. That established, you will receive a visit from another acquaintance of mine and Mr. Clew's. It will be a civil visit. You'll be shown certain papers. I think you can guess what they are."

"I've no idea."

"Yeah, you do. From Aubrey's ledger. And yes, my son took it."

"I'm . . . sure that I don't know what you mean, sir."

"Make the call."

Poole did make the call. It had its effect. Clew suggested that he take Harry Whistler at his word if he hoped to postpone meeting Jesus. The "associate" appeared at Delbert Poole's office with selections from the ledger in hand.

Who were these associates? His father wouldn't say. This was normal enough, a need-to-know thing, but it still annoyed him that Poole could be told while he, Whistler, who was central to all this, was being kept in the dark. He did, however, at least know Roger Clew. Clew had worked Europe for much of his career, his specialty being Intelligence. He had been to the house in Geneva many times. But Whistler hadn't seen him since the year his mother died. Clew was one of the speakers at her service.

His father said that Poole made a show of being shocked when his caller let him read a few pages. Poole swore that he knew nothing of any "loss or leakage" of property that had been seized. He denied that people who were otherwise innocent were targeted for punitive raids. This was interesting, said his father, because he hadn't been accused of targeting and looting the innocent. Poole said that he would certainly have a talk with Felix Aubrey and get to the bottom of this matter. The visitor said, "Let's go do that together."

Aubrey tried to stonewall, claimed the ledger was a forgery. The visitor advised Aubrey to rethink that point of view. She said that Harry Whistler had expected the denial. There was ample corroboration, she said, in the form of several sworn affidavits.

"She?" Whistler asked.

"A very capable she. Not that her gender is relevant."

"And what affidavits? Affidavits sworn by whom?"

"That's what Poole would like to know. Let him wonder."

"I . . . take it that there are no affidavits."

"If not, they'd be easy to come by and he knows it. There's

always somebody who'll flip or sell out at the mention of a possible indictment."

"Or the threat of a possible accident."

"Whatever."

"So, where was it left?"

"They behave. We'll behave. And you walk away from this, Adam."

Whistler was doubtful that they'd leave it at that. They'd fret for a while. They'd try to cover their tracks. But sooner or later they'd look for a way to try to regain an advantage.

"They must know that I've been spending some time in Silver Ridge."

"Sure they do. And they'd naturally wonder whether what you've been doing is turning whoever's on their payroll out there. They would wonder whether that's where those affidavits came from. They'll look into that and they'll satisfy themselves that their people out there had never heard of you before. They'll see that your only interest in Silver Ridge is a girl who happens to live there. They'll check her out. It should go no further. But of course you'll be watched while you're visiting."

"They'll tap the Gellers' phone."

"Well, of course. Wouldn't you?"

"Which would mean they'll be reading those faxes you send. They'll know that you're friendly with Kate."

"Adam, they read what I want them to read. Their content is innocent, and they serve as a reminder that I'm not as far away as I seem. They also suggest that you have more on your mind than causing trouble for them."

Whistler still wasn't sure. This all seemed too easy. And it wasn't like his father to leave so much to chance. Ordinarily, his father would probably have urged him to come over to Europe for a year or two. Stay away from Silver Ridge. Forget about Claudia. Or stay in touch, if he feels that he must. Better yet, bring Claudia to Europe.

He would also have made sure that Aubrey and Poole were left with no doubt that he was serious. He would have had the twins visit each of their homes late at night when they were in bed with their wives. They'd wake up to a gun muzzle stuck in their mouths. A twin would say, *"Hush. Don't wake up the nice lady. Harry Whistler asked me to drop by."* They would be asked to blink to show that they understood. The twin would say, *"For now, all I want is to give you food for thought about how easy I could make you not a problem. Blink again so I know you started thinking."* He'd get his blink and probably a squeal. *"That's good. Go back to sleep. I'll let myself out. Your alarm system sucks, I should mention."*

Maybe they'd done that. Or maybe these faceless "associates" had. But Whistler didn't think so. As far as he could tell from his father's account, it was simply a semi-polite office visit that laid out the terms of their parting of ways.

His father heard the silence. "What's bothering you, Adam?"

"Me walking away with them not even singed. You might have been a little too generous."

"Perhaps. But this thing's a done deal."

"If you say so."

"Adam, let it go. Forget about those turkeys. There will always be hypocrites; there will always be thieves. What we're short of is people like the Gellers."

And of course that was it. His father was being less thorough than usual because he was still playing Cupid. Add to that, he'd grown fond of Kate Geller himself. Initially, the idea behind all those faxes was to give the potential young lovebirds a nudge. They'd ended up nudging themselves in the process. His father's original intention had been clear right from that first day in Aspen. His hope was that the closer his son got to Claudia, the less he would care about things he couldn't change and find something more useful to do.

He said, "Adam, go. Get on with your life. Give Kate a kiss for me, okay?"

If indeed the plan was to get him refocused, that part of it was working fairly well. He found himself losing interest in Aubrey. He found himself being gentled by a woman who was so much better than any of those people that his heart did not have room for much else.

Still, one could not have called it a whirlwind romance. They had kissed; they'd held hands, but that was all.

She had already asked him, "Is something wrong, Adam?"

"Wrong? No, what could be wrong?"

"Well, you've never . . . I don't know. Never mind. It's okay."

"No, go ahead. If something's bothering you . . ."

"Nothing is. It's okay. Never mind."

Whistler never claimed to know much about women, but he knew that "never mind" never meant "never mind." Whatever it meant, he thought he'd probably find out before this latest visit was over. She said, "Let's go someplace quiet. Just us."

She said that she'd like to drive up into the mountains. They'd park and they'd walk a trail that she knew offered some fabulous views. He took that to mean no interruptions.

She hadn't said much while on the way up. Perhaps she was saving it for one of the views. He began to worry that she'd heard something somewhere and wasn't sure whether to confront him with it. They parked and started up the trail that she'd mentioned. Still nothing, but she seemed quite distracted.

Her distraction, and his own, almost got them both eaten. They had rounded a blind spot on the trail they were following and came upon a cougar and two cubs. The mother mountain lion had just caught a rabbit. She hadn't killed it; the rabbit was still kicking. She was probably teaching the cubs how to hunt. Occupied by that task, she hadn't heard their approach, or perhaps the scent of fresh blood had masked their own. The startled cougar snarled and braced for a charge, but seemed torn between going after these intruders and staying to protect her cubs and her lunch.

Whistler, on instinct, went into a crouch, first pulling Claudia behind him. He looked for a rock, a stick, any weapon, but there were none within reach. All he could think of was to slip off his jacket, maybe use it to blind the big cat if she charged.

He heard Claudia hiss, "Stop that and stand still."

She was at his side, one hand on his shoulder, the other on the jacket that he had removed to keep him from raising or flapping it.

"Don't crouch," she said. "Stand up straight so you look big. Now back away slowly and stare, stare her down. Don't look at the cubs. Only her."

Her voice, more than calm, had a cooing sound. She could almost have been singing a lullaby.

"Now turn, really slowly, and we'll walk down the trail."

"Turn our backs?"

"Do it, Adam. She just wants us to leave."

Whistler had no intention of turning his back, but he did start down the trail at her side. The cougar, in response, began to ease off as well. The mother cat's snarls and threatening feints settled down into something like muttering. She hissed at her cubs. The hiss was telling them to leave. The cubs hesitated, then scampered away. The mother grabbed the rabbit and followed.

Claudia was silent for several minutes as they made their way back down the mountain. Whistler was watching her, admiring her, while keeping one eye on the trail behind them lest the cat reconsider its menu.

When Claudia spoke, she said, "You weren't afraid."

"Oh, yeah? Tell that to my pulse."

She stopped and put a hand to his chest to feel its beat. "That's not even seventy to the minute," she said, "and we're hiking eight thousand feet up."

He thought that all she was trying to say was that she believed he'd been fairly brave. He said, "Back there? You're the one who took over. All I did was what I was told."

Another odd silence. She was walking very slowly. "Adam, will you answer a question?"

"Sure."

"Do you carry a gun?"

"Why would you ask that?"

"When you moved in front of me, you reached one hand behind you. You were reaching for the small of your back."

"I was not."

"In movies I've seen, that's where men carry guns. You're not carrying one now, but you reached for it."

"No, I didn't."

She reached behind his waist and felt for his belt at the spot where she'd seen his hand go. "Your belt is worn down there. No, the leather is flattened. What would do that, a clamp on a holster?"

"Claudia, it's just an old belt."

"I'd like us to go camping. Just you and me."

"Why camping all of a sudden?"

"I want us to go camping so that we can be alone. Two days, just us, no one else within miles. You can kick back and take all the time you need to tell me who Adam Whistler is."

"I already have. There's not much more to tell."

"The silences, Adam. All those long thoughtful pauses. Those times when I knew that you wanted to say something, but you couldn't quite bring yourself to say it."

"There's no wife or anything. If that's what you think."

"My mom got that much from your dad."

"There's no one. It's true."

"I also saw the look between you and your dad when Mom asked if there were brothers or sisters."

"There are none."

"You say *are*. Were there ever?"

Whistler took a long breath and let it out slowly. He picked up a rock and he threw it before answering.

"Claudia, not all evasions are sinister. I did have a sister. She died very young. It is not the sort of thing one would chat about at dinner. It remains a hurtful subject for both me and my father. I am asking you to leave it alone."

"Oh, boy."

They walked on a little farther. He asked, "Oh, boy, what?"

"It's personal and it's hurtful. I understand that. But you can't drop a thing like that with a thud and expect me to leave it alone."

A sigh. "For now, then. Please leave it for now."

"Could I at least know her name?"

Another breath. "It's Alicia."

"How young?"

"Nineteen."

"I have one other question. Then nothing more, ever, unless you bring up the subject."

"Go ahead."

"Is the subject so hurtful because you caused her death?"

Whistler blinked. "God, no. What would make you think that?"

"It's . . . more that I don't want to think it."

"Well, I didn't. She was in school in California at the time, and I was here in Boulder at UC. You thought what? Drunken driving? I ran us into a tree?"

"Adam, give me a break. Who wouldn't have wondered?"

"You saw regret and assumed it was guilt. I regret that I was so far away. I regret a hundred things that I wish I'd said or done. People always do when it's too late."

"I realize that, Adam. And I'm sorry."

"Let's forget it."

"I have another question—different subject—involves us. But maybe I'd better let it wait now."

He grunted. "Look who's talking about thuds."

"Well, it's a little personal. And you might take it wrong."

"When has *personal* stopped you? Dive right in."

"Better not."

"If you don't, I will tie you up and leave you for that cat. But don't let that affect your decision."

"Okay, here it is. Do you find me attractive?"

"Are you kidding?"

"No, I'm serious. Do you?"

"On your worst day, Claudia, you'd still be world-class. On the inside, you'd rate even higher."

She said, "Hmmm."

"Okay, what?"

"So, maybe it's the inside that's holding you back? You think you shouldn't mess around with Snow White?"

Uh-oh, thought Whistler. He could see what was coming. He said, "That's not it at all."

"Well, then, that's the other reason why I want to go camping. . . . I would like you either to make love to me, Adam, or explain to me why you haven't tried."

His color rose. He was no good at this. He said, "I don't know. I . . . guess I've been afraid. . . ."

"Of what? That you'd ruin it? You're not that straitlaced."

"Well . . ."

"And you can't tell me now that it's been fear of rejection. I think I just burst that bubble. Do you think I'm too young? Is that it?"

"Maybe partly."

"You won't ruin me either. My high school prom date did that."

"Could we just . . . back up to where you wanted to go camping?"

"And talking. That's part of the deal."

He nodded. "Okay. Next trip out we'll go camping."

"No, tonight. Let's go home and get my gear."

They did go camping. They talked for hours on end. And he told her a dozen well-rehearsed lies that he'd used as a cover for years.

He acknowledged that he'd sometimes carried a pistol but only when abroad in wild country like this. His work with NAFTA often took him to places where snakes and wild animals like that lion were common. There were also bandits who called themselves rebels and who've made a cottage industry of kidnapping foreigners and forcing families or employers to pay ransom. Personally, however, he had not had any problems.

"Just as well," he added. "I'm not good with guns."

"You were in the army, but you're not good with guns?"

"Claudia, I thought we were talking about handguns. Soldiers hardly ever fire them, let alone get proficient."

"And you're not?"

"I'd do just as well throwing rocks."

While camping, they caught a few trout and they cooked them. Over coffee, he told her a bit more about Alicia. He said he knew that he ought to be over it by now. She'd been dead for about thirteen years. She'd been a freshman at UCLA when he was a senior at Boulder. She went to a party in the posh Brentwood suburb and somebody slipped her some drugs. She was not used to drugs, never touched them before. She went into convulsions, died later that night.

"The person who gave her the drugs . . . was he punished?"

"There were several involved. They were all brought to justice."

"Was your mother still alive?"

"She had died the year before. She'd been ill for some time. The only good thing I can say about her dying is that she didn't have to know about Alicia."

She took his hand. She caressed it. "I'm very sorry, Adam."

She was looking at the back of his hand. Her fingertips ran across two of his knuckles. She had noticed before this that they were misshapen. She seemed about to ask what had happened to his hand, but she shook off the thought as unimportant.

"But, thank you, Adam. I'm glad that you told me. It's better than carrying it inside you."

They did make love. Shyly, awkwardly, at first. They had joined two sleeping bags by the zippers. Afterward, they said little. They just held each other. Then they fell asleep looking at the stars.

They woke up at first light and they made love again, this time with a bit less self-consciousness.

So he thought.

He marveled that a body so firm, so athletic could become so incredibly soft and yielding. It was tender, it was shy, it was giving. It was everything. But after the second time, as they held each other, she gave his shoulder a squeeze. With a sad little smile, she said, "It will get better."

Surprised, he answered, "That gets better? Better how?"

She said what women say. She said, "Shhh. It's all right."

He touched her face. "Claudia . . . you just lobbed a grenade. In my mind, I'm thinking how lucky I am and how wonderful that was for me. But I've disappointed you, haven't I? Have I?"

"I—thought it was the other way around."

"That you disappointed me? Are you out of your mind?"

"I didn't?"

"You couldn't. Not in any way, ever. Especially not making love."

She said, "You're sweet."

"But you're not buying it. Why?"

She said, "Look, Adam, I shouldn't have said anything. I'm not one of these women who has sex and then critiques it. But I did hope that this would get us over the hump—" She winced. "Sorry, Adam. Bad choice of words. But I don't think you had your heart in it."

She was right, of course. But so was he. Claudia wasn't the problem.

If his heart wasn't in it—not one hundred percent—it was because a part of him felt like a rat. It was all the lies and the half-truths—the evasions.

She deserved so much better than that.

8

He hadn't lied when she asked about his sister. He had told her the truth, bare bones though it was. It was certainly true that Alicia was clean. She did like to party and she was a flirt. She drank, but she never touched drugs. The party she went to in the Hollywood Hills was hosted by two brothers, two rich kids. They gave her a spiked Margarita.

The spike was GHB, a synthetic depressant, the first of the so-called date-rape drugs. The street dealers called it by a number of names, the most popular of which was "Easy Lay." It was odorless, colorless, but it had a salty taste. That was why the drinks of choice were Margaritas. Mixed with alcohol, a few grams would put the victim to sleep. Two drinks would pretty much guarantee loss of memory, and the sleep would deepen into coma. The brothers who were spiking her drinks gave her three. Then they carried her upstairs and they raped her.

It got worse.

The two brothers had also been doing cocaine. They ran out of it, wanted more, and called their dealer. The dealer lived in a house off Sunset. He drove over and he brought his partner. This was late at night; all the other guests had gone, except Alicia, who was in an upstairs bedroom. The first two offered to share her. They took turns. She wouldn't have known what was happening.

At some point, one of the two brothers realized that Alicia was barely breathing. Her heart would race, and then almost stop. Her skin had become cold and clammy. The brothers decided that they'd better get rid of her, maybe dump her in front of a hospital. They asked the two dealers to do it. The two dealers, however, had no such intention. They took her instead to the UCLA campus. There, they found a fraternity house that was having a party of its own. It was raining at the time. Everyone was inside. They left her barely alive, if not dead, on the lawn of that fraternity house. That was where she was found the next morning.

Whistler got the news from his father. A police lieutenant had called him. His father would be flying to Los Angeles from Geneva, but would not arrive until the next morning. Whistler didn't wait. He flew out at once. It was Whistler who identified her body.

An autopsy hadn't yet been performed but they'd done a preliminary blood test. They knew that the GHB had killed her. The police had also traced her movements that night. They knew the two brothers. Both had arrest records. Aside from arrests for simple drug possession, they'd been accused of using GHB before on at least one other occasion. But they were the sons of some studio executive who had always bought their way out of trouble. The brothers, shown a photograph, said she did seem familiar. They acknowledged that she might have been at their party, but if so, she'd left it well before midnight. The police were unable to make an arrest without an admission from someone involved. With DNA testing not yet in existence, the rape charge couldn't be proved.

Whistler, once again, didn't wait for his father. The police wouldn't give him the two brothers' names, but he took a taxi to the freshman dorms, where he got them from Alicia's weeping roommate. He went to see the brothers; he pushed his way in. The brothers were defiant. They told him to fuck off. He used his fists and a chair to beat them both half to death. He needed the chair because he'd broken several knuckles. A neighbor heard all the banging and screaming and telephoned the police. Whistler was arrested for assault at the scene. He spent half the night in an Emergency ward and the next half locked in a cell. His father came to see him the next afternoon.

His father, by then, had also seen Alicia. He came to the holding cell, his eyes cold and distant. His eyes eventually fell on Whistler's hands. One was bandaged; one was in a plaster cast.

Quietly, he said, "Adam, never use your fists. Heads, as you now realize, are harder than fists. But many things are harder than heads."

Whistler glared. "Alicia's dead."

"I'm aware of that, Adam."

"And you want to talk about my hands?"

"No, Adam, the subject is not being foolish. I will leave you to give it some thought."

His father left him in custody, declined to post bail, and flew back to Europe by himself. While he was in Geneva, and could prove that he was, the brother whom Whistler had hurt the less severely was released from the hospital and vanished. The second brother, whose facial bones he'd shattered, would face months of reconstructive surgery. That one, because he was kept in the hospital, was the luckier of the two. A day later, the two drug dealers were found, both suspended from a pipe in their basement. The brother who had vanished was also found dead. He'd been left to bake in the trunk of a car that was parked near the drug dealers' house.

The police questioned Whistler to ask him what he knew. That was the first that he'd heard of it. They declined to give details of how the drug dealers died, but the newspapers said that the scene was horrific. They had choked to death after being mutilated in a way that was meant to send a message. Whistler could guess what the mutilations were. He guessed that they'd choked on the same body part that they'd used to take their pleasure with Alicia.

The second brother soon vanished as well, but as far as Whistler knew, he might have survived. His wealthy parents had put guards on his room until they could arrange to have him airlifted elsewhere. They went with him, but they wouldn't have had much to come back to. Their Brentwood home, where those parties had been held, was burned to the ground in their absence.

These reprisals, their brutality, had shocked Whistler at first. Well, not shocked, perhaps, but they surprised him. Of course he knew who and what his father was by that time, but he'd never known his father to be cruel. He'd once heard his father reprimand an associate for maiming, then killing a man who'd betrayed him. "If you have to kill, kill. Don't get personal about it. Do it quick, do it clean, and be done with it."

He could not imagine that his father had specified a painful and horrifying death. Not even for what had been done to Alicia. But the twins, who had also watched Alicia grow up, might have had ideas of their own. Donald, especially, had been fond of Alicia. He had built her a dollhouse made entirely of wine corks when she was about eight years old. And as Whistler learned later, leaving people in car trunks was something of a signature of the twins. All this, however, was again just a guess. Neither they nor his father would speak of it again. All his father would say was, "It's done with."

Whistler, at the time, was still sitting in a jail cell. He had, as he was sure that his father intended, an incontestable alibi. But he was still charged with felonious assault, with intent to commit grievous harm. Other charges were added. Another assault. An inmate had attacked him while he was in custody; tried to stab him with a prison-made shank. That time, of necessity, Whistler used his feet and he used his plaster cast as a club. He took a few cuts as he went for the man's knees. He managed to connect and when he had the man down, he crushed the man's knife hand with his heel.

His father, at last, arranged for his bail. His father said he'd try to get the charges thrown out. The complainant had, after all, disappeared and the jail fight was clearly self-defense. The prosecutor, however, would not let him off, but he had a proposal of his own. If Whistler would enter the military service for an enlistment of not less than three years, all of the charges would be dropped.

Whistler learned, much later, that he could have gotten off. The enlistment condition was his father's idea. His father had thought that it would help him grow up. He thought that it might also keep him out of harm's way until the twins, or whoever, cleaned up some loose ends. The attack by that inmate was no jailhouse brawl. The father of the two who raped Alicia had arranged it.

"Not much of a story," he'd told Claudia's mother. *"One thing leading to another,"* he'd said.

Where it led, at the outset, was him learning how to kill. His father never taught him. The army did that. It might not have been what his father had intended, but it's something that the army does well. If Whistler had to do three years in the service, he decided that he ought to make the most of it. He spent his first year making up his college credits. He considered Officer Candidate School but opted for another kind of education at the Ranger School at Fort Benning. He became an Airborne Ranger. He was in the Gulf War. His team spent three weeks behind Iraqi lines during the chaos of the allied air attacks. His team's mission was recon until it was ordered to "disrupt the Iraqi chain of command." In plain English, that meant killing generals.

His team used Iraqi weapons for the task. This was to make the ambush scene appear to be the work of mutinous troops, most of whom were there under duress. The Iraqis, in reprisal, executed whole units that had merely been in the vicinity. That, in turn, however, led to hundreds of desertions. They probably saved more lives than they took. That, at least, was what their own general told them.

After that, the army found other ways to make sure that his training was usefully employed. Several of these involved little foreign wars that the public never heard much about. Some were incursions to extract personnel, but most of them were punitive raids against foreign-based terrorist groups. After that, increasingly, they went after drug barons.

Every branch of the service and many federal agencies had a role in the policy of drug interdiction. Most of these were set up to try to stem the supply. A hopeless task. They made almost no difference. At best, they interdicted one shipment in twenty, and many of those shipments were decoys.

The first punitive raids were authorized in response to the murder of government operatives in several of the trafficking countries. Well, not authorized, maybe. Such incursions were illegal. The teams that went in were made up of volunteers. They did what the law could not do. These raids were soon expanded to avenge other murders, such as those of reporters and honest officials, and even, in one case, a Catholic archbishop who'd become an annoyance to the traffickers. There were also raids that were made to appear the work of rival drug factions. The idea of those, as it was in Iraq, was to set them all killing each other.

That butchered family, those photos shown to Claudia, might possibly have been a retaliatory hit that grew out of one of his missions. Kate Geller had told him that the family looked Mexican and he'd certainly done work against the Mexican traffickers. The Mexicans had been known to wipe out whole families, including grandparents and children. But that family, much more likely, had nothing to do with him. Such a slaughter was a punishment that was usually reserved for one of their own who'd informed or had gone over to a rival. The people who did it would take photos and distribute them. If the victim had informed, they would send a copy to whatever competitor had enticed the betrayal. Briggs and Lockwood must have merely taken one from their files. Anyone could dig up a murder-scene photo and claim that so-and-so was responsible.

For a while, what he'd been doing had seemed right and just. His targets were all the most vicious of men and, in one case, a woman who was worse. He felt no ambivalence about it. The missions were exciting, a test of his skills, and the targets that he took out would claim no more victims. Again, as in Iraq, he told himself that he was saving lives in the long run. And by taking out targets who'd been killing too readily, he was sending a message to those who replaced them. In that sense, he served as a deterrent.

But as with interdiction, no lasting good came of it. Drug traffic, if anything, was increasing. The government was not about to admit that its policy of strict prohibition had failed. They looked for other weapons, other punitive measures. They took aim at the wealth of the traffickers. Laws were passed that permitted the wholesale seizure of property that was bought with drug money. Or alleged to have been bought. Or even rumored to have been bought. Although it took Whistler a while to see it, such distinctions were quickly ignored.

The seizure business had become a bonanza. At first it was only the DEA that had statutory forfeiture power. Well . . . that's not counting the IRS and Customs. Those agencies had always had that power. But then came the FBI, the FDA, the SEC, the Postal Service, even the Fish and Wildlife Bureau. This was not to mention some three thousand jurisdictions that set about looking for property to seize. Nor were drug-related gains a requirement. Almost any crime could result in a seizure. That included soliciting a hooker from your car. That's how some jurisdictions were getting new vehicles. And it's why so many more female cops were suddenly out working as decoys. This had nothing to do with suppressing vice. It had more to do with the value of your car. If you drove a Ford Pinto, you were safe.

As the seizure business became a major industry, a number of special units were formed. Delbert Poole's unit, as Whistler understood it, was tasked to go after "respectable" people who'd amassed their wealth not by trafficking, per se, but either by financing those who did or by helping to launder their profits. Delbert Poole had somehow heard about him and had put in a request for his services. Whistler suddenly found himself transferred.

His father didn't like the idea from the start. He'd also been saying that enough was enough. His father wanted him to come back to Geneva to take his place in the family business.

"Now it's a family business? Since when?"

"It will be if you join it. And it's more than a business. It's a way of life that answers to no one. I'd have thought that you'd miss it by now."

Yes, he did. From time to time. Sometimes he did have to answer to people whom his father would have ignored. But in the service, his achievements were his own. He wasn't just Harry Whistler's son.

"Adam, what's it called when your team goes in somewhere?"

"You know what it's called. It's called a punitive action."

"And the British army calls it 'remedial redress.' What would it be called if civilians went in?"

"We've been through this. I am not an assassin."

"If it quacks like a duck—never mind, I won't say it. But Adam, don't you see what a fine line you're straddling?"

"An assassin doesn't care who the target is. I reject far more than I accept."

"You reject or accept based on what you're told about them. Don't assume that you're always told the truth."

"Now you're saying I've been lied to. I don't think so."

"I'm saying it will happen sooner or later. Tell me about this new unit you've started with. You say it's run by civilians?"

"They're appointed by the National Security Council. I'm sure they've been thoroughly vetted . . ." He paused. "Unless you know something I don't."

"Not at the moment. I'll look into it, though."

"Yeah, you will, and then you'll tell me they're up to no good and that I'm just a pawn that they'll use and discard."

"They will have their own agenda. Can you doubt that?"

"I have mine."

"If you're . . . speaking of Alicia, you must let that go, Adam. I think she's been sufficiently avenged."

He was right, up to a point. He was almost always right. Alicia had always been in the back of his mind. One thing leading to another has to have a place to start. She was why he learned to do what he'd been doing.

Where it led, in the end, was to Claudia being shot. There was no direct connection. Just a chain of events. Except Claudia being shot was really more of a beginning. She'd been given back her life. And so had he.

But that day, in the hospital, he was still blind to it. He thought that what he'd had, what he'd almost had, was lost. He felt sure that if Claudia should come to her senses, she'd want nothing further to do with him. He knew that if she didn't, there still was no way that he would take advantage of her sickness. He told himself that all he cared about now was to see that his promise to her mother would be kept. That Aubrey wouldn't bother them, ever again.

He'd learned only one way to make sure of that.

9

He had no desire to confront Felix Aubrey. He had no wish to hear that toad of a man try to offer a deal or shift the blame. He would do this without any help from his father. He intended to simply put a hole in Aubrey's head and then pay a call on Delbert Poole.

The more he thought about it, Poole had to have known what his deputy, Aubrey, was up to. At least in broad strokes. The punitive part. He had to have known because Aubrey would have told him in order to cover himself. And Poole had seen the ledger. He knew about the ledger. He knew at least enough that, during that one meeting, he'd told Aubrey to put it away.

Poole, however, could deny that he'd known and he'd almost be telling the truth. Poole never approved anything, not in so many words. His practice was to either turn his back, saying nothing, or to cite a selection from the Bible. He would not cite the text, just the chapter and verse. He might say, for example, "Matthew 5:29. You'd do well to reflect on it, gentlemen."

Aubrey understood that the turning of his back meant, "Yes, but I know nothing about it." The biblical reference meant much the same thing, but it included God's approval as well. The operative text within 5:29 was the admonition, "if thy right eye offend thee, pluck it out . . ." Felix Aubrey would then order that someone be plucked. Most times it meant property. Sometimes it meant a life.

Whistler had been involved in a number of these actions, but his role had been limited to reconnaissance and disabling security equipment. In the beginning they seemed clearly

justified. The targets were all either criminal or corrupt, and
the evidence, though not actionable, was unquestioned.
They were rich men who funded major drug operations but
who kept a respectable front. But then he learned that some
who'd been targeted by Aubrey seemed to have no history of
involvement with drugs. All they had in common was that
they were rich and, apparently, had made enemies in Washington. Some might have made their money by questionable
means, but if so, that was none of Aubrey's business. He was
plucking them all the same.

Whistler intended to do his own plucking, but he couldn't
locate either Aubrey or Poole. Neither man had shown up at
the Center's office building, even though that building was
exceptionally secure. Their homes had been abandoned in
obvious haste. Whistler knew that because he had been inside both of them.

It came as no great surprise that they would go to ground
after learning of their losses thus far. They had to have assumed
that he'd be coming for them. He'd expected them, however, to
set out some bait and try to lure him into a trap. The least that
he'd expected was to find well-armed men waiting for him in
each of their homes. These men would have been told to try to
take him alive so that Aubrey could trade him for that ledger.
He doubted that they would have tried very hard. If Whistler,
therefore, had found them waiting in ambush, he probably
would have snapped one of their necks before departing as qui
etly as he'd come. He'd have left one there for the others to find.
It might cause them to rethink their career choice.

But there wasn't any ambush or bait. There was no attempt to take him at all. On the contrary, from what he could
learn, Aubrey's people had been given explicit instructions
to take no action against him. Whistler didn't understand it.
He could only guess why. Perhaps Aubrey and Poole were
having some trouble knowing whom they could trust to defend them. And, for that matter, they couldn't be sure of
who, or how many, they were up against. Whistler couldn't
say he blamed them. He didn't know either. He was going to
keep looking all the same.

* * *

On the fourth or fifth night of his hunt for Felix Aubrey, he was watching the home of an Aubrey family member who had profited from some of Aubrey's seizures. The home, quite a large one, was surrounded by a wall and had every security device. Two large German shepherds roamed the grounds. He had no reason to think that Aubrey would be there. Hiding out with a relative would not have been smart, even one who seemed so well protected. It was more that he'd run out of places to look.

He watched from his car until almost midnight. No one had emerged. The last lights had gone out. He decided not to bother going in for a look. He'd have to kill both those dogs to no purpose. In disgust, he reached to turn on his ignition, but froze when he sensed a movement to his rear. A shadow came forward. A hand tapped on his window.

A voice said, "Don't get nervous. It's me."

Whistler showed both his hands and he turned his head slowly. Donald Beasley was standing, arms folded, by his door.

He said, "Talk to me. Roll down your window."

Whistler let out a sigh and obeyed.

"This ain't too smart, is it? You know better than this. Never do things like this by yourself."

Whistler muttered a curse. "Where'd you come from?"

"Been around."

"How did you find me?"

"Never lost you, Adam. We got friends who been watching. Nice job, by the way, cracking Poole and Aubrey's houses, but didn't it get lonely inside?"

Whistler drew a patient breath. "Do you know where they are?"

Donald rocked a hand. "They can keep for right now. You been back to your apartment in Virginia?"

"Of course not," said Whistler. "That's the last place I'd go."

"That's good because you would have been dog food by now. What's the name of the guy we missed out in Denver? Not Briggs. The other one. The big one."

"Lockwood?"

"Yeah, that guy. Loose cannon. He's the only one after you. All the others crawled into a hole."

"Well? What about him? Do you know where he is?"

"There's him and another guy up on your roof. They've been there since the day before yesterday."

"Alive?"

"Hey, a guy wants to spend three days on a roof, the guy's a fucking moron; you let him. Anyhow, Dennis is down there with some friends. They'd have popped him if you had turned up."

"I keep hearing about friends. Who the hell are these friends?"

"Just friends," said Donald. "Don't worry about that. Anyhow, I got a message. Your father says sit. Don't do nothin' for a day, maybe two."

"What for? What's going on? Did he say?"

"He's working on a deal. Might be we end this."

"What kind of a deal? You mean one with Felix Aubrey?"

"Not him. It's with the preacher guy, Poole."

"I don't want any deal. All I want is to find them."

Donald Beasley spread his hands. "What, you're doing so great? A couple of days, we try some diplomacy. That don't work, then it's war. We go killing."

Two full days went by before his father finally called him. His father said that Poole had asked for a truce so that an understanding could be reached. Poole acknowledged that his people had overreacted to what *seemed* the "betrayal of their mission by his son." They had erred in deciding to punish "those two women" for refusing to be of assistance. He was mortified, he said, to learn that one had been shot. She'd been in his prayers ever since.

Poole offered guarantees, reparations, no reprisals, provided that he, Adam Whistler, would stand down. All criminal charges against Claudia and her mother had been dropped and would never be renewed. Whistler, in return, would leave the country for a year. Poole, during that time, would work to end certain practices that he'd "lately" come to realize were unjust. To that end, of course, he would need a certain ledger. That ledger was the only record, he said, of the errors that needed to be rectified.

"That's a load of crap," Whistler said to his father. "All he'll do is bury it deeper."

"He would if he got it. He won't. He'll get a copy."

"Then what's the point? Why would he make this deal?"

"To cut his losses. He's running scared, Adam. He'll sweeten it further, believe me. I'm asking you to accept it because I want you alive. And I want you to go back for that girl."

"I can't do that."

"From what her mother says, you weren't given a choice. Where you go, the girl goes, apparently."

"Do you know that she thinks she's my guardian angel?"

"Of course. Her mother told me. Gave me hell, by the way. Kate says that you told her they'd be safe now. That right?"

"I . . . said that I don't think they'll bother her again."

"Wishful thinking, Adam. They're a long way from safe. If we let this thing escalate any further, either Kate or her daughter are going to be snatched. You thought what, that they'd only try for you?"

Whistler grunted.

"This way you get Claudia out of their reach and I'll see that her mother is protected. And a year, just you and Claudia, doesn't sound like bad duty. I'd go for it, Adam. I'd give it a shot."

"Wait a minute. This year thing. Whose idea was that?"

"I told you. It was part of Poole's offer."

"So, it's nothing like the time you got that prosecutor to tell me I either go to jail or join the army?"

The line went silent. Whistler said to his father, "I guess that answers my question."

When his father spoke again, his voice had an edge. "Then you needed the army. Now you need this. I'm not trying to run your life for you, Adam. What you're getting is some time to sit back and examine it."

"I'm not trying to run your life for you, Adam." No, of course not. What would make him think that?

"Look, Dad—"

"Do it, Adam. You're not thinking straight. And you're too damned ready to kill."

Whistler couldn't disagree. At least not in this case.

"Say you're right. But with Claudia? I am not going to do that. You've got to know that can't work."

"What I know is that she might be good for you, Adam. I'm asking you to give it a chance."

"Yeah, but for how long? She's bound to snap out of it."

"That could take a little while. In the meantime, enjoy."

"Enjoy? Are you serious?"

"Yeah, I am. What's your problem?"

"With Claudia that would be like . . . like child molestation. I can't believe I'm hearing you suggest it."

"Adam, she's hardly a child."

"Have you tried speaking to her?"

"I've spoken to her mother. Granted that Claudia's had a change in perspective. But you're looking for diminished capacity, Adam. Sounds to me more like it's been heightened."

Whistler paused to rub his face. This was out of control.

"Say you're right," he told his father. "You're not, but say you are. Say Claudia and I ride off into the sunset. What makes you think that Aubrey and Poole will keep their end this time around?"

"For openers? They know they won't get another chance. I'll come after them with everything I've got."

"Yeah, but—"

"I told Poole that I would have stayed on the sidelines if they hadn't pulled that dumb-ass raid. I don't need a war either. I have better things to do. All I wanted was to help you walk away clean. No one had to have been hurt on either side and Aubrey wouldn't be in a wheelchair."

"Aubrey? What wheelchair?"

"You didn't know?"

"I'm the last to know anything. Someone got to him? When?"

"The night before last. Carved him up pretty good. So it's not as if he's getting a pass."

"Yeah, but fill me in. Who's this slasher we have? I know it wasn't the twins."

He said, "No, not their style. It was another old friend who caught Aubrey with his pants down. That's no figure of speech. Caught taking a dump. Did some surgery on his lower extremities. Do you know if he has any kids, by the way?"

"No, he doesn't."

"And he won't. Consider him *punitivized*. This guy not only does not walk away, he doesn't walk at all for quite a while."

Whistler blinked in disbelief. "And you still won't say who?"

"Later, maybe. Not now."

"But it is the same friend who cut Briggs out in Denver?"

An appreciative chuckle. "She does get around."

"The same one who went to see Aubrey and Poole?"

"No, that job called for someone with a bit more restraint."

"But both of them are women. Do I know them? Have I met them?"

"Yeah, you might have. Years ago. They're friends of a friend. You want to know names, but they aren't important. What's important is that the other side doesn't either. They could kill the twins, and you, even me, but they'd still have to worry about ghosts."

"Except Aubrey's seen the one with the knife. So has Briggs. They both know what she looks like."

"I doubt it. She's quick. I bet they never saw it coming. And as long as we're on the subject of friends, you're going to need one yourself. They've agreed to this deal, but you're right, they could rethink it. You're going to want somebody watching your back, and what better protection could anyone have than a flesh-and-blood guardian angel?"

"That's out of the question. Forget it."

"Even then," said his father, ignoring that response, "I think you'll want to keep moving. You've piled up a pretty good body count, Adam. I mean before this. There are people who'll remember. And Aubrey might be tempted to drop a dime and tell some of them where you can be found."

Whistler asked, "Are you listening to yourself? Is this the life I'm supposed to offer Claudia?"

"Of course I've made it clear that if you're harmed in any way, I'll assume that Poole and Aubrey were behind it. Even so, an extra set of eyes couldn't hurt."

"Now it's you who's not listening to me."

"About Claudia? Then go see her. Change her mind if you can. But we already know where her head is."

"I won't do this to her. And I won't let her do it. This discussion is over, so let's drop it."

"Adam . . . here's your choice. It's her or the twins. You decide. Don't make me decide for you."

The good humor had left his father's voice. Whistler knew better than to doubt that he meant it. This Claudia thing . . . it was completely absurd. But the thought of spending a year with the twins . . .

"Adam?"

"Just wait. I need to think about this."

"Not by yourself. Think it over with Claudia."

"Say I do. How much of a window do I have?"

"I'll get you the time. You go back out and see her. She'll be in the hospital for about another week. After that, she's coming here to convalesce."

"Coming where? To Geneva?"

"Did I mention that her mother will be coming here with her? I've arranged for their passports. They're not terribly well-traveled. I should think this would be a nice treat."

"When was all this decided?"

"They'll be here for a month. Did I mention that you're coming, too?"

"Hey, hold on."

"Left to me, you and Claudia would come and you'd stay, but not being the kind of father who interferes, I will leave you to make your own decisions. We'll need to discuss where you two ought to go. Does she sail, by the way? Do you know if she likes boats?"

"Okay, wait. You're right. It *will* be my decision. Don't give me this '*we need to discuss.*' "

"Colorado girl . . . mountains . . . probably not. We'll try her out on my boat when she's able."

"What do boats have to do with any of this?"

"Just a thought. I might know where there's a nice one."

The boat in question was the yacht he now owned. It was a 46-foot Tartan, custom-designed, and was worth nearly half a million dollars. It had a range of five hundred miles under power and no limit to its range under sail. With a shoal-draft keel that drew only six feet, it could anchor close to shore nearly anywhere. It was light tan in color with red scroll-work added. The name on the transom was *Me & My Gal.* It was among the agreed-on reparations.

The man whose house Whistler had watched, Aubrey's brother-in-law, had been the previous owner. He'd had it for less than a year. The original owner was a Florida banker who'd been charged with laundering drug-dealer cash and whose property had been seized and then auctioned. Aubrey saw to it that his brother-in-law was the only person making a bid. That bid, Whistler learned, was for five thousand dollars, an amount that would barely have paid for the dinghy, let alone for the yacht it was on.

He did fly back to Denver; he went directly to the hospital. He was glad to find Claudia considerably improved. By then she was able to sit up in bed. All the tubes, save one, had been disconnected. The only sign of her wound was a cervical collar with bandages showing underneath. She would need to wear the collar for some time. She could eat, feed herself, but only soft foods. Her mother had brought her a white satin peignoir to replace the stark hospital gowns. Her hair, no longer matted, had been washed and brushed. A little makeup made her color look the way it had before. She smiled, pleased to see him, but seemed not at all surprised. She was toying with a half-eaten lunch.

Whistler had decided that he would be firm. This whole

angel thing had to stop there and then. He would not let her waste one more day of her life clinging to a man who almost got her killed just because she heard voices in her head. He began by telling her the truth about his sister, of the hatred that drove him to hurt many people who'd had nothing to do with her death. He told her that he was a marked man himself. He told her that it was entirely likely that he'd have no future to share with her.

She asked, "Would you like my rice pudding? I'm full."

"No, I wouldn't. Have you heard a word that I've said?"

"I've been listening. And it's sad. But what difference does it make?"

Her voice was still raspy and still a bit labored. Her expression, however, was untroubled.

"What difference?" he asked her. "It makes all the difference. Claudia, it isn't just those people who hurt you. The list goes back long before them."

"Then, see?"

"See what?"

"You will need my protection."

A sigh. "Yeah, but wait. Maybe I don't deserve it. Were you listening when I told you—"

"That your past was less than wholesome? I already knew that. Those men showed me photographs, remember?"

He blinked. "You mean those photos where I cut the throats of children? You actually believed that I could do that?"

"You didn't?"

"No, damn it."

"Well, good. I'm glad to hear it. That one was a lie. But if you hadn't done some other things almost as brutal, what would have been the point in me saving you?"

She said this in the manner of a patient schoolteacher who was pointing out an obvious fact. To him, her logic was clearly deranged. To her, it was unassailable.

Very well. He would indulge it. But he'd try a different tack.

"By . . . saving me, Claudia, let's be clear on what you

mean. Does it mean that you'll be nagging at me to repent and become as saintly as you are? Because I'll tell you right now, if that's what you have in mind—"

"I'm saintly? Who said I'm saintly?"

"Okay, then angelic."

"Only guardian angelic. Otherwise I'm still human. Unless it turns out that I do have special powers, I'm exactly the person I was."

"I don't think so."

"And the light never said that it's my job to judge you. It just said I should save you by loving you, Adam. No biggie. I loved you already."

"No, you didn't."

"Now you'll say I only loved who you pretended to be. Sure, you left a lot out, but that was still you. You're nicer than you think you are, Adam."

"Listen, Claudia . . ."

"Here's another flash for you. I know you love me. All that's holding you back is that you think I'm nuts. Oh, and now you're afraid I'll be a pain in the neck. Don't worry, Adam. I came back as your angel. I'm not the Ayatollah Khomeini."

"Even so . . ."

"Want to hear me talk dirty? Would that ease your mind?"

"No."

"I know. I'll take you camping again. That broke the ice last time. Come to think of it, why wait? Move my tray, hop aboard, and let's get at it."

"Cut it out."

"Then get off this. Accept it. This thing's a done deal. If you blow town again, I'll hunt you down."

10

He stayed in Silver Ridge at her mother's house until Claudia was released from the hospital. He had dreaded the prospect, but her mother insisted. She said that her house was the safest place for him, "what with snipers all over the place."

"Um . . . what snipers?"

"Here and outside the hospital, too. And a couple are watching the police chief and mayor. Your father didn't tell you about that?"

"He did say that he would look after you."

Yes, he had. However, there were probably no snipers. Maybe one or two observers. Maybe even the twins. All his father had done was to call Mrs. Geller on a phone that he knew to be tapped. He told her that he had sharpshooters in place, but don't worry, they're experts and they're all well concealed. Just go about your business as usual.

Whistler had been reluctant to stay at her house for fear that she'd lay into him for even considering taking her daughter away for a year. She didn't, he realized, because she hadn't heard. His father was apparently saving that news until she got over to Geneva. Kate Geller had accepted his invitation, swayed by the prospect of a month's peace of mind while her greenhouse was being repaired. She wouldn't have to worry that a phantom sniper might pop some poor salesman who blundered to her door. More than that, he'd arranged for further medical care while Claudia rested and healed. Not least, Kate Geller would have that month to decide whether she should thank his father or strangle him.

Claudia was released and was able to travel. Her

mother had packed two suitcases for her and brought a
change of clothing to the hospital. She brought a pair of
slacks and a big loose-fitting sweater that fit over the cervical collar. Whistler had hired a private ambulance that
would take them directly to their plane. Claudia asked her
mother to ride up front for the forty-minute ride to Denver's airport. She said, "I need to have a private chat with
Adam."

Two minutes into the ride, she leaned toward him. In a
low voice, she asked, "You still think I'll be a nag?"

"No, I didn't really mean that."

"Still think I won't be any good in the sack?"

"I never said any such thing."

"Well, just so you know, the doctor said we can have sex
as long as it's nothing too athletic."

"Claudia . . ."

"Oh, Adam, lighten up. Don't you know when I'm teasing?"

"I'm still . . . having a little trouble with all this."

"But as long as we're on the subject of sex, aren't you
dying to find out what it's like? I mean, how many angels
have you boffed?"

"Um . . . we're still teasing? You're not serious, right?"

"On the other hand, angels don't do humans as a rule. For
me, it might be a real letdown. You think?"

She was watching his expression. She reached to take his
hand. She said, "Yes, Adam, I'm still teasing you."

He muttered, weakly, "I knew that."

She said, "Okay, Adam, all kidding aside. All I'm trying
to do now is make you comfortable with me. We've both got
to try to relax."

"I'm fine."

"No, you're not, and you've never been comfortable with
me, especially not after we made love."

"That's not true."

"Yes, it is, Adam, and now we know why. You were holding so much back. That's changed, but now there's this. You
do love me, don't you?"

"From the first day I met you."

"Then give us a chance. We'll be okay."

He had booked an overnight flight to Geneva, with a change of planes in New York. All three slept through most of the crossing. His father met their plane at Geneva's Cointrin Airport. His limo was waiting for them on the tarmac. The chauffeur had a wheelchair for Claudia. An escort car, engines running, stood near. Two bodyguards in it. Whistler didn't recognize them. The twins were probably still back in Denver, having seen to their safe departure.

Whistler's father, who'd arranged that they needn't go through Customs, was dressed in a business suit and tie. He had gotten a haircut and his beard had been trimmed. It seemed to Whistler that the look he was going for was that of a respectable businessman. He had greeted Claudia with a kiss on both cheeks after first kissing Kate Geller's hand.

Kate Geller nudged Whistler. "Is this the housebroken version?"

"Be nice," Whistler answered. "He's trying."

His father's home, in which Whistler had grown up, was a three-story town house on the Place Des Alpes. It was one of Geneva's many parklike squares and one of its better addresses. The house was, like its neighbors, of white brick and mansard-roofed, with a flower box at every window.

The house to its right was his father's as well. Whistler hadn't been inside it in years. From the outside it looked very much like the others. It was staffed and run like a small hotel with rooms for any visiting associates. It had two meeting rooms, one of which was a "bubble room" impervious to listening devices. The top floor was his father's communications center, staffed by several full-time employees. It probably contained more eavesdropping equipment than most foreign embassy buildings. Whistler doubted that Kate would be given a tour. She would have to be content with the residence.

Whistler's father had arranged to have Claudia's records faxed to his personal physician. He had also arranged for a visiting nurse who was trained as a physical therapist. The doctor didn't want her using the stairs, so his father had converted a first-floor study into a bedroom for Claudia. His father had moved out of his second-floor suite. That was where Kate Geller would stay. Whistler was given a room on that floor that had been his own, growing up. There was still another guest room on the second floor, but his father had chosen not to use it. That room had been Alicia's. That might have been the reason. Or perhaps he simply thought that for propriety's sake he should not be on the same floor as Kate. He opted to stay up on the third floor, where his driver and housekeeper also had rooms. Whistler knew them both well. They were longtime employees. Both did double-duty as bodyguards.

"It's so pretty," said Kate as she was being shown the house. "Very warm. And inviting. I'm surprised."

"You expected a barracks?" asked his father.

"No, in your case, a bunker. But a woman must have done this. Your wife?"

"Every stick."

The furnishings were an interesting mixture of styles. Mostly Empire, Queen Anne, and a little Swiss rustic, with rich Persian carpets on the floors. Good art on the walls, mostly Dutch—Vermeer and Mondrian—and a French artist's portrait of . . . well, Whistler's mother. She was in her early thirties when she sat for it.

A better word would have been *squirmed* for it, recalled Whistler. The artist had tried for a classical pose. Sitting straight, very regal, chin held high. She wouldn't do it. The smile, intended to be elegant, serene, looked like that of a woman who was trying not to laugh. Her eyes said, "I just can't believe that I'm doing this. Please don't take this seriously. This isn't me. Get me out of this gown and into some jeans. Oh, hell, go ahead. It's for Harry."

Kate saw that at once. "You must have had to tie her down."

"Not me," said his father. "I knew nothing about it. The portrait was a birthday surprise."

"You haven't told me her name."

"It was Andrea."

"She's lovely."

"Yes, she was. Even now, I'm still amazed that she married me. One would think that she could have done better."

"One would think," said Kate Geller.

"Beg your pardon?"

"Just agreeing."

"Well, feel free to contradict me any time."

Claudia had also admired the portrait, but she seemed to have something else on her mind. Whistler asked, was something wrong? She took him aside.

"You and I are going to have separate rooms on separate floors?"

"We . . . didn't sleep together in your mother's house either."

"Are you stalling?"

"Not at all. But what's the rush? You're still healing."

He was certainly stalling and a little afraid. That first time . . . the time that they'd made love while going camping had been awkward for its own set of reasons. They quickly became less self-conscious with each other, but Claudia had been right. There was still something missing. The only thing that made it fall short of being great was his awareness that he was still lying to her and that she would eventually find him out.

Now there were no more lies. She knew who he was, Well, sort of. She had yet to see that side of him. It was now more a question of who Claudia was and how different she thought sex would be. Would she expect celestial trumpets? An orgasmic supernova? There was only one way to find out, he supposed. He hoped that she would not be disappointed.

Kate Geller had overheard the exchange. While Claudia was being shown to her room, Kate nudged him again and said, "Adam, ease up. There's such a thing as thinking too much."

He asked, "How would you know what I'm thinking?"

"Daughters talk to their mothers. She knows that you have all kinds of misgivings. She said you told her that you love her. Did you mean it?"

"Oh, yes."

"Then be patient, Adam. You'll work it out."

"Working it out takes two rational people."

"You think love is rational? Who told you that? All you can do is follow your heart and dance to the music while it lasts."

"Yes, ma'am."

"On the subject of irrational behavior, Adam, something seems to be developing between me and your father. Would that bother you, by the way?"

"Not at all."

"Unlike yours, ours might not be a match made in heaven. Here I am, this hick who grows plants in Colorado. There he is, this, well . . . whatever he is . . . who's been known to do a different kind of planting."

"Mrs. Geller—"

"My point is, if I'm willing to dance with the Devil, why should you get uptight about an angel?"

"He's not a devil."

"I know that, Adam. He's only a man. And Claudia is still just a woman."

"Yeah, but—"

"You're looking that horse in the mouth again, Adam. There doesn't have to be any 'but.' You ought to try counting your blessings."

He supposed that he'd never thought of his father in terms of having a woman in his life. There must have been some since his mother died. But perhaps there were none who had gotten to know him before they had any idea who he was. Like Claudia and himself. Two very different worlds. As with Claudia and himself, maybe that was the attraction. Whatever. Here they were. And Kate Geller was right. They should dance to the music while it lasts.

Within a week he and Claudia were going on day trips, returning for her therapy sessions and treatments. They went out on his father's boat a few times. He taught her the basics of sailing. On land, he took her touring, a few trips by car, but mostly they traveled by train. He thought that travel by train would be less exhausting, so he bought Eurail passes for the two of them. Half of Europe was within a few hours by rail. He showed her some of Switzerland, some of France, some of Germany.

Claudia was thrilled, like a kid on Christmas morning. To begin with, she'd never been on a train. Most Americans hadn't if one doesn't count subways. In Europe, it's the best way to travel.

At first, he'd booked them a first-class compartment, but Claudia preferred to wander through the cars meeting and mixing with the passengers. She was very outgoing, much more so than he, and no one seemed able to resist her warm smile. Most of them spoke some English and, if they did not, Whistler would act as translator. She was very impressed to learn that he was fluent in most of the languages they would encounter. It had not occurred to her that he'd be multilingual, having grown up in the middle of Europe.

Europeans are often taken aback by the easy affability of Americans. This was not the case with Claudia at all. People seemed instantly comfortable with her. They would ask with concern what had happened to her neck. She would shrug it off as nothing and ask about them. She would want to know where they were going, where they came from, and she'd ask their advice on places to visit. If they'd brought a lunch with them, they would ask her to share it. If they traveled with children, she would play with the children. If they traveled with pets, she would ask to hold the pets.

Oh, yes. The pets. She would hold small dogs and cats in her arms and walk with them up and down the aisle. She would speak softly to them and they would respond with a lick or the touch of a paw. Whistler didn't realize what was happening at the time, but this was where the talking to animals began. He wasn't sure when they began talking back. Or at least when she started to hear them.

Even without her thing with the animals, Whistler had serious concerns. If the plan was for them to lay low for a year, that meant not attracting attention to themselves. But

Claudia was a magnet. One could not fail to notice her. And once noticed, everybody seemed to want to approach her. This was new. Well, sort of. She had always been approachable. But he supposed that when a woman is convinced that she's an angel, she's bound to radiate an extra measure of warmth. He half expected to see cripples hobbling after her to touch her. But it was nothing like that. They just liked her.

And there was a flip side that might not be so bad. No one seemed to be paying much attention to him beyond what was minimally polite. The attraction was Claudia. He was just, well . . . some guy. Compared to her he was almost invisible. That might not be a bad thing after all.

What mattered for the moment was that she was happy, especially when they would detrain and explore. To her, every vista was new and exotic. Not the cities so much. They'd become too modern-looking. Downtown Frankfurt, for example, could well have been Houston, having been almost totally rebuilt since the war. But dozens of quaint little villages and towns had survived the war undisturbed. A few looked like something out of *Hansel and Gretel*. She'd want to hop off the train and tour them on foot until she was thoroughly exhausted.

Whistler let that happen. He let her get tired. That way, getting home, she'd fall asleep right after dinner and the question of sex could be postponed a while longer.

It wasn't exactly that he dreaded the prospect. He knew that she claimed to have been pulling his leg on the subject of transcendent sex with an angel. But if she, in fact, had some unearthly expectations, how could he possibly live up to them?

"Adam . . ." He could hear her mother's voice in his head. *"Stop fretting. Just follow the bread crumbs."*

Kate Geller and his father had stayed closer to home. Kate had been right. Something seemed to be developing. Not that the going was entirely smooth. They had obviously already had the discussion about their two kids going off for a year. Whistler knew this because he had happened to hear a part of a subsequent discussion.

Well, he hadn't just *happened* to hear it; he'd eavesdropped. He was sitting in the study where Claudia was napping. He'd left the door ajar, although not for that purpose. Kate and his father had gone for a walk. They'd been out in the square feeding birds. As they came back in, he heard his father's voice asking, "How can I help you feel better about this?"

She said, "I'd take her and run if I had any sense."

"Except Claudia won't. She's quite comfortable with it."

"Harry . . . we both know she's out of her gourd. That aside for the moment, let's talk about you."

"We're just people, Kate. We're a family just like yours."

"No, yours is a family like the Mafia's a family. Mine is a family like the ones that go to church and then stop to pick up some Egg McMuffins."

He grunted. "In the first place, we are nothing like the Mafia. In the second place, Adam's always gone his own way. My hope is that this will redirect him."

"So it's true. This is part of a grand scheme you've hatched."

"Kate . . . I did not deal these cards."

"Oh, and who are those strange little men I keep seeing? There are two of them, right? Or have you cloned a whole bunch?"

"They're the Beasley twins. Donald and Dennis."

"They're part of the family?"

"You could say they're adopted."

"What exactly do they do besides lurk?"

"They do what members of a family should do. We take care of each other. We look out for our friends."

"I bet they also take care of your enemies, correct?"

Whistler heard another grunt. His father didn't answer.

Kate said, "Come on, Harry. Time to level with me. I promise I won't call the cops."

He said, "Only when there's no other way."

This led to a discussion of "those bozos and their bosses"

and why his father had let them off the hook. She said, "It isn't that I wanted you to stop all their clocks. It's more that you don't seem the kind of man who'd leave a thing like this unfinished."

Whistler wanted to hear this himself.

His father's answer was, basically, that they weren't worth the trouble. Bottom-feeders, he called them. Dime a dozen, he called them. He said that every government has them.

She said, "So you're saying that you, Harry Whistler, have no time for minor-league villains. The woods are filled with crooks who only steal millions and who kill on a scale that falls short of genocidal. Is that about the size of it?"

"No, nothing like it."

"Harry . . . then what the hell are you?"

As soon as she'd said that, Claudia coughed. His father walked over and pulled the door closed. Whistler couldn't hear very much after that. Too bad. Kate had seemed to have his father on the ropes.

He could only imagine what she must have been thinking. She must have concluded that Harry Whistler only dealt with James-Bondian villains. Maybe the kind who sat and stroked a white cat as they planned to unleash some doomsday device that would vaporize a dozen world capitals. It struck Whistler that his father might be letting her think so in order that, when he finally explained, his real business would sound almost boring. He wouldn't lie to Kate. He almost never lied. But he certainly would be selective.

Back at Aspen, he'd said that he counseled investors and that was essentially true. More or less. Or at least since the cold war had ended. He still did the odd job for this or that government, but mostly his clients were businessmen. These were entrepreneurs who wanted to invest in countries where shakedowns and bribes were the rule and where the law, far from offering protection, often needed protecting against. He would negotiate their agreements for them. He knew how to reach the right people to talk to. What made him special, and much in demand, was that he also had the means to enforce those agreements. "Keep your word, we stay friendly, we all make a fair profit; there will be other deals after this. Break your word, get too greedy, and you're going to get hammered. This is all the warning you'll get."

That warning would apply to all the parties involved. Every deal that he brokered had to work both ways. But the need for such enforcement was actually rare. Anyone on either side who was tempted to cheat knew that his father's response would be swift. There would either be a visit by one of the twins or by any of some fifty out-of-work former operatives of at least eight or ten different governments. They were KGB, CIA, Stasi . . . the works. Only a few were on his payroll full-time. The rest were used on an as-needed basis according to their individual skills. That pool gave him people who not only spoke the language but who knew how things worked within any given culture. As a group, they seemed to know where all the bodies were buried and who could be bought at what price.

His father valued these ex-agents, but he felt sorry for them. All that training and experience and they're scratching for jobs. He'd once said, "See these people? That's you. That's your future. You're an Airborne Ranger, Special Ops, highly trained, but how long do you think you can do it? There are thousands of you, Adam, and that's all you know. One day you're going to find yourself, forty years old, selling plumbing supplies at Home Depot."

Actually, he said things like that all the time. It was part of his ongoing come-back-home pitch. He didn't care much for government service. He didn't care much for governments either. Too slow, too much meddling, too little accomplished, and most of them don't really matter very much in the daily lives of their citizens. It's better to make your own world.

His father was by no means alone in that view. In fact, he had competitors in the same line of work, but there didn't seem to be much rivalry between them. As often as not, they helped each other. They all drew on the same pool of freelance ex-agents and often employed each other's specialists. In Moscow there was an ex-KGB general who did pretty much the same thing. His name was Leo Belkin, an old friend of Whistler's father. He'd stayed at the house next door many times.

The friendship between Leo Belkin and his father dated back way before the cold war ended. Belkin was still KGB at the time. One would think that they would have been enemies, but they weren't. Not that Whistler would have given that a thought growing up. One would also think that he would have wondered, growing up, why there were always guns and bodyguards around. But he hadn't. It must have seemed normal.

He didn't know why Belkin had popped into his head. Except that Belkin, and Russia, were perhaps the best example of why what his father did was needed. In Russia, say, you want to set up a company. You draw up a contract, you make your agreements, but say that the mafia—the Russian variety—gets wind of it and tries to muscle in.

No, wait. That's too obvious an example.

Say instead that some supplier, some partner, some investor, decides not to hold up his end of the deal. In most of Western Europe, you'd take him to court. To the East, however, there is no civil law that protects people trying to do business. The business environment in Russia today is much as it was in nineteenth-century America, when the robber barons were a law unto themselves and when many of them either had private armies or they'd rent one from the Pinkerton Agency. So unless you have a Belkin or a Harry Whistler, you have no real recourse; you will lose your investment. You might also end up being gunned down on the street. That happened in Moscow every night.

The other reason why Belkin popped into his head had to do with his mother's funeral. Belkin was there and tried to say a few words. But he'd always been a little bit in love with Whistler's mother. He choked up and someone had to finish his talk for him. Who was that? Roger Clew? No, he'd already spoken. No, the man who got up and put his arm around Belkin was another old friend named Paul Bannerman.

Bannerman, by then, was an almost mythic figure who had more or less invented this kind of consultancy. Whistler's father had worked either with him or for him until Bannerman, still young, still in his late thirties, decided that he wanted to call it a day and try to live a normal, quiet life. He went back to the States—this was well after the funeral—and maybe a dozen of his people went with him. Whistler had met most of them over time. He liked some more than others. Some were pretty scary people. At least two had struck him as borderline psychopaths, but Bannerman seemed to have them under control. One was a woman. He'd forgotten her name. In fact, several of Bannerman's people were women. They had chosen to follow him and were loyal to the death. It was much like the twins and Whistler's father.

The story is they moved to some town in Connecticut. Westbury . . . Westport . . . something like that. They bought homes and businesses, settled down, some got married. Settling down, living normally, was all that they wanted. Well, normal might not be the right word for how they lived, but they did do their best to mix in. The government, however, had trouble believing that settling down was all that Bannerman had in mind. Or maybe they saw all that talent he'd brought with him and decided to try to put his people back to work. Whistler didn't remember what the story was, exactly. But a lot of people had died who would have lived if they'd only just left him alone.

Bannerman . . . Wait . . . *The American friends.*

That had to have been Bannerman who supplied the extra help within hours of Claudia being shot. Whistler didn't know why he hadn't thought of that before. It had to have been someone well known to Roger Clew. So it must have been one of Bannerman's women who called on Aubrey and Poole with the ledger. Molly Farrell, maybe. She was Bannerman's right hand. Nice woman. Deadly. But still very nice. He remembered that she'd hugged him after the funeral. She handed him a small book of poems that she said his mother had given to her. She and his mother had been

very close. She said, "Adam, call me if you ever need to talk.
And if you ever need me, I'm there."

He'd lost touch with Molly, but he'd bet that it was her.
She would have been the one with "more restraint." And
the woman, therefore, who carved up Briggs and Aubrey
was probably one of Bannerman's scariest people and one
of the two whom Whistler thought to be psychos. It would
have been a tiny little redheaded woman who was known
for her work with a knife. Her name was Carla Benedict.
There were all kinds of stories. Come to think of it, Carla
had a sister of her own who was murdered years ago in
California. A serial killer was blamed for the murder, but it
turned out that he didn't do it. That serial killer, more to the
point, resented being accused of the murder. So he ended
up allying himself with Carla and helped her track down
the real killer. Whistler's father said it was true. It really
happened that way.

Last he heard, however, she'd settled down with some
Russian who had previously worked with Leo Belkin. An
ex-KGB major named Podulsk. Viktor Podulsk. That was
after she helped nurse him back to health, having shot him
by mistake in a Moscow hotel lobby. It seems that some
KGB goons had come looking for Bannerman. Carla was
ready to blow them away when Podulsk turned up where she
didn't expect him and . . .

Oh, never mind. Doesn't matter.

He could spend all day recalling Carla stories, many of
which he had trouble believing. And as for the story that
she'd finally settled down, maybe she liked to test her skills
now and then to make sure that she hadn't gotten rusty.
Whistler would let his father know that he'd figured out who
had helped him. His father might not confirm it, but he
wouldn't deny it either. Whistler would at least like to get
their addresses. Send some flowers to both of them, maybe.

Speaking of rust and the testing of skills, the sex issue finally came to a head. How it did and what happened was
nobody's business. Her mother knew. Somehow she could

tell. Claudia might have given her a nod or a wink, but he didn't think Claudia had gone into detail because he'd asked her not to and she'd promised. He certainly would not say a word to his father. If he did, he might never hear the end of it.

They had taken a train from Geneva to Cologne, a six-hour ride into Germany. At Cologne he rented a car and he drove her down the east bank of the Rhine. It's the best side for viewing all the castles. They drove south as far as Wiesbaden, turned the car in, and boarded another train home.

Because it was late, and a long ride to Geneva, he had booked a first-class sleeping roomette so that she could catch up on her rest. They took their supper in the roomette and had ordered a bottle of a decent French wine. The wine, combined with her prescription medication, made Claudia more assertive than usual. After the steward came and cleared away the supper trays, she reached to lock the door, snuggled against him, and murmured, "Are you ready to give it a shot?"

"Claudia, listen . . . you're a little bit smashed."

"No, I'm not. Well, a little. Anyway, let's just see."

She proceeded to unbutton his shirt and to lightly tickle his chest. She said, "This is where you put your hand on my thigh. Maybe even brush a hand across my boob."

"Claudia . . . I remember. It has not been that long."

"Then, Adam, let's do it. No more stalling."

This did not set the most romantic of moods, but she might have been nervous as well. He responded by starting to caress her cheek. Most of what he felt was her collar. She said, "Oh, yeah, wait. Let me take this thing off," and she reached for the Velcro that fastened it.

"No, no, leave that on." He tried to stop her.

"Uh-uh. I like to be nuzzled."

He didn't know where he was expected to nuzzle. Bandages covered her entire throat and neck. The entry wound's padding was half an inch thick. The exit wound's padding was twice that.

But the collar came off and so did her sweater. She turned

so that he could unhook her bra. When he didn't, she reached to undo it herself. "You can jump in whenever you're ready."

"Claudia . . . look, with the lurching of a train . . ."

"I can handle it, Adam. Now get with the program. Aren't you dying to find out?"

"At least keep the collar. I'd feel better if you do."

She reached for the light switch. "On or off?"

Looking back on that night, he could only hope that a crowd hadn't gathered in the hallway, listening. It would have heard gasps and low, throaty moans and it would have heard shouts of "Do you see it? Do your hear it?" followed by a few primal screams.

The first "it" in question was the flashing of lights that she thought had their origin within her. She thought they erupted from deep within her being and were strobing all over their compartment. The second "it" in question was the symphony of bells that seemed to go off in her brain.

"Yes, yes, I was right. Yes, yes, it's fantastic. Adam, can you *believe* this?"

That was another thing people would have heard as Claudia reached her most unearthly height and as he tried to keep her from hurting herself. The flashing lights were real but they were coming through the window. They happened to have been passing through Stuttgart at the time and the lights were more commercial than celestial. The bells were the bells that went off at every crossing. The motion of the train must have been the biggest factor. That and three glasses of Merlot.

She'd gone limp. She melted and lay snuggled against him. "Adam?" she murmured. "What did you think?"

"It's like . . . nothing I've ever experienced."

"I told you. Did I tell you?"

"Yes, you did. Those heightened senses."

"Oh, rats. Including pain. Now my neck hurts."

"Stay still. I'll get your collar. And I'll fold down the beds."

"Don't you move. Holy smoke. You were fantastic."

Actually, he knew, all he'd done was hold on.

She said, "There were bells. There were actually bells. I
thought ringing your chimes was just an expression."

"I know. First time for me, too."

"You could hear them?"

"Uh-huh. I could. But I'm not sure we're going to hear
bells every time. It's better if it's always . . . you know . . .
different."

She managed an "Mmm-hmm." She fell asleep in his arms.

It turned out that Whistler needn't have worried. They
made love just about every night after that. And each time
they made love was different and thrilling because Claudia had decided that it must be. Part of that, he supposed,
was that she was in Europe and every locale seemed romantic. If she didn't hear bells, she would hear other
things. One time she was sure that what she was hearing
was the sound of distant applause. It would rise and fall
the way it does in a theater when cast members take their
final bows. That embarrassed her some. It was only the
rustling of the wind in the trees, but she imagined it to be
some otherworldly cheering section that had dropped by
to check on her progress. For some time after that, she
would pull up the sheets so that spirits weren't able to
watch.

Claudia would still take some getting used to.

11

At the end of a month they all said their good-byes.
Whistler and Claudia packed their bags; the two parents
drove them to the airport. Whistler's father had asked Kate
Geller to stay and drive down to his lodge in Chamonix.
She agreed, but only for another few days. She said she had
a business to run. She told Claudia that she might miss her
a little. Not much, just a little now and then. She said she

was glad to have the house to herself and had intended to kick her out anyway.

"And you call me a liar?" Whistler's father said softly, after Claudia had moved out of earshot.

"Harry . . . shut up. Let's go. Get me drunk."

"Better not. You know me. I might take advantage."

"No, you won't. So I'll have to. Let's go."

Whistler and Claudia flew to Puerto Rico and from there to Tortola in the British Virgin Islands. That was where they took possession of the boat. He'd explained why they were doing this, and about the deal with Poole, and he'd given her every chance to protest that a year seemed a little extreme. After all, she wouldn't see much of her mother in that time. And a boat, he pointed out, might prove too confining for a girl who grew up roaming the Rockies. But she never hesitated. She agreed with his father. A year might be just what he needed.

During their outings on Lake Geneva, she had learned how to handle a boat fairly comfortably. Real competence would come with experience. On her own, she read books, watched instructional videos, and learned how to read charts and plot courses. He was pleased, though not surprised that she had thrown herself into it. She had never been one for half measures.

She no longer needed her cervical collar, but he'd asked her to bring it along just in case. They would hit rough weather sooner or later and she would be glad of the support. Her neck was largely healed and the therapy had done wonders. But the injury left her neck a bit rigid and some of her movements seemed almost robotic. What she'd lost in fluidity of movement, however, she gained in terms of a chin-held-high elegance. Whereas before, she had an outdoorsy look, she could now have been a model or a princess.

She fell in love with the Tartan on sight. She especially liked the name that he'd given it. He'd arranged to have the red scrollwork removed and the *Me & My Gal* sanded off. It was bad luck to change the name of a boat, but the old name

and scrollwork made it stand out too much. The new name
that he gave it was *Last Dollar.*

"Last dollar?" she asked. She didn't get it at first. "Did
this boat cost you everything you had?"

"Try again."

"Because you know I can work. There are plenty of
florists. And I used to waitress in college."

"Claudia . . . Last Dollar. Doesn't that ring a bell?"

She thought for a moment, then brightened. "The ski trail?"

"In Aspen." He nodded. "And on top, by the lift, what
happened up there?"

She grinned. "It's where we met. Oh, Adam, that's
sweet."

He supposed that he might have blushed a little.

"And it's so romantic." She threw her arms around him.
"It's the nicest thing you could have done."

"This yacht, by the way, will be in your name as soon as
you sign a few papers. Also two bank accounts, one Swiss,
one Grand Cayman. You won't have to work for some time."

"My name? Not our names?"

"You earned it the hard way."

"But what about you?"

"I've got you to take care of me. Come on, let's take a
look down below."

She thought that he should carry her over the threshold,
but that was hard to do on a yacht. He'd have to have slung
her over his shoulder and struggled to back his way down.
The mood of the moment might quickly have faded once she
whacked her head against the topside. So he took her by the
hand and led her down the several steps. She gasped at almost everything she saw.

The interior was solid mahogany throughout, polished to
a mirror-like sheen. Lalique crystal windows were set into
the bulkheads; the upholstery was cream-colored leather.
The main saloon was a miniature of a well-designed luxury
living room. Sliding panels concealed a built-in TV that ran
off a satellite dish. There were a VCR and a CD player and
speakers wired throughout. The walk-through galley had a

smaller-scale version of every modern kitchen appliance. The pantry and bar had already been stocked.

Whistler had noticed what sort of books she liked as she'd browsed his father's shelves in Geneva. He already knew what sort of music she enjoyed. He'd purchased and shipped a sampling of each. She had learned a smattering of German in their travels and she'd already had some inadequate French of the type taught in American schools. He bought her some tapes and texts from Berlitz. If she wished . . . and she did wish . . . he would have her nearly as fluent as he was well before their year had gone by.

Whistler led her to the chart room, just forward of the galley. It had been equipped with every state-of-the-art navigational and communications device. These included the basics—a cell phone, a fax, and an answering machine—plus a device that was called a Magellan. It combined a computer with a GPS, or global positioning system. It could send or receive instantaneous messages anywhere in the world.

"Your mother has a handheld version of this one."

"She does?"

"Or she will, by the time she goes home. So it's not as if we're dropping off the face of the earth. You can message back and forth all you like."

"I can tell her where we are?"

"It would be better if you don't for a while. These messages are hard, but not impossible to track. My father, however, will know where we are. This thing transmits a continuous signal that only his equipment will recognize."

He showed her the bedrooms, one forward, one aft. The aft cabin was the larger, more luxurious, of the two, but he'd opted for the smaller forward cabin.

"For who?" she asked. "You mean we still get separate rooms?"

"Oh, no. Not this time."

"Not ever again."

She didn't ask him why he'd chosen the small one. Actually, she preferred it, because overhead there was a tinted plastic hatch that opened wide. They could fall asleep look-ing at the same moon and stars that lit the skies over Col-orado.

Whistler's reason for preferring it, which he kept to him-self, was that anyone attacking the boat while they slept would assume that they were in the aft stateroom. Another minor precaution also probably not needed. But it was one that might give him an edge, however slight, should an un-welcome visitor come calling.

Claudia took her time exploring the boat. She went from place to place checking every switch and instrument, mak-ing notes on the function of each. She began to unpack for the two of them. While checking the closets she discovered a locker that was just below the main hatch. It contained a rack of armaments, two Kevlar vests, and an ample supply of ammunition.

"Adam, why all these guns? You said you were through."

"My father had them put there."

"His idea or yours?"

"I didn't have to ask. Every boat in these waters has some kind of protection. You've heard of carjackers? There are boatjackers, too."

"Like pirates? Really?"

"It doesn't happen every day, but it happens."

She reached to run her fingers over the firearms. They were, in addition to his own Beretta pistol, an Ingram MAC-10 with a thirty-round clip, a drum-fed shotgun with a cut-off stock, and an M-87 .50-caliber rifle.

"What's this rifle?" she asked. "I've never seen one that big."

"It's a military weapon. For snipers. Long-range."

She frowned. "You were a sniper? Is that what you did?"

"Um . . . actually this weapon isn't for people. It's for putting holes in equipment."

That seemed to be what she wanted to hear, and his an-swer was more or less the truth. He had once brought down a command helicopter with a rifle identical to this one. He had also disabled several ground-to-air missiles at a range of almost two miles. No explosion, just a hole that more than likely went unnoticed until they tried to fire the missile. That's when it would have exploded.

"What kind of equipment?" she asked. "Like a hull?"

"A hull or an engine. More humane than shooting people."

She nodded toward the shotgun. "That doesn't look so humane."

"It's called a street sweeper. Well, down here, a deck sweeper."

"I guess I'll need to learn how to use them," she said.

"No, you won't," he answered. "There won't be any trouble." He reached to close the locker. "Pretend they're not there."

"I'm supposed to protect you. I think I should learn."

"We'll see. There's plenty of time."

She said she thought that she should learn, but she said it with distaste. It was a reaction that he shared. He supposed, however, that as long as she'd seen them, he might teach her how to handle them safely. The shotgun, at least. It would be hard to miss with it. Twenty rounds to a drum, half buckshot, half slugs. It could probably cut a speedboat in half.

For the next eight months, *Last Dollar* was their home. They would wander with the breeze, no pattern, no plan. They would choose their next landfall on a whim. By their third month out, Whistler found himself believing that this might actually last. He'd kept waiting for Claudia to wake up one morning and realize that she must have been out of her mind. But Claudia never did. She never wavered.

At the outset, he'd intended that they'd keep to themselves and try to avoid probing questions. This was more out of prudence than from any real fear that someone might be actively looking for them. But as he should have known, that was not going to work. There were always other yachts in every anchorage they came to. One look at Claudia was usually enough to get them invited for cocktails. Those they met, however, seldom asked many questions that were of a personal nature. Most of them were on an escape of their own, although not in a fugitive sense. They were taking a break from whatever their lives were back in Toledo, Chicago, wherever. Only the here and now mattered to them. They might ask him where he came from, meaning where he'd been cruising, but they didn't much care what he'd done before this. The past seemed to be of no importance.

Even so, he and Claudia used assumed names. He would introduce himself as Kip, sometimes Greg. He thought these names suited the sort of young man who had a lot of time on his hands. Claudia would make up her names on the spot. She thought Fluff or Bootsy were the kind of names that went with a Greg or a Kip. The use of false names had begun as a precaution, but Claudia thought there would be no harm in having some fun while they were at it.

"Gotta keep it light, Adam. But don't worry. I'm watching. I'll never let anyone harm you."

Names aside, he'd asked Claudia to cover her scars whenever they would be with other people. The entrance and exit wounds were still vivid. Someone would be bound to ask what had caused them, and the subject was better avoided. Although Claudia was not at all self-conscious about them, she took to wearing little green or white scarves, knotted to one side with long trailing ends, whenever they were in company. He had bought her several. They looked good on her. Almost anything did. He had also requested that she try to avoid telling anyone that she was an angel.

"Why would I do that?"

"Just in case it comes up."

"Adam, that's hardly a thing people ask."

"Well, yeah . . . but if some guy says you look like an angel, you shouldn't say, 'Well, it so happens that I am.' "

She looked at him. "Adam, do you think I'm that dumb?"

"Claudia . . . far from it. All I'm trying to say—"

"I don't really mind that you think I have a screw loose. I don't even mind if some people think that I'm just some rich yuppie's bimbo. But please don't imagine that I'm stupid."

"Dean's list, remember? Of course I don't think that. And where did this bimbo thing come from?"

"I . . . overheard it."

"From someone who's actually spoken to you? Because anyone who's known you for more than three minutes—"

"No, just some kids who were walking past the boat."

That was one more thing about her. Her senses stayed heightened. She could hear and she could smell many things that he couldn't, and his own senses, he'd always thought, were fairly acute. Early on, he'd thought that these were more in her mind, but she'd usually turn out to have been right. So, okay, thought Whistler. Some kids called her a bimbo.

"Using names like Fluff and Bootsy, what else did you expect? Even without them, I'm still not surprised. I can't blame them for wondering what a woman like you is doing with someone like me."

At that, she softened. "Don't shortchange yourself. I've seen the way women look at you. They get goose bumps."

"The heck they do. No woman ever has."

"There are times, when you're quiet, you look dangerous, Adam. You look . . . I don't know . . . sort of coiled. It's a turn-on."

He grunted. "Can we get back to you?"

"Except when you smile. You have a little boy's smile. Go from one to the other; women melt at your feet."

"Yeah, I know. It's been my curse. So many women."

"Of course, with me, that cute smile came first. I had to wait to find out what a tiger you are."

He was starting to blush. She always did this to him. Whenever he tried to sit her down, be firm, she'd have him stumbling all over himself.

"Claudia, listen. All I'm trying to say . . . it's like when I asked you to cover the scars. You're hard enough to forget as it is."

"That's all you meant?"

"I should not have brought it up."

They both let it go. They quickly made up. That had been the closest they'd come to a quarrel since . . . well, those other quarrels weren't really quarrels either. They were minor disagreements; they'd discuss them and he'd yield. He had yet to win an argument with Claudia.

The bimbo thing never came up again, mostly because she abandoned those names and took to calling herself by rich girl's names such as Courtney or Valencia or Brittany. She might have overheard "spoiled bitch" a time or two, but no one calls a Brittany a bimbo.

That discussion, however, was *not* all he meant. There were two related subjects that he'd wanted to discuss, but that was not the time to pursue them with her. She'd reduce him to stammering again.

The first had to do with the *guardian* part of her being his guardian angel. There had been several incidents—her trying to protect him—that could have led to serious trouble. The first time, off Belize, a passing yacht radioed to say its compressor had shorted out and that it had run out of ice. It was during her watch; he was sleeping below. Claudia, recalling what he'd said about pirates, told the yacht to stand off and send over its dinghy with only one person aboard. They did as she asked and she gave them the ice. But she'd waited at the rail in her Kevlar vest with the deck-sweeping shotgun at the ready.

That skipper must have wondered what they had on board that commanded that sort of vigilance. He might easily have reported *Last Dollar* as being a suspected drug runner. Suspicious-looking boats were reported all the time. The motive for reporting them was financial, not ethical. The tipster would get up to twenty-five percent of the value of everything seized. But nothing had come of it. That yacht had not reported them. If it had, they would have been boarded soon after. Perhaps that other skipper was a runner himself.

"Claudia," he'd said, "please don't do that again."

"They were watching us, Adam. They were watching through binoculars."

"More likely, they were ogling a nice-looking woman. Next time, come and wake me, okay?"

"Okay."

"And I wish you'd leave the guns where they are unless there's a clear and present threat. You know what's just as good? Hold a cell phone to your ear. That almost always makes people back off if they don't have the best of intentions."

She nodded. "Okay, no more guns."

That, however, was only the first time. On shore as well, she'd be watching for signs that any stranger was paying them undue attention. Another time, on Grand Cayman, they were sitting in a restaurant and Claudia noticed that a man outside was peering in through the window. People do that every day. They're just looking the place over. But this one was wearing a dark business suit and Claudia was especially sensitive to suits, given her experience with Lockwood and Briggs. But he felt sure that anyone who might mean him harm would probably dress less conspicuously. They were, after all, in the tropics. This man, in any case, then entered the restaurant and seemed to be heading toward their table. Claudia tensed; her hand gripped her fork, and she was ready to spring. The man, to make a long story short, had only come in looking for a rest room. He was lucky he hadn't reached into his pocket or he might have had a fork in his ear.

More recently, in Martinique, Whistler had hired a diver to go down and clean the growth off the bottom of his boat. He'd neglected to tell Claudia that he'd done so. She heard the scraping noises and she saw the trail of bubbles from the scuba gear the diver was using. True to her promise, she did not grab a gun, but she was waiting to whack him with a spinnaker pole the moment he came to the surface. She didn't because—and this was the other subject—a pelican swooped down and landed on the deck. It squawked at her and it flapped its wings at her. Whatever that meant in pelican language, to Claudia it meant that the pelican knew the diver and was telling her that he was harmless.

When she told him about it, she still wasn't sure. She said that even when the diver came up, he seemed unable to look her in the eye.

"Were you . . . still talking to the bird at this point?"

"I'm serious, Adam."

"What were you doing?"

"I was doing that cell-phone trick that you taught me."

"Either way, I'm sure he didn't want to intrude. Those guys do their job and they go to their next one. So it's good that the pelican dropped by."

First she's bothered that the skipper off Belize was looking at her; now she's bothered that a dockworker wouldn't. With anyone else, he'd have called it paranoia. With Claudia, though, it was more like disappointment. She was his guardian; she was right in there guarding, but there never seemed to be any genuine threat for Claudia to guard him against.

Eventually, he might have to sit her down and risk her annoyance one more time. The subject wouldn't be excessive vigilance, however. It would be her thing about animals. He'd seen people watching her, wondering about her. She would speak to any bird that might land on the deck and she spoke to dogs and cats while ashore. Many people talk to animals. Nothing odd about that. But most people don't have discussions with them. Most people don't share with dogs and cats, met at random, the good news of the afterlife that awaits them. Most people don't nod and say thank you to pelicans. Most people don't take their advice.

As far as Whistler himself was concerned, if she thought she was an angel, so be it. She was entirely human in all other ways. She had the normal range of moods; mostly happy, sometimes pensive, but he never saw her sullen or brooding. He never saw a single sign of regret that she'd chosen, or been assigned, to be with him.

She missed her mother, but they'd swapped frequent E-mails using the Magellan device. And later, as there seemed to be less need for that precaution, they would speak on the phone once a week. Whistler knew that anyone determined to find him certainly could have done so by now, especially if Kate Geller's phone was still tapped. Days would go by, sometimes a whole week, without Felix Aubrey ever crossing his mind. That chapter seemed to be closed.

Nor had her mother been pining away back in Silver Ridge, Colorado. Kate had made two more trips to Geneva and she'd spent the Christmas holiday with his father in Paris, followed by a stay at Chamonix. That relationship seemed to have a future as well. Like Claudia, her mother was learning French and German. In fact, she and Claudia would test each other's progress in the course of their phone conversations.

She'd told Claudia that she was thinking of selling her business. His father had encouraged her to do so; stop commuting, and think about moving to Europe full-time. She didn't say whether they'd spoken of marriage, but they'd surely grown comfortable with each other. And Kate had received several offers for the business. Those offers were increasingly attractive because the garden center's business had boomed.

The boom in sales and traffic had come in the wake of all the media publicity that she had received as an aftermath of the drug raid. The wire services had written it up as a classic example of "jack-booted thugs" pounding down the wrong doors on bad information and hurting innocent people. A Denver paper ran a four-part series on the evils of the federal seizure laws. Kate had faxed the whole series to Claudia.

The Denver paper's editors were especially incensed by one of the provisions of those laws. That provision was called the "relation-back doctrine." They called it an affront to any fair-minded citizen, one that turned the Constitution on its head. That doctrine went far beyond seizing private property. Briefly stated, it said that all property was forfeit *from the moment* that it was involved in a crime. This was even if the government didn't learn of that crime until several years after the fact. For example, it said, say your son once used your phone to buy or sell a couple of joints. You never knew anything about it. But that buy then came to light in a subsequent prosecution. Your house, by law, was no longer yours. It had been used in the commission of a federal crime. It became the property of the federal government from the moment the call was completed. If you had been living in that house ever since, not only could the government put it up for sale, they could also charge you back rent.

As far-fetched as this example might seem, said the editors, it had actually happened to a family in Iowa. The town in which they lived had hired prosecutors to review old arrests and convictions. Many towns had done likewise once it came to their attention that "relation-back" was a gold mine. The job of these attorneys was to find seizure prospects, and these were not limited to drug crimes. Say your daughter once pled guilty to a shoplifting charge. She's contrite and has stayed out of trouble. A review of her record has shown, however, that she used your car to get to the mall, intending to shoplift when she got there. Your car, if you still own it, may be forfeit to the town. You may buy it back if you wish.

What the paper didn't know was that these scattershot events had since become institutionalized. Felix Aubrey, maybe Poole, saw real money to be made by supplying such towns with more lucrative targets and keeping a percentage of the spoils. Aubrey, as Claudia and her mother had seen, was not above planting evidence.

In her mother's case, though, there were public apologies. The police chief and mayor, perhaps mindful of those "snipers," had decried what they called a tragic mistake. Those responsible, they said, had been fired from their jobs and had left Colorado in disgrace. That reference, said Kate, was to those two policemen who hadn't been seen since the day after the raid.

She said, however, that dark rumors persisted. It had been whispered that the two missing cops were nourishing some of the fruit trees she grew.

She E-mailed him, "Adam, tell me they aren't."

He answered, "Not the fruit trees. Just the beeches."

She responded, "Adam, please say that you're kidding."

"I am. Copper beeches. Sorry, Kate. Bad joke."

"Adam, this is serious. And since when do you joke?"

He assured Kate Geller that he was just being silly and

that no one was buried on her property. Truth be told, he really didn't know where they were. Using those two to fertilize Kate Geller's soil did have a certain poetic appeal, but he knew that his father would not have allowed it. Those two cops were most likely in the trunk of a car that was sitting at the bottom of a lake. Even so, with those rumors, Kate's garden center was becoming a tourist attraction. The resulting new business was all well and good, but as Kate had said, "I'm not running a waxworks." The relentless attention was beginning to wear thin. Whistler thought that she'd probably take one of those offers. However, if a quieter life was her goal, she was not yet convinced that moving to Geneva would be that great an improvement.

Kate Geller had asked, *"Since when do you joke?"* Whistler was a little taken aback. He knew that he'd never been the life of the party, but he didn't think he'd been some humorless plodder who couldn't loosen up if he tried. He supposed, however, that he'd always been a bit distant, never quite comfortable with people he'd met who came from more conventional backgrounds. Especially after he was sent off to school. He never felt superior. It was not that at all. The truth is that sometimes he envied them. He had more in common with a . . . well, a Carla Benedict than he had with his fellow students and professors. His view of the world had already been formed. Their opinions, their ideals had seemed hopelessly naive. His father had said, "Keep your own thoughts to yourself. You're there to absorb, not to teach." So he never got over feeling like an outsider. He had never really made any friends.

But Kate's question made him realize how much he had thawed since he had been living with Claudia. Okay, he still wasn't a barrel of laughs. But he was much more congenial, less guarded, with people. He smiled more readily and people responded. He found himself able to make small talk with strangers without needing Claudia to break the ice first. And yes, he even made a joke now and then. But yes, "copper beech" was pretty lame.

As for their daily lives, they were active and full. The

boat was their home, but it was often in port. They would keep in shape by running, biking, and swimming, all of which were Claudia's triathlon events, but she tried not to show him up too badly. Most evenings while in port they would dress and go out, often with other couples they'd met. They would try different restaurants, catch up on new movies, or Whistler would take Claudia shopping. He would have to take her shopping because if he didn't, she would seldom buy anything for herself. He would have to watch her browse, memorize what made her smile, then go back later and buy it.

And yet Claudia loved to dress up and look good. She loved going out, she liked being with people, and people liked being with her. She just didn't like to spend money.

"Claudia, I've told you. You're a long way from broke."

"I know, but we need it to last."

"If you're worrying about me, I'm not exactly broke either. What else is bothering you?"

"If we did run short, how would you earn more money?"

"Not with a gun, if that's what you're thinking. I'll never go back to that life."

"But it's all you've ever done . . . and it's all that you're good at."

Whistler grumbled. "Thanks for the compliment."

"You've never missed the excitement, the danger?"

Now and then. But he answered, "Not in the slightest."

"Then we need to decide what we'll do with your new life. Maybe we should think about planting some roots. We'll need to if we're going to start a family someday."

"A family?"

"We're supposed to. I told you."

"Oh, of course. The white light."

"That's the plan, but don't sweat it. You're not ready yet. Don't get me wrong, Adam. I love our life together. But if there doesn't seem to be much need to protect you, I need to figure out what else the light had in mind."

"The light never spelled it out in detail?"

"No, just the big picture. Let me think about this."

* * *

"Let me think" often meant that she would have a discussion
with either a bird or the wind. He was never really clear on
what role she thought they played. He didn't think she saw
them as surrogate white lights or as actual messengers from
the world beyond this one. They were more like good lis-
teners, nonjudgmental and unbiased. He supposed that it
was better than talking to herself.

Whatever the case, it was during one such session that
Claudia decided it was time to head north. Her consultant,
however, wasn't much more specific than the white light apparently had been. The bird or the wind didn't lay out a strategy. It just told her, or agreed, that it was time to move on
and start looking for a place of their own.

This was after their uneventful stay in Antigua, during
which he had used his real name. Other boaters had offered
suggestions. They told her that springtime was especially
pretty all along the Sea Islands of the Georgia coast and in
South Carolina's inland waterways. They suggested exploring them until early May, and then sailing up to Maine
for the summer. To Claudia, this began to sound like a plan.
They could also decide on a place en route where her
mother could fly in for a visit. Perhaps his father could join
them as well. Claudia hoped so. She'd often spoken to him
via satellite phone, but she hadn't seen him for almost a
year.

Whistler knew that his father wouldn't go for that idea.
His father would be pleased to have a family reunion, but
he'd want to host it in Europe, on his turf. Put another way,
he wouldn't like the idea of the two of them being in the
same place at once. At least not in the States. Too tempting
a target.

Whistler knew that even going back by themselves might
not be the smartest thing either. But Claudia had gone to a
library in Antigua and had spent a day poring through cruising guides to the whole Eastern Seaboard. She had already
plotted the course they would take. To ease his misgivings,
they would swing wide of Florida. Too many spotters. Too

much Coast Guard activity. Too many random searches for drugs and for Haitians. The Coast Guard would find no contraband on board, but they'd wonder why he carried so many weapons and would surely check him out on their computer. They wouldn't find much there either; his records were sealed, but that would make them all the more curious. It was better, he decided, to avoid such encounters. They would stay a hundred miles offshore.

"Maybe we can send some birds on ahead."

He had said this, or muttered it, while marking a chart.

She looked at him, oddly. "Beg your pardon?"

"Your friends. Your birds. Let them scout and report. Better yet, do you know any porpoises?"

She sighed and shook her head. "Sometimes I wonder about you."

She wonders about *him*. "Never mind."

Spending a summer in Maine did sound nice. Claudia read aloud from her cruising guide about all the quaint little seaside towns, all the romantic rocky inlets in between, and the dozens of pine-covered islands offshore. They could pick one, drop anchor and dig for clams in the shallows. They could buy a trap, she said, and catch their own lobsters. They could pick wild mushrooms, blueberries and onions. She said, think of the money they'd save.

However, if they did elect to push on to Maine, they'd give the Washington area a wide berth as well. Nothing much nears that city without being monitored. No use rubbing their noses. Stay well out to sea. Especially don't cruise up the Potomac on the former *Me & My Gal*. All they'd need was Felix Aubrey to get wind of it and be tempted to drop a few mortar rounds on them.

He wondered if Aubrey could walk yet.

12

Vernon Lockwood had never liked Adam Whistler. He hadn't liked him, sight unseen, from the day he learned that Whistler would be joining their unit. Some Special Ops hotshot, was all that he'd heard. He and Briggs had gone in to ask Aubrey why. They could not understand why they needed him.

"This new guy," he said to Aubrey, "they call him 'the Whistler'? What is he? A spook? What's going on?"

Aubrey gave him that faggy little curl of his lip without looking up from his desk. "He is not 'the Whistler.' It's his name. Adam Whistler. His credentials have impressed our Mr. Poole."

"So that's his real name?"

"As I think I've just told you."

"Sounds more like a code name. Like some CIA bullshit."

"Unlike 'Vern the Burn,' it is not a sobriquet. Unlike you, he must not feel that he needs a nom de guerre in order to intimidate the stupid."

Little turd, thought Lockwood. He said, "What I hear, this guy can kill at long distance. So what? Any pussy can work at long distance."

"He's considerably more gifted than that, by all accounts."

"The other thing I hear, this guy's mostly a loner. What makes you think he'll play ball?"

"He will not 'play ball.' He won't even know the game. And you two are not to enlighten him. Avoid him."

It was Briggs who asked Aubrey, "So then why is he coming?"

"Because this was done before I could object. Mr. Poole, as you know, can see into men's souls. Or rather he can see that some men don't have one. You two, for example. Now excuse me."

Lockwood said, "I think I'll see what he's got. You care if I push him a little?"

"How little?"

"Just enough so he knows who's top dog around here. Let him know to keep out of my way."

Aubrey didn't answer. All he did was shrug. Lockwood took that to mean he had a green light to make Whistler think twice about staying. Whistler's first day was as good a time as any. He and Briggs caught Whistler alone in the washroom while Whistler was drying his hands. He said, "I'm Vern Lockwood. You heard about me?"

Whistler never looked up. "No, what are you?"

"I'm this." He opened his jacket to show Whistler his gun, his Glock with the custom hollow points. Whistler still didn't look, so Lockwood pulled it from its holster. He twirled it on his finger. That made Whistler pay attention.

Holding the gun, not on Whistler, just holding it, he said, "So it's clear, we don't want you. And me, I don't like you. If you stay, you and me . . . well, we're going to have a problem. You don't really want to mess with me, do you?"

Then Whistler sucker-kicked him. He would never forget that. All he'd done was show Whistler the gun. Briggs was standing right there, but he didn't do shit. Even Whistler stood waiting for Briggs to do something. Briggs didn't. He let Whistler walk out.

Later on, Briggs said, "That was your show, not mine. You were begging for a kick in the nuts."

"You saw that coming? Is that what you're saying?"

"You thought what? That the guy would piss in his pants? I think he's seen a gun before, Vern."

"Yeah, well, next time—"

"Next time don't just stand there. This guy is no pussy. Next time, put him down first, then talk."

There wasn't any next time. Not for weeks after that. Poole heard about the washroom. He said leave him alone. He said, "The darkness within him must be made to serve the light. Forbear, Mr. Lockwood. Forbear."

That was how Poole spoke. No one ever understood him. Anyway, Aubrey tried to keep Whistler busy. He kept him traveling, scouting targets for raids, but soon Whistler started asking questions. Why this target? Who is he? Where's the evidence that he's dirty? Then he wanted his instructions in writing. Even Poole began to realize that this guy had to go, but by that time it was too late. Aubrey's notebook, which was stupid to have in the first place, turned up missing from his house and it wasn't hard to figure who had taken it. Aubrey should have had him pop Whistler on the spot, but he wanted his ledger back first. Next we know, there's Whistler's father getting into the act. Whistler's father turns out to have some kind of juice. The father's not even here; he lives somewhere in Europe, but he still gets Poole to roll over. Poole is seriously spooked; he starts that "Forbear" shit again. Even Aubrey wimped out for a while there.

Well, screw this, thought Lockwood. You don't just let the guy walk. You at least try to find some kind of edge.

Lockwood said to Briggs, "I'll tell you what we do. Whistler knows these two women; it's this girl and her mother. They're why he's been going out to Denver. It figures that Whistler is porking the daughter, but it figures he wouldn't have told them what he does."

"That would be a good bet. But so what?"

"We go see them. We tell them who this prick really is. We wave the flag, maybe. We say that both him and his father are dirty. We get them to flip on whatever they know."

They did that. They tried that. It didn't work out. They went out there with all kinds of stuff from their files. They brought photos of killings they said Whistler had done. Briggs brought a report some shrink had written up, showing that Whistler was a sociopath. Except the profile wasn't Whistler's. It was Lockwood's own. It was from years ago, when he'd tried to get a job with the Central Intelligence

Agency. They had him do a bunch of tests and after that they wouldn't take him. Unsuitable, they said. Yeah, well, fuck you, too. He hadn't known that Briggs had brought it along until Briggs started reading parts of it to those women. This was Briggs's idea of a joke.

"What joke?" Briggs asked later. "You said scare them. That was scary."

"You couldn't have pulled Whistler's? You had to pull mine?"

"His is sealed. Yours was handy. I blacked out your name. Hey, it's not like it's news that you're one twisted fuck. That's what got you hired by Poole."

Aubrey wasn't happy that they went to see these women, especially when they got nothing out of it. Those women didn't scare; they just got mad. Aubrey reamed them both out. He said the damage was done. But he said, "Let's see what we can salvage."

He said, "What we need is to neutralize Whistler. Go find me something to trade."

They knew what he meant. He meant set them up and bust them. This was something they'd done a hundred times. They knew how. But who'd have figured that two nervous cops would start blasting at a shape that came out of the darkness. Fucking girl. It was an accident. They happen. And who would have figured that within, like, one day, Whistler has this fucking army invading the place. No one knows who they were or where they came from.

So now look at Briggs. Until then he had a face. They put it back together the best they could but his skin still looks like a lampshade. Briggs hasn't been worth a damn since.

And who does he blame? Not the woman who cut him. He blames Vernon Lockwood, is who he blames, for taking off and leaving him there. Well, two things about that. First, Briggs should have been on time. Second, only a dope would have hung around after knowing how much heat must have showed up in that town, what with everyone they knew disappearing. You get out until you know what you're up against.

This was all Whistler's fault. It was all Whistler's doing. But does Whistler get the bill? No, he goes off playing sailor. He's off with that girl who should have been dead like he doesn't have a care in the world.

And now look at Aubrey. Still can't walk without crutches. The word is he's minus a set of balls, too, not that Aubrey ever used the ones he had. The worst of it is, he gave Whistler a pass. He folded because Whistler has his ledger, but so what? All that money listed in it had already been laundered. All that real estate they seized, all that other stuff they took is so spread around over so many people that they'll never be able to track it all down. And all Aubrey has to do is cook some new books and say that the other one was a fake.

Aubrey doesn't know who cut him. Neither does Briggs. Briggs says by the time he felt the first cuts he already had blood in his eyes. Aubrey won't talk about what happened with him, but Lockwood had heard from other sources. The story is that Aubrey was taking a crap in a hotel room down in Richmond. He's sitting on the bowl, his pants down at his ankles, when this woman shows up out of nowhere. He says he couldn't see who because he's reading reports. Anyway, this woman grabs his pants, yanks them up, flips Aubrey ass-over so his head's in the toilet. She carves him up like a roast.

Lockwood knew who it was. It was the mother, who else? It was the mother of the girl who got shot. Aubrey, however, says that isn't right. They showed him pictures of the mother. He says that's not her. Not that he ever got that good a look because his face was in the shit he just took. And not that it makes any difference who's right. When a thing like that happens, you make somebody pay. Pick someone who's handy. Like the mother. She deserves it. From the day those two women threw them out of their house, he knew they were in this with Whistler.

Briggs says no, not the mother. He says leave her alone. He says she was there when they were stitching up his face. He says she was decent to him. She held his hand. See that? The guy's perspective is shot.

Next it's Aubrey and Poole who say leave it alone. Aubrey says this is an order. Aubrey and Poole want to let Whistler go. They not only let the guy get out of this clean, they let him take off with that girl who got shot and let him live the life of Riley on some boat these two gave him. They also gave him cash, must be two or three million. A good chunk of that came from Lockwood's pocket. Aubrey made Briggs kick in almost as much, but it was probably Aubrey who took the biggest hit. Or his relatives did. He cleaned most of them out. Poole started to say something about "rendering unto Caesar" until Aubrey told him to shut the fuck up. That was something, at least. At least Aubrey was mad.

Three times now, Lockwood had gone in to Aubrey with ideas on how to get even with Whistler. Okay, thought Lockwood, the money's gone, but there's a principle here. You let someone burn you and walk away clean, you got no credibility left. You have to let it be known that they did not walk away. You fix it so Whistler's never heard from again. He went off on a boat? Make him look lost at sea. It happens, right? Boats go down all the time. How can anyone blame us for that?

Aubrey doesn't want to hear it. He says forget it. He says let's just get back to work. The truth is, he's—what's the word?—he's traumatized right now. That woman who cut him cut deeper than she knew. He's scared she'll come back and he's scared of Whistler's father. But if you know she had to work for either Whistler or his father, if you make them go away, she's no longer in the picture. That makes sense, right? She's got to find some other work. The trick is, therefore, to get Whistler and his father, same day, both at once, and it's over. We either coordinate, same day, different places, or we wait until they visit for a birthday or something. What we don't do is sit with our thumbs up our asses, letting that bunch think they beat us.

Aubrey agrees. He won't say so, thought Lockwood, but he does. He could see how Aubrey was biting his lip and wanting, really badly, to get even with Whistler. All he'd say was, "You are to take no action. No action whatever. Am I clear?"

"You mean until we know we can't miss."

"There is no 'until.' There is no 'unless.' Must I write this on the back of your hand?"

"So, you're telling me—what? You got something else going?"

"Get out of my office, Mr. Lockwood."

This was very frustrating. It could have been over.

Lockwood could have had Whistler if they hadn't pulled him off. He and one of his guys had staked out Whistler's apartment. They were waiting on his roof. Rain or shine, they didn't care. Whistler would have shown sooner or later. But then Mr. Poole made this deal with Whistler's father. It's a standoff. It's over. They could make up their losses in a few months, tops, as long as Whistler's father keeps his end of the deal and doesn't go public with this thing.

This was wrong. It was dumb. No one keeps a deal like this. Someone hurts you this bad, you go for payback, big time. You watch for your chance and you finish it.

Twice now, since then, he'd almost got Whistler. He'd almost got Whistler and the girl in one shot. He'd gone after them on his own. A runner who owes him spotted their boat. It was on its way out of Belize. He told his guy, "Let them get out to sea. Then I want you to take them; send that boat to the bottom. If you can, board them first and take them alive. Have whatever fun you want with the girl and make Whistler watch while you're doing her. Let them know before you kill them that this is from me. This is payback from me and from Briggs."

His guy almost had them, but he had to back off. He got close to their boat, said he needed some ice, but the girl must have not liked their looks. She gave them some ice, but she kept a gun on them. It was one of those shotguns with a twenty-round drum and she looked like she knew how to use it.

Same guy, same runner, sees her again. This time, a

month later, it's on Grand Cayman Island. She's walking
down the street and Whistler is with her. They're walking
along holding hands. His guy was there for a court appearance on a charge that the magistrate ended up dismissing
after they'd talked a little business. Whistler and the girl turn
a corner, disappear. There were restaurants there; he knows
they must have gone in one. He looks in some windows and
he spots them, he thinks. He goes in this one restaurant to
make sure it's them, but then he gets spooked by the girl
again.

He says he gets a feeling that she recognized him from
last time down off Belize. He says he knows it's crazy because, that time off Belize, she never got a look at his face.
Off Belize he was watching her through a pair of binoculars from maybe four boat lengths away. On top of that,
he's now wearing a suit because of this court appearance
he had. He says there's no way that she could have made
him, but it's like she sensed it, he says. She looks like
she's ready to stick him with a fork. He kept going past
their table, took a leak, then went back out. He wasn't
going to try to take them alone, so he went back to his boat
to round up some crew. By the time they get back,
Whistler's gone.

After that, Lockwood told this guy to forget it. By now,
this guy's gone so mental on the girl that it's better to use
someone else.

The mother, all this time, is sending faxes and E-mails
and is talking to them on the phone. Lockwood had moni-
tors logging these calls, but they only got fragments of what
they were saying. A couple of times they were talking in
German. Since when do these women know German? And
since when, for that matter, does the daughter know guns?
Since when did she learn to smell trouble? The answer has
to be that she's learning this from Whistler, but what is he
training her to do? Be like him? They've got to be planning
some kind of move and the mother has got to be part of it.
The mother disappears for weeks at a time. She makes it
look like she's headed for Europe, but she's probably flying

a roundabout route and meeting up with them on some island.

The good news, thought Lockwood, is that now he'll know where Whistler is at all times. Another guy he uses flew down to Martinique after Lockwood had traced some of their calls there. This was Kaplan, the guy who was with him on the roof. Kaplan's not just a shooter. He does electronics. He was looking for a way to stash a tracking transmitter someplace on the boat Whistler lives on. But Whistler had this boat at a private marina that had security guards day and night. Kaplan had a hard time getting near it.

But one day he sees Whistler watching some kid who goes down and cleans the crap off boat bottoms. Whistler talks to the kid. He wants to hire the kid. The kid gets seventy-five bucks for the job. Kaplan asked the kid how he'd like to make two hundred. He flashes an ID, says he's DEA, tells him Whistler's a suspected drug runner. He shows the kid this little transmitter that looks like a domino tile. He gives him some stuff, Krazy Glue or some shit, and tells him to stick it under the rail at a place where it wouldn't be noticed.

And what almost happened? Same thing as before. The girl comes on deck while he's working below. She's walking along the deck, looking down. This kid can see her up through the water. He thinks she's on to him; he almost gives it up. But a bird plops down and distracts her long enough so he can slap the thing under the rail. Even then, he's sure that she knows what he did because of the way she's still looking at him. She also has a phone to her ear. She looks like she's reporting the kid.

But it ends up okay. They never found the transmitter. It showed where they were every day after that. They couldn't move that boat without him knowing it.

Lockwood didn't tell Aubrey about the first two. When Aubrey said, "You're to take no action," Lockwood decided that what Aubrey really meant was that he didn't want to know. Lockwood would have waited until he was sure they were dead and maybe the mother along with them. He did tell Aubrey about the transmitter, however. He wanted to see the look on Aubrey's face when he told him that he'd pulled it off.

He went into Aubrey's office. He said, "Ask me where he is. Ask me where Whistler is right this minute."

Aubrey didn't look up, but he turned a little red. "I have no further interest in that subject."

"He's in Antigua. Two weeks now he's been there."

Aubrey sat back. "You've been tracking him? Why?"

"Because somebody should. I got a stake in this, too. And I'll tell you what else. He's using his name. It's the first time he's used his real name."

"Which means?"

"I don't know. It's just different. Wait a minute. Here's why. He's saying, 'Fuck you, Mr. Aubrey.' "

Again, that faggy little curl of his lip. "I would think, Mr. Lockwood, if that were his intention, he would find a more direct way to say it."

"Okay, then you. What do *you* have to say?"

"On what subject, Mr. Lockwood?"

"On maybe how I did a good job here, for starters. On maybe how that girl, who you thought was just his squeeze, is turning into someone we should worry about."

Again, with the lip. Aubrey asked, "Meaning what?"

"Forget it. You don't care? Then forget it."

Aubrey hissed. "Mr. Lockwood, tell me what you have done."

"It's . . . just that I know more about them than you think." He wasn't going to mention the two hits he missed. If that lip curled again, he'd want to smack it. He said, "But, hey, let's forgive and forget. So what if they made you spend four months in a wheelchair. They're enjoying themselves. The girl's learning a trade. Let's let bygones be bygones. Be happy."

Lockwood turned to leave his office.

"Mr. Lockwood? One moment."

Lockwood stopped. He waited.

"You say you'll know at all times where that boat is?"

"Within thirty feet. Rain or fog, it won't matter."

"Then perhaps you've done well. I will give this some thought."

"Then we move, okay? You'll get the green light from Poole?"

"Never mind Mr. Poole. You just keep me informed. But you're to do nothing. Don't think for yourself. You saw where that got us the last time."

Lockwood darkened. "You're going to keep harping on that?"

Aubrey motioned toward the crutch that he still needed sometimes. "I'm reminded of the cost every day, Mr. Lockwood."

"Well, I told you before. If Poole hadn't pulled me off—"

"Mr. Lockwood, they knew that you were waiting on that roof. I am told that it gave them a chuckle or two. I will say it again. Do not think for yourself. Just report on Whistler's movements. Nothing more."

13

They did sail north after their stay in Antigua. They did swing wide of the Florida coast. His father called on the satellite phone.

He asked, "Adam, what are you doing?"

"Oh, you noticed."

Whistler knew that he would have. His father, at that moment, would be sitting at a screen on the top floor of the building next door to his house. He'd be watching a little yellow blip on that screen. He'd have seen that the blip was now north of the Bahamas. After that, there weren't any more islands. There was only the southeastern coast.

"Yes, I noticed," he said, "and your year isn't up. You remember the terms of the agreement."

"Of course, I remember. I also remember whose idea it

was. But don't worry; we only have a few weeks left and we're not going to make any waves."

"Where exactly are you headed?"

"We're just cruising along up the coast."

"I'm getting two signals from your boat again. Do you have your GPS on?"

"It's never off. You must be getting an echo."

"Well, instead of just 'cruising along up the coast,' why not swing more northeast and set a course for Bermuda? Tell you what, I'll fly over. We'll spend a few days."

"Claudia would like that, but not in Bermuda. She's got her heart set on Maine. Meet us there."

"You know better than that. Explain to her why."

"Wait. I'll put her on. You can try to explain. But her pelican has already given its blessing. In fact, I think this was the pelican's idea."

"Adam, what the hell are you talking about?"

"There's this pelican. It talks to her. And it scouts up ahead. But maybe you'd better not mention that last part. Sometimes she gets touchy about it."

"Adam . . ." Long silence. "Are you pulling my leg?"

"The pelican's an angel, too, by the way. It's been with us for months, keeps an eye on things for us. One good part about it being an angel is that it doesn't have those nasty bodily functions. It never leaves its droppings on the deck."

"Adam . . ."

"The pelican likes lobster, but it can't crack the shells. That's why it needs us to go to Maine for the summer. Myself, I'm looking forward to digging for clams. Think of the money we'll save."

"I get the picture."

"Knew you would. You're very quick."

"You've either been out in the hot sun too long or I'm seeing a touch of rebelliousness here." He said, "Fine. Have your fun. But watch yourself, Adam. You've had a good year, but it must have dulled your edge. Check in with me, will you? Don't leave me here wondering."

"I will. Don't worry."

"Um . . . that pelican business . . ."

"There's really a pelican. It does speak to Claudia. You thought what? That she's suddenly normal?"

Another long silence. His father was still doubtful. "You're lucky you're too big to spank."

Vernon Lockwood stepped into Aubrey's office again, a loosely rolled chart in his hand. He said, "Whistler's moving. He's coming this way."

"This way . . . meaning what, Mr. Lockwood?"

The bigger man placed the chart on his desk and spread it for Aubrey to see. A series of plottings were marked with an X and the Xs were joined by a line. "This shows where he's been. Look where that route takes him."

Lockwood traced a finger more or less in the direction that Whistler's boat seemed to be following. His finger came to rest on the District of Columbia.

"You're saying that he's planning an assault on us by sea? And without air cover? No shelling of defenses? No bombing of all our routes to the beach to keep our tanks from engaging him?"

"Hey, you wanted me tell you where he goes."

Aubrey groaned softly. "And you have, Mr. Lockwood. I would point out, however, that the course he is on might lead to Nova Scotia just as easily."

"Why'd he swing so wide of the Florida coast?"

Aubrey looked at the chart. "That would seem to have been the thing to do if he had no intention of going there."

Aubrey sat back. He saw Lockwood's color rising. Very well, he thought. A good dog deserves a bone. He decided to soften his expression and his voice. He said, "Mr. Lockwood, you're doing good work. But surely you see that no action can be taken until we know what Whistler is up to, if anything. Do you have any other intelligence?"

"Not yet. I wanted you to know something's changed."

"And I thank you. I do. You're a very good man."

"You mean that?"

"I do. You'll keep me advised?"

"I'll track him every inch of the way. Just one thing. If we take him, I get him. Agreed?"

"Who else but Vern the Burn would I call on," Aubrey asked, "to handle such a delicate matter?"

Claudia had realized that Maine would have to wait. It was only late April. There would still be snow in Maine. Her original thought would make the most sense. They would cruise the Georgia coast and the Carolinas until it warmed up farther north.

They did the Sea Islands, Saint Simons and Jekyll, never stopping for more than one day and a night. They continued up the coast until they reached Savannah. It was time to find a place to settle in for a while and use it as a base for further cruising. Whistler elected to bypass Savannah because he'd be expected to check in with Customs. He'd be expected to do so anywhere along the coast, but the requirement was seldom enforced in most of the smaller marinas. He found such a place a few miles farther north, just over the South Carolina border. He rented a slip at Palmetto Bay on the inland side of Hilton Head Island.

They refueled, reprovisioned, and settled in for a stay. The island would do nicely as their base. They rented a car and they toured Savannah. A week later they drove up to Charleston. Claudia was especially charmed by both cities. Both had large historic sections with gracious old homes that were virtually unchanged since before the Civil War. She'd described them to her mother over the phone. Her mother, who adored old homes with old gardens, and had never been to this part of the country, remarked that she'd love to see it someday. Claudia agreed that she must, but why wait? Hop a plane, she said, and fly into Savannah. Hilton Head had an airport, but it didn't take big jets. Just as well, she said, we'll all meet in Savannah. We'll do the town, then drive back to the island and maybe go to Charleston by boat. Adam doesn't think that his father would join us, but he might if you call him and nag him.

Whistler had to step in and disappoint them both. At least for a while, he said. He told Claudia that he'd rather sit tight for a time, see if anyone seems interested in their comings and goings. His father, in any case, would feel the same way. He certainly would never join them on a boat. It would be an unnecessary risk.

"Adam, I think that must be over. I do. Wouldn't something have happened by now?"

"I suppose."

"All we've had all year were those three false alarms. They were not even that. I was overreacting."

"No, you weren't; you were listening to your instincts, and that's good. The mistake would have been to ignore them."

"Well, next time I'll try to be a bit more selective."

"No harm, no foul. You did fine."

"And those people must know you're not looking for trouble. Don't you think they're content to let sleeping dogs lie?"

I would not be, thought Whistler, but maybe they are. "Let's keep our eyes open all the same."

Lockwood entered Aubrey's office with his chart once again. He asked Aubrey, "You know anything about Hilton Head Island?"

"It's where rich men go to play golf until they die. I gather that's where the boat is."

"They made a few stops, but this is the longest. And he still hasn't checked in with Customs."

"Implication?"

"What else? He's supposed to be out of the country, right? So the guy doesn't want it on record that he's back. Ask me, he's there for some kind of meeting and he doesn't want anyone to know it."

"A meeting with whom?"

"I don't know. His old man."

"Not likely, I think. He could meet with his father anywhere in the world without risking your steely-eyed scrutiny. Perhaps he has merely put in for repairs."

"For that, you haul the boat. He's just sitting. Hasn't moved. I'm telling you there's something going on."

"Without evidence?"

"Gut feel. I know I'm right about this."

"No, Mr. Lockwood, you *want* to be right. You are less than objective in this matter."

"So, okay, we find out. I can put someone down there. I can put someone Whistler doesn't know."

"What sort of someone?"

"Not to hit him. Just to watch. And let us know what he's up to."

"Someone to observe. Only that?"

"I'll send Kaplan. You know Kaplan? Oh, that's right, I guess you don't."

"Your electronics whiz, as I recall."

"Arnie Kaplan. That's the guy. He's the one who put the tap on the mother's house in Denver. He's the one who put the tracker on the boat."

"That phone tap fell short of being state-of-the-art. We were able to hear every fourth or fifth word, but that's better than nothing, I suppose."

"He says Whistler or his father must have jammed the thing somehow. You're going to down Kaplan for that?"

"Very well. This Kaplan. He is strictly a technician? He's a nonviolent type, am I correct?"

"Shit, no. What good's a guy who can't do what needs doing?"

"Mr. Lockwood—read my lips. He's to take no sort of action."

"He won't. Not till you say so. And not without me, I can have Kaplan there by tonight."

"Very well. Please keep me—"

"Advised. Yeah, I know."

"You're a gem among men, Mr. Lockwood."

Two weeks had gone by. There was no sign of trouble. Whistler had continued to use his real name and had used a credit card both to shop and dine out. He'd transferred some funds from his own offshore account into a bank on the island. Any one of these transactions should have sent up a flare if someone's computer was watching for evidence that he had returned to this country.

But there was nothing. No hint of interest. And, as he'd promised, he had checked in with his father. His father confirmed that his own equipment hadn't picked up any electronic buzz that involved either Whistler or his boat. He became more at ease. Perhaps Claudia had been right. He was becoming less alert, less watchful by the day. Islands seem to do that to people.

That was not to say that life was entirely idyllic. There were still decisions to be made. On this day, for example, he was faced with the question of whether to eat in or eat out. The decision was made for him when he saw a plump grouper that a fishing boat had brought in. On his dock were several fishermen who supplied the island's restaurants with the item called the catch of the day. Coming in, they would usually give a toot of their horns, a signal that boat owners should come take a look before the best of the catch was snatched up.

He bought the grouper. He decided on the menu. He had some creamed corn, fresh tomatoes, sweet onions. He and Claudia would eat beneath the shade of the Bimini. They would sip a chilled wine, admire the sunset, and then go for a nice long walk and a swim before settling in for the night.

The yacht club nearby had an unlit pool that was off in a corner, surrounded by trees, and almost never used in the evening. The water, after sundown, was warmer than the air. Most nights it gave off a layer of mist that made it all the more perfect for a languid swim. And all the more private should Claudia decide that her swimsuit was an unneeded hindrance.

If he'd stuck with that decision, there would still have been a shooting. If he'd stayed on the boat and cooked up the grouper, a man he'd never heard of would probably have been murdered by some other men he'd never heard of either. This island would no longer be so gentle a place, but neither he nor Claudia would have been involved. They would have been two miles away when it happened. And it wouldn't have turned into a bloodbath.

14

What had changed his plan was that Claudia had gone shopping. She returned to the boat with three new blouses she'd found, all on sale at a seasonal clearance. On the rare occasion when she did treat herself, she showed a girlish, almost guilty excitement. She would want to model them for him.

He was kneeling on the slip when she came down the ramp. He was cleaning the grouper, tossing scraps to the gulls. He stopped to admire her as she approached. So did everyone else on the dock. She couldn't wait to show him what she'd bought and to tell him how deeply the prices had been slashed. She set her shopping bag down and laid out its contents. She asked him what blouse he liked best.

Whistler never knew how to answer that question. His rule for offering an opinion about her clothing was to wait for her to give him a hint. She saw his hesitation. She said, "Wait. I'll try them on."

She stepped onto the boat and stripped off her top before he could say a word to stop her. She wore no bra; she seldom did. All that remained was her scarf. Never mind that other people were coming and going or that heads were popping up on other boats. Never mind that one dock boy would have walked into the water, had he not first bumped into a piling. This was another otherworldly thing about her. Ever since her white light sent her back as an angel, she had never displayed the slightest awareness that her body might have that effect.

Her nudity, however, lasted only a few seconds. She slipped into the first blouse and shook out her hair. She brushed a fawn-colored wisp from her eyes, looked up and awaited a reaction.

He said, "Hmmm." Noncommittal. Still neutral.

"Okay, wait."

She repeated the procedure with the other two blouses, two more intervals of unabashed nudity. All three had long sleeves, open throats, high, wide collars. She seldom wore any other cut. She rolled the sleeves to mid-forearm, tucked in the hems, and each time made a slow pirouette for his benefit. The first blouse had been pink, the second, emerald green. The third had blue-and-white vertical stripes and little epaulets on the shoulders. He guessed that she might have saved her favorite for last.

He said, "I like all three."

"I'm not keeping all three. That's extravagant, Adam. Pick one."

Three blouses were too much of an indulgence for Claudia. Never mind that they were living on a luxury yacht. The cost of painting the hull alone would have bought her five years' worth of clothing.

"Okay, the striped one. Very sharp. Very nautical."

"You don't like the second one? The green one?"

Bad guess, thought Whistler. "I like that one even better."

Her lips formed a pout. "You don't mean that."

"Claudia, listen. You'd look good in a trash bag. But if I have to pick one, it's the green one."

She fingered the fabric. "You should feel it," she said. "It's so very soft, very feminine."

"You don't need any help being feminine."

She blushed. A shy smile. "Let me see what I've got that goes with it."

She disappeared below. He could hear what she was doing. He heard the sound of hangers scraping as she rummaged through her locker. She would end up choosing white slacks, maybe tan. The slacks would determine the shoes. The bulk of her time would be spent on accessories. She would go through a half dozen junk jewelry earrings before deciding, he hoped, on the emerald studs that he thought went so well with her coloring. He had lied about the studs. He had told her they were fake. Otherwise, she might not have worn them.

She would rummage through her necklaces and try several on before settling on a simple gold chain. The right knotted scarf would come next. Rings and things would take a few minutes more. Hair and makeup perhaps another ten. When satisfied with the overall effect, her eyes would glaze over just a little bit as if asking the mirror, "What now?"

Whistler knew the answer because Whistler knew his lines. He called, "Are you dressed yet?"

"I guess. Want to see?"

She appeared in the hatch. She had opted for the studs. She had brushed her hair back so that they showed.

"Well, now you're too elegant for the meal I had in mind. Now we have to go someplace expensive."

"Oh, no. You bought that beautiful fish."

"We'll have it for breakfast. Let's go. Name the place."

"We don't need expensive. Someplace casual, okay? Let's just go grab a bite at Jump and Phil's."

She liked Jump & Phil's for a number of reasons, not least that it was moderately priced. And unlike most island restaurants that catered to tourists, Jump & Phil's clientele were predominantly locals who had moved to the island years before.

Conversations with the locals were generally more relaxed than those with short-timers or tourists. The latter always asked, "So, where are you from?" The locals seldom did because they didn't much care. Nor did they ever ask, "What do you do?" In that regard, they were like cruising yachtsmen. This island was a place where people started new lives. Who you'd been, what you'd done no longer mattered.

They'd been to that restaurant nine or ten times in the weeks since they'd put into Hilton Head. The young owners, Jump and Phil, had both introduced themselves and now greeted them on a first-name basis. When these two weren't tending to business, the one called Jump liked to work on his golf game and his partner, Phil, was a fisherman. Phil's boat, in fact, was berthed near his own at the Palmetto Bay Marina.

Their favorite bartender was a pleasant young woman who had made them feel like old friends. Her name was Leslie. She had a wonderful smile. She was very good-natured, very bright, quick-witted, and she seemed to know everyone on the island. Leslie, early on, had noted what they drank. Their drinks would sometimes be sitting on the bar by the time he and Claudia walked through the door. Scotch and water for him, a Chardonnay for Claudia. He would get a small wave from people he'd met there, but their eyes were always really on Claudia. Aside from her looks, it was that elegant carriage. Her neck had still not fully regained the suppleness that it once had.

Claudia never said so, not in so many words, but the other thing that she probably liked was how the place was laid out. It had a U-shaped bar set against a solid wall. The other three walls were mostly glass. If they sat, as they did, on the far side of the bar, they could see everyone who came in.

Whistler himself saw no great advantage in finding a bar with a wide field of view. If trouble did find them, it would choose its time and place, and not where he could see it approaching. It would certainly choose a quieter place, one with fewer pairs of eyes than were present. Although Claudia's vigilance had gone for little thus far, she was nonetheless convinced that a guardian angel ought always to be on her toes.

They were seated at the bar; their drinks were in place, and the tables were filling up quickly. Only one, by the fireplace, remained unoccupied and that one had a sign that said RESERVED. He'd thought that this restaurant didn't take reservations. But it was a Wednesday, and the Wednesday-night special was always a decent roast beef. That usually drew a good crowd. Among the other specials were a pasta creation and the catch of the day, another grouper. The sign called it Mustard-Crusted Grouper.

He did have his heart set on a good piece of fish, but to

order it might have made Claudia feel guilty. He also wasn't
sure that he could pronounce it without tripping over his
tongue. A Mustard-Crusted Grouper. Try saying it fast. So
he sniffed the air and said the roast beef smelled good. A
nice end cut would really hit the spot.

"You're not sorry that we came?" she asked.

"I'm with you. What's to be sorry?"

She poked his arm. "You're so full of beans, Whistler.
But you're also very sweet and I love you."

They both ordered the beef. She liked hers blood-rare. He
did not share her taste for almost raw meat. He'd told her
that he'd known cows to get well after they'd been hurt
worse than some he'd seen on her plate. Then she'd look
down her nose at his blackened end-cut slab. She'd say she
had beach thongs that were juicier.

Whistler had noticed the two men outside. They appeared a
few minutes after sundown. For an instant his thought was,
"Oh, no, not the twins," because the first one he saw had their
shape. But it wasn't the Beasleys. The two men were
strangers. There was nothing especially remarkable about
them. Both in their forties, both of medium height, one a little more portly than the other. The stockier one wore a base-
ball-type cap. His companion went bareheaded and he wore
his hair short. Whistler might not have given them a second
look except that they both wore zippered up jackets. The
evening was too warm for outer garments.

They were probably tourists, new to the island. Perhaps
they thought it might rain. Nor did their manner seem in
any way furtive. They were standing perhaps twenty yards
from the entrance, peering into the restaurant, scanning
faces. The one with the cap shook his head; he seemed annoyed. He muttered a few words to the other. The other one
nodded in apparent agreement. He gestured as if to say,
"Let's go see what's in the back." Perhaps whoever they
were looking for was in one of the neighboring establish-
ments.

There were three other restaurants behind Jump & Phil's.

A seafood house, a brewery, and an Irish Pub, plus a billiard room and cigar bar called The Lodge. Whistler followed their progress as they rounded the perimeter. They glanced in once or twice but at no one in particular. He half turned in his stool as they passed the wall of windows behind him. He made eye contact, briefly, with the one who wore no hat. The man showed no surprise, no hint of recognition. The other one never looked at him at all.

Whistler and Claudia had finished their salads and the bartender, Leslie, had brought their roast beef. Whistler, ordinarily, would have asked for a steak knife. His end cut, while tender, had a thick outer crust. But Claudia was blithely dissecting her steak with an ordinary table knife's serrated edge. She was showing off, he thought. He resolved to make do. He would try to avoid grunting as he sliced it.

The table by the fireplace had been occupied by then. A middle-aged couple, well dressed, had come in. The man wore a blazer; he had on a necktie. Whistler hadn't seen anyone wearing a tie in the weeks that he'd been on the island. They must have just got here. Complexions still pale. Hadn't doped out the dress code as yet.

The woman sat facing him, the man was in profile. The woman glanced up at Whistler, met his eyes for an instant. She looked away, then she looked back again. The second time around, she was squinting. For a moment, she looked as if she thought she might know him. Just as quickly, she apparently decided that she didn't. She apologized for staring with a flicker of a smile before turning her attention to the man she was with.

Her face had seemed vaguely familiar as well. Or not familiar, perhaps. She was more of a type. She impressed him as having that easy self-assurance that comes from good schools and good breeding. She had put him in mind of his mother. The man had more of a blue-collar look, but one that had picked up some polish over time. Gray-haired, he wore it combed forward, uneven. It was sort of a Julius Caesar cut. A waitress was taking their order for drinks.

A woman who was seated at a table in between appeared

to know the man, or at least who he was. She leaned in
toward the people who were with her at her table. She was
whispering to them. They turned their heads to look. The
man noticed and he answered with a shy little wave, but he
did not encourage a further exchange. Someone famous, apparently. An actor, perhaps. That would have explained why
they saved a table for him.

Claudia nudged him. "Those two outside are back."

Whistler hadn't realized that she'd noticed the two men.
He looked up at them without raising his head. They were in
the same spot, scanning faces again. And again they were
standing well away from the entrance, just out of the reach
of its lights. The bareheaded one had reached into his pocket
and pulled out a stack of what looked like brochures. The
other one took them, put them in his own pocket. They huddled together for a few seconds more. The hatless one
seemed to be giving instructions.

"You don't know them?" she asked.

"No, and they don't know us. Claudia, it's nothing. Eat
your dinner."

She said, "They're behaving pretty oddly, don't you
think?"

Whistler thought of the diver whom she'd almost clubbed
and the man on Grand Cayman who needed a rest room.
"Claudia, they're tourists. They just look a bit lost."

"No. It's not that. They're looking for someone."

He tossed a hand. "I'm sure that they are. They were
probably supposed to meet up with some friends and they
got their signals crossed as to where. It happens all the time.
No more to it than that."

She squinted. "I suppose. Look, one of them's leaving."

Whistler saw that the bareheaded one was walking
toward the parked cars. He watched him climb into the only
car there that had been backed into its space. That alone
made Whistler pay more attention. The car was a Buick,
older model, dark in color. Whistler noticed that the dome
light never went on. In his own cars, Whistler always kept
the dome light switched off. It was one of those things that

he'd learned from his father. Don't illuminate yourself un-
necessarily. It was possible, he supposed, that the bulb had
burned out, but it made him increasingly wary. He saw a
puff of exhaust; the man had started the engine, but he still
hadn't turned on his headlights. He was obviously waiting,
but his friend had disappeared.

"Where'd the other one go?" he asked Claudia.

"In those trees."

Whistler searched. He found him. The man's back was to
the restaurant. "What's he doing now? Can you tell?"

"He's pretending that he's taking a whiz."

From his posture and from the hunching of his shoulders,
he did appear to be relieving himself. Why there, however?
There were rest rooms all over. "You say he's pretending.
What makes you think that?"

"He's . . . using his hands for something else."

Whistler watched him more closely. She seemed to be
right. When the man finally straightened, there was no little
hitch that is seen when men fix themselves. His shoulder
never dipped to reach the bottom of his fly. Instead, both his
hands came up to his face. They were busy there for a few
seconds. When he turned, Whistler saw that he had altered
his appearance.

He had put on dark glasses, but that wasn't all. He had
placed a strip of bandage over his nose and another across
his right eyebrow. His face was effectively disguised. He
paused for a moment and looked down toward his companion. His companion revved his motor. Whistler saw the exhaust. This one nodded in response. He unzipped his jacket.
He took a deep breath and walked toward the restaurant. His
right hand had reached inside the jacket.

"He's here to hurt someone," Claudia whispered. "I think
he has his hand on a gun."

"More likely a practical joke. Just be cool."

"Then stop him and ask him. What if you're wrong?"

"If I'm wrong, it's still none of our business."

"I'll ask him."

The man pushed through the door without breaking

stride. Claudia had already slid off her stool. He grabbed her arm and hissed, "We need to stay out of this."

In the second and a fraction that it took him to say it, the man had crossed half the width of the restaurant and was headed toward the table by the fireplace. Too late, Whistler saw that he did have a pistol. He was pulling it from his waistband. It looked like an old army-issue automatic. As he cocked it, he shouted, "God is not mocked." In another half second, he fired.

The sound was a thunderclap. The pistol spat flame. The man at that table had seen what was coming. He had shoved the table forward, tried to tip it toward the gunman. The shot, aimed at his heart, struck the table's edge first and then caught him high in the chest. It spun him, knocked him down, but he hit the floor crawling. He gasped, "Not my wife. Don't hurt my wife."

There was instant pandemonium. Many screams, many shouts. Men were dragging women and children to the floor and some women were dragging their men. The man with the gun shoved the table aside, knocking the man's wife down with it. He was trying for a second killing shot.

Whistler was already on his feet. He had picked up his barstool and was ready to throw it. He felt Claudia's hand on his shoulder. He snapped, "Get down. Stay behind me." But her hand had now gripped the back of his collar. She said, "No, you. You stay behind me." She pulled him aside and then backward, off balance. He felt her free hand whip past his ear. He saw something silvery spin through the air and he realized at once what she had done.

The man with the gun went stiff, then lurched drunkenly. He tried to bring his left hand to his head, to feel for the thing that had struck him. But his fingers were flaccid; they would not obey his brain because his brain had lost much of its function. The handle of a table knife jutted out from his temple at a spot just behind his left eye.

That was Claudia's knife. Whistler couldn't believe it. It was simply not possible that Claudia could do that. And

not only Claudia. *No one* could do that. No one makes a
killing throw with that kind of a knife.

The searching hand quivered. It was going into a spasm.
It knocked the shooter's cap and dark glasses askew. His
other hand, the gun hand, began clenching on its own. It
jerked off several shots that went into the floor and into a
neighboring table. The recoil was forcing his hand to rise
up and the man was still stumbling about drunkenly. Now
the bullets were spraying the restaurant at random. One
struck a woman who had gotten up to run. She fell on her
face without a sound. Another smashed the back window
that faced a garden path. A man outside, watching, clutched
his stomach as if punched. Others near him were hit by flying glass. The whole pane collapsed, raining shards.

Again, all this happened in not more than three seconds,
in the time it took Whistler to take several long strides. He
had let the barstool fall and had focused on the gun. The man
who held it was no longer the issue. He seized the man's
wrist and jerked the arm downward, taking care to jam his
thumb inside the cocked hammer so that the gun could not
be fired again. The man was still flailing; he was clawing at
nothing. Whistler looked into his eyes as he pried the gun
loose. His eyes had no life. He'd been blinded.

Whistler grabbed him by the hair and twisted his head
until the man fell heavily at his feet. The impact altered the
angle of the knife, causing the blade to slice more of his
brain. The man reacted as if he had touched a third rail. He
stiffened, bucked wildly, then stiffened again. Whistler
dropped to one knee; he pinned the man with it. He felt for
the knife sticking out of the man's skull and ran his fingers
over its handle. He glanced back toward the bar where he
had last seen Claudia. He still could scarcely believe she had
done this. She was no longer there but he heard her voice behind him. She called, "I've got your back. Watch the front."

The place was still bedlam. Patrons scrambled toward
exits; some climbed through the smashed window; others
tried to crowd into the rest rooms. Whistler saw that one
man in a loudly striped jacket had stayed at the bar with a

beer in his hand. Straw hat, tinted glasses, mid-forties.
Whistler had seen him in this restaurant several times. The
man's expression was one of detached fascination, as if this
were a play he was watching. Whistler glared at him. "You!
Get off there. Get down," and the man quickly slid out of
sight.

Whistler turned his attention to where he'd last seen that
Buick. The driver, thought Whistler, might still try to help
the shooter. He could not have seen the knife. He could have
only seen the struggle. Whistler spotted the Buick, its high
beams now on. It was coming, not quickly, but deliberately.
Whistler could make out the driver's head and shoulders. He
was stretching and craning, looking for his confederate. As
he neared, the passenger window slid down, perhaps to give
the driver a better view, but perhaps for him to fire a weapon.
Whistler raised the automatic. He tracked the opened window in its sights.

He heard a scuffling of feet and glanced back just in time.
A young man, a big one, had risen to a crouch and was about
to try to jump him, try to grapple for the gun. Whistler had
no time to explain who was who. He swung the gun around,
froze the young man in his tracks, then chopped it against
his right ear. He wheeled again and sighted in on the Buick.
He saw that the driver had indeed raised a weapon. It looked
like a shotgun. Whistler squeezed off two rounds.

The glass entrance door deflected his shots, but they shattered the windshield of the getaway car. The driver ducked
down and the Buick leaped forward. Whistler heard frightened shouts and the squeal of cold tires as the driver took the
shortest way out. He drove over flower beds and took shrub-
bery with him. He hit one passing car and forced others off the
road as he steered toward the island's main parkway.

Whistler turned to check on Claudia. She was on her
knees. She was giving aid to the first man who'd been shot.
The man's wife was frantic but trying to help. She was
pulling wood splinters out of his flesh. Claudia told her to
leave them alone and instead put pressure on the hole in his
chest while Claudia felt beneath him for the exit wound.

With all that, she kept watching the back and side windows for any further threat from those directions. Whistler saw that the bartender was coming around to try to be of assistance. He waved her back and pointed to the bar phone.

He told her, "Leslie . . . call nine-one-one *now*. Shots fired, four down, maybe more hurt out front. And stay on the phone; don't hang up."

He stepped over toward Claudia, the pistol pointed skyward. He used his free hand to make calming gestures toward those who were watching him fearfully. He reached down to the floor and picked up a red napkin. He placed the napkin over a stray table knife and tucked them both under his arm.

He whispered to Claudia. "Come with me for a minute."

"No, wait. I found the bullet. It's almost out."

Whistler saw what she meant. Her fingers had located an oozing lump between the man's armpit and shoulder blade. He would have thought that it should have passed through. The ricochet off the table must have slowed it.

"What you're doing isn't helping. Come with me. I'll tell you how."

She looked up at him, confused, but she did as he asked. She told the man's wife to keep pressure on the wound. Whistler led her to the bar where her dinner still sat.

She asked, "I'm not helping? What should I be doing?"

Whistler waved that aside. He said, "Listen to me. We don't have much time. You never threw the knife and you don't know who did. There's a new knife in the napkin that's under my arm. I want your fingerprints on it and I want your food on it. Leave the knife up here on your plate."

"But what for?"

"Please, this once, don't argue with me."

"Adam . . . people saw me. They saw where it came from."

"They won't agree on what they saw, or what they heard either. You never called out, 'Watch your front. I've got your back.' You wouldn't because all you are is my bimbo, not someone who would interest the police."

"I understand."

"Wait to do the knife until I'm talking to Leslie. Wipe it first. It should only have your prints."

"Then can I go back and help? Even bimbos know first aid."

"Yes, but try to seem a little less competent."

From out front, he could hear the first distant sirens and he saw the faint strobing of Mars lights. He asked Leslie if she still had 911 on the line.

She nodded, blinking. Her chest was heaving. "The dispatcher . . . she wants to know who here is armed."

He removed the clip and saw that it was empty. He ejected the one remaining cartridge from the chamber. He tossed the pistol and clip onto a shelf behind the bar.

"Say the shooting is over. You have the only weapon. Make sure she tells the deputies not to get nervous. If they see people running it will only be your patrons. They may not have paid their bills, but don't shoot them."

She passed on his message. "Now she's asking who you are."

He ignored the question. "Say the shooter's accomplice drives an older blue Buick. His windshield is shot out, left front fender is smashed and the driver is armed with a shotgun. I suggest they put a roadblock on the bridge to the mainland."

Leslie told the dispatcher what he'd said, then listened. "She says I should tell you not to leave."

Whistler sighed within himself. There was no question of leaving Leslie and the owners knew where he lived. Two cars full of deputies would be down at the marina before he could even start his engine. He reached for his Scotch but thought better of drinking it.

Right now he and Claudia would be taking their swim if he'd said he didn't like either blouse.

15

Four Sheriff's Department cruisers had arrived on the scene and the ambulances came close behind them. The deputies, tan uniforms, approached with guns drawn, telling people outside to stand back. Whistler heard people answer that the danger was past, but too many were talking at once. One of the owners, Phil Henry, went out and tried to calm everyone down. He managed to explain what he thought had transpired. The deputies knew him. They holstered their weapons. Whistler kept his hands flat on the bar.

A fire truck and two emergency vehicles added to the light show outside. Soon the deputies were augmented by security guards from one of the gated communities nearby. A sergeant asked the guards, who were dressed in blue uniforms, to assist in both crowd and traffic control and in gathering all those who had witnessed the shootings.

Traffic control was made even more difficult as a television news truck tried to get through and the ambulances tried to get out. A car that the getaway driver had hit was also blocking part of the road. A few local doctors had been called from their homes to give aid to those who were less seriously injured. Most had suffered cuts scrambling out through broken windows. Others had been trampled in the general panic after the shooting had started.

The woman who'd got up and had tried to run was dead. So was the old man who'd been walking out back and had stopped to see what was happening. The shooter with the knife in his skull was still twitching but dead for all practical purposes. His victim had already been taken away. He'd gone into shock but had been more or less conscious by the time the first ambulance rushed him to the hospital. He was able to talk to his wife, who'd gone with him. The casualties included several people out front. At least three needed treatment for injuries they'd suffered when the Buick, escaping, knocked them aside. And the young man, the big one whom Whistler had clubbed, had a probable fracture of the cheekbone.

According to the squawks of the deputies' radios, the getaway driver had not yet been found, but a roadblock was in place on the island's sole bridge.

The ranking deputy was a sergeant, about Whistler's age. A black man, light-skinned, he wore wire-rimmed glasses. He already knew Leslie; he addressed her by name and asked her if she was all right. She was trembling a little, but seemed in control. He asked her several questions as he bagged and tagged the gun that she'd kept on the shelf behind the bar. She pointed out Whistler, who was sitting with Claudia, their plates still in front of them, their dinners gone cold.

The sergeant approached them, asked to see some ID. Whistler told him that he'd come out without his wallet. All he had was some cash and his rental car key. He offered to drive down to his boat and retrieve it, knowing that the offer was sure to be declined.

"Eddie, I know them," said Leslie. "They're regulars."

"And they live on a boat?"

She nodded. "I've seen it. They're on the same dock where Phil keeps his Grady-White."

He said, "Give us a minute to talk."

As Leslie moved away to help clear the bar, the sergeant asked their names and wrote them down in his notebook. He asked the name of the boat and for their telephone number. Whistler answered all questions. Claudia remained silent. Whistler summarized what had happened that evening, or at least what he said he had seen of it. The sergeant tried to question Claudia. She seemed too dazed to answer. She sat cleaning the wounded man's blood from her hands with a wet towel Leslie had given her. Her new blouse had his blood on it as well.

The sergeant left to interview five or six other patrons, all of whom were still stunned by what they'd witnessed. That one man who had stayed at the bar was not among them. He had had the best view. He'd seen everything that happened. Whistler hoped that he'd chosen to melt away and not become involved in the event. The sergeant finished with the others, then took Leslie aside and spoke to her again at some length. Finally, he came back to where Whistler was sitting. Claudia had still not made a sound.

"Mr. Wismer, is it? And Miss Kelly, is that right?"

Whistler grunted. He didn't correct him. Leslie overheard, raised an eyebrow, but said nothing. Whistler had deliberately mispronounced their names. He would explain why to Leslie a bit later. But for now he was starting to worry about Claudia. He had asked her to pretend that she was in shock, but he was not sure that she was pretending. The knowledge that she might have killed a man might only have begun to sink in.

"I need to go through this one more time," said the sergeant. "You say you two are tourists? You just happened to be in here?"

Whistler nodded. "As I'm sure Leslie told you."

"And you have no connection with the victim? The first one?"

"Connection? I've never laid eyes on him."

The sergeant gestured toward the corner where the man had been shot. "His name is Philip Ragland. He's down from Chicago. He has a TV talk show called *The Ragland Report*. None of this rings any bells?"

"Never heard of the man or his show."

"You're sure? He's pretty famous."

"I don't watch much TV."

"Good show. But controversial. Not everyone loves him."

Whistler gave a small shrug. "Evidently."

"According to his wife, he's had a number of death threats for things he's said on the air. His wife said he never took them seriously before. Never felt the need for a body-guard. Or did he?"

"You're asking me?"

"I suppose I am. You did what bodyguards do."

"What? Sitting over here eating my dinner while he's back in that corner getting shot?"

"Just a thought. Let's talk about what you did do."

He gestured toward the shooter, who was still on the floor, only then being readied to be put on a stretcher. The ambulance crew had strapped an oxygen mask on him. They were careful not to touch the knife handle.

"And you say you didn't stab him. Someone else already had."

"I was way over here when I heard the first shot. I heard screams, people falling. By the time I made out who was doing the shooting, that knife was already sticking out of his head."

"Well, Mr. Wismer, not everyone agrees. Some say you ran and stabbed him right after that shot. Others say you threw the knife just before you took him down. Some even say that Miss Kelly here threw it."

"Nobody threw it. You know that's ridiculous."

"I do? Why is that, sir?"

"Because I doubt that there's a knife thrower living who could hit a moving target at twenty feet, striking the man in the only spot where a blunt-ended knife was likely to pene-trate, especially a knife so poorly balanced as this one." He picked up his own. "Anyway, here's mine. It's still on my plate where it belongs."

"And so is Miss Kelly's. I see that. But whose prints would we find on the knife in that man's head?"

"You might find mine on the handle, not the blade. I felt it and thought about pulling it out, but that might have done even more damage."

"No idea who stuck him?"

"Someone near that table, clearly. How about that big kid who tried to jump me? Where was he at the time, do you know?"

"He barely remembers coming in here this evening. You clocked him pretty good with that gun."

"Had no choice."

The sergeant glanced at the dinner plates sitting in front of them. "You must like the food here."

"That's why we come in."

"So much that you went back and finished your dinner with dead and injured lying all around you. Miss Kelly here, I'm told, was giving CPR, but took time out to come over and grab a few bites. And this with his blood still wet on her hands."

"She looked faint. She was ashen. I made her come and sit."

"Sit and eat?"

"Officer . . . she was in a fog by that time. If she did push some food around her plate, what of it?"

The deputy looked at Claudia. She had shown no reaction. He said, "Fair enough. Let's talk about you. Did I mention that the witnesses are pretty shaken up?"

"You mentioned that they are confused."

"On the other hand, there's you, cool and calm as can be. You know about knives and you know about guns. You don't freeze or hit the floor when some guy comes in shooting. You deal with it like it's a walk in the park. What's your background? Where does this come from?"

"I don't know. I did spend some time in the service. Perhaps some old training kicked in."

"Half the men here were in the service, Mr. Wismer. Was your training anything special? What branch?"

"Infantry."

"Officer?"

"Noncom."

"Just a grunt? You don't look like you'd be just a grunt."

"Not everyone is officer material, Sergeant."

"True enough. Especially some officers I've met. Where did you train, Mr. Wismer?"

"Near here. Fort Benning in Georgia."

"Airborne, by chance?"

Whistler took a breath and nodded. "I was in the Seventy-fifth."

"That would . . . be the Airborne Rangers. That would start to explain it. Did you see any action? Like over in Iraq?"

"I was there."

"Me, too. I was Armor. Drove an Abrams. You?"

"Mostly recon. Look, Sergeant—"

"Name's Moore. Ed Moore." He touched a finger to his nametag. "This recon . . . would that be the First Ranger Battalion? Were you on one of those teams that went in early?"

Whistler nodded.

"Weapons specialist?"

"We all were."

"Yeah, that's right," said the sergeant. "You all had to rate Expert. So how'd you miss the driver of the getaway car?"

He had had no intention of hitting the driver. "He'd raised a shotgun. I fired to suppress. I snapped two quick shots through plate glass at an angle. I was lucky to even hit the car."

"But you put out his windshield. Did that cut him up, you think?"

"Might have. I couldn't see from in here."

The sergeant stepped away and brought his radio to his lips. He called the dispatcher, had her tell all other units that the driver, very likely, had cuts on his face. Whistler, meanwhile, was silently regretting that he'd had to say anything of his personal history. He was also regretting that this Ragland was well known. This was going to attract a good deal more attention than if it were a simple private grudge.

The sergeant ended his call, then walked over toward the entrance. Whistler saw him reach his hand toward the two bullet holes still discernible in what was left of the door. He was able to cover both holes with his palm. He returned to where Whistler was sitting.

"You just snapped those, you say."

"It was all I could do."

"Moving target. I know. We've established that moving targets are tough, but those shots went exactly where you wanted them."

Whistler shrugged a denial. The sergeant answered with a grunt. Then the sergeant surprised him by offering his hand. His face softened into a smile.

"I heard about some of the stuff you guys did. I've never met one of you before."

Whistler took the hand. He said, "Listen, Sergeant, one grunt to another, it's true that all we did was come in here for dinner. I'm not looking for a medal or my name in the papers. I wish now that I'd minded my own business."

"You have a reason for needing to stay out of this?"

"Not needing. Just wanting. We live a quiet life."

He answered, "Well, you're in it. But I'll do what I can."

Moore was looking at Claudia. Whistler followed his gaze. He saw that a tear had run down her cheek. Moore asked her, "Miss Kelly, will you be all right?"

Whistler answered, "I'd like to get her out of here now."

"Maybe one of the doctors should look at her first. Maybe give her a sedative so she'll sleep."

"She won't take a sedative. She won't even take an aspirin."

He told Sergeant Moore where the boat was berthed and that they had no intention of leaving the island. He said he realized that a formal written statement would be needed and that a coroner's inquest would be held.

"Take her home, Mr. Wismer. Go out the side door. I'll try to keep the media busy out front."

Before they left, he took Leslie aside and told her why he'd misspoken their names. It was purely for reasons of privacy, nothing more. The media would get those names from the police and those names would appear in the next morning's paper. By then, he said, they might no longer be of interest, all attention by then on the victim and the shooters. She could later, if she chose, call her friend Sergeant Moore and give him the right spelling for his records.

"Do you have a problem with that?" he asked Leslie.

She shook her head slowly. "I'm okay with it, I guess."

"You're sure?"

A slow nod. "And Claudia still didn't . . ."

"Didn't what? What is it?"

"And Claudia still didn't throw the knife at that man?"

He looked into her eyes. "No, she didn't. Thank you, Leslie."

She touched both their arms. "No, thank *you*."

They had left Jump & Phil's in the car he had rented. They had managed to avoid the photographers. They were on the road that led back to the marina. She still had barely spoken. She was hugging herself.

He reached to touch her. "How are you holding up?"

She answered in a whisper. "I don't know yet."

"Claudia, what you did back there saved a man's life. The one you . . . distracted . . . would have shot him again."

"He did shoot again. He killed two other people."

"That was my fault, not yours. I was not quick enough."

She turned her face from him. "You know that isn't true." She remembered that he'd wanted to stay out of this. That he'd tried to keep her from interfering.

"Claudia . . . those dead people . . . where are they now?"

"Where are they? They're dead. They're on their way to a morgue."

"Yes, but you know better. No one really dies."

She turned her head, looked at him, said nothing for a moment. Then, "Adam, I know what you're trying to do. I appreciate it, really, but don't."

He let up on the gas. He said, "No, hear me out. I remember when you told me about the white light. You said it's really there. You really see it when you die. So aren't they with your white light?"

"Adam, stop," she said firmly. "I know you don't believe that."

"What I believe is one thing. What you know is another. You know that right now they feel nothing but peace. You've been there. You know they're okay."

That's unless, of course, they were still in the restaurant, floating around, looking down from the ceiling. That's another thing people say they've done when they died. Then the long black tunnel, and then the white light. But wherever they were, saying this wasn't helping. Claudia had put her hands to her face and was rocking back and forth in her seat.

He said, "One more thing. The man you hit isn't dead." This was true, but then neither is a radish.

"Do you think he might live?"

"Well . . ."

"I didn't think so."

"Look, the damage was done when I took him down. There are people who've survived getting hit with an ax. He would have survived that little puncture of yours if the floor hadn't knocked the knife sideways."

"The floor or you?"

"Okay, me. But not you."

She did not speak again for a half mile or so. She had turned her face toward her window.

"Adam?"

"I'm here."

"How did you feel? I don't mean back there. How did you feel the first time you killed?"

"That was entirely different."

"How so?"

"It was in the Gulf War. It never seemed personal. I was also part of a team that was trained for it. And we did it at a distance. Not like tonight. We never saw the looks on their faces."

"It was personal later, though, wasn't it?"

"I suppose."

"And up close."

"Now and then."

"How did those make you feel?"

Whistler chewed his lip. He would rather not have answered. But he thought of one instance that he hoped would be of help. "Later on, down in Mexico, there were two men in particular. They had captured one of ours and they tortured him to death. They took their time. He took several days to die. Do you want to hear what they did to him?"

"No."

"What they did, they'd done to others. They'd have done it again. I did not feel an ounce of regret when I caught up to them. That man tonight must have done this before. Now he'll never hurt anyone again."

"Did you enjoy it?"

He took a breath. ". . . No."

"You must have felt something. What did you feel?"

"Not much. Not much of anything." Like stepping on bugs. "Again, you must remember—I was trained for this, Claudia. Don't look for me to have felt what you're feeling."

She thought for a moment. "What did Sergeant Moore say? He said that for you it was a walk in the park. He's right. You never batted an eye. You were so very calm and deliberate."

Whistler frowned. He did not want this discussion. "Claudia, this is not about me."

"You can be so gentle. You can be so kind. It's been hard for me to grasp that the Adam I know is a man so many people are afraid of. Are there two of you, Adam?"

"Of course not."

"Then you're able to separate who you are from what you do. How does one manage to do that?"

"I suppose . . . I don't know . . . I've never given it much thought. I guess you sort of keep it in a different place. A prizefighter does that. He leaves it in the ring. The man he is when he's trying to hurt someone is not the man he is when he's home with his kids."

"But that's not you, Adam. You're the same either way. I guess I'm still trying to understand that."

He'd had conversations with Claudia before this about how one becomes an Adam Whistler. His sister's death was part of it. She'd understood that. And the army had a good deal to do with it. But mostly, he supposed, it was the way he'd grown up. He'd had, by most standards, two excellent

parents. There was no lack of love and affection and guidance. He'd been taught a clear sense of what's right and
what's wrong, what is honorable and what is not. But he
would grant that the standards learned at Harry Whistler's
knee were somewhat more pragmatic than most.

"What I am, what I became, has no application to what
you did tonight in that restaurant. That was an accident. You
were trying to do your job."

"What job was that, Adam?"

"Protecting me."

"I didn't protect you. Not one little bit. All I did was pull
you off balance for a second. He wasn't going to shoot at
you anyway."

"Okay, so you protected someone else. The white light
didn't say just me, no one else. Did you expect that knife to
stick, by the way?"

"I don't know what I expected. I just wanted to stop him."

"So all you could do, sitting that far away, was pick up
what was handy and throw it. Where it hit was either inhu-
manly skillful, which you're not—wait a minute. Have you
practiced throwing knives?"

"No."

"Have you ever even thrown one? At a tree, for example?"

"Not that I can remember. I don't think so."

He had thought of Carla Benedict, a wizard with a knife.
But not even Carla could have done that.

"Do you think the white light might have guided your
hand? If that's the case, you can hardly blame yourself. As a
matter of fact—"

"You're humoring me, Adam. Please don't."

"I'll shut up."

Perhaps it was best not to say any more until she was
ready to talk. He'd been about to get off on the subject of
powers. They'd talked about that, whether angels have powers. Maybe one of those powers is to snatch up a knife and
make an impossible throw.

Except she also used to pitch. There's one answer. A good

arm. The throw might have been a million to one shot, but so is a hole in one playing golf, and those are made every day.

"You want to know what I believe in?" he said to her quietly.

"Not in any higher power. But you wait. You'll find out."

"I believe in you, Claudia. You're my higher power. If there's anything else, it will be frosting on the cake."

She said nothing. But she reached and she gave him a squeeze.

He parked the car and locked it. They walked down to the boat.

She asked, "Will there be trouble?"

"I don't know. Maybe not."

That business of mispronouncing their names might be useless, but he'd thought it was still worth a try. By tomorrow, maybe no one would care who they were because they'll have become minor players. The big story will be, and should be, this Philip Ragland. Who he was and who wanted him dead and why. And the hunt for the shooter's accomplice.

She said, "Let's take the boat out."

"That might not look good."

"Not far. We can anchor just out in the sound. If that deputy needs to find us, he'll see us out there."

He thought about that. "Sure, let's do it."

"I'd like to go to bed and I'd like you to hold me. That's all. Just hold me, all right?"

"Sure it is. We'll turn off the phones."

"And thank you, Adam. Thanks for everything you've said. You really are a special kind of man."

16

The next morning, Whistler was on deck before daybreak, but not to admire the sunrise. He had brought a portable TV with him and set it on a foldout table at the stern. He was eager to see how the shooting was reported on the local and regional news. He wanted to do so without waking Claudia. She'd had a troubled night before she finally slept. He'd heard her pacing the cockpit.

As he waited for the six-o'clock broadcasts to come on, he was struck by the utter tranquillity all around him. Every home on shore was dark. Few cars were moving. A soft breeze had risen out of the west. The events of last night almost seemed like a dream. They were not the sort of thing that ever happened in such places. He feared that the story, for that very reason, would attract much wider attention.

The news came on and, as he'd expected, the shooting was the opening lead. Whistler reached to turn the volume down low.

The local newscaster was a good-old-boy type, named Billy something or other. He began by announcing a "*Wild West–Type Shootout*" in a popular Hilton Head restaurant. As he spoke, film came on. It was all of the aftermath. Flashing lights, jerky cameras, police cordoning the area.

The newscaster gave the names of the three shooting victims. Two had been pronounced dead at the scene. The older man outside, who'd been shot through the glass, was a tourist from Ridgewood, New Jersey. The woman inside who'd got up to run was a real estate broker on the island. A photo of Ragland came on the screen. The newscaster said he was in "guarded" condition and that he was recovering from surgery. He said, *"More about Philip Ragland later."*

The *"alleged assailants"* got only three sentences. The shooter wasn't dead yet; he was on life support. He was given little chance of recovering. His *"suspected accomplice"* was still being sought. Neither man had been identified, no hint as to motive. Whistler, however, felt reasonably sure that Sergeant Moore had been right. Ragland's broadcasts had probably offended some wacko. It was certainly not a professional hit. A pro might still have done it in a crowded bar because a pro would know the value of confusion and panic. A pro, however, would have gone for a head shot. A pro would not have bellowed, "God is not mocked." He would have said nothing at all.

The newscaster, having glossed over the assailants, took a breath and launched into an excited account of how the *"enraged local patrons"* reacted. While some inside the restaurant attacked the first gunman, others outside tried to stop his accomplice, heroically risking their lives. But Whistler wasn't mentioned, not even as Wismer. The account made no reference to Claudia whatsoever. It mentioned the knife with which someone *"stabbed"* the gunman *"during the ensuing melee."* It said another patron then picked up the gunman's pistol and fired at the getaway driver outside. *"That patron has not been identified."*

Another video segment came on that had been shot by an on-the-scene reporter. It was shot from a distance through the shattered front door. It focused mostly on the EMS crew that was wheeling Ragland out on a gurney. Whistler saw himself and Claudia; they were still at the bar, but her head was down and his own was turned toward her. The camera caught them only in passing.

Whistler could hardly believe his good luck. He was one of the "enraged local patrons" at most. Just one of the crowd. So was Claudia.

The photo of Ragland reappeared on the screen. The photo had been posed, a publicity glossy. The newscaster's voice-over described Philip Ragland as a "tabloid

TV personality." Its tone struck Whistler as borderline contemptuous. Ragland, he said, had espoused such causes as *"abortion on demand and gay rights."* The phrase *"gay rights"* was said drippingly. He said that Ragland was also a leading proponent of *"making the use of drugs legal."* The newscaster noted that Ragland's positions ran counter to traditional values, and *"are not those of this station or its management."* He stopped short of suggesting that whoever shot Ragland might have done a community service.

Whistler switched channels, looking for a network station. He had almost forgotten that, except for resorts and the larger cities, this was still Bible Belt country. And this was a state that still had laws on the books forbidding oral sex of any kind, gay or straight. He was nonetheless pleased that Ragland's views were the story and that his own role was totally ignored. He found CNN's *Headline News*.

Whistler was dismayed, though not entirely surprised, to see that CNN had named the shooting as one of the morning's top stories. But again, its emphasis was primarily on Ragland, and its treatment was considerably more generous. Ragland's program was far from a tabloid TV show, according to this network anchor. It was known for supporting libertarian causes and had won any number of Emmys. Ragland and his wife had shared a Pulitzer prize in the field of investigative reporting. He had also testified at congressional hearings looking into—

"Good morning," said Claudia.

She'd awakened after all. She was standing below, looking up through the hatch while slipping into her robe. He looked for that big good-morning smile that he'd grown used to. She tried, but she couldn't quite manage it.

He said, "Hi, there. How are you feeling this morning?"

"A little better, I think."

"I heard you up here last night. I heard you talking to yourself. I would have come up, but . . ."

"It's better you didn't. I had things to work out." She

waved off the subject. She gestured toward the screen. "I didn't hear us mentioned. How are we?"

"So far, so good. We just might slip through the cracks. So far, we're not even a footnote."

"And the man, Philip Ragland?"

"He'll recover, thanks to you. Come on up and watch. I'll fill you in."

"In a minute. Let me put on some coffee."

Whistler turned up the volume so that she could hear. The phrase "libertarian causes" was repeated.

"Libertarian causes?" she asked from the galley. "What does that mean? Did they say?"

"Well, to me it means leaving people alone. Staying out of their personal lives."

"Adam, I know that. I meant in this case. Which cause was he for that got him shot?"

Whistler shrugged. "I guess we'll know when they've ID'd the shooter. If they have, they're not saying so as yet."

"Or what he's against. Is he antireligious?"

"Why? Because of what the shooter yelled out? That couldn't be it. His program would have dumped him at the first sign of that. But who knows what people get into their heads? Some nut might have thought he was the anti-Christ."

He changed channels again to another network station. This one, a Fox affiliate, was doing a piece about Ragland's opposition to the drug laws. The Raglands had been awarded their Pulitzer, it said, for a series on the *"more enlightened drug measures under way in certain European countries."* He'd also won an Emmy for a feature he'd done that condemned the asset forfeiture laws.

Uh-oh, thought Whistler. This was getting close to home.

The Fox commentator summarized that legislation. It had been enacted as a weapon against major drug kingpins, but had led to a number of outrageous abuses against people with no drug involvement. The commentator was citing examples. A California man owned several hundred acres of undeveloped land outside Malibu. Marijuana plants were found on the property. The owner lived elsewhere, had no criminal record, had no provable knowledge that the plants were on his land. Even so, the property was forfeit. Although the matter was still in the courts, some of that acreage had already been sold and the proceeds used to hire more police. Ragland charged that the seizure was a land-grab, pure and simple. The county had tried to buy some of that land, then they'd tried to condemn it without success. In the end, they decided just to take it.

In Massachusetts there was even a ship-grab. The Woods Hole Oceanographic Institute had an $80 million research ship. It was seized because a single half-smoked reefer had been found in the kit of a single crew member. The seizure made headlines. The press ridiculed it. Because of the publicity and the Institute's prestige, that seizure was soon overturned.

If the Institute had that kind of influence, however, most victims of seizures did not. Thousands of people had their cars and cash seized because the cash in their pockets had drug residue on it and those people were presumed to be dealers. Drug-sniffing dogs had reacted to the cash and that became probable cause for the seizure. The fact is, however, that trace amounts of drugs can be found on nearly any bill that's changed hands enough times. Especially cocaine and marijuana. Those two drugs cling more than most.

Almost none of those people who were stopped were ever charged. Their money was taken; they were sent on their way. Such victims could sue, but they almost never did. Some were guilty, surely. Perhaps most of them were. Some were carrying large sums in order to buy drugs and some to buy handguns for resale up north. Some were merely loading up on cartons of cigarettes at half the price that they'd pay in, say, Connecticut.

They'd accept the loss as a cost of doing business. But some, many hundreds, had no criminal intent. Some were merely on vacation. Some had won the money gambling. Some merely liked to carry a few thousand in cash for any number of reasons. Perhaps they had no credit, or they didn't trust banks, or perhaps they simply enjoyed flashing rolls. Their money would be seized and they would soon learn that the legal costs of getting it back would be greater than what they had lost in the first place. They would also be reminded that they still could be charged, and would be if they didn't go away.

Claudia was listening. "Like those articles Mom faxed us. But this makes it sound even worse."

Whistler nodded. "It's worse than you know. Your mother was not the first person to be framed and it isn't all just the police. Any vengeful ex-wife or ex-husband can do it. Any business competitor, any rival, and it's easy."

She handed him his coffee. "How easy?"

Whistler pointed to a house on the shore. A luxury home; it had its own private dock. "See that house. Let's say that my ex-wife owns it. No, wait, we'll rule out vengeance. We'll stick to simple greed. Say I don't know the owner. Never met him."

"Okay."

"One way or another, I get into that house. I stash a sellable quantity of cocaine in something that's likely to have the owner's prints on it. I tell the cops that I've heard he's been dealing. I say that someone told me where he keeps it, that he sells it from the house. My word is all they need in terms of probable cause to go to some judge for a warrant. Next they'll call in the DEA to make the actual raid. That's because when the feds are involved in a seizure, eighty percent of the proceeds, by law, revert to the local jurisdiction. If the locality should do it on its own, that amount would usually go to the state. The locality would rather keep the money."

"So, they find the drugs you've stashed . . ."

"The feds, by the way, will have first asked the owner whether he has any drugs on his property. He'll say no, and now there's another charge against him. It's a felony to lie to any federal official. When the drugs are found, that house is instantly seized. When the house is later sold by the U.S. Marshal's Service, I get ten percent of the take."

"That's unless he's found innocent. He probably would be."

"He might; he might not, but that wouldn't really matter. Guilt or innocence has very little to do with how the seizure laws work."

She said, "Adam, I find that hard to believe."

"You do? Why is that? Because this is America?"

"And because there's such a thing as constitutional protection."

"The Constitution means what the courts say it means. It protects individuals from unreasonable search and seizure—or at least it protects them in principle. But the courts have said that property isn't a person and does not rate the same protection."

She had closed one eye. "Then who does this man go to?"

"For what? To get his house back? He can bid on it himself. He might want to because that would be cheaper and quicker than trying to get it back through the courts. Either way, the man's reputation is ruined. If this happened, he must have been guilty."

"That's outrageous, Adam."

"Yeah, but it's the law. It's extortion, but it's legal. And it won't stop anytime soon. It's easy money."

"Laws can be changed. No one's trying to change them?"

"Ragland is, for one. And look what happened to him."

"Are you saying you think that's why someone wants him dead?"

Whistler shrugged, then shook his head. "No, not really. I've no reason to think so. Actually it's more that I'm hoping it isn't. I'm hoping that the motive will be some grudge that has nothing to do with you or me."

Whistler supposed that he had drugs on the brain. Oddly, however, if drugs had been the motive—or rather Philip Ragland's position on drugs—it's the traffickers who probably would have wanted him silenced as much as the antidrug side. Traffickers don't want the drug laws reformed. Take away prohibition and their business dries up. Whistler knew, however, that no trafficker had done this. They would not have been that sloppy or stupid.

If Ragland won his Pulitzer for a series of reports in favor of the "more enlightened European model," Whistler knew what Ragland's position must have been. It must have been much like his father's. Start by accepting the world as it is, not as you'd like it to be. There has never been a drug-free society. Scrap all the drug laws as they're now on the books. Adopt the successful Dutch and Swiss systems that emphasize treatment and containment. Let doctors treat addicts under strict controls instead of not letting doctors treat them at all. Recognize that addiction is an illness, not a crime, much the same as alcoholism. Decriminalize, therefore, all private use and put all your effort into choking off the source. Keep coming down hard on the traffickers.

Whistler reached to switch back to the CNN channel. It was still on Ragland. And a similar topic. This one mentioned that Ragland had personally funded a number of drug treatment centers.

Claudia asked, "But does drug treatment work?"

"Sure it does. What there is of it," he answered.

"I sure wouldn't think so from all that I've read. Doesn't only a tiny percentage stay clean?"

"Yes, but that's true of diets and of trying to quit smoking. Most people who try are going to fall off the wagon. However, while they're trying, and even if they fail, their consumption is down and that's something at least. Most will try again until it finally takes. But the government does not want to pay for treatment centers. They'd rather spend the money, up to ten times the money, to put drug users in jail."

An excerpt from one of Ragland's programs came on. No, it wasn't a program. It was Ragland at some hearing. He was testifying before Congress. His words startled Whistler because it almost seemed as if he'd picked up on Whistler's train of thought.

"Above all," he was saying, "start telling the truth. Admit that the drug war has been a disaster. Admit that most of what you've been saying about drug use is at best misleading and at worst an outright lie. Admit that the Dutch and

Swiss have been right and that what they are doing is working. Admit that addiction has gone down, not increased,
wherever commonsense laws have been enacted. Admit
what every honest clinician has long known: that cannabis
has never been a dangerous drug. If it's harmful, it's far less
harmful than alcohol and only slightly more toxic than coffee. Admit what's been known for more than three thousand
years. Admit that it's a medicine that can ease more human
suffering than almost any legitimate drug. Chemotherapy
patients and those suffering from AIDS are able to eat food
and keep it down. People racked by migraines can get instant relief. Give a little cannabis to a patient with glaucoma
and the pressure . . . that can *blind* them . . . is eased in two
minutes. Will you give it? No. Will you consider it? No. So
you force these sufferers, those who can afford it, to fly off
to one of the more civilized countries, one whose leaders
have listened to its doctors. One whose leaders, I might add,
are not gutless."

A gavel came down. "That will do, Mr. Ragland." The
hearing room had erupted into laughter and cheers.

Claudia asked, "It that all true?"

"Pretty much."

"Do those congressmen know that?"

"Some do. Most don't want to. That's why he said 'gutless.' Any congressman rash enough to agree, at least in public, knows he won't be in office very long."

Ragland, once again, was saying much the same thing.
"Some of you know what I'm talking about. But admit it?
You won't. You'd be called soft on crime. And as most of
you know, the stakes are too high to let a little thing like
truth get in the way. The war on drugs has become a big
business. Twenty billion a year, and that's just law enforcement. Add in all the prisons built to lock up drug offenders,
most of whom are there for personal use or for selling a mi-
nuscule amount. Add in the lost income of lives that have
been ruined by mandatory sentencing guidelines. Five years
for possessing five grams of crack, an atrocity against urban
blacks."

Ragland paused to study their faces. He said, "You're sitting there thinking, 'What makes that an atrocity? These animals are guilty, are they not?' The fact is that blacks use far less crack than whites. But they're there; they're available, you can pick them off the street and they usually can't afford a decent lawyer. The result? As we speak, there are more blacks in prison for simple possession of *just marijuana* than for all crimes of violence put together."

He said, "Add in police corruption   cops stealing and dealing. Add in more human cost—the muggings, the burglaries. Add in tens of thousands of women turning tricks in order to finance a need they can't control and despising themselves for what they've become."

The camera, tight on Ragland, pulled back a few feet to show some people nodding in agreement. Whistler recognized one of them. It was Ragland's wife. Same intelligent face. And she was, of course, a good deal more composed than she had been the last time he saw her. Her husband was still speaking. This was more than a film clip. The news show that was running it was letting it go on well beyond the sort of sound bites that were usual. Whistler guessed that this network agreed with Ragland's views, and was probably the network that carried his show. Ragland seemed to be just warming up.

He said, "Add in all the sick who are in chronic pain, people hurting so badly they wish they could die. Any doctor could ease their pain if you'd let them. But do you? No, you don't. Any doctor who prescribes enough pain drugs to help them risks having his license to practice suspended. You intimidate the doctor; you intimidate the pharmacist; you let the patient suffer, and for what? Because the DEA zealots say it sends the wrong message. Use drugs to feel better? Oh, we can't allow that. We can't let some old lady who's dying of cancer risk getting addicted to morphine, God forbid. We've got to protect that old lady from herself. Can't any of you grasp how imbecilic that is? Don't any of you have the guts to stand up and—"

A gavel came down. "You've been warned, Mr. Ragland."

"My black Lab had cancer. I had to put him down. But that dog was kept free of pain all the way and he died a calm and dignified death. My mother had cancer. She died trying to scream. Mr. Chairman, do you see an inequity here? It's okay to help my dog but not okay to help my mother. I wish to God that I myself had had the guts to go out and buy morphine on the street. But let's say I did. Let's say I decided to treat my mother as mercifully as I treated my dog. You hypocrites would have had me locked up. Not one of you would have—"

A gavel came down hard. "Mr. Ragland, that's enough."

"Very well, I'll change the subject. Let us talk about our children. We must protect them from drugs, must we not?"

"I believe that's what we're here for, Mr. Ragland."

"You're aware that our children can readily buy drugs. Most don't, but all of them can. Am I right?"

"Sadly, yes."

"Ask a child which drug is the *hardest* to buy. So hard that it's scarcely worth the effort. Can you name it?"

"I dare say that you're about to tell us, Mr. Ragland."

"The answer is booze. I'm talking alcohol, gentlemen. Vastly more common, vastly more harmful, but vastly more difficult to purchase. And why is that?"

"Because its distribution is controlled by the government."

Ragland nodded. "Correct. And controlled quite effectively. You used to prohibit it, did you not?"

"Mr. Ragland . . ."

"Distribution of alcohol is controlled by our government. Distribution of drugs is controlled by the mob. There's a lesson there somewhere if you look hard enough."

The gavel rapped again. The committee chairman was angry. He was telling the witness to be careful with his language and to forgo any further personal attacks on the honorable members seated there. But the people in the gallery seemed to be with Philip Ragland. A camera panned over them. Most of them were applauding. Several, here and there, had sour looks on their faces. Those several, no doubt, were there to testify as well, probably to rebut Ragland's arguments.

Whistler suddenly blinked. He leaned closer to the screen. He said, "Claudia, look. Those two men three rows back." He reached to point them out with his finger.

"Uh-huh. Who are they? Do you know them?"

"Oh, yes." He tapped the screen. "The bigger one—white hair, yellow tie—is Delbert Poole. The one who looks like a frog, that's Felix Aubrey."

"They're the ones who . . . ?"

"Yes, they are."

She squinted, surprised. "But they both look so . . . harmless."

"Well, they don't have horns and a tail."

"Especially Poole. He has a kind face. He looks—I don't know—so at peace with himself."

"That look is standard issue for the morally certain. Never mistake it for kindness."

"But even the other one. He doesn't look evil. He reminds me of some kids I went to school with."

"Kids you thought were dorks?"

"I have never used that word."

"Not you. You wouldn't. But you're right about the type. The kind who never had a date or got invited to parties. And who envied, even hated, those who did. Yeah, that would have been Aubrey. And Aubrey, I imagine, dreamed of someday getting even. I think you'd be surprised how many people like Aubrey find their way into government jobs."

Claudia leaned closer. "What's he holding in his lap?"

"Looks like a crutch. The short kind with a clamp."

"Is he crippled?"

"He wasn't. Must have been in an accident."

Whistler hadn't told Claudia that Aubrey had been visited. He saw no point in telling her now. In any case, the pan of the camera had ended. A voice-over announcer was wrap-

ping up the segment. He reminded the viewers that Ragland
had been shot, but that he was expected to recover.

"It's quite a coincidence, isn't it?" said Claudia.

"You mean seeing Poole and Aubrey in the same room
with Ragland? I wouldn't call that a coincidence."

"It doesn't make you wonder?"

"Yeah, it does, but it shouldn't. A hearing like that one
would have dozens of witnesses arguing for and against.
Delbert Poole is always testifying at these things. Poole and
Aubrey wouldn't care about silencing one critic unless he's
caught on to what they were doing. Even then, they wouldn't
have done it like this. They had nothing to do with last
night."

"Or you're hoping they didn't."

"No, I'm sure of it."

Claudia turned her head. She was looking toward the
shore. A sportfishing boat had left the dock and was motor-
ing in their direction. She reached below for a pair of binoculars. As she focused them on the approaching boat, she saw
a young woman in a sweatshirt and shorts stand up and wave
both her arms.

She said, "That's Leslie who's waving. From Jump and
Phil's. She's trying to get our attention. And that's Phil himself at the wheel. That's his boat."

Whistler stared. "Who's that with them? Is that Sergeant
Moore?"

"Yes, it is. Why would he be coming out on Phil's boat?"

"As opposed to a police boat? I can't imagine."

"Hold on. Leslie's trying to tell us."

Leslie had backed away from the wheel and out of
Sergeant Moore's line of sight. She brought a hand to her ear
as if holding a phone, then she spread her hands wide and
she shrugged.

"She's saying that she tried to call us, I think. Did you
shut off our phones?"

"Yeah, I did. I forgot."

"Now she's mouthing something. She's saying . . . he
knows. He knows what? That I did throw that knife?"

"He couldn't know that because that didn't happen. He probably knows our real names. That's okay. She's just letting us know that she had to tell him, but that doesn't explain why he's coming out with them."

"I guess we're about to find out."

17

Vernon Lockwood had called Felix Aubrey at his home as Aubrey was struggling to get dressed. Aubrey's dressing routine involved strapping on a brace that supported one atrophied leg. It also involved putting on an undergarment that absorbed a certain leakage that had plagued him. These reminders of his visit by that woman from hell did not start Aubrey's day on a positive note. Nor did any interruption, especially from Lockwood. He was not pleased to hear Lockwood's voice.

"Yeah, well, just listen. You're not going to believe this."

"Then I probably won't at the office either. See me then, Mr. Lockwood. It can wait."

"You want to know who cut you? I can make a good guess. I think it was that girl who's with Whistler."

"Mr. Lockwood—"

"Turns out she's as good as they come with a knife. You're not going to believe what happened last night. You're not going to believe why they stopped on that island. You're not going to believe who they're tight with."

"Mr. Lockwood . . . reflect. Think back, if you can, to when I was assaulted. Do you recall where Miss Geller was at that moment?"

"Where? Oh, the hospital? She was still there?"

"She'd been shot five days earlier. She was not in robust health. So you see, you're quite right. I'm not going to believe you."

"You're not? Then try this. She did a lobotomy on some guy last night. It was in this bar. My guy, Kaplan? He saw it. And now before you start giving me shit, ask me why her and Whistler were there."

"Mr. Lockwood . . . no more teasers. Blurt it out, if you will."

"They're down there to meet with Philip Ragland."

Aubrey listened as Lockwood related what his man on the scene had reported to him. "Kaplan's been there two weeks. Could have taken Whistler easy. You said just watch, so Kaplan did. You said he should see where they went, who they talked to, which was mostly no one you'd care about."

"What phone are you using to call me, Mr. Lockwood?"

"The cell phone you gave me. You said it's secure."

"It is. Now what's this about Ragland?"

"Let me tell it, okay? We got context here. My guy tailed Whistler and the girl to this bar. It's a bar they'd gone to a few times before this. They always try to take the same seats. They always sit like they're watching and waiting for someone, but until last night no one shows. Last night the place is almost filled when Ragland and his wife come waltzing in. They go to the one empty table. Whistler looks over to the table where they sat. The guy looks toward Whistler, kind of gives him a wave. Whistler pretends not to know him."

"You're certain it was Ragland?"

"You can turn on the news. But first let me tell you what's not on the news. Oh, wait. I didn't tell you that Ragland got shot."

"A significant detail, Mr. Lockwood."

"It's not too bad. I hear it looks like he'll live."

His man, Kaplan, said Lockwood, had a front-row seat. "He's sitting on the opposite side of the bar. For a minute, he thinks Whistler and the girl might have made him. They're looking up toward him and they're whispering. But then he realizes they're not watching him, they're watching someone who's standing outside. He turns around himself, sees two guys he doesn't know, but they don't look like much, so he ignores them. Two minutes later, one of these guys comes in, walks over to Ragland, yells something and shoots him."

"Yells what?"

"God something. Like a curse. He didn't catch it exactly. Anyway, by this time, Whistler's out of his stool. But the girl grabs Whistler; she holds him back and, swoosh, she nails the guy with a knife. She throws it. You got that? From way across the room. It's this plain old knife she was sitting there eating with. And remember, this guy's not standing still."

"Go on."

"Well, the guy, who's now got her knife in his head, stays on his feet, but the guy's one big twitch. Suddenly he's spraying the room. Two or three more get shot before Whistler can get at him. Whistler takes him down and he takes the guy's gun. The girl meanwhile runs to Ragland. She yells to Whistler, 'Watch the front, I've got your back.' Does that still sound to you like she's Little Bo-Peep?"

"Never mind the girl. Stay with Whistler and Ragland."

"Whistler clubs some other guy who was trying to jump him. I'm not sure what that was about. Then, after telling *my guy* to get down, he shoots through the window at this first shooter's partner, who by then is coming up with their car. Whistler misses him; the guy gets away. Whistler gets the girl and he makes her sit down and act like her dinner's all she cares about. Whistler tells the barmaid to call the cops. Oh, and this barmaid, here's what's funny about her. She not only—"

"Mr. Lockwood—never mind the barmaid either, if you please. Confine yourself to Whistler and Ragland."

"That was it. He never goes near Ragland himself."

"Never spoke to him. Nothing?"

"Not a word since Ragland got there."

"Then why would you think they know each other?"

"From what my guy saw, and he says he's pretty sure. First he saw Ragland's wife make eye music with Whistler, and then there's that wave I just told you about."

"Yes, you told me. But did Whistler respond?"

"He didn't get a chance because right at that moment,

Whistler's girlfriend spots these two jokers outside and she says, like, we better check them out."

"No idea who they were? Or why they shot Ragland?"

"My guy's first thought was that maybe it was us. He knew that you and Poole took some heat from Ragland's show. That's why he didn't wait for the cops to show up, but he hung around outside with the crowd. I told him, no way this would have been us. I told him we'd have done it cleaner than that. And most likely it's me who would have handled it."

"We would not have done it at all, Mr. Lockwood. Philip Ragland's an annoyance. Nothing more."

"Until now, you mean, because now here's the question: Why was Whistler meeting Ragland? What would Whistler be giving to Ragland?"

Aubrey was silent.

"You still there, Mr. Aubrey?"

"I'm here. I'm thinking."

"I say Whistler's going public. I say Ragland, pretty soon, is going to do another show and he's going to wave that ledger of yours. We all get indicted, all except Mr. Poole. Poole will say how he's shocked and disappointed. Meanwhile, Whistler walks away, this time for good. Whistler's already disconnected himself, and it looks like he had help from the cops."

"Meaning what?"

"Kaplan was watching while this cop talks to Whistler. He says the cop, at first, is trying to act like a cop while the other cops are around. Pretty soon, though, it's clear the cop is friendly with Whistler. He says the cop also huddled with the barmaid I mentioned. And this barmaid, like I tried to tell you before, there's something funny about her. She sees people blown away, but she never loses her cool; Whistler gives her instructions, and she does what he says. Later on, the cop gets there, she huddles with him, and he looks like he's taking instructions from her. Kaplan says—"

"Mr. Lockwood—"

"Oh, and then at the end there's these whispers between them. The barmaid pats their arms like she's saying, 'I'll handle this. You two make yourselves scarce.' Then Whistler and the Geller girl slip out the back way, and—"

"Mr. Lockwood, you're advancing a conspiracy theory that is ludicrous on its face. You're suggesting that Whistler has assembled a team that consists of almost everyone he's encountered on that island."

"What, this is nuts? Then tell me this. How does Whistler walk away? He goes out the back door, and from that minute on, it's like Whistler doesn't exist. You watch the news; you see nothing about Whistler. Not him, not the girl, not how she threw that knife, not how Whistler grabbed the gun and blasted away at the shooter's driver outside. It's all about Ragland. Ragland's got center stage. Pretty soon, now, he's going to do his solo."

"Philip Ragland is a national figure, Mr. Lockwood. That is why he'd be the center of attention."

"So you're blowing this off?"

"No, I'm going to think about it."

"If I'm right, don't think about it too long."

"I'll confer with Mr. Poole."

"Confer for what? Poole would hang us out to dry. We should move. You should let me take care of this."

This, from the man who took care of Whistler's women and nearly got them all killed or maimed. This also from the man who, acting on his own, once caused a Woods Hole research ship to be seized. Philip Ragland loved that one. It was worth a whole program.

As for the scenario suggested by Lockwood, it seemed unlikely in the extreme. Why would Whistler get in bed with Philip Ragland, especially? Surely Ragland was a critic of his government's drug policy, but he was only one of many, and a lesser one at that. Why would Whistler go to Ragland as opposed to, for example, CNN, *The New York Times* or *60 Minutes*? And why now, for that matter? Because his year was almost up? That year was the father's suggestion, not theirs. What possible relevance could that have?

And yet it was troubling. The coincidence, above all. Whistler sails to that island, hangs around doing nothing, goes

out to a restaurant one evening. Philip Ragland shows up on
the very same island and goes to the very same restaurant.
And yet if those two were planning to meet, would they not
have done so in secret? Why be seen together? Why would
Ragland bring his wife? Why go through a charade of not
knowing each other? According to Lockwood, they exchanged nonverbal greetings. That would seem to defeat the
charade.

"Mr. Lockwood, I'm in need of more information. Is
your man still on the scene surveilling Whistler?"

"Uh-huh. And he's checking out that cop and the barmaid."

"Forget about them. Is your man watching Whistler?"

"As good as he can. Whistler moved his boat. He's keeping it out on open water."

"Fly down there. Take our plane. You can be there by
mid-morning. All I want you to do is watch and report. Need
I add that you are not to let them see you?"

"Prick'll see me one more time before I shoot out both
his eyes."

"Mr. Lockwood, have you heard me? Did you understand •
me?"

"You said to just watch. That's okay; I can wait. Anyway,
first I want to mess up the girl. I want Whistler to know that's
for Briggs. Oh, and you."

Oh, and me, thought Aubrey. Good of him to remember.
"Leave at once, Mr. Lockwood. Call the minute you get
there. As for our Mr. Poole, he's less removed than you
think. Don't imagine that he is unindictable. I'll deal with
Poole and you'll do as you're told. I'll say again that you're
to take no action. Am I clear on that, Mr. Lockwood?"

"How about I take Briggs? Get him back on the horse."

Aubrey blinked. "You're not serious, are you?"

"What, because he's still mad? This could help him get
over it."

"Mr. Lockwood, I'm still not sure that you hear me. You
will not take Briggs, nor would he wish to go. Beyond that,
you're not going to a Halloween party. He would hardly
blend in with the populace."

"Yeah, I know. The face. I just thought—"

"Do not think."

"Hey, why do you always have to be such a shit? It's me thinking that fixed it so we know where Whistler is. It's me thinking that got him where we can get at him before he messes up what we got here."

"Mr. Lockwood, I'll remind you . . . No, I won't. Never mind."

"Just tell me we'll finish what we started this time. No more deals, no more payoffs. We just fix it."

"Oh, yes, Mr. Lockwood." But in my way, not yours. Depend on it, however. "We'll fix it."

18

As the boat that was bringing Sergeant Moore approached, Whistler took a moment to step belowdecks and switch on his cell phone and satellite phone and also his answering machine. He was halfway back topside when the satellite phone chirped. He reached for it, thinking that the caller might be Leslie.

He said, "Sorry. It was off. What's happening, Leslie?"

But the call had come from much farther away. His father's voice answered, "You tell me."

"Dad? Oh, hi." He tried not to sound startled.

"Good morning, Adam. I'm in need of reassurance. I'm hoping you'll tell me that you had no part in what happened on that island last night."

"You're talking about that shoot-out in some local bar? How did you hear about that?"

"Adam, we do have TV in Geneva. More specifically, we have CNN."

Oh, great, thought Whistler. Now it's gone international. His father had probably been at his computer checking every new wire-service update. He would also be looking at a little yellow blip that showed, within yards, the boat's location.

"Dad, we're not even on the island at the moment. We're anchored offshore and we're about to have breakfast. Some friends we've made here are on their way out to join us. I thought that's who was calling when I answered."

"If that's so, why would you ask this Leslie what's happening?"

"What's happening? Dad, that's just an expression. You know, like, 'How goes it? *Wie geht's?*' "

"Were you on the boat when the shooting took place?"

"No, we'd gone out for a nice quiet dinner. As a matter of fact, we were with these same friends. When they get here you can ask them yourself if you'd like."

The line went silent for a beat. "But you knew about the shooting."

"Everyone does. It's all over the news."

His father asked, "And you don't know this Ragland?"

"I'd never even heard of the man."

"Adam, I think you understand why I'd wonder. You would seem to have a good deal in common with the victim. By extension, so would Aubrey and Poole."

"Well, I'm not going to tell you that it didn't cross my mind. But all I know is what they're saying on the tube." He paused. "Look, Dad, our company's here. I've got to go help them tie up alongside."

"Why'd you turn off your phone?"

"So we wouldn't get called. Because every now and then, we'd rather not be disturbed. Will you stop with the suspicions? We're okay. We're just fine."

"And you're staying clear of trouble? You're sure?"

"Believe me, I've been doing my best."

"Kate Geller tried to call you. They get CNN in Colorado as well and she had the same uneasy feeling that I had. She was ready to jump on a plane. You should call her—no, wait—I'd better do it myself. Listen, Adam, while we're on the subject of Kate, let me ask how you'd feel if . . . after Kate sells her business . . ."

"She's found a buyer?"

"In a manner of speaking."

"You're saying it's you. Does she know that?"

"Not yet. Listen, Adam . . ." Another silence, this one longer. "How would you feel if, not now, but down the road . . ."

"You're thinking about getting married again?"

"I'm . . . thinking that I miss her. I like being with her. As I say, down the road. Nothing imminent."

"Have you asked her?"

"I've asked her to move here. I didn't say as what. I'm sure she'll have some thoughts on that subject."

"Well, my feelings are that I like you together. I'm sure that Claudia would feel the same way. Want to ask her yourself? I'll put her on."

"Not now. You talk it over. Let it settle for a while."

"Look, Dad, if it's us that's holding you back . . ."

"No, I have some things that need attending to first. In the meantime, leave the damned telephones on. I don't like it when you're out of reach."

Whistler waited for his father to break the connection, then he breathed a qualified sigh of relief. Ordinarily, he wouldn't have lied to his father, even though what he'd said had been technically accurate. If he'd told him the truth, he'd have to have told him how Claudia took out that shooter. It should be up to Claudia whom she'd tell, if and when. And God knows what his father's reaction would have been. He would surely have sent some people here to look after them. The twins, most likely. This island had been traumatized enough without those two. Anyway, depending on why Moore had come calling, their role in all this should continue to fade.

Phil had slowed his engines and maneuvered his boat abeam of the yacht's starboard quarter. Whistler dropped fenders so that they could tie up, but Phil said, "We're going to stand off and wait for Eddie. That okay? He said he wants to talk to you alone."

Whistler looked toward Leslie. She was gesturing again; she was pressing palms down, and she was nodding. She seemed to be saying that this would be all right. She mouthed the words, "*He's a good guy. Don't worry.*" Whistler next looked at Moore. He looked into his eyes. He saw a new interest, a new curiosity, beyond what he'd seen the night before. And he noted that Moore had brought a small briefcase with him. He wondered what Moore might have to show him.

Whistler answered, "Come aboard," and he held out a hand, waiting to help the sergeant climb the railing.

"Nice boat, Mr. Whistler. Good morning, Miss Geller." He smiled and added, "Yeah, I know your true names. Once the press was gone, Leslie told me why you fudged them. That isn't a problem for now."

"Coffee's on. Would you like some?"

"Thank you. I would. And I'd like to talk to just you, if I may." He turned to Claudia. "Would you mind very much?"

She looked into his eyes, rather strangely, thought Whistler. But she gave him a smile. She asked how he took his coffee. She said she'd bring it up when it was ready.

Whistler gestured toward the table at the rear of the cockpit and invited the policeman to sit. Moore asked him, very quietly, "How's she doing this morning?"

"Much better. How else can I help you?"

Moore didn't respond. He was looking toward the hatch as if hoping for another glimpse of Claudia.

"Sergeant Moore?"

"Huh? Sorry. I don't mean to stare. Miss Geller is an interesting young woman."

"Is she why you're here?"

"Well . . . a number of things. I could use that cup of coffee. This thing has kept me hopping all night."

"I'm sure it has."

"As to why I came out here with all that's going on, it's more about you than Miss Geller."

"Go on."

"I spent a little time sitting at a computer. I heard you when you said you didn't want to be involved, but I think you'll understand if I got curious about you."

Whistler shrugged. "I don't imagine that you found very much."

"Well, I did confirm some of what little you told me. Not much beyond that because your records are sealed. It's almost fair to say that you ceased to exist from about—what age—twenty-five or twenty-six?"

"A lot of people's records are sealed. You know that."

"You stayed in Special Ops? You're still army?"

"I'm inactive."

"You don't want to tell me what you did in Special Ops?"

"I think you know that I can't."

"Whatever you did, it must have paid very well." Moore took in the yacht with a sweep of his hand. "Or are you independently wealthy?"

"Good investments."

Moore sat back. He nodded. "I'm relieved to hear that. Special Ops has been known to do drug interdictions. All those drugs, all that cash, there must have been a few temptations."

"You heard me when I said good investments."

Another glance toward the galley. And again he dropped his voice. "Do you mind if I ask how you hooked up with Miss Geller? I guess I want to ask whether she worked with you, but I don't suppose you'd tell me that either."

"Sure, I will. She didn't."

"How long have you known her?"

"Look, Sergeant—"

"Call me Ed."

"I don't know you well enough. As to Claudia, I've known her for a year and a few months. She's had no connection with anything I've done. She's as gentle a creature as you'll ever meet, so suppose we leave her out of this discussion."

The sergeant raised a hand. "Try not to get sore. I have a reason for asking." He rubbed his chin and winced in a show of discomfort. He said, "Let's back up. I'm not here to hurt you. I'm not sure that I'm even here as a cop. Do you think we could talk man-to-man?"

"Are you wired?"

Moore's face took on a chill. "You can frisk me if you like. Or we could go swimming. We can have this conversation treading water."

Whistler was tempted not to have it at all, but he needed to see where it was going. Claudia had appeared at the hatch holding two coffee mugs in her hands. Whistler took a few steps forward. He reached for the mugs. She held on for a moment and said softly, "Be nice. If he wants you to call him Ed, call him Ed."

"You could hear?"

"And I can feel. He's an honest man, Adam."

"You could tell that by looking into his eyes?"

"I could tell that he's nervous. We both make him nervous. But, Adam, he did keep our names out of this. He wants to know that he didn't make a mistake. And I think he wants you for a friend."

"Why would he?"

"He admires you, Adam. You heard that last night. I think he wants to be like you."

"We'll see."

"He knows more about us than he's letting on. It's better if you let him be your friend."

Whistler was doubtful, but he said, "I'll be nice."

"He hasn't had breakfast. I'll put on some bacon. Ask Leslie and Phil if they'll join us."

"When? Now?"

"Not now. When you're done. Go finish your talk."

He hesitated. "Are you sure you're all right?"

"I'm better." She touched him. "I'm fine."

"You seem . . . distant this morning. Like you're in another world."

"No, I'm in yours. More than ever, I suppose. Go finish your talk with your policeman."

Whistler walked back aft, a little worried about her. Nor

was he sure that this meeting was so harmless. He knew that Claudia was right about one thing, however. The sergeant knew more than he was saying.

"Okay, man-to-man." He handed Moore his coffee. "Let's start with what's on your mind."

Moore looked over Whistler's shoulder. "She could hear us?" he asked. "I'm back here barely whispering."

Heightened senses, thought Whistler. Been that way since she recovered. He supposed that he'd gotten used to it himself. But he answered, "No. Just a word here and there."

Moore wet his lips, took a sip from his mug, and took a deep breath before speaking again. "The reason I wondered whether she worked with you . . ."

"You're not still on that knife question, are you?"

"You said she never touched it. That's what Leslie says, too."

"Then that ought to be that."

"Yeah, it might be as far as knives are concerned. What about other talents? What else can she do? Does she have any other special gifts that you know of?"

Whistler blinked at the question. It was not what he had expected. "What exactly do we mean when we say *gifts*?"

"The gift of hands? Healing? That sort of thing?"

"Ed . . . you've lost me. Where did this come from?"

"Ragland's wife . . . at the hospital . . . we spoke at some length. Her name is Olivia, seems like a good woman. She wants to see you both, by the way. She said she'd like to thank you in person."

"There's no need. Now what was this thing about hands?"

"She was saying how Miss Geller found the bullet in her husband and, well . . . with her hands, somehow worked it toward the surface."

"You're not serious."

"She's mistaken?"

"It's preposterous, Ed."

"Yeah, but I wasn't there. Mrs. Ragland was. In fact, where she was sitting, she was facing you, right? I'd say she must have had a pretty good view of anything that might have happened."

The knife again, thought Whistler. He said, "Yes, she might have until that first shot. After that, I suspect, her mind was elsewhere."

"Even so, she was calm and together when we spoke. Did you know that she was a reporter herself before she teamed up with Ragland? She's a Brit, by the way. BBC, I think she said. She used to be a foreign correspondent."

"Your point?"

"She's no flake. And she's not unobservant."

"Yet she thinks that Claudia can make bullets go away. Has she said this to anyone else?"

"Her husband. He has also asked to see you."

"Ed, what else have you told them about us?"

"Me, not a thing. I did confirm to Mrs. Ragland that your name is Adam Whistler, but only because she knew that already. Seems she called the bar last night. They were still there cleaning up. One of the waitresses told her."

Last night, thought Whistler? While her husband was critical?

"You're sure you've never met her?" Moore asked him.

"Absolutely."

"I got the impression that she's heard of you, though. It was nothing she said. Just a look that she had."

"If that's true, you would have asked her if she knew me."

"I did. She said no."

"Once again, then. That ought to be that."

Whistler did recall that she had looked familiar the first time he saw her in the bar. BBC correspondent. That must have been it. He might have seen her face on the tube at some point. He felt sure, however, that she couldn't know him. If Moore was right about her reacting to his name, it's entirely possible that she'd heard it before. A foreign correspondent for the BBC would probably have heard of his father. But if asked, he would deny that there was any relation. There must be thousands of Whistlers in the world.

That, thought Whistler, again should be that. Except that

this woman, this former reporter, seemed even more interested in Claudia. She seemed to have gotten it into her head that Claudia's some kind of a witch. And so, for that matter, has Sergeant Moore, an otherwise sensible man.

Don't you love it, thought Whistler? That's all we need. It was hard enough keeping the angel thing quiet. But Whistler remembered. He thought he knew what had happened. Claudia had located that lump in Ragland's back. The bullet had lodged near the surface. She'd said, *"Wait. I found the bullet. It's almost out."* All she meant was that it hadn't quite emerged.

Or he hoped that's all she meant. He surely hoped so.

Whistler said, "Okay, look. This is starting to get crazy. Shouldn't you be out looking for the one who got away? How far could he get in that car?"

"He abandoned the Buick within a half mile. He carjacked a new one, but it hasn't left the island. He did get some bad facial cuts, by the way. The car-jacking victims said he was a mess. What would you do next if you were him?"

"Me? I'd get Claudia to heal me."

"No, I'm asking."

"Better yet, I'd get Claudia to turn me into a bird. She can do that. It's one of her gifts."

He heard a crash from the galley. She might have dropped a pan. More likely, it was a warning. Be nice. And the deputy leaned forward, saying much the same thing. He said, "How about easing up?"

"Yeah, you're right," said Whistler. "Strike that one. I'm sorry."

"May I call you Adam?"

"Sure, now that we're friends."

"There's a lot about this I don't run into every day. This isn't an Interpol uniform I'm wearing. It's a small County Sheriff's Department."

"I said I'm sorry. I know that was rude."

"I'm not in your league, but I'm not Barney Fife. As for Miss Geller, I'm trying to be straight, so I should have told you

this right up front. I ran her name through the computer as
well. You say that you've known her for a year and some
months? Then you know she has a criminal history."

Whistler's eyes turned hard. "Keep talking," he said.

"Silver Ridge, Colorado? Denver Metro, I think. A year
or so ago—months after you'd have met her—she was
charged with trying to shoot two cops who had gone to bust
her mother for drugs. There's also a charge of possession
with intent on both Claudia and her mother, Katherine
Geller. You're telling me you didn't know this?"

"Ed, where did you get your information?"

"I told you. The computer. But it didn't pop right up. In
fact, it almost seemed to be misfiled."

"What file?"

"Some DEA offshoot. A policy think tank. Were you
DEA?"

"No."

"But you worked with them, right?"

"Now and then. Let's get back to those charges."

"I will in a second. One more about you. Did you ever
work Antiterrorist Ops? I think you know why I'm asking."

Whistler answered, "No, Ed, I do not know why you're
asking." And he didn't. He brushed that question aside. He
said, "Listen, Ed, those charges are bogus. Claudia never
shot at those cops. They shot her in the neck, then tried to
frame her. To this day, she has never used a handgun in her
life."

Was that true? Yes, it was. He'd never taught her to use
the Beretta. Only the shotgun and the M-87, a few practice
rounds out of each.

Moore glanced toward the hatch. He touched a finger to
his throat. "Shot her here? That the reason for the scarf?"

"Yes, it is. And she's never possessed or used a drug. I'd be
surprised if she's ever even seen one. In any case, those charges
were dropped. Her record was supposed to be expunged."

"Well, you see, that's what's funny. They were not ever
dropped, and yet there's no warrant, no wants. There is an
instruction. It says 'Do not detain. Observe and report, but

do not detain.' Now you're telling me you thought the charges were dropped. Can you tell me what you think is going on there?"

"You've observed. Have you reported?"

"Is it any of my business?"

"It's some people who've tried to get at me through her. I thought it was settled. We had reached a détente. Believe me, it is not police business."

"This was duty-related?"

"And it's classified, Ed. I'm not free to tell you much beyond that, but I'll owe you if you'll keep this to yourself."

"No connection to Ragland? To this case?"

"None whatsoever."

Moore reached into the briefcase that he'd brought on board with him. "I'll give you the printout of the file I found. And the reason I asked about Terrorist Ops . . . do the names Breen and Crow mean anything to you?"

Whistler shook his head. "They're the two from last night?"

Moore produced the file entry, the one about the Gellers, plus two other printouts of FBI want sheets. He placed the want sheets on the table facing Whistler. He said, "Leonard Breen and Joshua Crow. We've identified Breen. He's the one you took down. The one we're still looking for is Crow."

Both want sheets had photos, but the photos weren't mug shots. They'd been taken from amateur snapshots. That meant neither man had ever been booked. Whistler recognized the shooter, Leonard Breen, at a glance. The other was more blurred, but it was a fair likeness of the one who had waited with the car. Both men were wanted for unlawful flight to avoid prosecution for murder.

Moore asked, "You've never heard of these two before?"

"Me? Why would I?"

"Antiterrorist Ops. Thought you might have run across them."

"I've never worked domestic antiterrorist at all. That's the FBI's jurisdiction."

"Yeah, it is. And by noon, they're going to be here in

force. They've been looking for these two for a year and a half."

The FBI's involvement was not welcome news. Those people are slow, but annoyingly thorough. Whistler hoped that they wouldn't feel the need to reinterview all witnesses to the Jump & Phil's shooting. But perhaps they had enough on Breen and Crow as it stood.

"So you're saying Breen and Crow are known terrorists. What kind?"

"Fanatics. They're both Reconstructionists."

"And . . . what is a Reconstructionist, please?"

"Never heard the term? Really?"

"There are hundreds of groups. Most of them are just noise. What is it that they want to reconstruct?"

"The world. To get it ready for Jesus."

19

Felix Aubrey had pretty much made up his mind what to do about Whistler's reappearance. Was he there to meet Ragland? Maybe yes; more likely no, Mr. Lockwood's paranoia notwithstanding.

Almost everything about it was suggestive of coincidence. Did the two make eye contact? Indeed, they may well have. It was a small bar, after all. And Whistler, especially, would have made it his business to scan every face in the room. Would Whistler have chosen such a public place for an assignation with Ragland? That seemed very unlikely, but if he had, would Ragland's wife and the girl have been present?

And speaking of the girl, if she did throw that knife—improbable, but let's say she did. Let's agree that Whistler helped to pass the time at sea by teaching her some tricks of the trade. One would think, however, that if he taught her how to kill, he'd have told her not to dawdle after doing so. If there's one thing that Whistler understands very well, it's the value of melting away quietly.

So here, thought Aubrey, we get to the crux, the one thing that Lockwood was right about. Whistler did manage, somehow, to fade into the woodwork. Not a word on the news about Whistler or the girl, even though one would think, at the very least, that they'd be worthy of honorable mention. How he managed it, no matter; the point is, he did. The question: Do we let him get away with it?

We don't, of course. We let the word go forth. A leak from a confidential source. We let it be known that the mystery Samaritan is none other than a blood-soaked U.S. Government assassin. He's one of many, of course, but we'll give Whistler all the credit. We say, there he is, on that boat, go take his picture. Put it on your front pages, on your evening news broadcasts. Let the sons and the brothers of his various victims, meaning everyone who has ever been targeted by anyone, at last put a face to the stalker. Here he is; here's what he looks like; good hunting.

And here, as a bonus, are the people most dear to him. The girl, the girl's mother, oh, and yes, Whistler's father. Get them first, if you can. Save Whistler for last. Make sure that he knows why they died.

The beauty of this is that it's Whistler's own doing. His father had told Poole, "You touch him; I touch you." He said, "Don't even think in terms of an *accident*. No matter how random, no matter what the evidence, I'll assume that you people are behind it." Poole wilted, of course. He turned into a puddle. He as much as smeared lamb's blood across Whistler's forehead so the angel of death would pass him by.

Well, the game has changed. The advantage has shifted. Delbert Poole, no doubt, will blanch at the prospect of declaring open season on Whistler. He'll say, "You heard his father. We're bound to be blamed. The least that he'll do is go public with your ledger."

He'll blame us? How can he? Did we put him in that bar? Did we force him to take center stage with Philip Ragland?

Don't you see; it's the media that will do this, not us. Our
agreement with his father remains in force because we're innocent of any involvement.

Some days it's a pleasure to go to the office. Felix Aubrey
couldn't wait to present this to Poole.

The Center for Policy Analysis was housed in a purposely
nondescript building. Twelve floors of grayish concrete and
gray-tinted glass with a private garage underneath. All its
tenants had similar gray-sounding names. The Center for
this, the Committee for that, the National Council of whatever. Any curious outsider would be bored to stupefaction
just by reading the lobby directory.

If that curious outsider were to get past security, he or she
would not see much of a change. The tenants, on the whole,
were gray men and women who tried not to look at each
other. A new employee might say "Good morning" at first,
but such overtures would quickly be discouraged. They
could lead to small talk and, in turn, to indiscretions. What
each did was no business of the other.

Felix Aubrey, especially, preferred it that way, and all the
more since he'd been cut. His humiliation had been enough
to bear without being asked, "Oh, what happened, poor
man?" and knowing that the questioner was chortling inside.
They all knew. He felt sure that they knew.

On this morning, as usual, he came in through the
garage and used a coded card to call the elevator down. He
used the same card to select his floor. There would be no
admittance without it. The elevator rose, but it soon
stopped again to collect those who'd entered through the
lobby. There were several people waiting. Delbert Poole
was among them in his usual black suit, wearing one of his
usual yellow neckties. Something was missing. Aubrey
couldn't quite place it. Ah, yes. No lapel pin. Poole always
displayed some kind of a pin, depending on whom he
might be seeing that day. He had American flag pins, Put-
Prayer-Back-in-School pins, Just-Say-No pins, pro-life
pins, and a wide assortment of Christian pins, the most re-

cent of which showed a flaming sword in the hand of a militant angel.

Poole acknowledged Aubrey's presence with the barest nod as he stepped in and turned to face the doors. This was normal, not unusual, and yet something else was different. Poole's normal expression was a satisfied smile. Aubrey would have expected it, especially this morning, assuming that Poole had heard the news that someone had shot Philip Ragland. His expression, however, seemed glazed, almost haunted. No matter, thought Aubrey. Dyspepsia, perhaps. He would soon give Poole something to be haunted about before relieving him with a solution.

He waited until the other passengers stepped off. "You're aware, are you not, that Philip Ragland has been shot?"

Poole moistened his lips. He didn't answer.

"And no doubt you have prayed for his speedy recovery."

Poole swallowed hard. He said, "I had no part in that."

"No part in shooting Ragland? Who said that you did?"

"I do not choose to discuss it."

This was curious behavior, even for Poole. Poole normally would not volunteer a denial. To do so would suggest that there might be some basis for even considering that he might have been involved. His normal reaction was more likely to be a pious expression of shock.

Wait a minute, thought Aubrey. Poole must know about Whistler. That idiot, Lockwood, must have called him as well. If he has, he'll pay dearly for ruining the surprise.

"Shall I . . . take it that you've heard from Mr. Lockwood this morning?"

Poole blinked a few times. He asked, "Who?"

"I think you heard me."

"Oh, Lockwood. Your man? Why would I speak to him? I don't even know what his job is."

This again was normal. He chose not to know Lockwood. Very well. Rule out Lockwood. "Let me ask another way. Do you know who else was at the scene of the shooting?"

"I know nothing of that incident. I'm in no way connected."

"And of course you know nothing about Adam Whistler."

"Him? What about him? No, don't tell me," said Poole. "Whatever he's up to, you deal with it."

This was getting beyond curious. Could he really not know? If he didn't, what could possibly have him so out of sorts?

"Mr. Poole, I'll ask again, and this time I'll speak slowly. Are you aware that Adam Whistler and his lady friend were present when Philip Ragland got shot?"

The color drained from Poole's face. He seemed unable to speak.

"And did you know," Aubrey added, "that, acting together, they subdued the man who shot Philip Ragland? Did you know that they saved Ragland's life?"

Poole could only stammer. This was news to him, clearly. Aubrey, at least, could now enjoy Poole's discomfort, but he still didn't know why Poole had bothered to insist that he was innocent of any involvement. It was clear that Poole knew a good deal more than he was saying.

"Want to hear the best part? It was actually the girl. It seems that young Claudia has used her sabbatical to acquire a few lethal skills."

Poole gave no response. He merely tightened his jaw and averted his eyes. This also was normal. He could say he never heard.

Aubrey said, "Very well. Never mind. Here's our floor."

"Wait a minute," Poole whispered. He was chewing his lip. "You say Whistler . . . and the girl . . . ?"

"Too late. I don't wish to discuss it."

This was the sort of game that they played all the time except that this one, again, was somewhat different. Delbert Poole almost never asked a question directly. Nothing asked, nothing known, was his watchword. But Poole, it was clear, hadn't heard about Whistler. He had only known that Philip Ragland had been shot, and that news alone had affected him greatly. Then the mention of Whistler in connection with Ragland had nearly the effect of defibrillator paddles applied to his private parts.

Poole wet his lips once more. All he managed was, "Whistler?"

"We'll talk when you're ready to share."

When one has an advantage, one doesn't discard it without getting something of value in return. Aubrey said nothing further. He would go to his office. He would wait until Poole could stand it no longer. He would let Mr. Poole come to him.

It took longer than he'd thought. On reaching his office, Poole told Robert, his assistant—his bodyguard, really—to cancel his appointments for the day. Moreover, he'd be taking no calls.

"Will you be in prayer, sir?"

One had to know Robert.

"I am . . . always in prayer."

And one had to know Poole.

Before closing his door, Poole reached into his wallet and extracted a card key that he carried in its folds. Aubrey knew that the only card key lock in that room was the one to a cabinet that concealed a safe where Poole kept his private papers. He could hear Poole at the cabinet, yanking it open. He heard him say, "Shit." Poole never said, "Shit." Mr. Poole was indeed not himself.

Some ten minutes later, Poole burst from the room, a thick folder under his arm. Aubrey heard him tell young Robert to get up from his computer and to go get some breakfast, read his Bible or something. The assistant, a mountainous young fellow, obeyed. Poole watched him go and then sat at Robert's desk where Robert kept a photo, framed in turquoise, of his mother and a coffee mug that asked, "What would Jesus do?" Robert also wore a pistol strapped to his ankle, which was, one assumes, what Jesus would have done if he'd known what the Romans had in store for him. He would probably have used it on Judas.

Poole pushed the photo and the mug to one side and went to work on Robert's keyboard. He spent another ten minutes bringing up files. Every so often, he would reach his right hand to the lower right corner of the keyboard. Aubrey sel-

dom spent much time at computers, but he knew that that
was where the delete key was found.

Aubrey couldn't resist. He got up from his desk. He said,
"May I ask what you're doing?"

Poole's response was, "Damn you, Mr. Aubrey."

This was odd in itself. Delbert Poole never cursed.
Surely, he used "damn" or "damned" on occasion, but only
to describe the eventual circumstance of all but a few living
humans.

He said it again, "Damn you, Aubrey."

"But for what, in this instance? And what is it you're
erasing? And whatever it is, you wouldn't have to erase it if
you hadn't put it there in the first place."

Poole ignored all but the first part of the question. "Damn
you for this. This folder right here." He jabbed a finger at the
folder that, one assumed, had lately come out of his safe.
"It's your ledger, Aubrey. Your damnable ledger. Damn you
and your damnable ledger."

It was not the book itself. It was only a copy. Whistler's
father had kept the original. Aubrey said, "Now I'm confused. Yes, Whistler was there. But why is everyone leaping
to the conclusion that Whistler and Ragland are in concert?"

"Whistler. You've confirmed that? He's a part of this
now?"

An exasperated sigh. "A part of what, Mr. Poole?"

"What Crow did. With Breen. Those two shot Philip
Ragland. Breen is dead or near it. They've identified Breen.
They know that the one who escaped must be Crow."

Aubrey hadn't heard that the assailants had been named.
"And . . . who are these two? What have they to do with us?"

"Don't play dumb with me, Mr. Aubrey."

One should never admit that one doesn't know something. One should smile and say, "Oh, that," as if it's under
control. But Aubrey could not. This seemed much too important. He said, "I'm afraid I'm not playing."

"You're a liar, Mr. Aubrey."

"Ah . . . what if I swear . . . may my parents burn in
hell . . . if I have the least idea of what you're talking about?"

Poole threw back the cover of the folder at his side. He whipped through several pages, knocking some to the floor. He found one page, and he reached for a pen. He drew a great circle around a notation that was written in Aubrey's own hand.

"There. It says, 'Recon.' That is your abbreviation. It says, 'JC.' That is your abbreviation. Here it says, 'Idiotic.' That is your assessment. I ask you, who is the idiot now? Whose ledger got us into this disaster?"

Aubrey blinked. He remembered. Joshua Crow. The JC of his ledger was Joshua Crow. Oh, this was too delicious, if true.

"Crow. The Reconstructionist. Their money man. That Crow?"

All Delbert Poole could do was close his eyes.

"He's the one who throws bombs into gay bars and such? Now he's shooting our critics? With Adam Whistler watching? It's your own Mr. Crow whom we have to thank for that?"

"You as well. Don't be modest. You above all."

"You've given them millions. And it *was* idiotic. No, no, I withdraw that. It was lunacy, sir. Show me one thing that you've gotten in return, other than one of their ridiculous lapel pins. Which reminds me: I see that you've retired that pin. Or did one of their numbers come and rip it from your coat because you were tardy with donations?"

Felix Aubrey was instantly sorry that he said it. It evoked a crackpot rationalization that Aubrey had already heard several times. Poole felt perfectly justified in diverting this money. That to do so was illegal, a crime, had no relevance. These monies, themselves, were the wages of sin. The problem with that was that Poole no longer cared whether victims of seizures were innocent or guilty. It was enough, in his eyes, that they were probably immoral. "Honest men," he'd once said, "do not acquire great wealth. And some have been born into undeserved wealth that is better used doing God's work."

Felix Aubrey might not have objected to this if God's

work had involved such traditional activities as caring for
the sick and the poor. Well, truth be told, he would have.
Unless caring for the poor involved having them spayed,
spending money on them would have been wasteful. But
the work that Poole was funding envisioned nothing less
than a new and more terrible inquisition. Not that Aubrey
would have minded a burning here and there. He'd known
plenty of people who were long overdue. In fact, he still had
the list that he'd started in his teens. People who'd slighted
him, bullied him, belittled him. Grown women, later, who
would roll their eyes when he did nothing more than try to
speak to them. Some of these, as time went on, married
well, had lovely homes. Not so many have those homes
anymore.

Delbert Poole was still whining. Aubrey waited him out.
At the moment Poole was fretting that Whistler must know
that Poole, Breen, and Crow are connected. Well, he doesn't.
Almost surely. Aubrey couldn't see how. But Poole seems to
think that if he doesn't, he will. He thinks that Whistler will
remember those notations in the ledger—those sums that
were earmarked as Recon-JC—and instantly realize that
they must mean Crow and his Reconstructionist lunacy. Not
likely. Not remotely. There were hundreds of notations.
Whistler would have to focus on those few in particular and
make an improbable logical leap. The term "Recon" could
have any number of meanings. Given Whistler's background, the first of those meanings that would pop into his
mind would be that it was short for "Reconnaissance." And
"JC" could mean anything from Jesus Christ to the Junior
Chamber of Commerce.

Aubrey tried to remember when last he'd seen Crow. Two
years ago? Longer? Crow had come to see Poole. Whenever
it was, Crow and Poole had prayed together. The occasion
was when Poole advised Mr. Crow that he'd best not be seen
in this building again. Leonard Breen, it seems, had murdered two people, one of whom was Breen's former wife.
He had actually, literally, stoned them to death, and had
gathered an audience to witness the event. While he did so,

it was Crow who kept the audience at bay, describing what they were to see, and why, and distributing literature to them.

Poole realized, belatedly, that Joshua Crow had finally gone over the edge. He pointed out to Crow, as tactfully as he could, that this sort of thing could cause problems. He said that although it might not be a crime in God's eyes, the law would surely take a less enlightened view. The coming of Christ would solve that problem, of course, and we know that He is coming any day now. Until then, however, Poole thought it would be prudent if Crow were to make himself scarce. Crow agreed to do so. He took Leonard Breen with him. Those two took their show on the road.

"Mr. Poole, settle down. I'm in need of some answers. I take it that you've been in contact with Crow."

"Me? I have not. I have severed all ties."

"That's a fib, I'm afraid. I was here when you handed him some traveling money. I was here when you promised that you'd send him all he needed."

"I . . . recall no such thing. You're quite wrong."

"You have aided and abetted. That's a no-no, Mr. Poole. May we stop this little game and move on?"

"I need to pray."

"Yes, but first let us deal with the here and the now. Did you send Breen and Crow after Ragland?"

"I didn't. I swear it. All I ever said—"

"So, you have spoken to him. Was this recent? By what means?"

"He . . . sometimes leaves a message. He leaves a number on my pager. When I call, it is only to urge him to surrender."

Aubrey curled his lip. Save that line for the police. "Yes, but why does he call? Surely not to hear that. Does he call when he's in need of financial assistance?"

"No," Poole said sharply. Then he added, "Well . . . no."

"So the answer is 'partly.' Why else does he call?"

"He . . . wants me to know that he's . . . doing good works."

"He calls to inform you of his latest atrocity? That makes you an accessory after the fact."

"No, no. All he says is, 'Read the papers tomorrow.' "

"You say he calls your pager. Does he have a pager?"

Poole rose to his feet. He clapped his hands to his cheeks. "I . . . believe so. But I've never . . ."

"So you do have his number. You can reach him if you must."

"Call him now? After this? I would have to be insane."

"No, what would be insane is to let him be caught. What do you suppose he would say to the police? Will he agree that you didn't ask him to shoot Ragland?"

"He would. All I said was that Ragland was scheduled to address a conference being held on that island."

"Its topic?"

"It's nothing connected with us. It's some group that's in favor of infanticide."

"So this group is pro-choice. You told Crow that was the topic?"

Poole was rubbing his face. "I . . . may have mentioned it in passing. It was merely a discussion. I never intended . . ."

"No, you never do, do you? This time, however, you have a problem. Its solution can benefit us both."

Poole looked up at him hopefully. "You can . . . help to resolve this?"

"I can save your skin. I can make this go away. How much cash is in your safe at the moment, Mr. Poole? Say none, and this conversation is over."

"I keep a fund for contingencies. A few hundred thousand."

"A good start. It's now mine. In addition to that, I will want an amount that equals what you've given to Mr. Crow's church."

Poole stared, his mouth open. "You're talking three million."

"Not talking. Extorting. I'm extorting three million. You're refusing? Then have a good day."

"Wait a minute. What next? What if I agree?"

"You will make one more call to Mr. Crow's pager. You'd

better hope that he returns it. I will tell you what to say. After that, you will never hear from him again. Do you wish to know how I can assure you of that?"

"I must . . . trust in your good judgment. As always."

"So the answer is no. You're going to leave this to me."

"But Whistler . . . he's involved . . . what will you do about Whistler?"

He can wait, thought Aubrey. First things first. This took precedence. The task at hand was to put Mr. Lockwood in contact with our inconvenient friend, Mr. Crow. How to do so had already taken shape in his mind. Mr. Lockwood will see to it that we see no more of Crow. That accomplished, Aubrey would then make the call that would put Whistler's face on every front page.

"He'll have problems of his own, Mr. Poole."

20

Claudia, thought Whistler, had apparently been right. All Moore wanted was to know that he'd done the right thing in letting them distance themselves from the shooting. Perhaps admiration figured into it somewhere, admiration of Whistler for his Special Ops past. Or perhaps that admiration was directed more toward Claudia. Moore seemed not a little enchanted by her. Whistler felt sure that Moore would take no action on those charges still pending against her. He'd observed, but he would not report.

Whistler, however, would have one more score to settle if he ever met up with Felix Aubrey again. They had buried the charges against Claudia and her mother but had not, as they'd claimed, had them wiped off the books. He supposed that he should not have been surprised.

He would need to tell his father, but later, not now. His fa-

ther would ask him how he came to find out and he'd have
to admit that he wasn't quite truthful about having no involvement in last night's events. For now, though, he just
might get out of this clean. There was no need to worry his
father.

As for Aubrey's deceit, his father might not even care. He
might say, *"Big Deal. He kept a card up his sleeve. It's not
much of a card. He knows he can't go to trial. There's no
one left to testify, remember? The most he could do would be
to have them picked up and kept on ice for a few days, tops.
If he does, and tries to deal, I'll snatch his mother if he has
one. Forget it. Let him think he's been clever."*

"Yeah, but then what's the point of him keeping them
open?"

*"Adam, you heard. It's 'Observe, but don't detain.' He's
just trying to track you for his own peace of mind. As long
as you don't do anything that threatens him directly, he's not
going to risk taking action."*

"You're so sure?"

*"Tell you what. I'll send someone to torch Aubrey's
house. Just a little token gesture to show our disappointment that he's been less than diligent in showing good faith.
How about it? Would that make you feel better?"*

"I don't need the sarcasm. Never mind."

*"Then count your blessings. One is that cop. But if I were
you, I'd slip out of there tonight. Head due east and don't
stop until you hit Bermuda, which is where I wish you'd
gone in the first place."*

Whistler didn't need to hear another "I-told-you-so," not
even one that he was imagining. Getting out, and soon, was a
thought nonetheless.

Except he wouldn't feel right, ducking out on these people. Especially Leslie, who had lied to Moore for them. And
Moore, who might possibly have risked his job by trying to
give them a break. On the other hand, there's Claudia, who
might find it therapeutic to put some open ocean between
herself and this island. He would see. He would see how the
day goes.

* * *

Leslie and Phil had tied up and come aboard in response to the breakfast invitation. Leslie volunteered to set the table on the deck. She went below for a tray of plastic dinnerware. The printout on Claudia was still on the table. Moore slid it toward Whistler, who put it away. He did not conceal the want sheets on Breen and Crow because he'd already shown them to Leslie and Phil. He said the one with Crow's photo was being distributed to every place of business on the island. It would shortly be flashed on local TV and probably on CNN.

Moore said, "Someone will spot him if he's still on the island. And he is unless he got off by boat."

"You say the vehicle he car-jacked never made it to the bridge?"

"They couldn't have missed it. It's a white Dodge van with a rack of bikes on it."

"He might have used it to get to another," said Whistler. "Maybe one they'd stashed. Maybe one he could steal. Maybe he got past the roadblock last night before you had a physical description."

"Those facial cuts, remember? No one like that got past them. If he has any sense, he wouldn't have tried. He wouldn't have risked being trapped on a bridge. He's holed up somewhere on the island."

Moore said that there were hundreds of unoccupied homes owned by people who lived there part-time. Moore said, "If it was me, I'd pick one of the smaller ones, but one with a two-car garage. I wouldn't try a big one; most of them have alarms. I'd keep it looking empty and dark and I'd stay for a week if I had to."

Whistler shrugged. "But what would he do for supplies?"

"From what we can tell, he has everything he needs. The driver of the van said Crow was carrying a duffel. We know that Crow and Breen use a scanner when they travel, so that's probably what he had in the bag along with some weapons and, I'd bet, some explosives. He's got a first aid kit that came with the van and at least a week's worth of groceries."

"Groceries? How so?"

"He grabbed the Dodge van from outside a supermarket. He took it from a family that drove down here from Ohio and had stopped to load up on food. He got their food and their luggage along with their car, so he's even got new clothes to put on. The family was a couple with a teenage daughter. He whacked the father on the head with the shotgun and threatened the mother and the daughter. Called them sluts."

Leslie came on deck. "Called them sluts? What made them sluts?"

"They made the trip wearing tank tops and shorts. And the daughter wore a little gold cross on a chain. He ripped the cross off her. He said she defiled it. This guy has some issues with women."

Claudia, although she still seemed not quite herself, had prepared an impressive breakfast platter. In addition to the bacon and a thick western omelet, she'd cut some fillets from last night's uneaten grouper and she'd garnished the platter with melon and grapes. Phil Henry volunteered to serve as the waiter. He said that his own chef could not have done better. And he promised to reciprocate, buy them all dinner, as soon as his restaurant could open again.

"What sort of issues?" asked Claudia as she joined them on deck. "With women, I mean. I couldn't help overhearing."

Moore started to answer. Whistler held up his hand. "Too nice a breakfast for an unpleasant subject." Especially, he thought, one that touched on religion in the presence of a guardian angel.

But she said, "No, really. I'd like to know about those two. What kind of a person was the one I—?"

"Saw outside?"

It was Leslie who blurted the completion of her sentence to keep Claudia from saying, "the one who I skewered." The near slip went by Moore . . . or he pretended not to catch it. Leslie snatched up Crow's want sheet. "You mean this one," she said.

"Adam's right," said Moore. "This can wait until we've eaten."

But Leslie pressed Moore so that Claudia wouldn't. She seemed to understand that Claudia still needed to hear that what she'd done had been justified. Leslie said, "It's already on all of our minds. To tell you the truth, I've been feeling almost sorry for the one who somebody stabbed in the head. If I shouldn't, that's what I need to know."

She said this while looking directly at Whistler. A touch of overkill there, but his eyes said, *"Nice move."* He then glanced at Phil and again back at Leslie. His eyebrow arched into a question. She answered with the smallest shake of her head. It meant, *"No, I haven't told Phil that she threw it and I won't. Now will you please relax? Eat your breakfast."*

Whistler had to look away. He tried to keep himself from smiling. This young woman was clearly Claudia's friend and she seemed to be one well worth having. All the same, he'd prefer that their friendship not develop to the point of them sharing their innermost thoughts. Let Claudia do that with her birds.

Sergeant Moore had already pulled more sheets from his folder. He said to Leslie, "Believe me, you're not going to feel sorry." He turned to Whistler. "Do you mind?"

Leslie said, "No, he doesn't. Unless Claudia does."

She didn't. She said, "I'd like to hear it."

Whistler learned that tank tops and little gold crosses were the least of what offended Crow and Breen. This past fall, they'd pipe-bombed a family planning center in a suburb of Lexington, Kentucky. The bomb killed one nurse and maimed another. At another such clinic in Buffalo, New York, they had shotgunned a doctor and a teenage girl while the girl still had her legs in the stirrups. They did not, however, limit their victims to those of the pro-choice persuasion. They'd tossed Molotov cocktails through the entrance door of a crowded gay disco in Atlanta. No deaths, but several young men were disfigured.

There was never a doubt that Breen and Crow were the

assailants. To begin with, they always took credit for their
work through messages that they left on the Internet sites of
the Reconstructionist Church. Nor were these attacks hit-
and-run operations. They would linger long enough to ha-
rangue any witnesses on why the flaming sword was
brought down on these sinners. This was why, said Moore,
they had chosen to shoot Ragland in a restaurant that was
filled with other diners. Breen had probably prepared a few
verses from Scripture that he'd shout as he backed out the
door. He would probably have strewn a few pamphlets
about. A stack of them were found in his pocket.

Whistler remembered seeing those pamphlets. He'd
thought they were tourist brochures. And he thought of Delbert Poole. He didn't know why. Yes, he did; it was this citing of biblical verses. Poole would do that all the time. But
something else nagged at him. Something else about Poole.
Whatever it was, it eluded him.

Leslie asked, "These two would actually give sermons?"

"Crow did from the start. I'm getting to that. Unless
you'd prefer that I stop."

"No, go on," said Claudia.

"You're sure? It gets grimmer."

"Adam." She reached to touch his hand. "Are you okay?"

She asked because she saw that his mind had wandered.
He was still seeing Poole . . . and now Aubrey . . . in his
head. He knew that his mind was searching for a connection
just because of that biblical business. It was silly. So unlikely. He'd already decided that Aubrey, at least, would
never have allowed this to happen.

"I guess we're lucky," said Leslie, "that they didn't throw
a bomb."

Moore explained that they've only used pipe bombs and
firebombs when their victims were randomly chosen. They
seemed to prefer guns when the victim was specific. That
lessened the chance that they would miss. A bomb might
have missed Philip Ragland entirely. It might also have deaf-
ened everyone in the bar. They wouldn't have heard any
parting words that these two had probably prepared.

"Their spree," he said, "began two years earlier in their hometown of Springfield, Missouri. Breen's wife, it seems, had moved out of their trailer and had taken up with another man. Crow pointed out that this made her an adulteress. They found them together, not in bed, but at a Wendy's. Breen and Crow walked in armed with shotguns."

Moore said they ordered the couple to get down on their knees, facing and embracing each other. Breen used a roll of duct tape to wrap them together while Crow kept other patrons and employees at bay. Breen's wife was screaming, begging for help. The new boyfriend tried denying there was anything between them. Breen stuffed napkins into his mouth.

Crow herded the dozen or so patrons and employees to the rear of the fast-food service counter. There were two small children among them. Crow told this group that they were not to be harmed, that instead they'd been honored to witness God's wrath. Crow then told Breen it was time to pass judgment. Breen went back outside where he gathered up some rocks that had lined a bed of flowers near the entrance.

On his return, Crow announced to the assemblage that they were in the presence of adulterers. Crow said that they'd been tried before God and convicted. He then quoted a number of scriptural texts that dealt with the penalty phase. He said that adulterers were to be stoned. He asked if any present were doubters, nonbelievers. If some were, they kept that to themselves. As they looked on in horror, Breen started his work. He began hurling stones at his wife and her companion from a distance of five or six feet. They were frantic, screaming, trying hopelessly to dodge them. Although Breen missed them as often as not, enough stones had hit them, crushed their shoulders, smashed their faces, that soon the floor and walls were splattered with their blood. Crow told Breen to end it. Breen went out for bigger stones. With these, he pounded each of them to death.

That done, Mr. Crow began handing out pamphlets describing the mission of his church. He gave each of the children a little lapel pin depicting a fiery sword. He had to pin them on himself because the children were in shock. One of them, to this day, was still unable to speak.

Moore paused. "I did warn you. This is not table talk."

He was looking at Claudia. Her expression had gone cold. She said, very softly, "Go on."

Moore glanced toward Whistler. Whistler said, "No, that's enough."

"No, I need to hear it," said Claudia.

"Well, so far we have adultery, abortion, and being gay. These are the big ones, but they only scratch the surface. Crow will kill you for some twenty different sins against God and the list gets longer all the time."

Whistler asked, "What was Ragland's?"

"You heard that yourself when Breen walked in shouting 'God is not mocked' before he shot him. Ragland, on his program, did a segment on them. From their point of view, he blasphemed."

"He did mock them?"

"Not at all. But he did warn against them. As it happens, I saw that program myself. I remember him saying that every faith, his own included, has its bigots and its lunatic fringe. In that program, he cited a number of groups who are opposed to almost any civil liberty. Kingdom Come was just one of the more extreme groups."

"And Kingdom Come is . . . ?"

"The Reconstructionists' church. Crow and Breen were both early members. Crow, in fact, was their treasurer. Breen never made it past the sixth grade, but Crow is no trailer-park type. He's a college graduate, majored in accounting, had a nervous breakdown, then he had his epiphany. He'd been hearing demon voices in his head for some time. Jesus showed up one day, drove them out, and told Crow that Crow was one of the chosen. He tried street preaching, then he found the Reconstructionists. He turned out to be a whiz at fund-raising, but Kingdom Come finally expelled him from the church. They say he was too militant, even for them, and besides, he'd have seizures and froth at the mouth every time they didn't let him have his way."

"Seizures?" Whistler asked. "Epileptic, you think?"

"Or some other short circuit. Whatever, it scared them. Anyway, he left and took Breen along with him. Crow went out and tried to start his own church. He calls it the Legion of the Flaming Sword. He hands out a lot of those lapel pins."

Whistler asked, "And how large is this legion?"

"Seems to be just Breen and Crow, but they must have some backing. They've left no paper trail because they only use cash. The FBI is sure that their cash has been replenished and yet there's no indication that they've robbed anyone. Somebody has to be funding them."

"And the aim of that someone and these two is . . . what? To kill everyone who sins? They would seem understaffed for such an effort."

"Well, I guess they've decided to do what they can until some more converts get into the game. In fairness, however, to the other Reconstructionists, killing sinners is not their priority. They're certainly radical and ultra right wing, but they don't go around killing people. They prefer to use the political system, backing candidates who share at least some of their views. As I mentioned, they seem very well funded. Most of them are devout; they're very sincere; but they think that they shouldn't just sit around waiting for the Second Coming of Christ. They believe in preparing the way."

Moore proceeded to brief them on the mind-set of a creed that produced men like Joshua Crow. Reconstructionists, he explained, are those who believe that before the Second Coming of Christ, all civil institutions need to be replaced by a system based on biblical law. Since Jesus, they say, intends to do that when he gets here, they ought to get the ball rolling now.

That law, as they interpret it, mandates the death penalty for a lengthening number of offenses. These include all the basics: murder, rape, and the like, but also nearly anything under the heading of acts by consenting adults. Homosexuality is at the top of the list, but there's also incest, adultery, of course, and any unmarried sex. Oral sex and masturbation are out of the question, whether

one is married or not. Having an abortion is a capital offense. So are blasphemy, witchcraft, and drunkenness.
Spreading false religions, meaning any but theirs, will be
punishable by death if and when they get their way.

Add divorce and the reading of prurient materials, and
the reading or teaching of evolution, for that matter. Add the
sale or use of recreational drugs. Add rebellion by children,
disobedience to parents. The kids get two warnings, then a
stoning. Some add smoking to the list of forbidden activities. Although the Bible makes no reference to smoking, neither does it say that it's permissible.

Claudia had been silent throughout this recitation. Her
expressions, however, were easy to read. There was sadness,
mostly, and a shaking of her head. There were flashes of
anger mixed in. Whistler was glad to see the anger because
it probably meant that any guilt she might have felt had been
replaced. He was also glad of her silence. It meant, he
hoped, that she'd resisted the urge to describe her more
benevolent theology.

They had finished their breakfast. Moore needed to get
back. Leslie and Claudia brought the dishes below while
Phil tried to get his motor started.

Moore gave Whistler his card and offered Whistler his
hand. He said, "I'm glad to have met you. The both of you."

"Same here."

Moore said nothing for a moment. He was looking down
at Claudia. He said, "Maybe the two of you can buy me a
beer if I ever run into you again."

"That sounded like good-bye. Does it mean we can
leave?"

Moore shrugged. "As a cop, the answer is no, but I'm
sure you're thinking about it. If you don't leave, however, I'd
stay out here at anchor on the chance that Crow decides to
pay you a call."

"He's no threat to me. He couldn't even know my name.
Anyway, all I did was take a shot at him and miss."

"I think we all know that you both did more than that. But
that isn't the point. The point is how this nut sees it. In his

mind, you interfered with the will of God. I wouldn't put anything past him."

Whistler thanked Sergeant Moore, shook his hand one more time, and he thought, By midnight, we're gone.

Claudia watched Phil's boat leave. She gave Leslie a wave. She said to Whistler, "This might be it."

He asked her absently, "This might be what?" His thoughts were on getting the fuel tank topped off.

"Do you remember when I said it was time to move on? That I needed to find out what else I should be doing?"

"I remember. So let's go. We'll move on to Bermuda."

"It's not finished, Adam. I think I need to meet them."

"Meet who? Wait a minute. You mean Ragland and his wife?"

"I think so, Adam. I think I'm supposed to. I think I might have been sent to Jump and Phil's last night."

Uh-oh, thought Whistler. He could see where this was going. A thing like this happens, people get killed, and the people who've survived it start to look for a meaning. There wasn't any meaning. A plane crash has no meaning. It's just a random tragedy. They happen.

Most people, however, don't think that they're angels.

He said, "Claudia, trust me. You were not there on a mission. We've been to that restaurant a dozen times. We went there to eat, nothing more."

"But you said that the white light might have guided my hand. I know you don't believe it, but you said it."

"To save Ragland's life? Okay, say it did. Good job. You did it. It's over."

"Except . . . look at all the ways in which our lives and his have crossed. Don't you start to feel a bond? A connection?"

"None whatsoever."

"But the things he's against are the things you're against. What if somebody else tries to stop him?"

Oh, damn, thought Whistler. Now where was she going? And wherever it was, do we try to be rational? No, we don't. That never works. Not with Claudia.

He said, "I think we need to get this angel thing straight. I am not anyone's guardian angel. The only angel around here is you, and you're assigned to me, not to Ragland."

A patient sigh. "We're pretending now, right? We're pretending that you believe it?"

Okay, so we're maybe *semi*-rational, thought Whistler.

"Say, I do," he answered. "You're mine, no one else's. This should be an exclusive arrangement. So, the next time you get tapped to do a job on the side—"

"Tapped by . . . ?"

"The white light. It didn't want Ragland killed. Thanks to you, but mostly it, he'll have many more years to tilt at every windmill in sight. You're out of that now; you're back with me and your pitching days are over, by the way. You're no longer available to come in as a reliever just because you happen to be handy."

She lowered her eyes. "Don't make fun of me, Adam."

"Oh, no," he answered quickly. "That's not what I'm doing."

"Then you're humoring me. Don't do that either."

"Humoring you would imply disrespect. There is no one I respect more than you."

"Then oblige me with the truth. Say what's really on your mind."

"Okay, *my* truth." He put his hands on her shoulders. "I think that us being in that bar was pure chance. I think your throw was partly a good arm, but mostly luck. No one guided your hand; that was you being you. And you, by yourself, without any white light, are as good a person as I've ever known. I'm as proud as I can be of how you've dealt with this, Claudia, but I'm asking you—please let's just go."

She looked into his eyes. She seemed surprised by what she saw in them. She said, "You're afraid. I've never seen you afraid."

He nodded. "Absolutely. This scares me."

"And it's me you're afraid for?"

"I can't lose you, Claudia."

"And you think that you might because . . . I live in a

dream world. The white light isn't real. There's just me being me. You're afraid that I'll try something like that again, believing that I can do it again. You think I really can't and I'll get killed."

He nodded again. "That would sum it up. Yes."

"You're afraid of that man who is still on the loose?"

"I'll feel better when he's caught. Or when we're gone."

"Do you think he'll be caught?"

"He won't get away. Not if he's still on this island."

"Maybe he doesn't care about getting away. Maybe he'll try again at the hospital."

"If he does, he's dead meat. Ragland's bound to be guarded. Ragland doesn't need us to protect him."

She said, "I'm sure you're right. But this just doesn't feel finished."

"It isn't. It's ongoing. But we've done our part. Unless you feel a need to be thanked, there's nothing to be gained by seeing Ragland or his wife."

"I'm not looking to be thanked. It's more like . . . I don't know. I feel that there's much more to this than we know. Do you remember the time that other boat needed ice?"

"You, um . . . think that's tied in with this?"

"Well . . . not really."

"See that? Yes, you do. And that's way from left field."

"Okay then, maybe not. But I remember what you said. You said it's never a mistake to go with my instincts. The mistake would have been to ignore them."

"All the same . . ."

"Adam, this all ties together somehow. Don't ask why I think so. I just do. I can feel it."

"Sweetheart, six degrees of separation, remember? We've met hundreds of people who know hundreds more and that goes on ad infinitum. Everyone connects if you look long enough. I don't want to look. I want to quit while we're ahead."

"I know, but what's the harm in dropping by for a minute? Leslie and Phil said they're going to."

"When was this?"

"They said so in the galley. They thought that they should. After all, he was shot in their restaurant."

"Good, then. They can convey our best wishes. We're not going. I'm putting my foot down."

"If we don't, his wife will only come here. You heard Sergeant Moore. She was asking about you. She'll probably show up on the dock."

"If she does, she won't find us. I intend to be at sea."

"But in the time it would take to get everything organized . . ."

"Claudia . . . listen to me. Sit."

He told her that he really did understand why what happened here didn't feel finished. He said, even if we put this whole angel thing aside, the encounter with the Raglands did *almost* seem fated. The drug law connection, the seizure connection, seeing Aubrey and Poole behind Ragland at that hearing. This is where human nature kicks in. We think, if it's fated, then this ought to lead somewhere. And it would, more than likely. But we can't let that happen.

He asked her to focus on their primary goal. Stay away from the cameras, stay out of the papers, and leave the way they came in. He reminded her of how lucky they'd been in that Ragland was the much bigger story.

"I understand, Adam. But we've done that, I think. The media would have been out here by now if they had any interest in us."

"Claudia . . . Ragland. Ragland is media. *The Ragland Report* is a network TV show and his wife was a journalist herself. People like the Raglands tend to ask questions and they tend to have cameras around."

"We could ask them not to."

"Not what? Ask questions? How could either of them resist? Mrs. Ragland already thinks you're a . . ."

"What?"

"Never mind. And by the way, did you do something to Moore? Did you somehow get into his head?"

"Like how?"

"Never mind. Forget I asked. And we're not going."

Whistler turned away from her. He would hear no more of it. This time, for once, he was going to have his way. They would not go near the hospital. They would not go ashore. That was it. No more discussion. It was over.

21

Joshua Crow, as Sergeant Moore had predicted, had found an unoccupied house in which to rest until he could gather his thoughts. He had made his selection within an hour of the shooting. It was in an older section called North Forest Beach, a non-gated, non-guarded community. Quite a few of the houses there were dark.

The one he had chosen seemed ordinary enough. Not likely to attract any notice. The street that led to it was rutted, unpaved, and this house in particular seemed weathered, neglected. This was all to the good, Crow decided.

There were other small houses on either side, but a fence blocked the view of the neighbor to the right and a wall of bamboo shielded it from the other. Best of all, this house had a two-car garage. Its neighbors only had carports.

Perhaps he would find another vehicle inside, but at least there should be room for the van. He broke into the garage through a window at its side and disabled the electric door opener. He raised the door by hand and brought the van inside. He closed the door behind it, then allowed himself a scream. He screamed, then held his breath until he thought his lungs would burst. He bit into the pad of his thumb. He started humming. The humming always calmed him. It brought him good thoughts. It helped him to remember that the Lord's work had been done. Philip Ragland was in hell where he belonged.

There was no other car, but there was a boat of sorts. It was covered by a blue plastic tarp. Crow stripped the tarp off

and let it slide to the floor. The boat was one of those little
Jet Ski things and it sat on a miniature trailer. He knew
nothing about them, but he'd seen children using them, so
they couldn't be too difficult to operate. A last resort,
surely, but it might be an option if he had to slip away over
water.

He broke into the house through the door from the
garage. Once inside, he flipped a wall switch to make sure
that there was power. There was, but he would keep the
house dark. He went back to the van and unloaded its contents, first stacking the bikes to one side. He brought in his
duffel, his shotgun, his scanner, and some of the luggage
that had come with the van. The van's owner was roughly
his own size and shape. Somewhat taller, but his clothing
would fit well enough. There were two sets of golf clubs. He
brought one set inside and then wondered why he'd done
that. He didn't like golf clubs. He didn't like golfers. The
game was surely an invention of Satan, devised to keep
Christians from going to church. He found the first aid kit.
All these vans seemed to have them. He brought it into the
house with the groceries.

In the darkened kitchen he used a small flashlight to find
an electrical outlet. He plugged in the scanner and turned it
on low, listening to the traffic of policemen. It was all about
him, although not by name. He was variously "the wheel-
man" and "perp number two." They knew about the van and
were only now describing it. He had found this house just in
time.

Crow doubted that there would be a house-to-house
search, surely not before they've checked every parking lot
and street. By then, the Almighty will have pointed the way
by which he could continue on his journey.

But this time he'd be alone. He would no longer have
Breen. Poor Leonard had been hurt. He must have been shot.
The reports on the scanner didn't say how severely. Crow
wasn't sure how it had happened, exactly, but he'd heard all
those shots; he'd seen Leonard wrestled down. And that
bodyguard of Ragland's, whom they'd both failed to notice,

had seen him approaching and had fired at him before he could come to Leonard's aid.

Would Leonard talk? No, probably not. But that wouldn't matter. They would soon know who he is. Fingerprints are checked very quickly these days. And if Leonard had escaped, he would have saved them the trouble. If he and Leonard had managed to get off this island, he'd have told them, with pride, who had done this night's work. He'd have told them it was they who slew the beast.

No use worrying about Leonard. The Lord was his shepherd. For now, thought Crow, he'd best clean himself up. He found a half-bathroom; it was just off the kitchen. Because it had no window, he could turn on the light as long as he kept the door closed. He brought the first aid kit in with him.

Crow was dismayed by what he saw in the mirror. The right side of his face was nearly covered with blood. Tiny shards from the windshield were embedded in his cheek. One had come within a whisker of his eye. There was a cut on his nose; there were others on his hands, and his jacket, wet with drippings, had a dozen tiny punctures. No wonder those two females in the van were so frightened when he counseled them about their mode of dress.

He wished now that he'd thought to solicit a donation of any cash they had on them. He had only about sixty dollars in his pocket. He had at least twenty thousand hidden here and there, but most of it was several states away. He had a thousand or so more in their other car, but they'd left that car a few miles off the island after Leonard had acquired that old Buick. He might need to find an interim source of funds.

He had pulled out the shards that had pierced his skin. They left wounds but not terribly big ones. He washed away the blood and was pleased to see that his face, although pitted, seemed almost unmarred compared to what he had expected. A little ice, some ointment, should do the trick. Perhaps they would look more like blemishes than cuts. At a distance, they might not be noticed.

He would rest. That was the main thing. He'd go into the

living room and lie down on the sofa. He would gather his thoughts and his wits and he'd pray. He would not ask for deliverance. He had no doubt of his deliverance. The Lord would show him the way.

The next thing he knew, it was morning, full blown. He looked at his watch; it was a quarter past nine. He had slept so soundly for nearly ten hours that not even the scanner had roused him. He felt his face and hands. His wounds were less tender. The ointment he had used had done its work.

He spent fifteen minutes listening in to the scanner. The traffic that he heard provided few clues as to how the search for him was progressing. They were talking about grids that their cars were patrolling, but the grids were identified by three-digit numbers. Those numbers meant nothing to him. A large-screen TV sat across from the sofa. He found the remote and switched it on.

He tried several channels before coming to one that was showing his face on the screen. He should not have been surprised that they'd identified him so quickly. Even so, it still came as a shock. All they had, however, was that same old photo. It was grainy, indistinct; it had been lifted from a crowd scene and he wasn't even looking toward the camera. With a change of clothing, a hat, some cosmetics, he would look like a thousand other men on this island. If only he hadn't been cut.

There were other surprises. All of them were unpleasant. Leonard Breen was near death; he was on life support, and that evil Philip Ragland was not only still alive; he was well enough to talk to the police. And the commentator seemed to be honoring Ragland. He was talking as if he were a hero.

The news was almost too much to bear. Leonard's sacrifice seemed to have been in vain. And more, Leonard hadn't been shot after all. Someone had stabbed him, stuck a knife in his head, and nobody seemed to be sure who had done it. Why not? he wondered. How could they not know? At least fifty people were there looking on. Could it possibly have been Ragland's wife? And what about that man with the gun? Who was he? There was no mention. All the media seemed to care about was Ragland and his anti-Christ views. But the media, at least, was informative in one way. It said that Philip Ragland was recovering, under guard, at the Hilton Head Medical Center.

Crow began to have a vision. He was seeing himself at the hospital complex. He'd acquired the smock of an orderly somehow. He was pushing a mop cart or some similar conveyance in which his shotgun was hidden. But wait. Not just the shotgun. He still had some explosives. He had a brick of plastique and a container of thermite. He had fuses, detonators, lengths of pipe in his duffel. He had never put a bomb together himself. That was Leonard's expertise, but he had watched him assemble them.

In his vision, he had already visited Leonard. He'd told Leonard that in minutes Ragland's room would be a furnace. Philip Ragland, his wife, and anyone guarding him would find out what awaits them in hell. Hearing this, Leonard died with a smile on his face. Or Crow assumed so. He couldn't be sure. He was suffocating Leonard with a pillow at the time. He knew that Leonard would have wanted that assistance.

But this vision, thought Crow, left some questions unanswered. He hoped that this vision was only a suggestion and not a specific instruction. If a sign, it fell short of helping him to see how he could get out of it alive. He would wait, he decided. There might be another sign.

As if in response to his wish for such a sign, he heard a buzzing sound coming from his duffel. The sound was his pager. It was in there with a number of cell phones he'd collected during his travels with Leonard. He knew at once who the caller must be. The only two people who could reach him in that manner were Leonard and their patron, Mr. Poole. It seemed very unlikely to be Leonard.

Crow supposed that he ought to return the call promptly, but he wasn't sure that he could bear the rebuke that was probably Mr. Poole's reason for calling. His worst fear was that Poole might cut off his funding. Or suggest that he re-

tire, his work still undone, his place in the rapture still un-
earned.

Crow couldn't blame him for being upset. He had not
done well for Mr. Poole in this instance. Philip Ragland
would now be more famous than ever. More people would
listen to his poisonous views. More innocents would be
murdered before they could be born, more young people
would be lured to depravity and ruin through drugs, homo-
sexuals, and Hollywood films.

This cannot be allowed. He would silence Philip
Ragland. He might, however, be in need of assistance. His
God, the true God, unlike that of the Muslims, does not ap-
prove of suicide missions.

He would call Mr. Poole. He'd reaffirm his resolve. They
would pray together. They would find a way. He could also
use a few hundred dollars.

All that Aubrey could do now was wait and hope that Crow
would respond to the page. Poole felt sure that he would, but
Poole was dreading it.

Delbert Poole, like himself, kept a number of cell phones.
Aubrey had provided them; they were specially made. Each,
in its way, was secure. Poole had marked each of the phones
he used with different symbols, depending on their purpose.
The one Crow would be calling, if indeed he did call, was
marked with a fish, the Greek symbol for Christ, to which
Poole had added the fin of a shark. A shark, thought Aubrey.
Now we have Christian sharks. He would not have thought
that Poole had that much imagination. At least he hadn't
added a halo to the shark.

"You're clear on what to say?" Aubrey asked.

Poole nodded, eyes closed. "I'm not a very good liar."

"That may be, but you are a most excellent believer. Believe this. You won't enjoy prison."

As they waited for the call, Aubrey found himself wondering what the Devil would think of all this. One often
hears the phrase, "Give the Devil his due," but we really
never do, he thought, do we? Old Lucifer has to work at such

an awful disadvantage. Bad location, to begin with. Rotten climate. Poorly lit. Tens of thousands of clerics preaching against him and never a word of his side of the story. That's what happens, of course, when God writes all the books. One would think that he'd open a Web site, at least.

Beelzebub.com. It could be a moneymaker. Think of all of the businesses that would leap at the chance to advertise their wares on such a site. Arms merchants. Porn dealers. And the Mafia, what's left of it.

Poole's fish phone chirped. Poole blanched, then wiped his palms on his chest before picking it up with his finger-tips. He cleared his throat, swallowed, and said, "Yes?"

He listened for a time, then reached for a pen. He scrawled the words, "very distraught" on a pad. Aubrey saw it and whispered, "We'll fix that."

Poole was saying to Crow, "I'm so sorry about Leonard. But it isn't for naught. You've done better than you know. Are you safe at the moment? Are you alone? Are you in hiding?"

Poole listened to Crow's answer and nodded to Aubrey. Crow's response was in the affirmative.

"Now listen to me carefully." Poole had lowered his voice. "There is more important work that needs to be done. I can't elaborate just yet, but you'll be very excited. My immediate concern is to get you off that island. I have people on their way. They will help you."

Poole listened again. He made a note on his pad. Aubrey read it. The note read, "What about Breen? He doesn't want to leave Breen in their hands." Aubrey took the pen and wrote, "Already made arrangements. Breen to be rescued, leave everything to us. Get Crow's location, then get off the phone."

Poole repeated the first part and went on to the second. "Joshua, where are you at the moment? . . . No, no, an address, a specific location . . . You don't? Very well. Go and look."

Poole whispered to Aubrey, "He doesn't know the address. He's gone out to check the street sign. You say you've already made arrangements for Breen?"

Aubrey sneered. "Of course not. Breen no longer matters. By the way, has Crow ever seen Lockwood?"

"Not that I can recall. I don't think so."

"Describe him. Can't mistake him. Always wears a dark suit. Neck is wider than his head; he was born without lips and his eyes are as dull as a goat's. He'll be with a man named Kaplan. I've never met Kaplan. Tell Crow that he can trust both these men with his life."

A minute later, Crow was back on the phone. He gave the address: 22 Lagoon Road. He described the house, painted blue with black shutters. He gave its approximate location. Poole wrote it all down, then described Vernon Lockwood, omitting the reference to his eyes. He told Crow that Lockwood will be bringing an associate. He said that both are reliable men, and that Crow will be in very good hands.

"Are they what? Are they saved? Well, we're . . . working on that. I'm sure that they're both committed Christians at heart. For the moment, let's put that aside."

Poole covered the mouthpiece. An exasperated sigh. He said to Aubrey, "He's correcting me now. He's saying that one never puts that question aside." Poole removed his hand. Crow was saying something else. "Repeat that please, Joshua. Will they what? Bring money? Oh, all that you'll need. You will not have to worry about money."

Very true, thought Aubrey. "He's to wait there," he whispered. He looked at his watch. "They should arrive in another two hours at the most."

"Two hours," Poole repeated. "Go nowhere. Stay indoors. Your deliverance will soon be at hand . . . um, say again?"

Poole listened. He grimaced. "No, forget about Ragland. We'll take care of him. No, you mustn't . . . very well . . . they will help you finish Ragland. God cannot be mocked. I agree."

He disconnected. He was wringing his hands.

Aubrey said, "That last part . . . them helping him get Ragland. You were not being serious, I trust."

"No, no, that was only to shut the man up. I am not entirely stupid."

Aubrey picked up the pad with the address and the directions. He said, "What you are is entirely too modest. You have the makings of an adequate liar."

"Oh, shut up."

"Calling someone named Arnold Kaplan a Christian might strain this fellow's credulity a mite. On the whole, though, you didn't do badly."

Delbert Poole bit his lip. "You will see this to its end?"

"Oh, yes. And with dispatch. When Lockwood checks in, I will give him his instructions. I will have him take hold of your lunatic friend and—"

Poole's hands went to his ears. "Just . . . deal with it. Please."

"Good as done," said Aubrey. He rubbed his palms together. "Now let's go and have a look in your safe."

22

Kate Geller was airborne, somewhere over Missouri. She could hardly believe that she was doing this. She supposed that she'd panicked when she couldn't reach Claudia and when Harry said that he couldn't either.

At two in the morning, half asleep, bad dreams, she thought, What's the harm in booking a flight? She probably wouldn't take it; they were probably just fine, but she thought she'd feel better if she had one reserved. She got up and went into her computer.

The earliest flights, it showed, were all full. One departure would leave Denver at 6:10 A.M. nonstop to Atlanta, change planes to Savannah. From Savannah there was an air taxi service that would take her to Hilton Head Island. Given on-time connections, no major delays, she could be there by 2 P.M. Eastern.

This was silly, she thought. All those hours in the air.

Then showing up and learning that she'd done it for nothing. She'd arrive at—where was it?—the Palmetto Bay Marina and find them both sunning themselves on the deck. Too dumb, she thought. It made much more sense to stay put by the phone. On the other hand, it would be a nice surprise. It had been much too long since she'd seen them.

Okay, she decided. She would book it just in case. She wait-listed herself on the six-ten flight and on one that would leave at seven-fifty. Harry called once again, still no luck getting through, and she told him she was thinking of grabbing a flight. He said don't, just sit tight, he'd get back to her.

Now she was wide awake. She flipped on the TV. Perhaps there would be more news of the shooting. She surfed all the channels and found one station that was showing the restaurant where the shooting took place. Police cars all around it, windows shot out. The camera scanned the restaurant; she could see inside. She saw an ambulance crew taking one victim out and policemen milling around. There were people at the bar. A couple. Just a glimpse. Then the camera swept past them. All she saw, really, were the tops of their heads. They were both hunched over the bar, looking down, as if having a private conversation. The woman wore a green blouse. Her hair was something like Claudia's. Several shades darker, but that might have been the lighting. And the man's shoulders seemed considerably narrower than Adam's, but of course that's what happens when you hunch them. Still, it could have been Adam. It could well have been them both.

She wished that she'd recorded the segment she'd just seen. She could play it back freeze-framed and be more certain. She turned on her recorder and stayed with that station, but the segment was not shown again.

By then it was almost five in the morning. She threw a bag together and drove to the airport. She told herself, "What you're doing is stupid. You're letting your imagination run wild, convincing yourself that that had to have been Claudia. You saw her for maybe a half second. Go back home. Get some sleep. Wait for Harry to call. You probably won't get a flight anyway."

But there she was; she was almost at the terminal. She found herself parking and going inside. She found herself watching as the Delta flight boarded and she heard the clerk call for any wait-listed passengers. Before she knew it, she was on board. What the heck, she decided. This visit's overdue. She would try them again from the plane.

She fell asleep in an aisle seat. By the time she woke it was two hours later. She checked her watch. Half past ten, Eastern time. The seat back in front of her held a phone. She tried the boat's number; same result, no one answered. She considered calling Harry Whistler again, but Harry, she assumed, would not have gotten through either. And he'd probably give her a good bawling out for getting on that plane without telling him. She'd be there in a few hours. She would call Harry then. She would call him as soon as she saw for herself that his son and her daughter were well.

An ocean and part of two continents away, Harry Whistler was having misgivings of his own. Adam had assured him that he wasn't involved in that mess of the previous evening. But Adam had seemed just a trifle too breezy in dismissing his father's concerns.

The more he thought of it, however, the more he felt sure that Adam was probably telling the truth. Even if Adam had been near the scene, he would have known enough to mind his own business. Secondly, he'd know better than to get involved with a high-profile character like Ragland. Add to that, the assailants had since been identified as a pair of religious fanatics. Two men he'd never heard of from a church he'd never heard of. No conceivable connection with Adam.

He placed a call to Kate to tell her as much. He could now tell her that they're fine, they're having breakfast, not to worry. The boat's out at anchor; they're out of harm's way, not that there was any harm in the first place.

No answer from Kate. He got her machine. It was barely

after six in the morning, her time. He said, "Oh, Kate, please tell me you didn't. Please tell me that you're not on an airplane." He tried her twice more; still no answer.

He went to his computer and hit several keys. A long list of codes filled the screen. He chose one of these and hit several more keys. A list of flights came on. He typed in one more code. This time a passenger list filled the screen. He scanned it and muttered, "Goddamn it."

He tried the boat again and got another machine. He tried Adam's cell phone. Again, there was no answer. With a growl, he cursed Adam under his breath. When he'd asked him to leave the phone on from now on, that meant be available, be reachable. He slid his chair to a different screen. He typed in another series of digits and waited for a blip to appear on the monitor. It appeared, but the boat's position had changed. The boat seemed to be back at its slip.

He returned to his console, hit a few more keys, this time the code for a pager. In less than a minute, his telephone rang. Donald Beasley was calling him back.

"Donald, I'm afraid I need to fly to the States. This is very short notice, but can you two go with me?"

"You gotta ask? Yeah. But how short? Like right now?"

"Oh, heck. Never mind. This doesn't make any sense."

"It's Adam again, right?"

"That's the thing. I don't know."

He explained, very briefly, the who, what, and where. He told Donald about his exchanges with Kate. He'd confirmed, he said, that she was en route. She would get there and find that there was nothing amiss. All this flying around would be pointless.

"Yeah, might be," said Donald. "But you got a bad feeling?"

"With nothing whatsoever to support it."

"Nah, that ain't you. There's something. What is it?"

"Well, whatever it is, I can't pin it down. There's a dim little light that keeps blinking in my brain. I move toward it, but it just floats away."

"Some connection between Adam and this guy that got shot?"

"I think so. I just can't seem to place it."

Donald said, "Harry, you know what I think? I think you worry too much about Adam."

"Yeah, maybe."

"That one time a year ago, when Claudia got shot, he wasn't thinking straight and I don't blame him. But you didn't raise any pussycat, Harry. Adam's good. He can handle himself."

"He . . . always could when he's been on his own. But, Donald, you just said it. He's got Claudia to take care of."

"Meaning what? She gets hurt and he'll lose it again? Harry, it was you who put them together. It's a little late to have second thoughts."

Harry said, "Oh, I'm not. At least not about that. She's the best thing that's happened to him."

"Maybe all it is . . . you miss him. It's been a long time."

"Yeah, it has been. And I do." Harry paused for a moment. "I don't suppose you know anything about churches."

"Now you want to talk churches? Like what? What they teach?"

"Ever heard of the Reconstructionist Church?"

"I don't think so. What's that? Like a cult?"

Harry shrugged. "All religions started off being cults. No, you wouldn't know anything about churches."

"I wouldn't? Who says? Me and Dennis grew up Catholic."

Harry blinked. "You're kidding. Did you really?"

"Yeah, we did. With the nuns. And then the Jesuits after that. Me and Dennis even served Mass a few years."

"You're . . . telling me that you were an altar boy, Donald?"

"What, you don't believe me? I could give you some Latin. Back then, all the priests always asked for me and Dennis. They liked that we came as a set."

Harry chuckled at the vision that had formed in his mind.

"See that? You laugh. But you seen us in church. We went with you at least three times I can think of."

Silly me, thought Harry. In fact, they had. They'd been to his wedding when he married Andrea. And then to her funeral. And to Alicia's a year later. He damned sure didn't want to add Adam's.

"Hey, Harry?"

"Hmm?"

"Where'd this church question come from?"

"I don't know. It's that dim little light I can't reach. Forget it. It's probably nothing."

"You keep saying nothing, but it's something. Let's go. Worst case will be that we wasted a plane ride, not to mention forty grand worth of fuel."

"Yeah, I guess."

"Except . . . you feel up to it? How's your back?"

"It's holding up."

"Maybe just me and Dennis should go. How 'bout that?"

"And leave me sitting here? I'd go nuts."

"Okay, but figure ten hours is the soonest we could be there. That gets us in when?"

"Early evening their time."

"Are you worried what can happen in the meanwhile? Ten hours?"

"Yeah, I am. I suppose that I am."

"So call Bannerman. He could have someone there in, like, two. You thought about that, am I right?"

"Yes, I have."

"So make the call."

"About something as insubstantial as this?"

"Harry, the guy is a family man himself. Him and Susan have a kid of their own. He'll understand."

"More likely, he'll think I must be losing my grip."

"No, no. What he'll think is Harry Whistler is his friend and Bannerman takes care of his friends. He came through for you in Denver, am I right?"

"That was real."

A patient sigh. "Let me ask it this way. Let's say Carla Benedict came over to, say, Munich. The next day it's on the news that some guys got cut up. A female assailant; the cops don't know who. Bannerman hears about this and he starts to wonder if maybe, just maybe, these guys pissed her off."

"Because she's in the same city?"

"Same country. Wouldn't matter. His head tells him, no, this is crazy, no way. But his head then reminds him that she's not tightly wrapped and that when we hear 'knife,' we think 'Carla.' Now—don't misunderstand me. Me and Dennis like Carla. So, when I say that the lady is not tightly wrapped, you know I'm not trying to be negative."

"I hear you."

"Who would Bannerman call to get this checked out? No-brainer. It's you. Same with him."

"Yeah, you're right."

"No question."

"Um . . . Donald?"

"What?"

"This example you used—Carla Benedict in Munich—that was strictly hypothetical, correct?"

"It was just a for-instance. It could have been Zurich."

"Donald, what I meant . . ." Harry sighed. "Never mind."

"You gonna call him?"

"I'll try him right now."

"We using the Gulfstream? I'll see it's gassed up. Talk to Bannerman, then be ready in about twenty minutes. Me and Dennis are outside in twenty minutes."

Harry Whistler had tried to reach the boat one more time before placing his call to Paul Bannerman. As with Kate, he got Adam's machine. He again tried Adam's cell phone. The result was the same. Adam, he thought, could have no excuse for not at least having his cell phone at hand. And why, he wondered, had they brought the boat in? Why, for that matter, had he moved in the first place?

He knew that he was getting himself worked up and that it was probably over nothing. But he said he'd call Bannerman and he would.

At this hour, Bannerman should be at his office on the Post Road in Westport, Connecticut. Bannerman had bought a travel agency there. He'd chosen that business, well . . . because he'd been everywhere, but largely because of the computers. No one ever wonders why a travel firm would need so many computers. Bannerman, like himself, believed in keeping in touch. He liked to know what was going on in the world and especially what was happening around him.

A number of his people owned other small businesses. There were a few shops, a restaurant, one worked as an electrician, and one had joined the police force. The electrician, by now, had probably wired every building whose occupants were of interest to him, including, of course, police headquarters. But primarily, Bannerman had acquired these businesses for them in the hope of keeping them busy, out of trouble. And to make friends. And to spread themselves around. And to avoid congregating together too much, the better to melt into the community.

It worked up to a point. Most behaved, by and large. And nearly all of them started to make friends. Bannerman had assumed that this was a good thing until one of his people, one Billy McHugh, was revealed to have been thinning the town's population for the benefit of his new friends. Bannerman blamed himself. He thought he should have known. Billy was a huge man, about fifty years old, whom many thought of as a monster. He'd probably never had a normal friend in his life, but he was loyal to Bannerman to the death. Bannerman had put him to work tending bar in a restaurant that was run by Molly Farrell. He thought that regular interaction with customers might elicit a few social skills.

Mario's? Yes, Mario's. That was the restaurant. It was down by the Westport railroad station, very popular with the locals and commuters. Over time these regulars had come to know Billy, and some, inevitably, started telling him their troubles. Some would tell him the troubles of others. A woman, for example, might have just left the bar and a customer might say to him, "There goes Sally, poor gal. She's afraid to go home. Her husband beats the shit out of her for no reason. It's a shame. Somebody ought to do something."

Any other bartender might listen and sympathize, but Billy, his concept of friendship still evolving, undertook to

solve some of their problems. He solved ten or eleven before
Molly caught on. She confronted him, then had to tell Bannerman.

Bannerman was unhappy with him, to say the least. But
Bannerman soon had more to worry about than the recent
rash of "suicides" and "accidental deaths," all of which Billy
admitted. He soon had to fight a short but bloody war
against those who wondered why he'd come back to this
country and just couldn't believe that he had no grand
scheme except to try to live a quiet life.

If they couldn't believe that Bannerman was *just* a travel
agent, and if they couldn't believe that Molly Farrell was *just*
a restaurateur, imagine the trouble that they had believing that
Carla was just a librarian. Well, not now, but she had been. She
had always liked books. However, she always kept her books
locked away because she thought that if others knew what she
read, they would know far too much about her. The fact is that
her tastes were in no way bizarre. It was not as if her shelves
were lined with books that explored her own abnormal psy-
chology. She read good literature, mostly, and some history, bi-
ography, and she loved the poems of Elizabeth Barrett
Browning. She couldn't read those without crying.

Carla solved her need to keep her reading habits private
by opening a small bookstore in town. Just as no one would
wonder about Bannerman's computers, no one, she reasoned, ever thinks twice about what a bookseller reads. Her
partner in the bookstore, and apparently in her life, was the
KGB major whom she'd nearly shot to death when—

The phone was ringing. His call had gone through. The
travel agency's receptionist had answered. He said his name;
she asked him to hold; she'd said, "You'll want a private
line. Just one moment."

In a blink, Harry heard Paul Bannerman come on. "Hello,
Harry. Glad you called; I've been thinking about you."

Bannerman always spoke in a calm, quiet voice. It had
often reminded him of Adam's. Same gray eyes as well.
Very soft, oddly gentle except when they weren't. He could
have been Adam's older brother.

They exchanged a few pleasantries. How was Susan? How's the family? He learned that Bannerman's daughter just had her sixth birthday and that Susan was pregnant again.

Susan's father, Raymond Lesko, a great bear of a man, was then living in Switzerland himself. He was a former New York cop who once nearly killed Bannerman after someone else had nearly killed Susan in reprisal for something that Bannerman had done. It wasn't Bannerman's fault, but we know how fathers are. In any case, it worked out; a friendship gradually developed, and Lesko—who had been long divorced from Susan's mother—married into the powerful Brugg family of Zurich. In fact, Lesko and the former Elena Brugg then went on to have a child of their own. Late in life. Harry, who had often had dealings with the Bruggs, had been invited to attend the child's christening. Since then, he and Lesko had become friends themselves.

Bannerman asked about Adam and Claudia. "Still together? It's been what—about a year?"

"Just about."

"Well? Is it working out as you'd hoped?"

"Yeah, it is," Harry told him. "I think it's made all the difference. I think he's grown up a lot."

"Grown up?"

"Well . . . let's say that it's made him more balanced."

"Harry, Adam's a long way from being a kid. You're the only one who thinks of him that way."

"You never thought there was something . . . incomplete about Adam?"

"Like in you before Andrea? Like in me before Susan?"

"Me, especially, but good point," Harry answered.

"You can't be Adam's father forever, Harry."

"Yeah, I can. So will you be. Wait and see."

"Well, anyway," said Bannerman, "his year's almost over. Are you still planning to bring him in with you?"

"It might take a little selling, but yes."

"And what about Claudia?" Bannerman asked. "Do you think she'll stick with him?"

"I hope so. I'm betting that she will."

"At least as long as she thinks she's his guardian angel. Does she still?"

"She more than thinks it; she's sure of it."

Bannerman said, "Well, then maybe she is. I'll tell you who believes it. It's Carla. Carla says Viktor had a similar experience after she put those holes in his chest. Viktor saw the white light himself."

"You're saying Viktor came back as her guardian angel?"

"No, he was only told that he should forgive her and that Carla should stop sending people his way."

"Whose way? Viktor's?"

"No, the white light's. So now she only tries to cut them. I suppose that's progress," said Bannerman with a sigh. "I mean, it's not up there with the conversion of Saul, but she has developed a spiritual side. She's been doing a good deal of reading about it. Carla's sorry that she never met Claudia, by the way. She said that she'd like to compare notes."

"That . . . sort of brings up the reason I'm calling. Adam and Claudia are back in the state. They're down on Hilton Head Island."

"Oh, really?"

Harry Whistler took the 'Oh, really?' to mean that Bannerman had been watching the news about the shooting. Bannerman added, "Small world."

"Well, it isn't that small. And neither is that island. The place must get a million tourists a year and—"

"Even so, you think Adam had a hand in it?"

"I asked him; he said no, but I'm not sure I believe him. Now you'll ask me why I doubt him and I simply don't know, but Adam's been making himself hard to reach. And my friend, Kate Geller—"

"The girl's mother?"

"Uh-huh."

"Is that 'friend' as in 'lady friend'?" Bannerman asked.

"Okay, more than a friend. And she doesn't like it either."

Kate Geller, he explained, was on an airplane at that moment. She'd arrive, assuming that her flights were on schedule, on the island in roughly two hours. He said she'd flown there against his advice. He could reach her on the plane, but it would do little good. Having come that far, she'd keep coming.

Bannerman asked, "So you're coming yourself?"

"Yeah, I am."

"With the twins?"

"Yes."

"And this is all on gut feel. You have no reason to think that this has touched you or Adam. Aside from Olivia, I mean."

"Aside from who?"

"Olivia Ragland. She's what I meant by 'small world.' "

"You're . . . talking about Ragland's wife? What about her?"

"You do remember her, don't you?"

"Paul, I have never met Ragland or his wife. And Adam said he'd never even heard of them."

"You may not have met Ragland, but you have met his wife. Her maiden name was Torrey. Olivia Torrey. She worked as a BBC stringer, remember? Harry, she's been to your house."

"Wait a minute."

"And she and Molly Farrell have been friends for fifteen years. Molly's been trying to call her all morning. They met at about the same time."

He did not remember. No, wait. Yes, he did. And Adam could have met her as well.

He said, "Paul, this is bothering me more by the minute. Too many dots are starting to connect."

"I know, I'm getting that feeling myself. But how do the Recons fit in?"

"The what?"

"The shooters. Those two Reconstructionist characters."

Recons, thought Harry.

Recon-JC.

Aubrey's ledger. Those entries. Joshua Crow. Recon-JC was that dim little light that kept floating just out of reach.

"Harry?" Bannerman had heard the silence. "Did you just connect another dot?"

"Yeah, I might have. That ledger that started all this. Either Adam knows damned well how this all ties together or he's out on a limb and he has no idea. Kate Geller sure as hell doesn't."

"So you're . . . thinking Felix Aubrey is behind the try on Ragland. Just to shut Ragland up? Why would he bother?"

"I don't know. You're right. It wouldn't make any sense."

"We both might be reaching. Just as I did last summer. You remember. That business with Carla."

Harry felt his stomach tighten. "What business was that?"

"Those two knifings in Zurich. I guess you were away; I spoke to one of the twins. Knowing Carla was there, it seemed worth checking out."

"Oh, yeah." Oh, for Christ's sake. "Yeah, they told me she was clean."

"So I owe you. Tell me what you need."

23

The plane that Lockwood had taken to get to the island was one of two aircraft in the Center's employ. Both were kept in a hangar out at Ronald Reagan Airport. Both always had a pilot on standby. This was the little one, the Lear, their smallest model. He didn't like to use it, not because of its size, but because its pilot was a pain in the ass who didn't always do as he was told.

He preferred the bigger one, the Hawker 700. He liked that one's crew a lot better. The Hawker had been seized from an air charter service out in Oklahoma somewhere. A residue of cocaine had been found in its baggage hold and its owner had been unable to account for it. Its pilot and co-pilot, the same two as now, were the ones who had planted the cocaine residue and then blew the whistle on their boss.

What they got in return was a soft job with Aubrey and a portion of the Hawker's market value. And that wasn't even the best part. Once the Hawker was signed over to the Center, it became immune to further searches and sniffs. That meant that the crew could moonlight running drugs with zero risk of ever getting nailed. Lockwood had to like people with that kind of initiative as long as they knew where their bread is buttered.

It was those two who flew him out to Denver last year. It was also them who got him out of there fast when the shit hit the fan in Silver Ridge. They didn't argue when he said, "Let's get out of here. Now." They didn't ask him, "We don't wait for Briggs?" They just went. They were not like the jerk who flew the Lear.

But the Lear was heading down to Florida anyway, so Aubrey told him to use that one. Lockwood asked, "He drops me off? Then how do I get back?" Aubrey answered, "Buy a ticket."

Little shit. That's what he said.

The flight to Hilton Head took an hour and a half. The Hawker could have made it in an hour. Before landing, he told the pilot to make a low pass over Palmetto Bay. He wanted to try to spot Whistler's boat. The pilot said he had to circle in from that direction anyway, but not below eight hundred feet. The pilot said, "You want lower? Use binoculars."

Someday soon, thought Lockwood, he would knock this guy's teeth out.

But for now he would let him have his way.

Whistler's boat was not where Kaplan said it would be. It wasn't out at anchor, but Lockwood did spot it. The boat was on its way in. He could make out Whistler and the girl at the wheel. Or rather Whistler was steering. She was standing behind him. She had her arms around his waist and her face up by his neck as if she was cooing in his ear. From a thousand feet up, Lockwood couldn't be sure, but he didn't think Whistler looked happy.

You want to see unhappy? I'll show you unhappy. Lockwood wished that this thing carried napalm.

The Lear was down within another five minutes. As it taxied toward the terminal, Lockwood spotted Arnold Kaplan. Couldn't miss him. He was waiting on the Tarmac.

Lockwood, on the whole, was satisfied with Kaplan. You could give him a job to do and it's done. Three things, however. He argued too much. That time they were waiting for Whistler on his roof, Lockwood nearly threw him off for all his bitching. The second thing was that he wore stupid clothes. He liked to wear hats like Greg Norman, the golfer. Flat hats, wide brim, curled up at the tips. He wore horn-rimmed glasses, big frames, red lenses. And he always wore these ugly sport jackets that had patterns that looked like they came from a beach chair. You could spot him in a crowd a mile away.

These were not the best outfits to wear on surveillance, but he couldn't make Kaplan understand that. Kaplan did, however, know a little about bugging. He didn't know a lot, not as much as he claimed. Aubrey was actually right about that. Most of what Kaplan knew, he had learned on his own. He got books about it from Delta Press; it's a catalog that sells manuals on shit like that, including how to make bombs. Also, he'd hang around Radio Shack trying every new eavesdropping toy they got in.

"You know the tap on the mother? It's better now. It's good." Kaplan said this as Lockwood climbed out of the plane and waited for the overnight bag he'd brought with him.

"Never mind out there. Let's just worry about here."

"No, listen; this is good. I just got off the phone."

"Tell me in the car. Let's get down by that dock."

Kaplan's car was the third thing. He always drove a big Cadillac, a red one, no less. Try to tell the guy he looks like a pimp and he says, "That's the point. It helps me stand out. That's until I don't want to stand out anymore. After that, I go "poof." I disappear.

What he meant, not that Lockwood thought it made any sense, was that all people see is the wrapping. Take away the wrapping; he's invisible. He had once said to Lockwood, "Look at you, for example. All the time these black suits. Your idea of changing outfits is to buy a new belt. It's like wearing a sign that says, 'I'm a fed' because that's how feds dress in the movies."

He was right about one thing. Black suits look official. For a long time he wore dark glasses as well because dark glasses make people nervous. But then one day Briggs told him he had scary eyes. Briggs said, "You got eyes that look at people like they're already dead. They even scare me. You should use that. Lose the shades." This was back before Briggs became a wuss.

They had reached Kaplan's car. Kaplan said, "Can I finish?"

Lockwood lit a cigar. "Go ahead. Someone called you?"

"I was saying," Kaplan told him, "that I just got off the phone with the guy who's been monitoring her calls."

"You mean the mother."

Kaplan nodded. "Correct." He said he thinks the mother might be on her way here. Maybe even Whistler's father, from the sound of it. "On top of that, something else is going on here. There was a very strange meeting on that boat this morning. This deputy sheriff; he's that sergeant, the black guy. He goes out to see Whistler along with the barmaid and one of the owners from the bar where this happened."

"Wait a minute. They had a meeting? You saw this?"

Kaplan nodded. "Through binocs. But I saw it."

"Fucking Aubrey. I told him. He thought it was bullshit."

"I saw what I saw. But wait, let's back up. Let me finish with the mother and the father."

"Fucking Aubrey."

"The mother calls the father, like at midnight last night. She gets him in Geneva, where it's dawn. She says she's calling him because she can't get through to Whistler. She asks the father, did he hear about the shooting? She says she just saw it on TV out there. The father says, yeah, he just heard."

"That's all he says?"

"Well, mostly he's trying to calm the mother down. She says she's trying not to worry, but she's getting a bad feeling. She knows who Ragland is and she knows what he's against. He's on this crusade against the drug laws and seizures and against guys like you who don't want them changed because then you'd have to steal someplace else, no offense. She knows that him and Whistler seem to have a lot in common because Whistler's no pal of yours either. She says she also remembers saying to Whistler, 'Try not to get my daughter shot again, okay?' The father tells her that no way would his kid put her in danger, but he says, don't worry, he'll check."

"So he calls Whistler?"

"He tried. He couldn't get through either. He calls her back an hour or so later and he says he'll keep trying, but he's sure it's okay. He says she shouldn't jump to conclusions. He says his kid wouldn't go to someone like Ragland without talking it over with him. He says he'd certainly never get the girl mixed up in it."

"Then his father's lying or he doesn't know dick about what his son turned her into."

"I saw her in action, remember? Let me finish."

Lockwood twirled a finger. "Short version, okay?"

"What am I, *Reader's Digest?* Details are important."

"Get to where the two parents are on their way here."

"Well, the mother's bad feeling isn't going away. She tells the father she's tempted to jump on a plane and go down there and see for herself. Whistler's father says don't, but maybe she did. The father tried to get her this morning, her time, and all he gets is her answering machine. He says, 'Kate, pick up, or call me right back so I'll know you didn't do something foolish.' He says, 'Kate, I spoke to him. His phone had been off. Don't worry, they had nothing to do with that shooting. Everything seems to be fine.' "

"So . . . he's lying to her?"

"Or his son lied to him. You want my guess? It's his son lied to him. Because then he sounded like he's starting to wonder. He starts to say, 'Okay, maybe I'd better . . .' but he doesn't finish the sentence. I think he's going to fly over himself. What else would follow 'Maybe I'd better'?"

"Did you check with the airlines?"

"I got somebody on it. If I'm right, she gets here this afternoon sometime. The father gets here early this evening at best."

Time difference, thought Lockwood. They're all here by tonight, maybe all on that boat. That's why Whistler's bringing it back to the dock. This could be too good to pass up.

The boat reminded him. "You said Whistler had a meeting?"

"With this deputy who questioned him after the shooting. Also with the barmaid I told you about. Also with her boss from the restaurant."

"That's this morning?"

"Cozy, right? They all met for breakfast."

"But what for? Why the meeting?"

"Ask me, I'd have said to get their stories straight," said Kaplan. "Remember, all three of them covered for Whistler. Whistler and the girl don't get a peep on the news. Here's the question. Why should these three people cover? What is Whistler to them?"

"You got an answer?"

"Yeah, I do. It's like I thought. Gotta be they're old friends. Gotta be they knew him from way before this."

"Except Whistler's a loner. He doesn't have any friends."

"Vernon . . . they're out there having breakfast on his boat. He takes the boat out there, he shuts off his phones, and they're having this meeting, passing papers around. Does that sound antisocial to you?"

Lockwood's mind had been elsewhere. "Wait a second. What papers?"

"How would I know what papers? I'm on shore with binocs."

"Well, the stack—was it thick? Like they copied, say, a book?"

Kaplan blinked. He asked, "What book would that be?"

"There's this book Whistler stole. It's none of your business. But did it look thick like a book?"

"I couldn't see."

"The cop who was there. What did you learn about him?"

"I asked around a little. That was all I had time for. I found out he was army before he was a cop. I found out he was over in Iraq for Desert Storm. Whistler, too, am I right? Whistler did Special Ops. The cop could have been in Whistler's outfit over there. It's a stretch, but it wouldn't surprise me."

Lockwood grunted, then shrugged. In his head he could see Felix Aubrey's lip curling. *"Mr. Lockwood, we had more than a half million troops there. That is hardly a definitive connection."*

He asked, "The barmaid. You get anything on her?"

"Hard to say. She comes and goes. She seems to travel a lot. She doesn't work anywhere full-time."

"She travels, huh? Like where and for what? Is she maybe an advance man for Whistler?"

"Um, Vern . . . she tends bar. Whistler drinks in that bar. Let's not make any huge fucking leaps here."

"Yeah, but say she knew him before. Say she's a lot more than you think."

"Like what, for instance? She also waits tables?"

"That woman, the knife, who cut Briggs and Aubrey. No one knows what she looks like. What if this could be her?"

Kaplan grimaced. "I think you need a nap."

"No, let's run with this a minute. Say you think that's who she is. Say maybe you were wrong about who threw that knife. Say maybe it turned out to be her."

"Um . . . except we know it wasn't. This is make-believe, right?"

"What we're doing is maybe improvising a little. What would Aubrey do if he thought it was her?"

"Vern . . . her who did what? You're losing me here."

"Her who did all of it. Her who cut Aubrey."

"First you're thinking it's the mother, then you're thinking it's the daughter. The daughter, since last night, becomes the much better bet."

"The daughter's got an alibi from when she got shot. I forgot that. She couldn't have done it."

"So you're going to go to Aubrey and say, 'Hey, guess what? I narrowed down the suspects; here's where I come out. The knife had to be someone who knows Whistler, correct? Who'd know the guy better than his bartender, right?' Vern, you're asking to be shit on again."

"We'll get proof."

"What proof?"

"I don't know. I have to think."

"Explain to me, though. The point of this is . . . ?"

"To get Felix Aubrey off his ass, is the point. This could do it. This could just maybe do it."

"Vern, you gotta trust me. This is too fucking dumb."

"Arnold, you never had your balls cut off, did you? It does things to your cogitative faculties."

"Your what?"

"It fucks you up, Arnold. Read a book, for Christ's sake."

Lockwood opened the overnight bag that he'd brought. On top was a pistol that he'd wrapped in a towel, along with spare clips and a silencer. Underneath were several cellular phones. He selected the one that was marked with an "A." It was specially coded. It reached only one party. He flipped it open and pressed the redial button.

"Vern, who are you calling?"

"Aubrey said to check in; I'm checking in."

"Hey, do me a favor. Leave me out of this, okay?"

"You kidding? It's you who gave me the idea."

"Take credit. With my blessing. You got my permission."

"You want to quit whining?"

"Take that nap first, okay?"

Lockwood raised a hand, telling Kaplan to shut up as he heard Aubrey's voice saying, "Speak."

"Mr. Aubrey? It's me. Are you sitting down? You're not going to believe what I found out here."

"No, no, no, Mr. Lockwood. Put all that aside."

Felix Aubrey had listened with growing dismay to the

drone of Vern the Burn's recitation. The mother coming, maybe. The father coming, maybe. Adam Whistler and his out-of-thin-air co-conspirators meeting for breakfast to plan their next move. The proof? They were seen with sheets of paper. The boat is at the dock, now an easier target. We finish them all when they get here—and a bonus. Jill the Ripper has at last been unmasked. She is revealed to be some cocktail waitress who has honed her skills in an island saloon by sectioning lemons and limes.

The man's a marvel, thought Aubrey. Never fails to astonish.

"Mr. Lockwood—now listen. There is more urgent business. I want you to put Whistler out of your mind."

"You don't care we know who cut you? I got sources. It's her."

"And of course I believe you." You damned fool, thought Felix Aubrey. "But even she can wait. This is much more immediate. Do you have a street map? Look up Lagoon Road. Yes, I'll wait. You want number twenty-two."

Aubrey drummed his fingers until Lockwood came back on. Lockwood said, "Yeah, I got it. What's there?"

"Not a what; it's a who. A very dangerous man; his name is Joshua Crow. He is one of the two who tried to kill Mr. Ragland. As we speak, he is waiting for you and your associate. Listen carefully now. Are you listening?"

"I'm listening, but how did you know this?"

"He was identified this morning. It's been on the news. I need you to see that he harms no one else. Am I clear in my meaning, Mr. Lockwood?"

"Yeah, but wait a second. What's this guy to us?"

"You need only know that we don't want him found. I am giving you that task, Mr. Lockwood."

"This . . . phone we're on. You're sure this is private?"

"Mr. Lockwood, you have just proposed a mass murder. Only now do you ask if this phone is secure? If you're speaking to me on the phone that you were issued, yes, I assure you, it's secure."

"Yeah, okay, then what's this 'Am I clear in my meaning?' You're so sure, let's hear you say it in plain English."

"I suppose I'd best," said Aubrey. "There must be no mistake. Mr. Crow is to vanish, never more to be seen."

"That's not plain English. That's like 'Get him out of town.' "

Aubrey sighed. "Never mind then. The reward will go elsewhere. It is double the amount that you're accustomed to, Vernon. Tell you what—let me speak to your associate."

"What for?"

"You said he's a man who does what needs to be done. Perhaps I don't need you, Mr. Lockwood."

"Yeah, well, he works for me. You want to deal, deal through me. What he'd get, though . . . it's extra? Not out of my end."

"It is extra. In this case, twenty thousand."

"And all we got to do is—"

"Kill the man, Mr. Lockwood. See that he is no more. End his life. Do away with him. Rub the man out. Have I covered every nuance, Mr. Lockwood?"

"Yeah, I get you."

"Make him vanish, Mr. Lockwood. Do it now; do it thoroughly. You're to leave no trace that a man such as this ever blemished the bosom of mankind."

"That he what?"

"No trace, Mr. Lockwood. Not so much as a footprint. Especially any papers, communications devices, any diary, if he has one. Every trace."

"Hang on a sec, okay? I gotta confer."

Aubrey heard a tiny blip as Lockwood pressed his mute button so that he could speak privately with his man. Typical of Lockwood, thought Aubrey. The man sees a mute button on a phone that he's been issued and assumes that the mute function actually mutes. He's never wondered why anyone would issue a phone that is capable of excluding the issuer. Aubrey's own did work, of course. Lockwood couldn't hear him. But he could hear Lockwood's every word.

"Did you know they made the shooters?" Lockwood asked his man, Kaplan.

"Yeah, a little while ago. Guy named Breen's the one who took the knife in his head. Guy named Crow is the leader. He's still on the loose."

"Nice that you told me. Next time tell me these things."

"Okay, but so what? What are these guys to you?"

"I'll tell you what they are." Lockwood gestured toward his cell phone. "You know what this sounds like, what Aubrey is saying? This sounds like Aubrey sent these guys after Ragland. They fucked up; now Aubrey doesn't want them caught and questioned. He wants us to pop the one named Crow."

Kaplan said, "Did I tell you? I *thought* it was us. You remember I said why I didn't hang around is because I thought that maybe it was us."

"Wait a minute," said Lockwood. "It could not have been Aubrey. Aubrey didn't know about any of this until I told him myself."

"Maybe that was an act."

"Nah, he didn't know. He asked all kinds of questions. If he knew, he'd have just made some faggy little crack like, 'We have it well in hand, Mr. Lockwood.' "

"But it's him who wants him whacked. He didn't tell you how come?"

Aubrey almost could hear Lockwood's primitive brain struggling to achieve a synapsis. Success came more quickly than Aubrey would have thought. Lockwood asked, "Hey, wait; what did you say the guy yelled? I mean the one who walked in and shot Ragland."

"I said I couldn't make it out, but it sounded like a curse. On the news, though, they say he yelled, 'God is not mocked.' "

"A religious nut?"

"Yeah, they're both religious nuts. All this has been on the news."

Aubrey listened as Lockwood thought for a moment. Lockwood said, "Wait a second." He pressed the mute button. He said, "Mr. Aubrey? Give us one more minute. We're strategizing, okay?"

"Take your time, Mr. Lockwood. Think it through, by all means." Lockwood pressed his useless mute button once more.

Lockwood said to Kaplan, "That's the answer. Religious. It had to be Poole who sent these two after Ragland. Aubrey knows this and now he has to cover for Poole."

"Poole's the same kind of nut?"

"I used to think he just talks it, but, yeah, I think it finally messed with his head. Whatever he is, he controls all the money. If Aubrey's doing this to cover for Poole, Aubrey's getting a bundle for doing it."

"So?"

"Maybe we have an opportunity here. I gotta think about this."

"Speaking of which," said Kaplan, "you were talking about my end. How much is my end if I help you with this?"

"Five grand. That's on top of what I pay you."

"Make it ten."

"It's ten," Lockwood answered, "if I like what you do. See that? I take care of you, right? After this—well, we'll see, but I'm getting some ideas. After this, you could make a lot more."

"After this comes Whistler?"

"I don't know yet. Let me think. Right now, let me get rid of Aubrey."

Felix Aubrey could barely restrain himself from screaming into the phone. He wanted to say, "Mr. Lockwood, you ass, did you hear me when I told you not to think? You're not equipped for it. Your neurons fire blanks. The reason why you're always outsmarting yourself is that yourself is even denser than you are."

But he didn't.

Aubrey waited until he heard the mute button's blip. He asked, "Are you there, Mr. Lockwood?"

"Yeah, we're done."

"And your strategy, no doubt, is reduced to the following. You knock on Crow's door, you identify yourself. He will let you in because he expects you; he thinks that you've come to assist him. Without further ado, you will shoot him. You will

gather up everything belonging to him and you'll put it in a bag
to take with you. You put the bag and Mr. Crow in the trunk of
your car. Not his, your own; they'll be looking for his."

"Hey, I know how to do this, Mr. Aubrey."

"You will find a quiet spot; it will be well off that island,
and you will dismember his body. You'll dispose of those
parts that would aid the authorities in identifying the corpse.
Ideally, the body should be totally consumed along with the
contents of that bag. Is this your plan in essence, Mr. Lockwood?"

"Yeah, like that."

"And of course you wouldn't go back to that island.
There would be no need because—listen to me closely—I
have plans of my own for Adam Whistler. He's to be left in
peace for the moment."

"Left in peace? When we *have* him? I need twelve hours,
tops. Then we'll have every one of them all in one place."

"Mr. Lockwood, reflect. By no means do you have them.
What you have is a hope that they might be assembling. Further, you hope that they'll gather on that boat showing reck-
less disregard toward a foe of your caliber. You envision . . .
what? A frontal attack in a busy marina? Or perhaps you see
yourself rigging a bomb and blowing them out of the water."

"No bomb. Bomb's are quick. He's not going to die
quick."

"Ah, yes," recalled Aubrey, "you want him to suffer. And,
oh, you would like to rape the girl in his presence, then
slowly peel her face from her skull. Was that just the girl? Or
the mother as well? Forgive me, I had taken careful notes of
your fantasies, but I don't seem to have them at hand."

". . . Hey, screw you, Mr. Aubrey."

"Are you hearing me, you cretin?" Aubrey's voice became a hiss. "I've given you a task. Go and do it. Only that.
Don't go anywhere near Whistler. Don't depart from my instructions in any particular without calling to check with me
first. Am I clear?"

"We'll go get this Crow guy. After that, we're gonna
talk."

"I do so enjoy our exchanges, Mr. Lockwood. I'll be counting the hours. Good-bye."

24

Whistler was still grumbling as they got into their car and drove out of the Palmetto Bay Marina. He made a right turn toward the new Cross Island toll bridge. It was the shortest route to the hospital.

Claudia was pleased that he'd consented to take her. Consented, however, was not quite the word. If he hadn't, she'd have gone to see the Raglands on her own. He had lost that argument with her.

She'd said, "Adam, this is something that I have to do. I think I'm supposed to. Come with me."

He then tried to dissuade her by making a show of taking two weapons from the locker. They would not, he told her, go anywhere unarmed as long as Crow was at large. He had shoved his Beretta into his belt and he took the MAC-10 plus an extra clip. He placed the submachine pistol in a large canvas tote and covered it with a sail bag. He took both Kevlar vests and put one on himself, under a baggy gray sweatshirt. He insisted that she wear the other. He told her that he wanted her to keep the vest on until they set sail for Bermuda. He said he didn't care how hot she got. He said he didn't care if the vest made her look fat. That was the price she was going to pay for—

"Adam," she asked quietly, "what are you trying to do?"

"I'm trying to get it through your head that it's dangerous out there."

"Am I supposed to say, 'I guess you're right; it's not worth it'?"

In fact, that's exactly what he'd hoped.

She'd said, "Tell you what—let's not do this halfway.
Let's take the deck sweeper with us."

"Listen, Claudia . . ."

The gun locker was still open. She reached in and got it.
She squeezed it into the canvas tote. She said, "There. We're
covered. At short range, at least. But what if this Crow
plunks away from a distance? Then we'll want your big
rifle. You know, the *humane* one? Let's go. I'll carry it out to
the car."

She was up through the hatch with the M-87 before he
was able to stop her. He said, "Claudia, get back here. Don't
wave that around."

"Your trunk open?"

"No, it's locked. Bring that back."

"Adam, are you coming or must I go alone?"

By that time she was striding up the dock toward the
ramp with the sniper gun under her arm. She passed some
sailors who were hauling a boat, too busy to notice, thank
God. He had no time to lock up the boat, but he threw a coil
of line across the hatchway. He snatched up the tote and he
followed. They got to the car. It was close by, thanks again.
He opened the trunk; he'd lied about it being locked, and
threw all of the weaponry into it.

Claudia climbed into the passenger seat and waited for
him to join her. When he did, she poked his leg. She asked,
"Are you mad?"

He answered, "I'm not speaking to you."

"Yes, you are. You're going to remind me that I'm nuts."

"Nuts is what you are in general. This, specifically, is
willful. I am very upset with you, Claudia."

"If I hadn't grabbed those weapons, you'd still be back
there stalling. I have to go, but not without you."

"To willful, add scheming. And manipulative."

"Start the car. I promise to be good from now on."

"Will you do as I say?"

"I'll try to do as you ask. What is it that you'd like me
to do?"

That still sounded willful, but it opened the door. She

agreed that his wishes should not be ignored, especially regarding their mutual well-being. He outlined—suggested—
the rules of engagement. Having agreed that it did make
sense to go armed, she agreed that if the hospital had metal
detectors, they would abort the Ragland visit. If they got to
Ragland's floor and there were people in his room, they
would also abort and return.

"And if you see a camera of any description?"

She nodded. "We're out of there fast."

"And if Ragland is alone? Or just Ragland and his wife?"

"I go in by myself. You don't want to; that's okay, and I
only stop in for two minutes."

Fat chance that he'll be alone, thought Whistler. They'll
leave and maybe she'll come to her senses before any damage is done.

"And if he's alone, or only him and his wife?"

"I don't know. I'll just see what sort of feelings I get."

"No, you know what I mean. What are you going to say?"

"We tried not to get involved because you're a married
man. I'm not supposed to be with you. I'm a silly little
bimbo, but I did want to help. I learned first aid and CPR at
beautician school in Toledo. They made me take first aid because I wasn't good with scissors and I kept nipping off
parts of cars."

"Claudia . . ."

"As for you, you're a lawyer with three kids at home
and a wife who has all the money. She doesn't know that
you've been screwing her beautician. If she finds out,
she'll dump you and she'll take all your toys, including the
boat, which she owns, not you. You'll deserve it because
you're a scum-sucking rat, and, oh, by the way, I think I'm
pregnant."

"Um . . . Claudia . . ."

"If I have to be a bimbo, Adam, you can be a rat."

This was not, of course, what they had discussed. She
was simply to look in, say hello, how are you feeling?
Sergeant Moore said you wanted to thank me. The best way
to thank me is to say no more about it. We're very private

people and we hope you'll understand that we'd rather not be bothered by reporters. If the thrown knife comes up, she has no idea how anyone could think that she could do that. This would be a true statement. Well, sort of. If she's asked about the bullet she's supposed to have moved, that one's easy; just explain what really happened.

"I'm teasing you, Adam," she said. "I'll be good."

"Just remember. Two minutes. I'll be waiting down the hall."

Kaplan was almost sure that it was Whistler who passed them going northbound on the Cross Island Parkway. A beige Ford Taurus, man driving, woman with him, heading in the opposite direction.

"You're sure?" Lockwood asked.

"It looked like them, yeah. But, we're coming to the bridge. Let's see if their boat is still out there." The arching bridge afforded a view of Palmetto Bay and the Sound. Kaplan glanced toward the place where Whistler's boat had been anchored.

"Boat's gone. No, there it is. It's tied up at the fuel dock."

Lockwood said, "I know. I saw from the plane. You got any idea where they're going?"

"Who knows?"

"The airport, I bet. The mother's coming in, right? Let's go down there and check out the boat."

"Didn't Aubrey say don't go anywhere near?"

"That's near Whistler. He's not there. We just go look around."

"What, we go climb on board? What if that wasn't them? He sees you, he blows off the top of your head. How about we do what Aubrey says for a change?"

"Screw Aubrey."

Kaplan raised a hand. He said, "Vern, we're not stopping. If you do this, you are strictly on your own."

"You'll see who does the blowing. It's not going to be Whistler."

"Good. You can practice on the Crow guy."

"Why would Aubrey want to give Whistler a pass? What are these 'other plans' he says he has?"

"Ask him later. Right now, let's take care of the wacko."

From the bridge, they stayed on Palmetto Bay Road. Two miles farther, they approached Sea Pines Circle. "We go straight here," said Kaplan, "but just off to the right is where the shoot-'em-up was."

"Where? One of those buildings?"

"That bar on the end. Jump and Phil's."

Lockwood said, "Swing in there. Let's take a look."

"For what? It's boarded up."

"It's good I get the lay of the land here."

With a shrug, Kaplan turned to the right off the circle and proceeded for another hundred yards. He said, "On the left. See? Windows covered with plywood. Oh, wait. It looks like they're open."

There were outside tables on a tree-shaded terrace that was off to one side of the restaurant. There was an outdoor bar and a built-in TV for customers who wanted to watch sports events. A waitress was setting the tables for lunch and another was stocking the bar. The one at the bar was . . . oh, yeah . . . that girl, Leslie. The two owners were sweeping up the last of the glass.

"See the blond one?" Kaplan pointed. "That's the one who you tried to tell Aubrey was probably the one who carved him up. She look like a killer to you?"

"So, who does?"

"You, for one. It's like you're wearing a sign. You also can't get two whole sentences out without talking about killing someone."

"Whistler's girlfriend . . . she look like a killer to you?"

"Good point," said Kaplan. "Her, I wouldn't have guessed."

"Let's get closer to this one. I can't see her face."

"Vern, she can't see yours either. You should keep it that way."

"You said she was on the boat with Whistler and those others? Then she knows what that meeting was about."

"So we what? Order brunch? Ask if she'll fill us in?"

"Just go in and swing around so I can see."

Kaplan did as he was told, but he didn't like it. He didn't need Leslie to look up and spot him. She knew his face from all those times at the bar. She'd probably noticed his red Cadillac from all the times he'd pulled up in it. She'd remember how he ducked out last night before the police could show up. It could enter her head to take down his plate number and give it to that cop friend of hers. Not likely, but possible. Why take the chance?

"Which reminds me," he told Lockwood, "we have to boost another car."

"What's the matter with this one?"

"We're going to hit Crow leaving this parked out front? I also don't need his blood and fibers in my trunk. You're sure that you've done this before?"

"Don't get smart."

"Fine. I'll shut up. Let's go boost."

"You know what we should be boosting? That bar girl, is who."

"Vernon, I don't want to hear this."

"We sweat her a little. Like you said, she fills us in."

"Then what? No, don't tell me. That's two sentences already."

"If I can't touch Whistler, you know what we should do?"

"I told you. I don't want to hear this."

"We finish with her and we cut off her head. We toss it in the back of Whistler's boat. We toss it back where they were eating their breakfast. There's a word for that. What's the word?"

"Fucking sick?"

"A calling card. That's it. From me to him. That's what I think I'll do before we're done here."

"Vernon—"

"Not now, though. You're right. Let's find a car."

Harry Whistler was airborne in the Gulfstream 4. His pilot, Erich Bierman, who once flew for Lufthansa, had been with him for more than ten years. The co-pilot, younger, had been with him for five.

Captain Bierman had computed the amount of fuel that
would be burned while crossing the Atlantic from Geneva.
That fuel, once consumed, would leave the plane light
enough to land on Hilton Head airport's short runway. Taking off, fully fueled, would not be possible, however. They
would have to reroute through Savannah or Charlotte, refuel,
and fly back from there.

Just as well, thought Harry. He told the captain that he
and the twins would get off the plane on the island. The captain would then take off at once and make at least three ad-
ditional stops. That way, anyone tracking his plane would
find it harder to know whether he was on board and where
he seemed to be heading.

He didn't like the idea of both twins flying with him, but
he'd had little choice in this case. He had always preferred
that the twins be split up and arrive at different times by different means, but dressed alike. Even Kate had once thought
she must be losing her mind when she saw the same little
man keep popping up in what seemed to be two places at
once.

As the Gulfstream reached altitude, he tried Adam again.
And again, he got an answering machine. He said, "Adam,
pick up. Is anyone there? Damn it. Okay, listen to me."

He related, briefly, his discussion with Bannerman. He
recounted his realization, or suspicion, that the entries for
Recon-JC in Aubrey's ledger must refer—*might* refer—to
Joshua Crow. He said that, if so, it must be assumed that
Aubrey and Poole were involved in the event.

He said, "They may not have been . . . they *should* not
have been . . . unless they have both gone out of their minds.
But you, for your safety, must assume that they were."

He said, "As to your claim that you yourself were not involved, I am no longer able to believe you. I don't know how
or why or when this began. I can only assume that during
your travels you ran into Olivia Torrey. I'm trying to assume
that you didn't know what her husband did for a living. I'm
assuming, in short, that you blundered into this because I
hope that you wouldn't be stupid enough to . . ."

He paused, then added, "Sorry, Adam. I'm a little upset. I know that you're smarter than that. I'm reminded, however, that your transmitter had an echo ever since . . . where was it? . . . Martinique. I'm the stupid one for not realizing before this that a second transmitter would have that effect. If it's there, then someone has been tracking you, Adam. My guess would be Aubrey, but it could be almost anyone, some unfinished business from your former vocation. Find it, get rid of it, but do so offshore. Get that boat away from the dock."

He said, "We're on our way to Hilton Head Island. We'll arrive between five and six this evening and we'll do a pass before landing. I'll expect to see that boat where you'd anchored it this morning. You'll know my plane, but do not meet my flight. I want you to stay in one place."

He said, "One more thing, and please do not argue about it. Some of Bannerman's people are on their way down there. Figure about two and a half hours. I think you'll know them if you see them, but pretend that you don't. They're not coming down to fight anyone's battles. They're to look out for you and that's all."

He closed by giving his son the number through which he could be reached while in flight. Donald asked, "You're not telling him Kate's coming?"

"No, if he knew that he might go to the airport. Claudia would certainly want to."

"Except, the thing is, she could have called them already. Maybe that's why they're not on the boat. Maybe they already went to get her."

Harry Whistler shook his head. "Too early by far." He fished for a note containing Kate's flight information. It said that she should just be approaching Atlanta, where she'd have to change planes to Savannah. He buzzed Erich and asked him to contact her flight and ask that she be summoned to the cabin.

"By the way," he said to Donald, "Bannerman thanked me for looking into that business with Carla."

"With Carla? Oh. That thing in Zurich, you mean?"

"The thing you said was 'just a for-instance.' "

"Me and Dennis didn't think we should bother you with that. She was there for a visit with Lesko and Elena. She went for a walk; two punks tried for her purse, and one of them whacked her in the ear. And it wasn't a knifing; it was more like a whittling. What Bannerman was afraid of was that she went hunting. You know, like she used to. She'd go out, like, looking lost to see who would take advantage. She doesn't do that no more. This was random."

"So she claimed?"

Donald shook his head. "Nah, it's true. She really doesn't. Her boyfriend, Viktor, the KGB guy, made her promise she wouldn't take chances like that. I mean, not just for the hell of it."

Harry Whistler threw up his hands. "Yeah, but damn it . . ."

He didn't finish because the captain had buzzed him. The contact with Kate Geller's plane had been made. Kate Geller was now on the line.

She spoke first. She said, "Harry, don't give me any grief. I'm long overdue for a visit."

"Kate, it's all right. Do they know that you're coming?"

"They will now, but I only got their machine. How about you? Did you speak to them?"

He said, "I spoke to Adam early this morning. They're fine. They were having some friends out for breakfast on the boat. But it got me thinking. It *has* been too long. So, I'm on my way over myself."

"You're calling from your plane?"

"Yeah, I thought I'd pop in."

A brief silence. "From Geneva? That's what you call popping in?"

"Well, it's not as if Denver is just down the street. If you can be impulsive, why can't I?"

A longer silence. "Harry . . . what's going on?"

He said, "Okay, I won't kid you. I'm worried about them. There are things about this I don't like."

"But you did speak to Adam? That was the truth?"

"It was, but he hasn't answered since. However . . ."

"So you don't know whether they're fine or not? Harry—yes or no? Were they in that bar last night?"

"Yeah. I think so, but it could have been strictly by chance. What happened might be part of something much larger and I'm not sure that Adam is aware of it. I've no reason to think that they're in imminent danger, but I've taken some measures to protect them all the same until they're well clear of that island."

Another brief silence. "You're scaring me, Harry."

"You're booked through to Hilton Head's airport, correct? When you land, I want you to wait in the terminal. A friend of mine, a woman named Molly Farrell, will be flying in a half hour later."

"What kind of a friend? Like the twins are a friend?"

"This is someone you'll be more comfortable with but, yes, Molly Farrell is a pro. She'll have another woman with her, very small, red hair. The other woman's name is Carla Benedict. Carla is . . . well, unusual, but these two will protect you. I don't want you to go anywhere without them."

"Protect me? Damn it, Harry—why do I need protection?"

"This is nothing new, Kate. You've been protected all along. Like it or not, it comes with knowing me."

"Then I'm better off not knowing you, aren't I, Harry?"

"For today? No, you're not. So you'll do as I ask. Tomorrow, you can do as you please."

25

Arnold Kaplan was having serious doubts about hitching his star to Vernon Lockwood. They'd be driving down the road, looking for a car to steal, and Lockwood would be saying, "Let's get this one or that one." He'd be pointing at cars that were parked outside stores. It's like the shopper wouldn't look out and notice.

Kaplan had picked out the car they would use. He had found it in a lot behind a Bi-Lo Supermarket by a sign that read "Employee Parking Only." An employee's car was not likely to be missed before the end of the shift. It was a beat-up green Pontiac, maybe twenty years old, that probably belched oil by the quart. On the plus side, it had four doors, a big trunk, and a car this old was low-tech enough that he wouldn't need tools to hot-wire it.

Lockwood argued, of course. "What, this piece of shit?"

"Vernon, would *you* look for *you* in this car? This is not a car people take notice of."

"That's if it starts. Go try. I'll park this one."

"Park the Cadillac, where? You mean here in this lot?"

"Down the end. Pick me up down the end."

Nobody, thought Kaplan, can be that fucking dumb. He reminded himself that neither was Lockwood. Not always, at least. But it's like he wears blinders. It's like he has room for only one thought at a time and his only thought now—and for, like, the past year—has been what he wants to do to this Whistler.

Kaplan started to explain that when the owner comes out, he is likely to call the police. The police will come and they'll see this red Cadillac that no one who works here seems to own. The police will then wonder—never mind. It's not worth it. He told Lockwood, "We'll leave it up the road."

Up the road was beach parking. Lots of cars. Lots of spaces. From there they were only two minutes away from where the wacko was hiding. They found the house, 22 Lagoon Road. Kaplan pulled up in front and cut his engine.

He said to Lockwood, "Let's get out nice and slow. Let the guy look us over so he sees we're not cops."

"He'll know we're not cops. He expects us."

"He also has a shotgun and is maybe a bit tense." Kaplan lowered his voice. "Here's a plan."

"I make the plans."

"Okay, then here's an option for you to consider. We wait until the guy waves us in. You introduce yourself, then you introduce me. I shake his hand, I hold on, and you shoot him."

"That's good, I guess. Except first shut the door."

No shit, thought Kaplan. "Good suggestion. Where's my head?"

"Give a tap on the horn. We don't have all day."

"Oh, damn. On your left. Is that him?"

A man was approaching, dressed in golfing attire. He had come from behind a thick bamboo hedge that ran from the side of the garage to the street. The man had a golf bag slung over his shoulder.

Lockwood's hand went to the gun that was still in his bag. He said, "Yeah, I think. What's with the golf?"

Arnold Kaplan was almost too stunned to speak. The man walking toward them looked ridiculous. He wore powder blue shorts that showed bone-white legs. His golf shirt was pink and his jacket was yellow. He wore a floppy hat, orange, that said "Cincinnati Bengals." The clubs in his bag had those novelty head covers. On his longest club, his driver, was a fluffy orange tiger. Another club had one of those happy-face things. On his feet were two-tone golf shoes that clacked on the driveway. His face and hands were dotted with little round Band-Aids. He had the kind of eyes that said, "*You must be the underlings.*" Lockwood spoke first. He said, "You'd be Crow?"

"I am *Mister* Crow. Are we ready?"

"Ready for what? You were supposed to wait inside."

"You would be Lockwood. The description was accurate. I was not told this other man's name."

Kaplan was busy scanning their surroundings in the hope that no one would see this. Slowly, reluctantly, he got out of the car. Lockwood said, "This is Kaplan. Now answer my question. What's going on with the golf?"

Crow frowned. "You said Kaplan? That's a Jew name, is it not?"

"It's an alias," said Kaplan. "Don't sweat it."

"Why are you dressed in such gaudy attire? Why not a suit and tie like your associate?"

Kaplan couldn't believe this. It's the pot and the kettle. Lockwood said, "Hey, look. Never mind what we're wearing. What the hell are you doing standing out in the open, especially in an outfit like that?"

"When in Rome, of course. Don't you realize where you are? There are golf courses everywhere one looks on this island. There are thousands of men who are dressed in this manner. It makes an effective disguise."

"Except here," said Kaplan, "they understand mix and match. You look like some hick from Ohio."

"Ohio. Precisely." Crow did not seem offended. Just the opposite. He seemed pleased with that appraisal. He said, "These garments belonged to a man from Ohio. They flock to this place from that state for some reason. All the wiser to adopt their taste in costume, don't you think?"

"What's all over your face?" Kaplan asked. "That the windshield?"

"Not any longer. These are bee stings."

"Come again?"

"Or should I say they're from wasps? Either one. Doesn't matter. I am reminded that golfers are stung on occasion while hunting lost balls among the trees. So if anyone should wonder what I'm doing at the hospital, I will answer that I have come there from the golf course in order to have these stings treated."

Lockwood stood blinking. "What is this about a hospital?"

"The Devil's spokesman still lives. But we'll see to that, won't we? Everything that I'll need is in this golf bag."

Kaplan asked, "This spokesman—you mean the TV guy, right?"

Crow narrowed his eyes. He was studying Kaplan. "You look and sound Jewish. Are you sure you're not Jewish?"

"See, that's part of the act. Like you and your bees. Fact is, my name's O'Malley, Southern Baptist, Jesus loves me. Now, tell me . . . you intend to try for Ragland again?"

"Of course. That's why you're here."

"Who says?"

"Mr. Poole."

"Wait a minute," said Lockwood. "No one said that to me. We're only here to help you get away."

"Where they'll never find you," Kaplan added with a smile. "And now that we've met, I can't wait."

Kaplan could have done without saying that, he realized. His meaning, however went over Crow's head. But Crow would catch on in another few minutes if they ever got this turkey off the street.

The Jesus guy said, "Yes, but first you must assist me. My work isn't finished. All you two need do is create a diversion while I finish what poor Leonard started. Oh, and first I'll need you to locate his room."

Lockwood turned to Kaplan. "Who's Leonard?" he asked.

"Vern . . . please. Not now. Not out here."

"He's the other guy, right? The one who's a vedge? He's the one the girl stuck with the knife."

"Vernon . . . not now, for Christ's sake."

But Lockwood already had got Crow's attention. "What girl?" he asked, startled. "A woman did that?"

"We'll tell you all about it inside," Kaplan answered. He started to walk toward the door. "Front door open?"

Crow shook his head. "No, go through the garage. But first answer my question. Are you saying that some barroom tramp attacked Leonard?"

"Yeah, that's it pretty much." Kaplan shot a hard glare at Lockwood, asking him, please, if they could leave it at that. He lifted the nearest of the two garage doors. He saw the Dodge van with Ohio plates. It had two bikes leaning against it. Inside, he saw luggage and groceries strewn about. Another set of golf clubs. A couple of beach chairs. The keys were still in the ignition. He said, "Let's all get in here before someone sees this. Mr. Crow, would you show me to the bathroom?"

"Off the kitchen."

"Would you show me? I'm suddenly not feeling so good."

All Kaplan wanted was to get this man indoors. Never mind the front hall. Shove him into a bathroom. Throw him into the shower, pop him once in the head, then open some arteries to let the guy drain. That's poetic, come to think of it. This way, he dies kosher. He dies fast and easy; the shower cleans the mess; it makes chopping him up that much easier.

This was Kaplan's new plan until Lockwood started thinking. You can tell Lockwood's thinking when he suddenly has lips. He starts pushing at them with his tongue. Lockwood said, "Wait a minute. You don't know about Whistler?"

"Vernon . . . do you mind? Get him into the garage."

The Jesus guy asked, "Who is Whistler? Who's this girl?" But he did step through the overhead door. At least he was out of public view.

"Whistler is the one who tried to shoot you last night." Lockwood said this as Kaplan pulled the door down and shut. "He's the one who gave you all your bee stings from the glass. The girl is the one who knifed whatzizname—Leonard. She should not have done that to poor Leonard."

Kaplan glared at him again. "Hold that thought, okay, Vernon? First I need him to show me the bathroom."

Crow's eyes had become slits. "Where are these people now?"

Lockwood turned to Kaplan. "It's only right he should know." He said this in all innocence, as in "What's fair is fair."

Kaplan had enough. "No, I'll tell you what's right. What's right is we do what we're paid for, okay? Vern, I know you. I don't like where this is going."

Lockwood said, "Hold your water. Let me think."

This man thinking, thought Kaplan, was never good news. He was going to tell Crow about Whistler and his boat. He was thinking what we'll do is show him the boat. He was thinking, *"Aubrey said don't touch Whistler, so we don't. We let this guy whack him, both him and the girl, and then, after that, we finish Crow."*

Sure enough, Lockwood said, "They're still around. They're on a boat."

"You will point them out to me?"

"My pleasure," said Lockwood.

"But the hospital first. Those two will have to wait."

Kaplan couldn't help asking, "What did you have in mind? You waltz into this hospital and blast him?"

"So to speak," Crow answered. He patted his golf bag. "As I've said, I have everything I need."

"So what's in there?"

"My shotgun, of course, and I've made us some sandwiches. I've brought a thermos of milk for myself and two bottles of Snapple iced tea. I'm sure that you're accustomed to a proper lunch, but we may find ourselves pressed for time."

"Good planning," said Kaplan. "Never shortchange nutrition."

"There is also my scanner to keep track of the police. There's some literature that I wish to distribute while we are departing the hospital. Oh, and of course the explosives."

Lockwood's eyes came to life. "You got explosives?"

"Three bombs. They should suffice. They use thermite. Very hot. I assembled them while I was waiting for you."

"And how do you plan to deliver these bombs?"

"As I've told you, I will need you to create a diversion so that I can get near Ragland's room. You will do that by setting off one of these bombs. They're quite safe; they have timing devices. I will then use the bigger one on Ragland himself. That explosion will create still another diversion. I will then make my way to poor Leonard's bed. You will have located it for me. I have decided to use the third bomb, if needed, to send Leonard to the glory that awaits him."

Kaplan said, "I need that bathroom. Come show me."

Lockwood knew what this meant. He said, "Wait. Hold your water."

Screw this, thought Kaplan. He would pop the guy right here. He said, "Vern, back away a few feet." You don't want this schmuck's brains on your suit.

Lockwood said, "Will you wait? We got new options here." He asked Crow, "You got stuff for more bombs?"

"Only these."

"But you don't need all three for the hospital, right? For your guy, all you do is pull a plug."

"That or a pillow. I've considered a pillow." Then Crow almost smiled. "I can see what you're proposing."

"One for the boat. We keep one for the boat."

"Vern . . . don't do this."

"I'm just thinking," said Lockwood. "You don't like it, go inside."

"Screw it. I'll wait in the car."

26

The campus of the Hilton Head Medical Center was a sprawling, modern-looking affair that was located close to the airport. There were several low buildings that housed doctors' offices. There were two larger structures at the campus's core. One of these housed facilities for treating outpatients; the other was the actual hospital.

Whistler had made several passes in the Taurus, getting a feel for the campus. He looked for unusual activity. He saw none. Just patients and visitors coming and going. No police presence that he could see. It was quieter than he'd expected.

Whistler patted his pockets. "Did you bring the cell phone?"

"No. Did you forget it?"

He answered with a dismissive grunt. The cell phone, he thought darkly, must have slipped his mind as Claudia went charging up the slip with the M-87 in her hand. He spotted a sign for a public phone at the entrance of the outpatient building. He pulled up to it, got out, and called the hospital building. He asked what room Ragland was in.

The operator told him that she'd been instructed not to give out that information. She said that the Raglands were not taking calls, but that he could leave a message if he wished.

"No visitors either?" Whistler asked hopefully.

"Only those preannounced and approved."

"Does that include the press?"

"I think especially the press."

"Well, how is he doing? Is he still in ICU?"

"Sir, I can tell you that he's listed as stable. That's all I'm permitted to say."

Whistler thanked the operator and broke the connection. He returned to the car and told Claudia what she'd said. He said, "So there you have it. No visitors."

"Adam, she said without prior approval. They've both asked to see us. That means we're approved."

"But we're not preannounced. We're not going to be either. We wouldn't know what we're walking into."

"Adam, park the car. You can wait in the car."

"You're not going in there alone."

"Then come with me."

He said, "Hold it. You promised that you'd do as I ask."

"Not when you're going to look for every tiny little reason to keep me from seeing him, Adam. I mean, those people you used to go after—didn't some of them have NO TRESPASSING signs? Would you have said, 'Well, that's that,' and gone home?"

"Big difference, Claudia. What I did was . . . never mind. If you want to go in by yourself, go ahead."

"You'll follow me anyway, so come."

Another lost argument. But this time she was right. He would not have let her out of his sight. He picked a parking spot that was near the main entrance, one that wouldn't be easy to block in.

As with most hospitals, the building had two entrances. The main entrance was more like that of a hotel, designed to seem inviting and comforting. Double doors led in to a lobby area that was furnished with comfortable chairs. Off the lobby were the gift shop and snack bar. A reception desk stood at the far end. Two pleasant-looking women sat behind it. Volunteers. Their job was directing visitors to patients or to say that no visitors were allowed. He had probably just spoken to one of them.

Claudia had begun to approach the double doors. Whistler said, "Wait, we're not going in that way."

"Do you see metal detectors? I don't."

He said, "I don't either, but they might be built in. We'll walk down and around to the Emergency Room entrance. Look worried and they won't even notice us."

That had always seemed true of Emergency Rooms. Look sick, you're a patient. Look worried, you're a relative. No one will bother to ask who you're there for. At most, they will point you to the waiting room. The doors almost never had detection devices. Too many policemen coming through at all hours. Too much urgency to worry about security.

As Whistler had hoped, no one paid them much attention. They walked directly through the waiting room and past Intensive Care. Beyond was an elevator bank. Near the elevator doors he found a directory that listed the various wards. The Trauma ward was two levels up.

He said to Claudia, "You remember the rules."

"I look for his room. If he has company I keep going."

"And if he's guarded?"

"You're hoping he will be, but he won't be, Adam. Because if he is, I have to abort. But I'm supposed to see him, so he won't be."

Whistler sighed. No use arguing. He pressed the button.

The elevator stopped on the main entrance floor. A visiting family was waiting to get on along with an aide who was pushing a wheelchair. Whistler and Claudia backed up to make room. He heard a voice from the corridor say, "Would you hold the door, please." His heart sank when he thought he heard a faint British accent. He thought, No, this couldn't be happening.

He was staring at the floor when the woman stepped on. Sure enough, it was Olivia Ragland. She still wore the dress that she'd had on the night before. She was carrying a small plastic bag from the gift shop in addition to an oversized purse. The bag seemed to contain a number of toiletries. A tube of Colgate toothpaste showed through it. She also carried a number of pink message slips that she must have picked up from the reception desk. Phone calls, no doubt, from family and friends and probably some from reporters. She smiled as she thanked the nurse's aide who'd held the door. She barely glanced at the others in the back of the car before turning and facing the doors as they closed.

Whistler reached to take Claudia's arm. He squeezed it and held it as if to say, *"Stay back. Don't get off when she does."* But Claudia, at that moment, reached with her free hand and lightly touched Mrs. Ragland's shoulder.

Whistler groaned, perhaps audibly. He looked skyward, helpless.

Ragland's wife turned. She met Claudia's eyes. Her expression was one of shocked recognition that quickly softened into something like awe. Whistler realized in that instant that Ragland's wife knew that the knife had come from Claudia's hand.

She whispered, "I'm so glad. I'm so glad that you came." She added, "You, too, Adam. Nice to see you again. You don't remember me, do you?"

The door to the third floor slid open.

27

Kaplan's first thought as he slid behind the wheel was to start up this sucker and go. Go back to beach parking, get his own car, and split. He'd be doing himself a big favor. He would also, however, kiss off the ten grand that was coming to him for doing Crow.

Another thought was to go back in and shoot him. That way, he'd be doing a favor for Lockwood, but Lockwood, at first, might not see it that way. Lockwood just might pull his

own gun and shoot him. No, wait. Lockwood couldn't.
Lockwood's gun and his silencer were still in his carry-on.
The dick-head was in there unarmed.

Armed or not, thought Kaplan, he would still be pissed
off. Lockwood might wait until they finished chopping
Crow and he'd say, "Sorry, Arnie. You go in the hole with
him. You shouldn't have forgot who's in charge."

Who's in charge is Aubrey. But tell that to Lockwood. If
Aubrey only knew the shit Lockwood was thinking . . .

"Now there," he said aloud, "is a thought."

Lockwood's carry-on bag was still in the well of the front
seat where Lockwood had left it. Kaplan reached in. He
thought, yeah, there's the Glock. He picked it up and pulled
back the slide to see if there was a round in the chamber.
There was. He ejected it. He put it in his pocket. Doing so
might just possibly give him an edge if push should come to
shove with Vernon Lockwood. Beneath it in the bag were
those cell phones Lockwood brought. Kaplan reached in; he
found the one with an "A." He thought, okay, let's think
about this. How does he explain this to Aubrey?

Gotta tell him the truth; they're with Crow; they haven't
popped him. Tell him two reasons. One is Lockwood, one is
Poole. The way Crow's talking, Mr. Poole must have called
him after Lockwood got finished with Aubrey. Poole told
him we'd help him get Ragland, which is nuts. He wants to
get him in the hospital with bombs.

He'd tell him Lockwood lights up when he hears this
guy has bombs. He says we have to save one for Whistler.
Now, an hour ago, Lockwood said no bombs, but of course
that was when he didn't have one. The way he's talking
now, he wants to use Crow to blow up Whistler's boat and
everyone on it. He thinks the whole family will be on it by
tonight.

Yeah, Lockwood shot his mouth that it was Whistler and
the girl who rained on this guy's parade. This gives Crow a
motive and this way Lockwood's clean. But we're only
clean if he leaves Crow's body so there's no doubt that Crow
did this and not us. Except Lockwood, probably, won't do

even that because Lockwood wants Whistler to know it was
him. So Lockwood's in there thinking, maybe he goes in
first. He does some knee-capping maybe, makes everyone
hurt, then he sets off the bomb and he cooks them. It strikes
me that this might depart from your objectives and maybe
you should want to have a talk with him.

That's good, thought Kaplan. That's all he would say. Mr.
Aubrey might appreciate the call.

"He plans to do what?"

Aubrey made him repeat it.

"And you're sure that Poole called Crow a second time to
suggest this new idiocy with the hospital?"

"That's according to Crow. I can't swear."

Aubrey thought for a moment. He remembered the first
call and how it had ended. He told Kaplan, "Wait a minute.
There was no second call. Crow was only told that to ap-
pease him."

"Yeah, well, someone better tell that to Lockwood."

"Mr. Kaplan, are you able to dispose of Crow yourself?"

"Yeah, I guess. But what about Lockwood?"

"I'm coming to that."

"I still get my ten grand?"

"Yes, of course. And by the way, that amount was not
ten."

"Well, Lockwood said five, but it's ten if I do good. I
hope I'm doing good with this call."

"Lockwood's cheating you, sir. The figure was twenty. I
am now prepared to double that for you."

"Um . . . this phone's okay? You're sure about that?"

"I am," Aubrey promised. "Speak freely."

"You're saying pop them both?"

"That would seem to be prudent."

"That would seem worth a medal for my service to hu-
manity, not that I would refuse the forty grand. But, hey,
with respect, I don't know about this."

"If you're asking for more . . ."

"No, I'm not. That's not it. Not that I wouldn't like to be

kept in mind if you need someone new for Lockwood's job. But popping them both? We're talking two bodies. And Lockwood's no bantamweight, remember."

"Are you . . . handicapped in some way, Mr. Kaplan?"

"Mr. Aubrey, let me describe what you're asking. Two bodies, one trunk. Put them in, take them out. I either dig a big hole or I haul them to a swamp. This, I gotta tell you, is how handicaps happen. Could be I get crippled, can't finish. I also have no one who's there as a lookout in case, I don't know, some bird-watchers show. What I'm saying is I'll need some assistance."

Aubrey said, "Hmm. I suppose you have a point."

"You got a suggestion?"

"Are you able to delay them? Keep them under control?"

"Sure. I go shoot them. If I do that, however, I don't hang around. I'm not going to sit in that house with two stiffs."

"You can't hold them at gunpoint?"

"How much time are we talking?"

"The . . . assistance you need will be forthcoming, Mr. Kaplan, but not for two hours or so, I would think. Can you keep them under control for that long?"

"Not with guns. That's too long," Kaplan told him.

Lockwood might be a schmuck, but he's a dangerous schmuck and he's going to know he's been downsized. The other guy listens to voices in his head and he thinks he has God on his side. Either one has got to figure he has nothing to lose. They're going to make a move and he's going to have to shoot them. That would put him back where he started.

"Tell you what, though," said Kaplan, "I can keep them both busy. Crow wants us to scout out the hospital first. We can kill a lot of time doing that."

"But you can't leave Crow alone. Take him with you when you do that."

"What, ride around with him? You seen this guy lately?"

"The problem?"

"This guy," said Kaplan, "looks like Dracula with zits. That's if Dracula took up golf and he shopped at Goodwill."

"Dracula with . . . zits?"

"Forget it. Don't ask. I know we can't let him out of our sight. We'll throw a sheet over him or something."

"And see that he behaves. I'm relying on you."

"How and where do we hook up with whoever you're sending?"

"Actually, I'm thinking of coming myself."

"You personally? For what? When I said I needed help—"

"You didn't mean an undersized cripple. I know that."

"No offense, you understand."

"None taken, Mr. Kaplan. But there seems to be a need for some management control, lest there be any further surprises."

"Not just you, though, right? I do need the help."

"I am more than your help. I'm your future, Mr. Kaplan. But no, I won't be coming alone. Where do you suggest that we meet?"

"Best bet, I think, is right here at this house. You look for our car. It's a big old green Pontiac. If it's there, we're inside and if it isn't we're out."

"If the green car is there, what then?" Aubrey asked him.

"You give three quick honks so I know you're outside. I cover Crow and Lockwood, then I call you in. If you don't see the car, you come in and wait. Come in through the garage. There won't be any locks. We get back, you be ready to surprise us, okay?"

"That sounds like a plan, Mr. Kaplan. Well done."

"Mr. Aubrey, they're coming. I gotta go. Just get here as soon as you can."

Aubrey stared at the phone. He was talking to himself. He said, "Felix, that might not have been smart. An impulsive decision, not at all like you. It is thug work. It is why we hire thugs."

But the more one tells a thug not to think, the more he makes the attempt. So Mr. Lockwood, already the cause of much damage, has once again decided to act on his own. A simple man, he has devised a simple plan. Kill everyone. That's his solution.

It never seems to occur to people like Lockwood that his victims might have minds of their own. They might not do what he needs them to do; they might not be where he wants them to be. Contingency plans, consequences, flexibility; these are alien concepts to such men. That is why one insists on utter obedience. Do this, do that, do not depart from my instructions. Do not think. I repeat. Do not think.

Aubrey asked himself, "Why am I telling myself this? Why am I repeating what I've said to Lockwood at least a dozen times in the past? Why not send to have him shot and be done with it?"

But he knew the answer. It would bring no satisfaction. For in truth he blamed Lockwood for all that he had lost. The money was the least of it; there would always be more money. His legs, however, would never regain what minimal strength they'd once had. Certain bodily functions would never be restored. Although he'd never been very attractive to women, at least he didn't think he was seen as grotesque. But now he had to waddle about like a duck. Or a frog. Yes, that's right. "There goes Kermit, the frog." He'd overheard that one, two, or three times. "Like a hemorrhoidal gnome" was another.

No, the only satisfaction would be watching Lockwood's face as he told Lockwood why he was going to die and why he was first going to suffer. And among those reasons would be what was done to Briggs after Lockwood abandoned him in Denver. Briggs despised him for that. That's why Briggs would come with him. He would invite Mr. Briggs to do to Mr. Lockwood what Lockwood would like to do to the girl. Strap the man down and cut off his face and then show him the result in a mirror.

Well, perhaps not. Briggs would probably decline. Briggs would say, "Let's just shoot him and go home." All the same, he'd make the offer. It's the thought that counts. And it might, as Lockwood said, get him back on the horse. It's true enough that he's never been the same.

Briggs and . . . we need muscle. Mr. Kaplan wants muscle. Robert would do, Mr. Poole's young assistant.

Robert's also a bodyguard who does not have much to guard because Poole won't come out of his office. Aubrey reached for his intercom and buzzed Poole's • extension.

"Mr. Poole, I'm in need of a strong and willing back. I'm going to borrow Robert for the day."

"I . . . might need him," Poole answered, dry of mouth.

"Mr. Poole, you're in a building that is virtually a bunker. Take a pill, get some sleep; this will soon be behind you."

"You'll see to . . . ?"

"Yes, I will. Now tell Robert to come see me. Tell him that we're going to expand his horizons. Above all, make it clear that he's to do as he's told. He is not to think or speak until tomorrow."

28

As Whistler had expected, a guard had been posted outside number 231, Ragland's room. But not a policeman. A security guard. He was armed, but he was yawning. Not much of a deterrent. The guard barely glanced at Claudia as Claudia approached him, led by Mrs. Ragland, hand in hand.

"*You don't remember me, do you?*" she'd asked.

He presumed that she didn't mean from last night. She had left him to wonder what she did mean. Whistler had waited near the elevator bank. That had been his intention. It was part of the agreement. And so far, the only part that had gone right.

Mrs. Ragland emerged from the room a while later. She'd left the plastic bag but she still had her purse. More to the point, she had also left Claudia. Whistler muttered to himself in disgust. So much for two minutes, he thought. Mrs. Ragland approached him, but more tentatively this time, and once almost stopping and turning around. He supposed that she was reluctant to be missing whatever she thought Claudia might be doing in that room.

She asked him, distractedly, "Have you ever been shot?"

"I've . . ." He stopped himself. He said, "No, ma'am."

"He's sleeping," she said. "They've been giving him morphine. Miss Geller said she'd like to sit with him a while. She said that's if you wouldn't mind."

Yes, I mind and she knows damned well that I mind. But all he said in response was "How is he?"

"He's alive. Thanks to you two. That's the main thing."

"I meant the wound itself. I'd heard it isn't too bad."

She said, "Well, it's high. And no organs were affected. You'd think that a shoulder wound wouldn't be serious. Western heroes in the movies shrug them off, barely wincing. But the shoulder is a complex bit of machinery. He might not regain the full use of his arm."

"I hope that you'll be pleasantly surprised, Mrs. Ragland."

He'd said that to offer his good wishes, nothing more. But it caused her to brighten and look into his eyes. An expression of . . . what? Of gratitude? Hope? Her face then turned and looked down toward the room. It was as Whistler had feared. She thinks Claudia's in there healing him. Coming here had been a terrible idea.

"Look, Mrs. Ragland."

"It's Olivia, Adam."

"Olivia . . ."

"You still don't remember me, do you?"

A helpless shrug. "You do look familiar. I thought that you looked familiar last night. I'm still not able to place you."

"Well, it's been a long time. I wasn't sure either. You've filled out and matured quite a bit."

As she said that, she reached and touched a hand to his chest. She said, "In fact, you've gained weight since I saw you last night. What's that under your sweatshirt? A vest?"

Whistler backed away. "Mrs. Ragland . . ."

She said, "Claudia, too. She seems a little top-heavy. I

tried to get Philip to wear one, but he wouldn't. How good
are those things? Would one have helped him at that range?"

"Mrs. Ragland . . ."

"Olivia."

"Where have we met?"

"Fourteen years ago, Adam. It was at your mother's funeral. We spoke for a few minutes afterward."

"Wait a minute. You're saying . . ."

"Yes, I did know your mother. I knew her quite well. We
met in Chamonix two years before that. Do you still have the
place in Chamonix?"

"My father does. Would he know who you are?"

"Harry would have known me as Olivia Torrey. This was
long before I met and married Philip. But he might not remember me. It's been all these years. And I really only
spoke to him three or four times. He didn't like having me
around."

"Why was that?"

"Because of my job. BBC correspondent, Paris Bureau at
first, then Geneva. No, Adam, it wasn't a personal dislike. He
warmed up toward me some when he saw me at the funeral.
He heard me sobbing aloud when Leo Belkin tried to speak
and again when Paul Bannerman had to finish Leo's eulogy."

That last part had certainly happened, thought Whistler.
But she didn't have to have been there to know it.

"You call Belkin 'Leo,' as if you were friends. How well
did you know Leo Belkin?"

"Not well. He said call him Leo, so I did."

"And you knew who he was?"

"Then? A KGB general. And you were in your third year
of college, I believe. You were going to school somewhere
out west. Colorado?"

Whistler still couldn't place her. That's assuming this was
true. There'd been dozens who'd offered their condolences
to him. He said, "I wasn't aware that there were journalists
at the service." In fact, they'd been told to stay away.

"I wasn't there as a journalist. I was there as a friend. I
was sitting with some of Paul Bannerman's people."

"Now you're saying you knew Bannerman? How?"

"Through your parents, of course. He often came to Chamonix. After he spoke, or rather after the service, Molly Farrell and I walked with you for a while. Molly said that she'd send you a book. Do you remember?"

He began to. "Yes," he said, "and she did. Can you tell me what sort of a book?"

"A small volume of poems that she got from your mother. That was my book, Adam. My poetry. I wrote it."

It came seeping back. He remembered it, some of it. He did not recall hearing her name at the time, or else he'd heard it but hadn't retained it. He did, however, remember the name that was on the jacket of that slim little volume. He'd looked at it many times since. Olivia Torrey. The book's title was *Shimmerings*. This woman was telling him the truth.

He said, "Your hair was longer. You were wearing . . . the same dress?"

"Hardly the same, but close enough. Basic black."

"You had lilacs pinned to it. I remember the lilacs."

"Your mother loved lilacs. That's why I wore them. I sent a bouquet to your house a year later, after I heard about your sister. I'd have come to her service, but I wasn't invited. Your father kept that one very private."

"Yes, he did."

"I think I'd better tell you how I came to know your mother. We did meet in Chamonix, as I've said. We did become friends. We skied together quite a lot. But I went there contriving to meet her, get close to her."

Whistler made a mental shrug. A great many people did. But he asked, "To what purpose, Mrs. Ragland?"

"The old story . . . young reporter looking for her big break. Writing poetry didn't put my name up in lights. Most of us had heard of your infamous father, but nobody knew much about him. I'd hoped to do a feature on him, followed by one on Paul Bannerman, Leo Belkin, and maybe a book about all three of them later. I thought it would have made a heck of a book. Molly Farrell, alone, would be worth a

whole chapter. Then there were the twins, and the crazy one,
Carla. Oh, I had a ton of anecdotal material. Men like John
Waldo and Anton Zivic and that monster, the silent one—
what was his name?"

"I would guess you mean Billy McHugh."

"Are they still with Paul Bannerman in Westport, do you
know?"

"I'm . . . told that they've all settled down. Even Billy. I
would leave that alone, if I were you."

She said, "Oh, believe me. I have no intention."

"This book," he asked. "You never wrote it, I assume?"

"I couldn't. Your father found me out very quickly. I'm
sure he warned your mother, but she didn't avoid me. Far
from it, she took me under her wing and suggested other
subjects more worth writing about. I took her advice and it
worked out very well. In fact it led, much later, to my meeting Philip and collaborating with him on a few. We shared a
Pulitzer prize. Did you know that?"

"Your report on enlightened drug policies," he said. "I
just saw that on TV this morning."

"Some of the others fed me subjects as well. They were
using me, of course, but I couldn't complain. I went from
being a stringer to a featured reporter on the strength of
some of the material they supplied. I heard stories from
them that could have brought down whole governments.
They wouldn't let me use them, but they told them."

"They were . . . probably just having some fun with you."

She smiled. "Oh, no. I checked a few of them out. They
seemed to have something on everyone."

Yes, they did. And still do. Selective extortion. An essen-
tial tool of the trade.

Her expression became wistful. "Those were heady days,
Adam. You all lived in a very rarefied world."

"One that seems to get smaller by the minute."

"They allowed me to penetrate the outskirts here and
there. Do you want to know something? I was never once
afraid. But of course I had your mother to protect me."

He shook his head. "They wouldn't have hurt you."

"You don't think they might have if I'd written that book?"

"No, but you would have wasted your time. No publishing house would have touched that material."

"I know. Your mother told me that. So did Molly."

"And you met Molly Farrell through my mother, you say?"

She nodded. "And the poetry connection."

"Did you know who Molly was and what she did by then?"

"I'd heard stories. I doubted them. She seemed too nice . . . and too young. She was only a few years older than you were. Me, too. I was only twenty-six at the time. By the way, how old is Claudia? Same age? Even younger?"

Whistler didn't answer. He glanced at his watch. He looked down the corridor toward Ragland's room, wishing that she would come out.

"Oh, and here," she said, reaching into her purse. She produced the message slips that he'd seen in her hand when she stepped through the elevator doors. She sifted through several, then said, "Here, you see? It's from Molly. She called twice this morning from a number in Connecticut. She's asking what she can do to help."

Oh, damn, thought Whistler. "You've spoken to her?"

"I only got her machine. This is her calling back."

"When you . . . spoke to her machine, did you mention my name?"

"I was tempted, but no. It was clear that you wanted no part in this mess. Or that you wanted Miss Geller kept out of it."

He said, "I do. At least until we're gone. As for Molly, you'd do well to take her offer of help. You can't get much better protection." He gestured toward the private security guard who was leaning against the wall, his arms folded.

"For the moment," she said, "I feel very safe. Is Claudia what I think she is, Adam?"

"A witch?"

"I was . . . going to say another Molly Farrell, for example. But since you bring it up—"

"She is neither of those."

"If you say so."

"And I do. There's nothing special about her."

She reached to touch his arm. She said, "Adam, believe me. I know that the two of you saved Philip's life. I would never do anything to hurt you."

He took a breath and nodded. "I believe you."

"Would you like to see Philip?"

"No, we have to be going."

She kept her hand on his arm. She didn't want him to leave. "The one who shot him—Breen—isn't here anymore. A helicopter took him an hour ago."

"Really? Why and where, do you know?"

"To a hospital in Savannah. They're better equipped for brain injuries, I'm told. I've also been told that his brain's been sliced in two, so it's hard for me to see why they'd bother. Mr. Breen, I'm sure, won't be answering any questions as to where that other lunatic might be hiding."

"And you're satisfied that it's only those two? That they acted strictly on their own?"

She nodded. "Unless you know something I don't."

He said, "Not at all." He knew he shouldn't have asked. No use troubling her with the unlikely thought that Aubrey might be somehow involved. "And I'm sure they'll find the other one soon. All he cares about now is getting away. I'm sure he won't try again."

Whistler said this more to ease Olivia's mind than as a considered opinion. A fanatic might do almost anything. As he spoke, his eyes had been roaming the corridor. He'd have hoped that this floor would have been less accessible. Getting up here had been far too easy.

She seemed to have guessed what he had been thinking. She said, "I have a pistol. It's here in my purse. I had it last night, but . . . you know, it was so quick." She opened her purse to let him see it.

He looked in. He frowned. "That's a twenty-five caliber, isn't it?"

"No good?"

"If you'd used it on Breen, that thing wouldn't have stopped him. Not unless you put half the clip in his head. Can you shoot well enough to do that?"

"I . . . had one quick lesson when I bought it."

He asked, "Do you think you could shoot if you had to?"

"If that man showed up here? In a heartbeat."

Against his better judgment, he reached into her purse and withdrew the ineffectual pistol. He replaced it with his own, the Beretta from his belt. "There's the safety," he said, pointing. "Flip it off and its ready. But only use it if you have to, okay? Keep in mind that these bullets can pass through several walls. You don't want to hurt the wrong person."

"You won't need this yourself?"

"I'll make do."

"Thank you, Adam."

"Would you . . . feel better if I left my vest with you? I mean for your husband. Drape it under his blanket."

She seemed about to say yes, but she shook off the impulse. "You wore it for a reason. You keep it."

She had lowered her eyes. She was fingering her dress. He could see several places where she'd tried to rinse the blood that had been on her dress since last evening. She said, "I'm sorry, I know I'm a sight. I haven't had the time to bathe and change."

"We could send over some of Claudia's things."

"Thanks, but our hotel is bringing my bags." She bit her lip as if she'd had another thought. She said, "Adam, on the subject of bewitching . . ." She stopped when she saw the look on his face. She asked, "Aren't you starting to trust me a little?"

"You want to know about Claudia. There's not much to tell."

"My husband thought she was an angel."

Oh, boy. "She gets that a lot. It's the face."

"No, I mean he really thought that she came down from heaven. She told him not to be afraid, that he wasn't going to die. She told him that it wasn't his time yet."

Claudia hadn't mentioned that they'd had that exchange. "She came from a barstool, Olivia."

"I know where she came from. And I saw what she did. I still don't quite believe it, but I saw it."

"A lot of people saw different things."

"Uh-huh. And I realize you're counting on that. How do you and your father find these women?"

"I don't know. Just . . ."

"Lucky? Say that and I'll slug you."

"How did Ragland find a woman like you?"

29

Kaplan had managed to kill forty minutes by claiming intestinal distress. Twice they got in the car; twice he said, "Sorry, guys," and went running back inside to the crapper. But that left Lockwood and Crow alone to talk. They were cooking up something. He couldn't hear what. But it had to have been about Whistler.

Lockwood finally said, "Screw it. We'll go out by ourselves." Kaplan had to say, "No, I'm all done here. I'm flushing."

He thought he might stall them for another twenty minutes by pretending that the car wouldn't start. But Crow, it turned out, knew how to steal cars. Crow saw that he was crossing the wrong wires.

This left more than an hour before Aubrey said he'd show.

Kaplan had no wish to be driving around in a stolen car for that long. By now, the green Pontiac should have been off the island and the wacko should have been in the trunk. But the Pontiac's owner, some checker at Bi-Lo, was probably on an eight to four shift and probably wouldn't miss it until the shift ended. There was good news and bad news on that subject.

The good news was that if the theft was reported, they'd

hear that right away on Crow's scanner. The bad news was that the cops wouldn't treat it as a routine report of a stolen car. They would have to assume that the booster was Crow and they'd instantly have their eyes open. And if they spotted this car, what was it they'd see? They'd see two men in front and some clown in the back, sitting up, big as life, not even hunkered down, holding his golf bag between his knees with those stupid head covers on his woods.

Lockwood said, "First stop is that boat Whistler lives on."

"I thought you said the hospital's first."

"New plan. Me and Crow want to check out the boat."

"What for?"

"Just drive. We'll decide when we get there."

"Vern . . . we've been through this. These were not your instructions."

"You want to argue? Get out of the car. You can walk back and stay in that house."

"Vern, this car had a purpose, remember? It isn't for riding around in."

"We got time."

"Also, this car doesn't have tinted windows. Don't you see how fucking weird we're going to look?"

"Weird, how?"

"Well, there's me in what your friend here calls 'gaudy attire.' There's you in your fed suit, which also stands out in a place where the only black suits are in coffins. And your friend's dressed in golf clothes a Polack wouldn't wear. This is not your everyday car pool."

From the back, Crow asked Lockwood, "Is this man your subordinate?"

"Yeah, he is and he's going to shut up now."

Kaplan did. He kept driving. He reached Sea Pines Circle. The wacko said, "Wait. I know where we are. That restaurant. Let's drive by that restaurant."

"We already checked it," said Kaplan.

"The owner and the barmaid. They were part of this, you say?" He had asked this question of Lockwood.

"Yeah, they're all in this with him. They were out on his boat. You did good when you messed up their restaurant."

"Let me see it."

"Vern . . . ?"

"Our friend here wants to see it; let him see it."

Kaplan groaned within himself. He should have shot them at the house. Lockwood must have told Crow about Whistler's breakfast meeting while he was on the phone with Mr. Aubrey. Kaplan entered the circle, made a three-quarter turn, and came out within sight of the restaurant.

"There it is. You happy?"

"Get closer," said Crow.

"Nooo . . . I don't think so." He tapped Lockwood's arm. "Take a look. It's crawling with feds."

He'd spotted two men in suits and two more in blue jackets with big FBI letters in yellow on the back. The two in blue jackets were taking pictures of the tire tracks that Crow left when he drove through the pedestrians. The two suits were near the bar that was set up outside. They were talking to the owners, this time both of them together, and Leslie, the barmaid, was standing nearby. She had changed her clothing since they'd driven by earlier. She'd put on dark slacks and a burgundy blouse and she'd run a brush through her hair. She seemed too well dressed to be tending bar, especially for a lunch crowd outdoors.

"Yeah, I see them," said Lockwood. "Keep going."

"Too late. The girl spotted us. No, wait. Maybe not."

Leslie's face had turned toward them, but she wasn't looking at them. She was looking at a car that was directly behind them. Kaplan glanced at his mirror and he muttered, "Oh, shit." The car right behind them was a cop car.

But its occupant, it turned out, wasn't watching them either. As Kaplan kept going, the cop car turned in. It pulled into a space and a deputy got out. Leslie was already walking toward him.

Kaplan said, "See that cop. He's that sergeant, name of Moore. He's the deputy who was with them on the boat."

"They're in everything, aren't they?" said Crow.

"Come again?"

"The mud people. They're everywhere. They're in everything these days."

Kaplan asked. "What the hell are you talking about?"

"The blacks. But no matter. They are all going to hell. As are all of the Hebrews, Mr. Kaplan."

Kaplan grimaced. "Hey, dick-head, do me a favor. Take your golf bag and lay it down on the floor. You look like you're doing a puppet show back there with your dumb smiley face and your tiger."

Crow hissed, "You're not wise to provoke me, Mr. Kaplan."

Lockwood slapped at Kaplan's arm. "You heard my friend. Cut the crap and just drive. Make a turn up ahead and let's go look at the boat."

"Make a turn where? There's no other road. We have to go back the way we came."

"Then pull in someplace and we'll wait a few minutes till the barmaid goes back to the bar. That make you happy?"

Thank God, thought Kaplan. Another few minutes killed. "That does make me feel better. Thank you, Vernon."

Lockwood used the time to further mess with Crow's head. "The cop's there," Lockwood told him, "to back up Whistler's story. Him, the barmaid . . . and now it looks like both the owners . . . are still covering for Whistler and the girl."

Crow nodded. "Yes, you've said that. But why?"

"Because like I told Arnold, they all knew each other. They're in some kind of cult that worships Satan."

"Vern . . ."

"The bartender—name's Leslie—she's a priestess with this cult. When they have their black masses, she does all the chants. See the outfit she's wearing? Red and black. That's what they wear. It was her who first spotted your partner coming in. She's the one who gave the knife to the other one, Claudia, so that Claudia could throw it at Leonard."

"Hey, Vern—"

"Arnold saw the whole thing. You can ask him."

"Vernon . . ." Arnold Kaplan's expression was pained. "Where the hell are you going with this?"

Lockwood ignored him. He had turned to face Crow. "And you know something else? They were laughing about it. Out on the boat they were doing imitations of how Leonard was twitching and shaking. They thought that was very hilarious."

"Fucking Vern!!"

"Arnold watched from the dock. He had binoculars. Right, Arnold?"

Kaplan started to protest, but instead he said, "Shit." He said, "Keep your heads down. Don't look."

"What's the matter?"

"The barmaid, damn it, is now watching us. She's pointing us out to the cop, for Christ's sake."

"Okay, go. Not fast. Just keep going."

Leslie wasn't sure of what she'd just seen. That Pontiac was one of hundreds of cars that had cruised by the scene of the shooting that morning. Passengers gawking. A few slowing to take snapshots.

This car was older, more beat-up than most. But the thing that had caught her eye, she supposed, was the odd mix of passengers inside. In the back, a golfer sat holding his clubs. Clubs are normally carried in the trunk. And the two men in front weren't dressed to play golf. The one in the passenger seat wore a suit. He was dressed like these FBI agents. And the driver, a man who seemed upset about something, was dressed like a . . . wait. Wait, she knew him.

She was sure of it now. She had recognized the driver. Straw hat, tinted glasses, and that hideous striped jacket. She did not know his name or anything about him except that she'd seen him at the bar several times. And the car he drove then was a red Cadillac. She had seen it when he pulled up and parked it.

And that man, she now remembered, had been there last night. He'd come in a few minutes after Adam and Claudia and had sat at the opposite end of the bar. He would have to

have had a clear view of the shooting but, if so, he didn't
stay to be interviewed.

She'd said, "Ed, see that car? The green one? Three
men?"

"The Pontiac? What about it?"

"Well, the man at the wheel . . . Oh, it's nothing. Never
mind."

The green Pontiac had passed them. It was moving away.
The FBI, she'd decided, didn't need another witness. And if
this one, indeed, had seen everything that happened, he
would only make things difficult for Claudia.

She said, "Ed, those agents are finished with me. I'm
going to drive down to the hospital."

"That's why you changed? You look very nice."

"Well, I couldn't go in shorts and a sweatshirt."

"What about Phil? Didn't he want to go?"

"He still does, so does Jump, but they can't until later.
Their insurance adjuster's coming over. I thought I'd stop on
the way and see if Claudia wants to come. She told me that
she'd like to see him."

"Mrs. Ragland would like that, but you'll need advance
clearance. I can call her from my unit if you wish."

She answered, "Sure, thanks. That will save me some
time. Tell her I should be there in about thirty minutes. Tell
Phil I should be back here by two."

30

Olivia Ragland wanted to know what Whistler had been up
to these past fourteen years. She said, "Last I heard, you
went into the service." He told her that was pretty much it.

"So you've gone your own way? A more normal existence?"

"It has been. For the past year, at least."

"And your father is well? Is he still in Geneva?"

Whistler answered yes to both questions.

"He's someone who knows what it's like to be shot. Did it have any lasting effect?"

Whistler squinted. "My father? When was he ever shot?"

"You're saying he wasn't?"

"I think I'd have known."

She shrugged and said, "Then I must have heard wrong. Who knows how these stories get started? This one said that he'd been laid up for months, that he very nearly was paralyzed, I think. Some fragments had lodged against his spine."

"He's . . . had some back problems. Maybe that's how it got started. When was this supposed to have happened?"

"I guess let me think—well, it doesn't really matter. You're saying it was only a rumor."

"But when was it?"

"Oh, a long while ago. Let's see. First your mother." Olivia was counting in her head and on her fingers. "Then you lost your sister about a year later. This would have been a few months after that. I remember thinking how bad luck comes in threes."

"Did the rumor mill tell you who shot him and why?"

"Adam, did it happen or not?"

"Just tell me."

"It was someone involved in the death of your sister. Or rather, it was someone who paid someone else. The story is that your father meted out his own justice to several of the men who were responsible. The story is also that he missed one or two and that oversight came back to haunt him."

That studio executive? And the son that survived? This would have happened, if indeed it did happen, soon after his father packed him off to the army. Ridiculous, thought Whistler. He would have known. His father's back problems had nothing to do with that sad episode in Los Angeles.

He saw that Claudia had stepped from the room. He said, "Olivia, I'm pleased to have met you again. And my father's just fine, by the way."

"I'm glad."

Claudia approached them with a soft little smile. Whistler noticed that she seemed to have regained her figure. She said to Olivia, "Your husband is awake. I think he's beginning to feel better."

Olivia blinked. She asked, "How much better?" She glanced down toward his door as if she expected her husband to come prancing through it, all healed.

Whistler said, "Olivia . . . steady."

"He's not hurting," said Claudia. "He could raise his arm a little."

Whistler said, "That's the morphine. Great stuff."

Olivia asked, "Did he remember you, Claudia? Last night he wasn't quite sure that you're real."

"He still wasn't, at first."

"The morphine," said Whistler.

"But he is now," said Claudia. "He wanted to touch me. We held hands and that seemed to make him feel better. Now he's asking for you, Mrs. Ragland."

Whistler asked, "Where's your vest? Did you leave it with him?"

Olivia had noticed. "Yes, she did. I'll go get it."

"Let him keep it," said Claudia. "I don't really need it."

"She means," said Whistler quickly, "that we're leaving the island."

Olivia curled her lip. She said, "Adam, relax. I know that she does not think she's bulletproof."

I wish I knew that, thought Whistler. He said, "We'd better go."

Olivia touched him. "Can't you stay for a while? Give me a minute to look in on Philip. You can't just walk out of our lives after this."

"I'll call you when this settles down."

"You promise?" She reached into her purse for a card.

He took the card from her. "I promise."

"It won't be another fourteen years, will it, Adam?"

This last question startled Claudia. "You . . . two knew each other?"

Olivia nodded. "From a long time ago. He'd forgotten."

Whistler said, "I'll tell you all about it in the car. Right now, let's go get the boat ready."

Kaplan had pulled off Palmetto Bay Road to listen to the traffic on the scanner. He'd feared that the barmaid's cop friend had got curious and called in a license plate check. But he heard nothing on the scanner. Nor had the cop thought to follow them. Kaplan would have seen him go by.

He pulled out again and proceeded toward the bridge. He told Crow, "From the bridge you can see Whistler's boat. Can't miss it. It's the biggest one down there."

But Lockwood said, "No. We need to see it up close."

"Close how? You mean you want to drive down there?"

"Yeah, we do."

Kaplan explained what "driving down there" entailed. There was only one road into Palmetto Bay. There was no other way in or out. Once there, they'd have to park and walk down a long ramp before finally reaching the boat slips. There's no cover. It's all open. They would stand out too much. The Goodyear blimp would have an easier time getting down there without being noticed.

"By Whistler, you mean?"

"By anyone, Vernon. None of us look especially yacht-ish."

"Let's just worry about Whistler. He might not be there. We'll check out the lot for his car."

You want a car? thought Kaplan. So, okay, we'll find a car. He turned down the road, drove to Palmetto Bay and into its complex of restaurants and shops. The parking area was half filled with cars. Kaplan spotted a brown Toyota sedan. "There it is. He's back. So let's go."

"Arnold, cut the crap. Whistler's driving a Ford. Check out the rest of the lot."

Kaplan cursed beneath his breath. He had hoped that Lockwood hadn't noticed the make when Whistler's car had passed them on the bridge. He cruised up and down the several rows of parked cars. Whistler's car was not among them. Whistler hadn't returned.

"Okay," said Lockwood, "pull up near the ramp. Me and Mr. Crow will get out and go take a look. You stay with the car and keep watch."

"You're serious, right? You and Crow, dressed like that. In broad daylight, you're going to take a stroll down the dock."

Lockwood paused to unwrap another cigar. That done, he reached into his overnight bag and extracted his Glock and the silencer. He screwed the silencer into its tap and placed the gun back in his bag. He said, "Mr. Crow, I think Arnold has a point. Strip down to your golf shirt and shorts, okay? All the other golf shit can stay here."

"I'll need my golf bag."

"You don't need the whole bag; just give me the thing. I'll carry it down there myself."

Kaplan watched in dismay as Crow unzipped his golf bag and withdrew what was clearly a bomb. It was ten inches long, three inches across, made of PVC pipe wrapped in duct tape. At one end was a clump of electronic devices bound together in a haphazard fashion. There was a timer, two batteries, and what he knew to be a fuse except this one looked more like a toy.

Kaplan blinked. Oh, Christ. That's exactly what it was. The fuse was the kind that hobby shops sell as part of a rocket-building kit. It was the kind that teenagers tell each other about when they talk about blowing up their high schools. Except they probably know better than to use plastic pipe. You might just as well pack it in cardboard. Unless . . .

Kaplan said, "Wait a second. Is that fucking thing live?" Unless what's packed in it is thermite.

"Not yet," Crow answered. "One must first set the timer."

"And you're going to do what? You're going to plant that on the boat?"

Lockwood slipped it into his overnight bag, taking care not to cover his gun and his cell phones. He said, "It's insurance. It's for later."

Kaplan threw the gearshift into park and scrambled out of

the car. Lockwood ordered him back. He said, "Get in here. Drive us closer."

"Screw you. You want to do this? From here you can walk."

"You hear me? I told you to get back in the car."

"Vern . . . kiss my ass. I'll see you later."

Lockwood, for once, didn't bother to fight him. Kaplan watched, arms folded, from behind a parked pickup as Lockwood and the wacko climbed out. Leaving the golf bag was a modest improvement but, still, there they were, the suit and the golfer where everyone else was dressed in deck shoes and grubs. Lockwood, however, had the sense to tell Crow to walk at least twenty feet behind him. This was after he realized that the golf shoes still clacked.

Beautiful, thought Kaplan. Here they go with their amateur bomb, Crow wearing shoes that make sparks on the pavement, Lockwood with a lit cigar in his mouth, and they're both on their way to a fuel dock. If God was good, if God had a sense of humor, he would finish this whole thing in one loud *ka-boom!* Talk about not leaving a trace.

"Arnold? You call me if Whistler shows up."

"Call you for what? Where the hell could you hide?"

"Lots of other boats down there. We'll duck in one until it's clear. You just keep your eyes open up here."

Kaplan watched them go until they sank from his view on reaching the ramp to the docks. He wished that he could call Mr. Aubrey again but Lockwood had the Aubrey phone with him. His impulse was, once again, to drive off. He could go to the airport; he could sit there and wait until Aubrey showed up with some help. But that was no good because God only knew what these two might do if he stranded them here. They'd have to snatch another car and throw its owner in the trunk because they couldn't leave someone who could give their description. They might even decide to stay near Whistler's boat and take Whistler and the girl when they got back. And Mr. Aubrey had said, "I'm relying on you." He said, "See that they behave until I get there."

He would stay, thought Kaplan. He would give them

twenty minutes. In the meanwhile, he would check out the contents of the golf bag and see what he was dealing with here.

Whistler waited until they'd returned to the car before he told her how and when he'd met Olivia before. She responded, "Did I tell you? I knew it."

"No, you didn't."

"Well, not that you'd known her, but I felt a connection. I was right. She was practically family back then."

"She knew my mother and she went to her funeral. That's all. You're reading too much into this."

"Adam, how can I help it? This all ties together. Don't you feel that it all ties together somehow? Don't you feel that we have to find out how?"

"Claudia . . . I'm leaving. Are you coming with me?"

"What kind of a question is that?"

"It's a man who is asking the woman he loves to get out before someone else gets hurt."

"And you'd leave without me? Is that what you're saying?"

"Not a chance. I was trying to be forceful."

"Then we'll go."

This was what he'd hoped to hear, but it was still a surprise. "You're . . . not going to say, 'Let's see how this plays out'? You're not going to insist that we stay?"

"If you want to leave, I'll leave with you, of course. I've a feeling that we're not going to get very far, but sure, let's give it a shot."

"And you have this feeling . . . because why, exactly?"

"Because I think we were sent here. I told you."

"Claudia, wait a minute. This impression you have. Is this what I have to look forward to with you? A new mission from the white light every few months? Because I'll tell you right now, if that's how it's going to be—"

"You'd leave me?"

"No."

"Then you'd what?"

"I'd just hate it."

She leaned into him. She embraced him. "I know. And you're right. I can see how this could get a little creepy for you."

"Claudia, what happened back up there with Ragland?"

"We just talked and held hands for a while."

"Did you know that he thought you were an actual angel? I mean the kind that materializes out of nowhere?"

"I do now. He still did when he opened his eyes."

"Did you tell him last night that it wasn't his time? That he shouldn't be afraid? Did you say that?"

Claudia frowned. She was trying to remember. "I . . . suppose I might have said something like that. But so did his wife. We both said he'd be okay. It wasn't meant to be a prophecy, Adam."

"You're saying you were only encouraging him. Good."

"Except he still thinks I made his bullet come out. Did you know that he thought I did that?"

"Yes, I did. On the boat. From Sergeant Moore."

"Do you think there's any chance that it could possibly be true? Do you think I could have possibly done that?"

"You didn't."

"I wouldn't think so either, but there in his room . . . all I did was hold his hand and he felt better."

"He felt better because he was under sedation. He felt better because he expected to feel better just by seeing you and having you touch him. I feel better myself every time I see you smile. None of this is miraculous, Claudia."

"Okay."

Uh-oh, he thought. "That's it? Just okay?"

"Well, I don't know why you're resisting this, Adam. He felt better. He was happy. Who cares why?"

"I suppose."

"First you're afraid that I think I'm immortal and am going to be unpleasantly surprised. And now you're afraid that I think I'm a healer. You think that every time I see someone on crutches I'm going to want to run up and touch him. It's nothing like that, Adam. I just held the man's hand. Wow, talk about reading too much into things."

"It's what other people read into it, Claudia. I know something about reputations."

"Want to screw?" she asked. "Would that lighten you up?"

"Claudia . . ."

"Adam, I'm making a point. Mystics and healers who think they're immortal almost never think in terms of a romp in the sack. That should give you a clue. I'm still me."

"Which reminds me . . ."

"Of course, screwing is healing. It does wonders for tension. Unless you've been hanging out in bathhouses lately. That would crank up the tension on my end."

"Which reminds me," said Whistler, "of what I think is sexy. I have a fetish for women who wear Kevlar vests. They make me soar to new heights of unbridled passion. Too bad you no longer have yours."

"I see what's coming."

"If you were to wear mine until we're well out to sea—"

"Smoothly done. But you keep it. No one wants to shoot me."

"Claudia—"

"Adam"—she touched him—"I can't lose you either. End of discussion. Let's get back to the boat."

"We can be out to sea in an hour."

Lockwood hated to admit it, but Kaplan had a point. A guy wearing golf shoes would tend to stand out on your average marina or boat. Crow had left a trail of little patterns of punctures in the planking all the way to the fuel dock. But they'd come this far and no one paid them much attention. Whistler's boat was ten feet in front of him.

He'd approached it from the stern with one hand in his bag. The hand gripped the Glock with the silencer on it. This was just in case. He would prefer not to need it. From the looks of the boat, he would not.

The first thing he noticed was the open hatch. Knowing Whistler, it was almost too good to be true, even without last night's shooting. He stepped closer and listened for sounds from below. There was nothing. Not even a radio.

Someone had left what looked like a crab trap next to the gasoline pumps. He told Crow to go get it, pretend that he's crabbing. Do it facing the ramp, sing out if someone comes, try not to get stuck to the planks.

"Do you know how to set the bomb's timer?" Crow asked.

"Like any alarm clock, right?"

"Pretty much. But how do you know when they'll be here?"

"Figure dinner. They all should be here about then."

"I'll want to watch. I'll want to be back here."

"Don't worry. I'll make sure you're around."

Not alive, thought Lockwood, but somewhere around. He spotted a little hinged plate on the deck a few inches inside the railing. It seemed to be a gas cap, just like on a car. He said, "Good. Now we know where the tank is, Mr. Crow. And it figures that the tank is nice and full."

"In that case," said Crow, "I'd dispose of that cigar."

Lockwood puffed it. "It's okay. It's almost out."

He stepped aboard *Last Dollar* with his bag in one hand and his other hand still on his Glock. But no question about it—there was no one below. A tangle of rope had been left across the hatch. On purpose? he wondered. Let's assume it's on purpose. Gently, he placed the bag on the deck. He used one hand to anchor the coil and the other to ease the loops to one side as he backed his way down through the hatch. Once inside, he reached out to get the bag.

The boat's main saloon seemed the most likely place. It was where they would probably gather. He looked around for a cabinet or drawer in which he could place Crow's contraption. There were several in the galley; it adjoined the main saloon, but they all were stocked with utensils or food and seemed likely to be opened once the guests were on board. Same problem with the bar. They'd be using the bar. He found a hatch on the floor of the main passageway with a chrome-plated ring at one end. He lifted the hatch. Underneath was the engine. He got down on his knees and reached for the fuel line. He tried to loosen it. It gave. But only a little. He felt cool moisture on his thumb and forefinger. Not much of a leak, but it might leak a lot more once the engine was started and the pressure increased. Whistler might smell the gas, but he'd think it's the fuel dock. With luck, he wouldn't bother to check.

Lockwood looked for a place where the bomb could be stashed. Near the engine would be good, but he could see no nook or cranny where the bomb would be completely out of sight. Better not trust his luck in this case, he decided. If Whistler did lift this hatch, he would spot it. Lockwood knew what he'd do. Stick it under Whistler's bed. If he put it just under the foot of the bed, that was also just about where the fuel tank should be. He walked back to the stateroom. This was perfect, he thought. Very carefully, he set the timer.

He was on his way out when he saw a blinking light on a panel that held all kinds of instruments. He paused to look, but he was hesitant to touch any of the boat's electronics. They all had black sign plates that said what they were, but he knew very little about such devices. Lockwood was afraid that he might mess something up and then Whistler would know someone had been here. Kaplan would know what these instruments were. He could call him and ask, but that would just bring more bitching. Kaplan needed a lesson in who's boss around here. That could wait, though. One lesson at a time.

Lockwood leaned closer to that one blinking light. He saw that it said "Mailbox" beneath it. There were buttons nearby that said "Play" and "Delete." Oh, hell, he thought. It's just an answering machine. And if it was blinking, that probably meant that Whistler didn't know he'd been called. He decided to chance it. He pressed the "Play" button. In an instant he heard an electronic voice. It announced that two messages were waiting.

He played the first. It was from the girl's mother. It only confirmed what Kaplan had known. She was on her way to the island. But the way she spoke, it also confirmed that this would be the first that Whistler knew of it. Lockwood hit

"Delete," not entirely sure why, except that, in general, it seemed an advantage to know things that Whistler didn't know.

He played the second message, this one from the father, this one much longer than the first. The father's coming too; he would arrive before six. Beyond that, this message was a goldmine. Kaplan had been right; Whistler'd lied to his father and said he'd been nowhere near the shooting. Not only does his father now know that he was lying, his father has doped out that Aubrey and Poole are connected with Joshua Crow. Or at least he suspects it. He doesn't sound sure. He sounds like he thinks they could not be so dumb as to want to pop someone like Ragland.

The father had also somehow figured out that this boat must have a tracker on it somewhere. He says find it, get rid of it, then move the boat out; keep it away from the dock. The father then mentioned some other names. A woman's name first. Olivia something. It sounded like Olivia Tory. The father thinks that Whistler must have met her in his travels, but he doesn't say who the hell she is.

Lockwood tried to think, but the name drew a blank. The father also mentioned somebody named Bannerman. This Bannerman, he says, was sending some help . . . it sounded like to watch Whistler's back. The father says that's all; they're not going to fight your battles, but they'll be there in a couple of hours.

Lockwood looked at his watch. Two hours from when? It had to be from when they saw Whistler on the bridge, so that's less than an hour from now at the most. The mother could get in even earlier.

Lockwood wondered why the father never mentioned the girl's mother. You'd think he would have wanted them to meet her flight, but now they can't because they don't know she's coming. So where was Whistler going when they saw him on the bridge? Can't be to the airport. The hospital, maybe. Which would prove that he's in bed with Ragland.

Lockwood hit "Delete" on that message as well. Now Whistler's in the dark about a whole lot of things, especially

about Aubrey and Poole. Hey, Mr. Aubrey—do you see what
I just did? I just covered your ass again for you. And now
I'm going to cover it once and for all. I'm going to finish this
thing.

He was tempted to meet the mother's flight himself, just
to see the look on her face. Hello again, lady, remember me?
Remember when you threw me out of your house? Remember me standing with my foot on your neck after my cops
shot your daughter? You and me, it's time that we had a little talk. Like, for instance, what happened to those cops after
that? Whistler killed them, right? Yeah, but him and who
else? Who were these people who showed up in town and
had all of us not knowing what hit us? Who was the one who
caught Briggs at the airport? Who was the guy who snatched
that Silver Ridge judge and scared him so shitless, he saw
double?

But he wouldn't meet her flight. No point. Let her come.
She would have a look on her face soon enough when that
bomb blows her ass out through the hatch.

Speaking of which . . . he climbed back out on deck. He
walked to the stern and leaned over the rail. He ran his fingers along a ridge that was formed by the trim on the transom. His fingers found the tracker. It was still there, glued
tight, where Kaplan said it would be. Not that it would matter much longer.

His cell phone chirped. It had to be Kaplan. He hit a button and asked, "Are they back?"

Kaplan's voice said, "No, but get out of there now. It's
Leslie, the barmaid; she just drove in. She's got to be headed
for that boat."

"What for? They're not here."

"Vern, she wouldn't know that. Don't talk. Just get off
that boat fast."

The phone on Whistler's boat was ringing again. He'd
have liked to stay and listen to who else might be calling, but
Kaplan was right; he would have to get off. He glanced
around the dock. He no longer saw Crow. He said into his
cell phone, "Crow's not here. He with you?"

"No, he's not."

"You don't see him?"

"Oh . . . damn. Yeah, I see him. Top of the ramp. It's too late; the girl's gotta walk past him."

"Okay, be cool. She won't recognize him. She won't know me either. I'm coming."

"Vernon . . . oh, Christ. He's walking up to her now. He's talking to her. Why's he talking to her?"

"I don't know."

"Well, I do. I bet it's your cult-priestess shit. He's grabbing her, Vernon. Get up there!"

31

Kate Geller's final leg, from Savannah to Hilton Head, was only a twenty-minute hop. Upon landing, she went to a phone in the terminal and tried once again to call the boat.

And again, no answer. She got the machine. She hung up without leaving a message. If she had, she reasoned, it might only cause confusion. They would have played the message, God only knows when, and perhaps be on their way to this airport after she had already been met.

She thought it best to sit tight, to wait for Harry's two friends, these women he was having flown in.

"They're your protection," he'd said. "You're to do as they say. Get used to it. It comes with knowing me."

He didn't really say, "Get used to it, Kate." He would never be that disrespectful. And of course she knew that she'd long been protected. Those snipers he'd posted throughout Silver Ridge—whether real or a bluff—did protect her. And then the twins, who were certainly real. They'd pop up out of nowhere in the damnedest places, but they no longer bothered her quite as much. She was almost beginning to enjoy them.

She understood it. She did. This need for protection. But she hadn't been nice to Harry at all. She'd said, "Then I'm better off not knowing you."

What a bitch. That wasn't fair. They were both upset. Especially Harry, being so far away and not knowing what Adam had got himself into. In the end, she'd bet, it would probably be nothing. A misunderstanding. Two parents who panicked. Adam and Claudia were probably on some beach. They would all get together; she and Harry would feel foolish, then they'd break out a bottle of wine and forget it.

Speaking of wine, she wouldn't mind a glass now, but she'd probably better stick with something lighter. She went to the snack bar, bought some hot tea to go, then walked back to the airport's departure lounge. There was only one lounge. It served all the flights. She would sit and wait for these two women to arrive. Harry said that their names were Molly and Carla. He said that she'd like them. No, he said she'd like Molly. He had trouble finding the right word for Carla. "Unusual" was the best he could do.

She found a copy of the *New York Times* that someone had left in the lounge. That someone had left the crossword partly done with at least two mistakes that she could see. She pulled a pen from her purse and went to work on it.

Another ten minutes had hardly gone by when she heard a plane coming in. Soon it taxied up to the gate. She saw no airline markings; it was a private plane, one of those with a tail that seemed too large for it. So soon? she wondered. Harry said a half hour. She watched as the door of the plane swung open and she waited for two women to step out.

But its passengers weren't women. Two men emerged from it. From their dress, they were businessmen or lawyers. The first of them was young, very large, with short blond hair. He carried a briefcase in one hand. The second was older, perhaps forty, and bald. The second one stood with his back to her. They waited at the door as a third man appeared. This third man handed a crutch to the bald one. The third man was small, rather homely, enfeebled. He needed their assistance to manage the steps as he climbed from the executive jet. Once down, he moved stiffly, bow-legged, with a limp.

The three seemed to be waiting. They made no move toward the lounge. Their pilot and co-pilot joined them for a moment. They had a brief discussion. The two pilots re-boarded. Kate's eyes returned to her puzzle.

She'd been watching their arrival, although not with much interest, but something about them was troubling her. She looked up again and as she did, the bald-headed man raised an arm and he waved it, gesturing toward someone outside. A moment later, a car pulled up. It was black, a big sedan, a Lincoln Town Car. The driver got out; he carried a clipboard; he handed it to the bald man, who scribbled something on it. A rental car, she realized. Delivered to planeside. The small one must be someone important. The bald one turned and, for the first time, Kate was able to see his face clearly.

His skin. It shone. It was almost like parchment. She realized with a shock that she'd seen that man before. She'd seen him when his face appeared normal, if unpleasant, and she'd seen him when he had very little face left. She'd held his hand. She'd comforted him. She'd told him that she forgave him.

His name—what was it? Yes, Briggs. It was Briggs.

During that moment of recognition, the three men got into the car. The younger one with the briefcase climbed behind the wheel. And Briggs if that was Briggs—held the rear door open and helped the one with the limp climb in. He then stepped around, got in the front; they drove off. The man who had delivered their car to them was approaching the departure lounge door.

Kate stood as he entered. She raised a hand. She said, "Excuse me. That man who just signed . . ."

"Yes, ma'am?"

"Those men who just flew in. I think I know one of them. Might his name, by any chance, be Briggs?"

The man looked at his clipboard. He shook his head. "He initialed the receipt, but it's just a scrawled line. Could be Briggs, but it could be almost anything."

"But . . . wouldn't you know who rented the car?"

"Well, I know they're government, but that's about all. The order comes in on a twelve-digit code. We don't even have to bill. It just gets paid."

"I don't suppose you know where they're staying."

"No, ma'am, I surely don't. He's a friend, did you say?"

"I . . . knew him before he got hurt."

"Looks like a burn. Your friend been in a fire?"

"No, it wasn't a burn. He was . . . cut. Flying glass."

"Well, the one with the limp who got in the back seat, he called the driver Robert; that's the only name I heard. I'd say you could wait and ask the pilot if you like, but I don't think he'll be coming through the terminal."

She looked out toward the plane. It was taxiing away. It appeared to be headed across the runway to the other side of the airport. The man said, "Over there's where the private jets park. It's where I'll pick up the car later on."

"Later on. You mean today?"

"Or tomorrow, the next day. They never tell us how long."

"Well, thank you," she said. "I'm . . . probably mistaken."

"Wish I could have been more helpful. Good-bye, now."

She began to pace. She didn't know what to do. In the first place, she couldn't be a hundred percent sure that the man was actually Briggs. If it was, she'd have expected to see the other one with him. What was his name? Oh, yes. Lockwood. And that younger man was definitely not Lockwood.

But that did look like Briggs, so let's assume that it was. Let's assume that Briggs didn't have the good sense to look for another line of work. That would mean that he's still working for that man, Felix Aubrey, the one who Adam said looked like a toad. She had never seen Aubrey. Not even a photo. But the little man with them, the last one off the plane, did fit into the frog family somewhere.

But there was also that limp and his bowlegged walk. You would think that if anyone described Felix Aubrey, there would be some mention of his physical impairment. On the other hand, frogs are bowlegged.

All right, hold it, she thought. Do you see what you're doing? You're letting your imagination run wild. Except you knew, you just *knew* that Aubrey might be involved from the moment you heard that Philip Ragland had been shot. Philip Ragland had railed against people like Aubrey. Aubrey and that other one, Poole. And if those two were involved, then Harry was right. Adam was definitely involved in that shooting. That was Adam at the bar in that film clip she saw. And the woman sitting with him was Claudia.

It was all she could do to not hail a cab and go looking for Adam and Claudia herself. But where to start? She did not know the island. All she knew was that the boat was berthed in a place called Palmetto Bay, which apparently was the one place where they weren't. As hard as it was, she would have to sit and wait for Harry's friends to arrive.

As if in answer to a prayer, she thought she heard another airplane. It sounded like a low whistle as it passed overhead. The sound became more distant; it seemed to be leaving. The whistling sound changed its pitch, became deeper. She realized that the airplane was turning to land.

She saw it at last. A smaller jet than the first. Also privately owned, from the look of it. But this one did not taxi up to the terminal. It turned off to the right where the private planes were parked. She rushed to the window to see as best she could. It had stopped, its door had opened; there were people disembarking. And again, there were men. She saw two of them get off. They seemed unremarkable, casually dressed. Within seconds they had disappeared from view.

The plane, however, was moving again. It approached the single runway, she assumed to take off, but it kept on coming; it was crossing toward her. She held her breath as the aircraft approached and, once again, it came to a stop. The door opened and a small set of stairs folded out. It was them. Now she saw them. Two women.

Her first reaction on seeing them in the flesh was something that approached disappointment. She'd expected two women, but these were . . . just women. She'd expected, she supposed, a pair of amazon types. Hard as nails, no nonsense, chewing gum. But the taller one had a look that, even from a distance, made her seem very friendly and approachable. She was nicely dressed in a skirt and a blazer. Dark hair, long and flowing in the afternoon breeze, framed one of those faces that easily smiled. Sad eyes, though. Not unhappy. Just the way they were shaped. So this has to be Molly Farrell, she thought. She's the one Harry said she'd be comfortable with. Kate began to understand why.

The smaller one looked even less the part of what one would expect in a bodyguard. She was a redhead, very tiny, not much over five feet. She wore her hair short, in an elfin cut. She was dressed much more casually; she wore blue jeans and sneakers and a tight-fitting turtleneck sweater. Kate guessed that she was a size two, if that. From a distance, she might pass as a fourteen-year-old girl, although she was probably somewhere in her forties. Her face, while not unpretty, showed almost no expression. She was constantly moistening her lips. This one would be the "unusual" one. This one would have to be Carla.

They both saw that she was watching. Molly nodded an acknowledgment. They waited until the pilot, an older man, deplaned and opened the luggage compartment. He drew out a soft duffel for each of the women and placed them on the Tarmac at their feet. He said something to Molly. They both checked their watches. The pilot raised a finger and he shook it at Carla. His expression seemed pleasant; it was not a threatening gesture; it was done in the manner of a kindly parent reminding a child to behave. That pilot, thought Kate, must be more than just a pilot. It was clear that he knew them both well.

As the pilot turned and reentered the aircraft, the rental car man, the same one, pulled up, delivering a small gray Mercedes sedan. As before, he had a clipboard. Molly took it, scrawled something, then she motioned to Kate, inviting her to come out and join them.

As Kate pushed through the door; the man saw her and smiled. He said, "Hi. Any luck with your friend?"

She said no.

"I just passed them again. Couple miles down the road. They'd pulled over to look at a map."

"Which direction?"

"Down island." He made a vague gesture with his thumb. "They were headed south along the main parkway, but there must be a dozen hotels down that way. Have you thought about calling the hotels?"

"That's a good idea. Thanks. I might do that."

Molly waited for the rental car man to leave before introducing herself. She offered Kate her hand and she introduced Carla. Carla kept her hands at her sides, but her expression seemed to soften a bit. She said, "I'm looking forward to meeting your daughter. Is it true that she—"

"Carla, please," said Molly. "That will keep."

Molly said this to Carla rather gently, thought Kate. Kate said to Molly, "Um . . . this car that you've rented . . ."

"What? Why a Mercedes? We're told that they're commonplace on this island. Especially in this color."

She was saying, Kate realized, that it wouldn't stand out. That's the sort of thing professionals consider, she supposed, but that wasn't what she wanted to ask. "Actually, I meant the way you signed for the car. Does that mean that you work for the government, too?"

Molly shook her head. She also saw through the question. She asked, "What friend was he talking about? Who else could you know on this island?"

Kate told her about the other plane that came in. She told her about the man who she thought was one of those who had raided her greenhouse. She'd thought it was the bald one whose face had been cut, but now she wasn't so sure. He'd arrived in that plane with two other men, one of whom might have been Felix Aubrey.

Carla's eyes lit up. Molly's didn't. She seemed doubtful. She asked, "Have you ever seen Aubrey before?"

"No, I've only heard him described."

"Felix Aubrey does not get around very well. He had . . . suffered an injury to his legs."

"This man limped."

Still that doubt. "A small man? In his forties? Odd-looking?"

"With two younger men, both much bigger than he is. One, if I'm right, is the man named Briggs. I didn't know the third one, but his first name is Robert. The man who brought their car heard him called by that name."

"So they picked up their car from the man who brought ours?"

"He delivered a black Lincoln Town Car."

"Did you get the plate number?"

"I didn't think to. I'm sorry."

"And the plane that brought them. Still here, or has it left?"

Kate pointed to it across the field. "That's it."

"The Hawker?"

Kate answered, "I don't know them by make. It's the one to the right of that Texaco fuel truck." She asked, "By the way, those men who got off your plane . . . were they just commuters or did Harry send them, too?"

Molly answered vaguely, "Don't worry about them." She chewed on her lip. She turned to Carla.

Kate watched as the two of them looked at each other. No words were spoken. Molly narrowed her eyes and Carla answered with a shrug. The narrowing of the eyes seemed to ask, *"Could it be?"* The shrug seemed to say, *"I don't know. Let's find out."* Carla reached to pick up one of the duffels. She walked back toward the plane that had brought her.

"Carla? Just check. Do you hear what I'm saying? Don't do anything more than ask around."

Carla wet her lips. She said, "I'll find my own ride."

"Carla? You heard me?"

"I heard you. Where will you be? You're still going to see Olivia first?"

"Yes, we are."

Carla said, "I'll catch up to you later."

Kate watched as Carla reboarded her plane. It started to taxi at once. It was headed, she assumed, to the far side of

the airstrip where the other plane in question had parked.
Kate turned to Molly and asked, "Who's Olivia? And why
aren't we going to the boat?"

"We're not going to the boat until we know who's where.
Adam and your daughter still don't seem to be on it. Olivia's
a friend who I've been trying to reach. She is also the wife
of Philip Ragland."

Kate blinked in surprise. "Wait a minute. You know
them?"

"Not the husband," Molly answered, "but we all knew
Olivia. Adam has met her, if that's your next question, but
that was a long time ago."

"So . . . he *was* in that bar and it *wasn't* by chance. What
the hell did he get my daughter into?"

"Mrs. Geller, we don't know yet. Olivia will."

"So that *was* Felix Aubrey who flew in with his thugs.
They're here after Ragland? To finish the job? Or are they
after Adam this time?"

"We don't know."

"You can't guess? It's one or both. Why *else* would he
have come?"

"Mrs. Geller, either one would be abysmally stupid.
Whatever else Felix Aubrey may be, there is nothing stupid
about him."

"You're sure? I'm not. And what if you're wrong?"

"If he's here for either reason, he will die here."

32

Kaplan, so angry that his eyes were wet with tears, could
barely keep his mind on his driving. First Lockwood and the
wacko go down to that boat, which Lockwood had no business going near. The next thing you know, the barmaid
shows up and walks into a fistfight with the wacko.

Not just a tussle. An actual fistfight. Crow sees her coming, says she caught him by surprise. She sees the look on his face and backs away. He thinks, "She must know me," and he goes to grab her, calling her a slut and all other kinds of shit, including a spawn of the Devil. He grabs her by her blouse and he rips off her sleeve. Next he grabs her by the hair and starts smacking her face. She responds with a hard right cross of her own that knocks him square on his ass. He gets up with blood pouring out of his mouth from a punch that made him bite through his tongue. He tries to square off, swinging both arms like windmills, but he's wearing these golf shoes with spikes on the bottom. The guy might as well be on skates.

The barmaid sees this and goes for his knees. She takes him down with a leg sweep. She pounces on his back and has Crow in a chokehold before Lockwood can get to the top of the ramp. She doesn't see it's Lockwood, but she must have heard him coming. She must have thought maybe it was Whistler. Whatever she thought, she never looked up and Lockwood coldcocked her with his gun butt.

Kaplan, by this time, didn't have any choice. He had to zoom down, pick up Lockwood and Crow, and get them out of there fast. There were people who saw it, but they ducked behind buildings when they saw that Lockwood had a gun in his hand. Kaplan got there, yelled "Get in," but Lockwood said, "We can't leave her." He picked her up, threw her in the backseat, and shoved the wacko in there on top of her. Lockwood jumped into the front and they burned rubber backing out.

Kaplan raced out to Palmetto Bay Road where they almost hit a kid who was crossing on a bike. This happened because Kaplan was turning left while Crow was yelling, "No, we're going right." Kaplan tried to ignore him, but Crow swatted at his shoulder. Crow screamed into his ear, "Why are we going this way? This isn't the way to the hospital."

Kaplan wasn't sure that he heard Crow correctly because the guy's bleeding tongue was all over his mouth and he sprayed half the car when he yelled. Kaplan said, "You think what? We're still going to the hospital? Is that what you seriously think?"

"Those were your instructions. You'll obey them."

What he actually said was, *"Doze weh yo izuctions."* "You'll obey them" came out as *"Yobayem."*

"Joshua, shit-brain—look down on the floor there. Have you noticed that anything's different?"

His answer, in real words, was, "I'll see that she's quiet. I'll keep her in the car while you scout."

"You'll see that she's quiet? Like you did back at the dock? If she wakes up, she'll kick your ass again, pal. We're going back to the house."

Crow started to rant. Kaplan couldn't understand him. But at least he was mostly spraying Lockwood this time. Lockwood was just sitting there, stone-faced.

Kaplan nudged Lockwood. "Will you shut this guy up?"

All Lockwood could say was, "This is bad."

"Yeah, well," said Kaplan, "I doped that out myself. Would you care to enlarge on your assessment?"

"Just drive."

Kaplan heard a squeal from the well behind his seat. The girl had come to, but the squeal was more than that. It sounded like something else was hurting her. He looked into the mirror. Crow was sitting high up. He was sitting on his golf bag and he seemed to be bracing. He was putting his weight on her back with those spikes.

Kaplan hit the brakes and pulled over to the side. He threw the car into park, spun in his seat, and reached with both hands to grab Crow by the shirt.

Lockwood said, "Arnold, not here. Let's just go."

Kaplan had already pulled Crow forward between them, dragging him over the seatback. He stiffened his thumb and jammed it under Crow's jaw. Near its hinge he pressed upward as hard as he could, his thumbnail crushing a cluster of nerves that ran from the jaw to the brain. Crow could only gag. His eyes almost popped. Kaplan would have kept pressing until Crow blacked out if Crow hadn't bled all over his sleeve.

Kaplan eased off a little. "That enough? You want more?"

Crow said something that sounded like "Yak."

"Can you reach your shoes? Slip out of your shoes. Let me know when you're down to your socks."

Crow reached and groped. He slid them off. He said, "G-agh."

"I'll tell you what you're not going to do anymore. You're not going to open your fucking mouth unless somebody asks you a question. You're not going to touch that girl again except to hold her down with your feet." He said, "Vernon? Tell this schmuck that you made all that up, all that Devil-worshiping shit."

"I said let's go. Let's get out of here, Arnold."

"Say it. Don't you fuck with me either."

"Arnold, she's still a friend of Whistler's, remember? I couldn't just leave her there, could I?"

"You could have—never mind. You're right. Let's just go."

Kaplan shoved Crow back and put the car in gear. He eased the Pontiac into the traffic. Crow sat back there gurgling, trying to swallow, holding his throat in both hands. Kaplan tried to calm himself by taking several deep breaths. He said to Lockwood, "Vern, check the scanner. See if anyone called nine-one-one on this yet."

If someone had, and had given a description of this car, they'd be lucky to make it back to the house. He thought about finding another car fast, but the problem was transferring the passenger load. It would not go like clockwork with this bunch.

A new sound from behind him interrupted his reasoning. It seemed the kind of sound that somebody would make when they're trying to be very quiet. No breathing, no nothing, just a dull scraping sound. He said, "Hey, Josh. Is your hand in that golf bag?"

The sound stopped abruptly. All was still.

He said, "Josh, I'm going to guess that your hand is on your shotgun. You're trying to slip it out of your golf bag, but you can't without rattling your clubs, am I right?"

Not a sound.

"Say you pull it loose, Josh. What's your plan after that? Were you going to blow my head off while I'm driving?"

"Um . . . num."

"Was that yes or no? It did not sound decisive."

Now a faint rattling sound. The schmuck was still going to try.

"Or else you figure with the shotgun, I'll go where you want. Like you'll make me turn around and go for Ragland again. But the reason, Josh, why that's not a good plan . . . if I hear one more rattle, I'll pull over again. What's different this time is I'll kill you."

Crow eased his arm out of the bag and sat back. He resumed his breathing and gagging and glowering. Lockwood had the scanner up to his ear. He said, "Nothing yet on this car."

"Keep listening. You'll hear it. We got maybe five minutes." Kaplan looked up at Crow in the rearview mirror. He said, "Now, Josh, if you'll try to behave, me and Vern here will get you off this island. That's all we want and that's what we're going to do. Vern, tell him that's what we're going to do."

"Yeah, that's right."

"He can finish off Ragland some other time. Vern, tell him that this Ragland shit is over for now."

Lockwood nodded his agreement. "No hospital now."

"No nothing, right. We do what Aubrey said."

"First we wait."

"Wait for what?"

Lockwood said, "I still want Whistler. We stay until that boat of his blows."

"Which is when?"

"Four hours," he said. "Little over four hours."

"Fine by me. We sit tight until then."

Which is horseshit, thought Kaplan. You don't have four hours. You have until Mr. Aubrey shows up. The minute he shows, you're both organ donors. As if anyone would want what's left over.

"Something's happened down there," said Claudia, craning, as Whistler drove over the Cross Island Bridge. For a moment, from the highest part of the bridge, nearly all of the marina was in view.

Whistler tried to look. The moment had passed. He asked, "What was it? Could you see?"

"People running around. A man waving his arms."

"Near the boat? Our boat?"

"No, up near the shops."

"An accident, maybe. We'll know soon enough."

By the time they drove into Palmetto Bay and reached the side road that led to the docks, Whistler saw that a small knot of people had gathered. They seemed to be watching the approach of his car. No, not his car, he realized. They were looking beyond him. Perhaps waiting for an ambulance, he thought.

He had to park in a space that was up near the shops. The much nearer space that he'd left had been taken. He and Claudia got out and proceeded toward the ramp. Another yacht owner whom he knew by sight was approaching from that direction. Whistler asked him if he knew what all the fuss was about.

The man answered, "I didn't see it myself. Man and a woman got into a fight. From what I hear, the woman was cleaning his clock. Some guy in a suit dragged her off him."

"Was anyone hurt?"

"I don't know. They took off. I guess someone thought they should call the cops anyway. Like the cops aren't busy enough since last night."

Whistler smiled an acknowledgment. "Yeah, you'd think so. Thanks."

He and Claudia reached the ramp that led to the fuel dock. But Claudia, by then, had been walking more slowly. She had fallen a few steps behind him. He saw that her eyes had narrowed a bit. Her head was cocked to one side. It was a look that Whistler had come to know well.

He said, "Go ahead. Say it."

"A man in a suit?"

He knew that she had a thing about suits. When you live on a boat, you don't see very many. It was possible that the

last suits she'd seen were those worn by Lockwood and
Briggs. Oh, and then there was also that man on Grand Cayman whom Claudia was ready to stab with a fork. He
grunted to himself. First a fork, then a knife. Perhaps they
should stay out of restaurants altogether. Either that or give
her plastic utensils.

He said, "Claudia, all kinds of people wear suits."

"Down here? At a marina?"

"One with four seafood restaurants. Bankers and lawyers
wear suits every day and some of them come here for
lunch."

Still that frown, that hesitation.

"Tell you what," said Whistler. "I'll call Moore and ask
him." He patted his pocket where he'd put Ed Moore's card.
"I also need to call my father and come clean with him, but
I'm not looking forward to that conversation. We'll put
Moore at the top of the list."

She asked, "What about the weapons? They're still in the
trunk."

"We're not going to need weapons."

"There's been trouble here, Adam."

"There's been some kind of fight and it's none of our
business. Either way, there are too many people around.
They'll have to stay where they are until it's dark."

She seemed very uneasy, but she knew that he was right.
Perhaps she was sorry that she pulled that stunt earlier. He
patted his waist and said, "We'll be fine. I still have a handgun under my belt." Not much of a gun, but a gun.

They continued down the ramp and onto the dock. He
could hear a siren in the distance. They proceeded to the fuel
dock where the boat was tied up. He hesitated before climbing aboard, not because he sensed that there was anything
amiss, but because he'd left the cabin unlocked. But the coil
of line that he had tossed across the hatch was still draped
pretty much as he remembered it. Whistler also noticed that
someone had been crabbing. The trap was on the dock. It
had left a recent puddle. He saw no bait, not even residue of
bait. Perhaps someone had merely been cleaning it.

Claudia asked him. "Is anything wrong?"

"Not a thing. Go ahead." They stepped aboard.

She gathered the line and hung it from a cleat as Whistler stepped down through the hatch. The siren that he'd heard had grown louder. Whistler found his cell phone where he had left it. It was under the jacket that he'd meant to wear but had forgotten in his rush to leave the boat. He checked the answering machine. It showed no new messages. Claudia had begun to climb down from the deck. He became aware that she'd stopped halfway. Once again, her eyes narrowed. Once again, her head was cocked.

She asked, "Adam . . . what do you smell?"

He sniffed and he shrugged. "We *are* at the fuel dock."

She shook her head slowly. "Not gas. Besides gas."

He gestured toward the galley. "I can still smell our breakfast."

Again she shook her head. She said, "Someone's been here."

He'd seen nothing that seemed to have been disturbed. He asked her, "Why do you think so?"

She said, "It's a man. A man has been in here."

"You're . . . saying you smell him? His aftershave? What?"

"No, a cigar. Don't you smell a cigar?"

He tried to. He couldn't. But he felt sure that she could. Claudia could catch a scent on a breeze like no one he'd ever met. He thought it likely, however, that what she was sniffing had wafted through the hatch from a neighboring boat. Perhaps whoever owned that crab trap outside had been puffing on a stogie while he used it.

When she spoke again, her voice was quiet, but firm. She said, "Adam, I want you to listen to me."

"I am. I'm listening. What is it?"

"That man—the big one—who came to our house. The one who smelled of cigars. It was him."

Whistler blinked. "You can't mean Vernon Lockwood."

"I can and I do. I can smell him."

"Sweetheart, you're saying he was here on this boat?"

She said, "It's strongest right here." She was at the chart table. She reached across to the panel of instruments above it. She said, "They both wore dark suits when they came to Mom's house. You told me that they always wore dark suits."

"The . . . um, man we just spoke to didn't say it was dark. He didn't say big. He didn't mention a cigar. All he said was a guy in a suit."

"Adam, do you doubt that I smell a cigar?"

"No, I don't. But to tell me it was Lockwood's cigar . . ."

She said, "Then let's ask. Let's find out what he looked like. All those people up the road must have seen him."

Whistler heard a squeal of brakes in the distance. He realized that the sirens had stopped. He said, "Okay, we'll walk up there, but only to eavesdrop. When we hear a description, we leave. Fair enough?"

His cell phone chirped before she could answer. He flipped it open. His father, most likely. But the caller was the sergeant. He thought Moore had read his mind. Sergeant Moore, however, sounded upset. Moore asked him, "Adam, are you on your boat?"

"Yes, we are. We just got here."

"Who is 'we'? Is Leslie with you?"

"Leslie Stewart?" Whistler asked. "No, she isn't."

"Have you seen her at all? She was coming to get Claudia. From there, she was going to the hospital."

"Claudia and I just got back from there ourselves. What's wrong, Ed? What's going on?"

"Look, I just pulled into Palmetto Bay. We have a report that a woman has been beaten and kidnapped. From the witness accounts, it sounds like Leslie. They ripped off part of a blouse like the one she was wearing. Oh, shit. Now I see Leslie's car."

Claudia was standing a few feet away. She was staring at the phone as he held it to his ear. He raised a questioning eyebrow. She nodded in response. She mouthed the words, *"I can hear."*

"Ed, you said 'they.' What did the witnesses see?"

"Three men, a green Pontiac and, goddamn it, I saw them. They were crawling past Jump's. This must have been why. They must have followed her down to the marina and—oh, Christ. I think one of them had to be Crow."

Moore paused to swallow. He was more than upset. He seemed to be blaming himself.

"Ed, slow down. Why might one of them be Crow?"

"Witness description. His face all patched up. He called her a slut and something else about the Devil. Who the hell else could it be?"

Whistler had felt his own stomach tighten, but he forced himself to speak slowly. He asked, "And the others? You have descriptions on the others?"

"Golf shoes."

"Beg your pardon?"

"They say Crow was wearing golf shoes with spikes. Why would he walk around wearing spikes?"

"I don't know. Ed—the others. What did they look like?"

"One had a gun. He whacked Leslie on the head. Then he threw her into the car. Dark suit, late thirties, linebacker build. He had a cigar in his mouth."

Whistler's mind was spinning. Crow and Lockwood together? As unlikely as it seemed, he knew that Claudia was right. Vernon Lockwood had been aboard their boat. He felt a cold fury rising within him. In his mind, he saw Lockwood touching Claudia's things and for that alone Whistler would kill him.

Moore said, "Talk to me, Adam. You there?"

Whistler, with effort, kept his voice calm and even. He asked, "And the third man? You said there was a third."

"Third man was the driver. Late forties, striped jacket, straw hat, tinted glasses. This is someone who I *think* Leslie knew before this. Do you know either one? They sound familiar?"

That didn't describe Briggs, but it did sound familiar. "Not offhand," he lied. "Have you broadcast those descriptions?"

"Green Pontiac, three men is all that went out. The rest of

it's going out now." Moore paused. He took a breath. He asked, "Adam . . . why Leslie?"

"You say she knew the driver?"

"She sounded that way."

"And she's seen the flyer on Joshua Crow. She knows that his face was marked up. You say you think they followed her here. She got out of her car and they grabbed her?"

"That's what it looks like," said Moore, "but why her?"

"Ed, you just said it. They thought that she'd made them."

Moore answered, "Wait a minute. That couldn't be right. She was halfway down to your boat when this happened. Crow didn't chase after her and grab her from behind. He was already down there. He was coming from there."

Whistler felt a chill. He said weakly, "I don't know."

"Is this about you? Were they down here after you?"

"Ed . . . I don't know. We'll be right up there."

33

Poole's bodyguard, Robert, slowed the Lincoln to a crawl as Lagoon Road came into view. The first mailbox he could see showed the number 18. The house two lots beyond it was blue with black shutters. He pointed. He said, "There it is, Mr. Aubrey. That blue house must be twenty-two."

"Good house," said Briggs from the passenger seat. "Set back and it's got a two-car garage. Got a privacy fence on one side of the house and what looks like a jungle on the other. Good choice by Crow. Even better for us."

Aubrey leaned forward, one hand on Briggs's shoulder. "I do not see the car. Do you see a green Pontiac anywhere on that street?"

Briggs shook his head. "It's not there." He seemed glad of it.

If it had been, thought Aubrey, they would have followed

Plan A. All they'd need to do is pull up and tap the horn. Kaplan would hear it, know that they've arrived, and promptly
shoot Lockwood and Crow. Tidier, perhaps, but less gratifying than actually witnessing Lockwood's comeuppance. Less
gratifying, certainly, for our Mr. Briggs, who would prefer to
see to Lockwood himself, But Briggs would want to preface
the deed by telling Mr. Lockwood why he's killing him. He
would say, "See this face? You left me behind. You saved
your own ass and they gave me this face. So I'm going to kill
you, you son of a bitch. But first I'm going to shoot off most
of your own face before I put a couple in your gut."

Or words to that effect. Something melodramatic. But
that sort of confrontation was out of the question. You don't
warn a man like Lockwood. You don't let him know what's
coming. Best to smile, say, "Hi, Vern," and then shoot him.

Young Robert, it develops, detests Lockwood as well. It
seems that Lockwood once tried to intimidate Robert in the
same way he'd tried to intimidate Whistler. Robert, who is
even bigger than Lockwood, might have given a good account of himself had his boss, Mr. Poole, not told him to
"forbear." Poole counseled him to turn the other cheek,
which he did, so Lockwood, predictably, then slapped him.
Well, we'll see, thought Aubrey, who gets slapped this time
around. We seem to be left with Plan B. We wait.

"We're here earlier than Kaplan expected us," he said. "But
that's good. They're still out. Kaplan's keeping them busy."

Briggs scanned the street. He said, "We don't know how
long. We better get inside while we can."

"You're quite right. Robert? Take us up to the driveway.
The garage should be unlocked. Briggs and I will go in.
You will then leave this car on one of the side streets, but
not one that Mr. Kaplan is likely to use."

Robert's feelings seemed hurt. "I'd have thought of that,
sir."

"Forgive me," said Aubrey. "I know that, of course. It's
just that so much has gone contrary to instructions, I find
myself micromanaging. I'm sorry."

"I understand perfectly, sir."

"When you walk back—excuse me. How *will* you come back?"

"I won't walk up the street. I'll come around through the woods in the back of that house. If you will unlock the back door for me, sir . . ."

"That is where Mr. Briggs and I will wait for you, Robert. We'll try not to start the party without you."

Whistler, after breaking the connection with Moore, took Olivia's small-caliber pistol from his belt, checked the barrel, and chambered a round. He slipped into his jacket. He put the cell phone in his pocket. He said to Claudia, "It was Lockwood, no question. Remind me not to doubt you again."

She said, "Let's go help them find Leslie."

"We'll do what we can. Let me think for a minute."

"While you're thinking, they could be killing her, Adam."

"You want us to do what? Drive around? Look for their car? That's why I didn't tell Moore that we know Vernon Lockwood. That's exactly what Moore would have us doing with him."

"Wouldn't that be better than standing here talking?"

No, it wouldn't, thought Whistler, because if they found Lockwood, he wouldn't be able to kill him on sight. Not with the sergeant looking on.

He said, "Let's try to figure out what we're up against first. The third man, the driver . . . we've seen him before. He was there last night when the shooting took place. I've noticed him several times before that."

She remembered. She asked, "The far side of the bar?"

"Facing us, his back to the door."

Whistler grimaced as he realized that he should have known. The striped jacket, he told Claudia, was the only person there who hadn't ducked for cover when it started. He'd seen it all. The best seat in the house. Whistler had to shout for him to get down when Crow drove up outside and raised his shotgun. Whistler should have wondered why he'd seemed so detached. No fear. Fascination. Didn't want to miss a thing.

She asked, "Could he have been a lookout for Crow?"

"No. Too surprised. He didn't expect it. He was there watching us, and now we know he's with Lockwood. This means that Lockwood must have known for some time that you and I are back in this country."

He must have, thought Whistler, but how? The answer to that was any number of ways. The most efficient of those would have been electronic. That double signal. That must have been it. His father had said that he was getting an echo. Since when? Since Antigua? No, before that. Martinique.

Whistler said, "There's a tracker somewhere on this boat. They've known where we are for two months at least."

She did not seem alarmed. She said, "And yet nothing's happened."

"You call all this nothing?"

"No, I mean that we've been here for more than three weeks. If they wanted you, Adam, they had every chance. Yet until last night, nothing happened."

"What's changed," he said, "is Crow. Them tying in with Crow. I just can't imagine why they'd do that. Or how."

"But they did. What's the simplest answer to how?"

He stared for a moment. "They already knew him. They had to have known where he'd be, how to find him."

"Of course. And therefore? Who put them together?"

"You . . . want me to say Aubrey. This does not sound like Aubrey."

"But Crow is a lunatic. A religious fanatic. What does that suggest to you, Adam?"

He nodded. "You're right. That would point to Delbert Poole."

"Okay, what's the simplest answer to why?"

"To silence Ragland. But that's where you lose me. Aubrey wouldn't have touched this, and Lockwood works for Aubrey. Lockwood doesn't take orders from Poole."

"You're assuming that Lockwood wouldn't act without orders. And if, as you say, there's a tracker on this boat, why would Lockwood feel the need to come aboard?"

Good question, he thought. To plant a listening device?

Or, just as likely, some other device. Whistler felt the hairs on his neck begin to rise. He remembered Moore saying that Crow had used bombs. Remote control, maybe? Lockwood's thumb on the button?

He stepped closer to Claudia, his lips to her ear. He whispered, "Don't touch anything. Climb back up the steps."

Her eyes widened. She understood and obeyed. Without a word, she went first. She reached the cockpit, where she waited for him. She pointed to some marks on the fiberglass deck. They were scuff marks. From street shoes. Whistler saw them and nodded. They had to be Lockwood's. She stepped over the rail and onto the dock. She pointed to another set of marks that she'd found. Spike marks. Those golf shoes. Crow had been there as well. They followed the spike marks all the way up the ramp. They were safely away from the boat.

Whistler saw Moore's patrol car. Another had joined it. Moore was standing at the door of his car, speaking into his radio; his back was turned toward them. Another deputy was talking to a small knot of people. Must be those who had witnessed the abduction. A few others had gathered and they stood on the fringes. Whistler saw two men among them who looked vaguely familiar. A big man and a smaller one, both middle-aged. The big one had the build of a wrestler. They reminded him of . . . never mind . . . it couldn't be. He took Claudia's arm and steered her toward the steps that led off into the warren of restaurants and shops.

She asked, "Why this way? Are we ducking the sergeant?"

"If we don't, he's going to hold us. Let's try to get to the car."

"What then?"

He said, "Claudia, I need you to do something for me. If we can get to Jump and Phil's, I'm going to drop you off there. Wait there for me. Stay by the phone."

"While you're doing what?"

"While I try to find Leslie."

"By yourself? How would you even know where to start?"

"I . . . know how Lockwood thinks. That might help me."

She looked into his eyes. She saw that they'd turned cold. She asked, "Is it Leslie you're thinking about?"

"She'll be with them if I find them. And you said it yourself. I won't find them standing here talking."

"I'm going with you, Adam. You go nowhere without me."

"Look, this morning, when you said that you're in my world more than ever, I didn't correct you. But you're not. You never will be."

She said, "Adam, that's not your decision to make."

"Yeah, it is. And I've just made it. You will wait at Jump and Phil's. I don't want you with me on this one."

Arnold Kaplan had almost reached North Forest Beach when he heard the description of their car on the scanner. Green Pontiac, three men, one young woman, partial plate. At least one of the occupants may be armed.

He said to Lockwood, "Few more blocks. We're almost there."

Another bulletin came on, this one much more detailed. It identified the victim of the "probable abduction." It gave her full name, Leslie Stewart. It described the two men who'd forced her into the car and the clothing that was worn by the driver. It said that one of them might be Joshua Crow, the man wanted for the shooting of Ragland. It further identified Miss Stewart, the victim, as a bartender at Jump & Phil's. It said that as such, on the previous evening, she had witnessed the shootings in that restaurant. She might have recognized Crow before he made his escape. She might have spotted Crow again at Palmetto Bay. He knew it and attacked her and seized her.

No, thought Kaplan, that is not how it happened. It happened because this fucking loony in the back . . .

He swung off the main road to a narrow street that looked like it might wind back toward the house. Up ahead, he saw that the paved road was ending. After that it was dirt. That looked right. He'd go that way.

He said, "Leslie, Miss Stewart . . . can you hear me back there?"

She coughed and she squirmed. She could hear.

He said, "Miss Stewart, we're not going to hurt you. I give you my word. No one hurts you."

Lockwood glanced at him sideways. Kaplan knew what he was thinking. Lockwood's eyes said, *"No way we don't snuff her. She's seen us."* But Kaplan was thinking, *"No, she's only seen Crow. You, she only heard, but it doesn't much matter. You two are going to get a bullet in the head just as soon as I can stash this girl someplace."*

Leslie's voice, scared and muffled, came up from the well. She asked Kaplan, "What did you do?"

He answered, "Do where? You mean down on the dock?"

"What did you do to Claudia? What did you do to Adam? If you hurt them . . ."

"We didn't. They were not even there. None of us have seen them. It's the truth."

Lockwood snapped, "What's this? True confessions? Shut up."

"No use scaring her more than we have to," said Kaplan. He asked Leslie, "By the way, what were you doing there?"

"I was . . . going to the hospital. I . . . stopped by to see if they wanted to come."

"See that?" said Lockwood. "I told you. They're tight. They knew each other long before this."

"Leslie?" Kaplan asked her. "How long have you known them?"

"I don't know. Two weeks. Maybe three."

"And just from the bar. You only know them from the bar?"

Lockwood asked, "And what's this? Now you're feeding her lines?"

Kaplan answered, "She's telling the truth."

"That she hardly knows them? You're kidding me, right? Then what was that meeting on the boat with that cop? You yourself said they looked very cozy."

Kaplan said, "So let's ask her."

"I'll ask her myself."

Lockwood turned in his seat. He looked down at Leslie's head. He pushed Crow's headcovers out of the way so that he could see her face looking up at him. He asked her, "You saw what the girl did to Breen?"

"I . . . no," she said, swallowing. "I'm not sure what I saw."

"See that?" he said to Kaplan. "She's still covering for them. They're both fucking killers and she's covering for them. Why is that, do you think? They're big tippers?"

Look who calls who fucking killers, thought Kaplan. He answered, "Let's just leave it, okay?"

But Lockwood never did know when to shut up. He asked Leslie, "Whistler showed you Aubrey's ledger, am I right?"

"His . . . who?"

"On the boat. This morning. He was showing you papers. They were from Aubrey's ledger, am I right?"

Kaplan sighed and asked Lockwood, "Did you hear what you just told her?"

"I'm not telling her anything she doesn't know. I'm right about this, Arnie. She knows."

"Vernon . . . do you think we could avoid using names?"

"Doesn't matter."

"And you showed her your face. Do you realize you did that? Back when you hit her, she did not see you coming. She never saw your face before just now." You dumb shit.

"So what? Doesn't matter. Watch the road."

You're right, thought Kaplan. It's not going to matter. He surveyed the road ahead and he checked his rearview mirror. Up ahead, all he saw was a garbage truck making its house-to-house rounds. Behind him was an oil truck on its way to make deliveries. He saw a taxi farther back, but the taxi was turning. It all looked nice and normal, nice and quiet.

But while watching through his mirror, he had also noticed Crow. Crow had hardly made a sound, except some gagging and coughing, since Kaplan had warned him that he'd shoot him if he spoke. Kaplan thought he had recovered from the thumb in his throat, but now Crow looked as if he was choking to death. Kaplan nudged Lockwood. He said, "Check out the wacko."

Crow's eyes were shut, his fists were clenched, and his face was the color of pastrami. Small drops of bloody spittle squeezed out through his lips. Kaplan realized he was holding his breath.

"Hey, Crow," said Lockwood. "What the hell are you doing?"

Crow began to hum softly, atonal, low-pitched.

"That's how babies look," said Kaplan, "when they're trying to shit. Hey, Josh, are you having some rectal discomfort? What that comes from is having your head up your ass; but don't worry, you'll feel better soon."

Crow made no response. "I think he's praying," said Lockwood.

"Either that, or he's trying to levitate," said Kaplan. "Hey, Josh, can you do that? Have you factored in the roof? The roof could be a problem if you're trying to float away."

Crow began rocking in time with his humming. He opened one eye. It was glaring at Kaplan. He exhaled a blast of air and he threw himself forward. He clawed at Kaplan's throat with both hands.

Kaplan cursed. The Pontiac swerved. Lockwood's fist shot out. It caught the side of Crow's head. Crow fell back, but he quickly recovered. He raised both feet and tried to kick at Lockwood. Kaplan touched the brakes to slow the car down because the crew of the garbage truck was a half block ahead and they didn't need the garbage guys seeing this. Crow kicked twice more at Lockwood. Lockwood cocked his fist again, but then he said, "Screw this." Instead, he reached for his Glock.

Kaplan said, "Put that away. Just keep the putz off me."

"This guy's fucking nuts."

"I been telling you that."

"So let's save ourselves some trouble. He goes now." He raised the Glock.

"No, don't," said Kaplan quickly. "We're here to help him, remember? Just keep the guy off me. No guns."

Lockwood blinked, confused. "Will you make up your mind?"

"I remembered our instructions, is all."

Kaplan didn't want him shot for a number of reasons. The most obvious reason was that Leslie was there and she'd be an eyewitness to murder. That likelihood, however, would cut no ice with Lockwood, because in his head she was on borrowed time. If Lockwood did pull the trigger, however, he'd notice that nothing much happened. Lockwood might then realize that the last time he checked, his gun had a round in the chamber. He might realize, therefore, that if someone removed it, that someone could only have been Arnold Kaplan. This would not be good. Not here, not now. It could cause an untimely falling-out.

"Vernon . . . the gun. Put it down now, will you please? Hey, Leslie? How's it going? You okay?"

A muffled "No, I'm not okay, damn it."

"Well, as long as you're back there, keep an eye on him, will you?"

"Me watch *him*? You want me to watch *him*?"

"Just keep your eyes open. Sing out if he moves. Not for long. We'll be stopping in a minute."

"You're crazy. You know that?"

"Some of us more than others. Are you watching? What's our friend doing now?"

"He's . . . curled up hugging his golf bag and humming. He opened a zipper that runs down the side. There's some stuff spilling out of the bag."

"What kind of stuff, Leslie? You see any plastic pipe?"

"No, it's food. A sandwich. And two bottles of Snapple."

"Watch out that he doesn't pick up one of those bottles."

"He can't. They rolled down on me."

"Especially watch out for any white plastic pipe. Make sure you can see both his hands."

"What's this white plastic pipe?"

"You see it or not?"

"No, I don't. And he's back in a fetal position. Hey, where are you guys taking me?"

"To a house. You'll be more comfortable. Trust me."

"And you're not going to hurt me?"

"You'll be tending bar tomorrow. In the meantime, try to roll with the punches."

Next left turn, then a right . . . that should be Lagoon Road. Get to the house, get this car in the garage. First order of business will be Leslie. Tie her up. Use Crow's duct tape. Stick her in a closet. Put a radio in there with her and turn it up loud so that she maybe can't hear what happens next. What happens next is Crow and Lockwood go down. Boom-boom, two head shots, then at last there's peace and quiet while he waits for Aubrey to show. After that, he disappears. He leaves disposal to Aubrey. He had earned the right to bail on any digging.

But digging was later. This was now. First things first. He'd considered taking Lockwood's gun and popping them both with the Glock. No noise would make Leslie even less of a witness. But that would involve holding these two at gunpoint and trying to get Lockwood to hand over his weapon. Lockwood wouldn't because he would know he'd been crossed and might decide he had nothing to lose. It could get tense. So boom-boom, two quick shots. Noisy is better than sloppy.

He found Lagoon Road at the end of a side street. From there, the house should be three streets to his right. As he made a right turn he glanced up that same side street and noticed a car that was parked there. That car bothered him for some reason. He tried to think why, and then he realized what it was. He'd seen no other cars that were parked in the street. All the cars around here were in driveways. And that car, in addition, was a black Lincoln Town Car. This was not a Lincoln neighborhood. It was a minivan neighborhood. Minivans, SUVs, and a few pickup trucks. Even so, it was three streets away from the house.

Kaplan put it out of his mind.

34

Whistler, once again, had wasted his breath telling Claudia that she couldn't come with him. He was tempted to leave her, to drive off without her, but that would have left Claudia with no place to go except back to a boat that might blow at any time. Or if not, she'd be found there by Moore.

They made it to the car without being seen. Shielded by other cars in the lot, he popped the trunk and reached in for the canvas tote that held the Ingram MAC-10 and the deck-sweeper shotgun.

"I'll take those," said Claudia. "You drive."

He said, "You won't take them. You won't even touch them. I'm putting this bag on the floor at your feet, but that's only so that I can reach them."

"As you wish."

"Keep them covered with that sail bag. Don't touch them."

"I heard you."

"I'm still dropping you off at Jump and Phil's. It's the one place where you'll be safe."

"And I think you heard me," she said. "No, you're not." She climbed in with the bag and both weapons.

Okay, thought Whistler, he'd have this out with her later. On the other hand, it might not matter in the end. He realized, of course, that there wasn't much chance of him spotting the car that took Leslie. But he knew that there were only so many places where that green Pontiac could have gone.

"They went that way," said Claudia. "Up Palmetto Bay Road."

"I'd like you to be quiet."

"They still went that way."

Whether this was intuition or a thought-out conclusion, he agreed that she was probably right. They would have turned left out of Palmetto Bay. They would not have risked being trapped on the bridge.

"And they would have kept going," she said.

"Going where?"

"Through the circle. They wouldn't have turned."

Whistler knew that going through would have made the most sense. On reaching Sea Pines Circle, there were three ways to go. Turning right would have led them past Jump & Phil's to the gated community of Sea Pines. They would not have risked being seen from Jump & Phil's, not after being spotted there the last time. Nor would they try to get past the Sea Pines gate in a car that was so easily remembered.

"Keep going through the circle," said Claudia.

"I heard you."

He did so because that had been his intention. The green Pontiac almost certainly would not have turned left onto the island's main parkway. They would have to have assumed that an alarm had gone out, and the parkway was the first route that would have been covered because it led off the island. And they might have a scanner. Crow probably used one. That was how he'd avoided being caught all this time.

It seemed likely, therefore, that they'd driven through the circle and headed due east toward the ocean. They'd pass one other gated community, called Shipyard. They would not have gone there either, for the same reason. There were several hotels, but he could rule them out as well. They would hardly have booked a hotel room. That left private homes, as Sergeant Moore had suggested. Moore thought that Crow would find an unoccupied home. The way to bet, therefore, was North Forest Beach. If so, they were trapped. They had no place to go. And if so, Sergeant Moore would soon realize that as well. Those police not assigned to specific intersections might then mount a house-to-house search of that area.

Claudia sat staring forward, sometimes upward. She might

have been looking for birds; he didn't know, but he thought it best not to ask. With birds on his mind, he was suddenly startled when he thought he heard the chirp of a bird inside their car. In that instant he realized that it was his cell phone. It was probably Moore calling, asking where they had gone.

Claudia turned her head toward the source of the sound. She said, "You'd better answer that, Adam."

"I know who it is."

She squinted. "No, you don't. You'd better answer it," she said.

With a sigh, he pulled the phone from his pocket. He thumbed it open and put it to his ear. He heard the words, "Adam? Is that you?"

It was a woman's voice. It was Olivia Ragland. He did not recall giving her this number. He glanced at Claudia, wondering how she could have known. He said, "Yeah, it's me. Has something happened?"

"Someone here needs to speak to you. Hold on."

Whistler grumbled to himself. He thought it must be her husband. But the voice that came on was another female voice. Low, soft spoken, almost gentle, but all business. He knew that voice. He knew it before she spoke her name.

She said, "Hello, Adam. Where are you at this moment? And is Claudia with you? This is Molly."

This was a surprise, but something less than a shock. He might have guessed that she would have grabbed a fast flight after failing to make contact with Olivia. And he'd have thought that she might have been a touch more cordial. It had been fourteen years, after all.

He replied, "She's with me. We're in my rental car. Molly, give me a number; I'll call you back later. This isn't a good time to talk."

"Adam, Aubrey's on the island. Did you know that?"

His stunned silence answered for him. He managed, "You're sure?"

"So is Aubrey's man, Briggs. And another man named Robert. Robert's in his late twenties, a big man, blond hair. We don't have a last name for Robert."

Whistler had to pull over. He saw a curb cut ahead. It was the entrance to the Bi-Lo Supermarket. He said, "You're describing Delbert Poole's bodyguard. Are you sure you don't mean Vernon Lockwood?"

"It's not Lockwood. That one was already here. Listen, Adam—"

"Just a minute. You knew that? How long have you known that?"

"Not long. Listen, Adam—"

"And who is *we*, Molly? Who else came down here with you?"

"A few of us flew down at your father's request. We're here strictly to keep you from harm and that's all. As we speak, your father is en route with the twins. Harry knows that it was you in that restaurant last night. Claudia's mother suspected it as well and decided to fly in on her own. Harry asked us to intercept her and we have. She's in talking to Ragland at the moment. Take my number."

Whistler shook his head in disgust. "Molly, why am I the last one to hear this?"

"Because you've been out of reach. Now you're not. Take my number."

An inward groan. "I don't believe this," he said. But he memorized the number of her cell phone.

She said, "We've all had trouble knowing what to believe. We doubted that you were in that restaurant by chance."

"We were."

"I know that. Olivia told me."

"Has Olivia said anything about Claudia's . . . performance?"

"Privately. Only to me. Did that happen?"

"Yes, it did."

"You taught her?"

"Me? I couldn't have done that myself. Please do not, in any case, tell her mother about that. The story is that neither of us used that knife. Let's keep it that way if we can."

"Except Claudia knows. How is she handling it, Adam?"

This question was Whistler's first inkling thus far of the old Molly Farrell that he'd known. The nice one, the kind one, the compassionate one with whom he had skied and played tennis.

He answered, "I'm not sure. We'll see how it settles. Molly, on my way out of Palmetto Bay, I thought I recognized a couple of men. Would one of those men have been Billy McHugh?"

"Billy and John Waldo. You slipped past them, I take it."

"You're in contact with them? Tell them not to board the boat."

"They've . . . surmised that Lockwood had been there for a reason. You think he's rigged something?"

"I would bet on a bomb."

"Billy says that three men kidnapped a young woman. Two of those men would be Lockwood and Crow. Do you have a name for the third?"

"No, I don't, but he witnessed what happened last night. So did the girl who they kidnapped," said Whistler.

"Which is why they took her?"

"That would not have been the reason. I am probably the reason. Look, Molly, I have to get moving."

"Adam . . . where are you?"

"Out looking for them."

"You're out looking for that green Pontiac by yourselves? Adam, you're up against six of them now. Are you trying to get the both of you killed?"

"Well . . . Claudia's more afraid that it's Leslie who'll be killed. She would not find that easy to live with."

"Adam, where are you? Please tell me precisely."

"Molly, hold on." He pressed the mute button. He asked Claudia, "How much could you hear?"

"Most of it. Who is Molly?"

"That's a long story. Later."

"My mother's here? Really?"

"And in very good hands. Don't worry about her. Molly will want us to sit here and wait for two other men to come and join us. They're not far away. They're old friends of my father."

"Men who've done this sort of thing? Like the twins?"

"Men who've been doing it since before you were born. We'd be foolish not to wait for them, Claudia."

"How long?"

"A few minutes."

"But not longer than that. I can't stand knowing that they've got Leslie."

That was easy, thought Whistler. And it was a relief. If he knew Molly, she'd tell those two to lock Claudia in the trunk until Aubrey was dealt with one way or the other. He'd be all for it. He'd apologize later. But if Molly was there at his father's behest, she'd be as likely to tell them to stuff him in with her. And those two could do it if they got within reach. He would damned well make sure that they didn't.

He released the mute button. "Are you looking at a map?"

Molly answered, "I am. Go ahead."

"Find Sea Pines Circle. We're a mile and a half above it. We're in a beige Ford Taurus. We'll be waiting, right-hand side."

"I got it. I'm putting you on hold."

He heard a click and the line went still. He assumed that she was calling John Waldo or Billy. He held the phone to his ear for what must have been a full minute, much too long for Molly just to tell them where he is. They were probably discussing such options as the trunk.

He heard another soft click. Molly came on again. She said, "That was Carla. She's somewhere near you. You remember Carla Benedict, don't you?"

"Oh, yes."

"Did you know that it was Carla who cut Briggs and Aubrey?"

"No one said so, but it wasn't hard to guess."

"Listen to me, Adam. She knows where they are. She denies it, but I don't believe her."

"How could she?"

"Trust me; she could. The 'how' part can wait. She is on her way to meet you. I want you to hold her. Keep her there until Billy or John Waldo can join you. One of them will stay near the boat. Introduce her to Claudia. Let them talk."

"Um . . . what for?"

"She's only coming to meet you because Claudia's with you. Otherwise, she's like you; she works mostly alone. She might try to take that bunch by herself."

"With a knife?"

A patient sigh. "No, Adam. Not with a knife. She is quite well equipped to take out six men, but I'll say again, that is not why we came here. We're here to protect you; get you both off this island. Your father needs you to . . . be healthy."

He had heard the hesitation. A near slip. That wasn't like her. He asked her, "Molly, is my father okay?"

"Your dad's fine."

"Can I believe you?"

"He'll live longer than you will, going after six men."

"Let me ask you something else. Has he ever been shot?"

She said, "Adam, he's fine. We were talking about Carla. She knows, by the way, what Claudia did. I know you'd prefer that I hadn't told her, but it sold her on stopping whatever she was doing and agreeing to rendezvous with you. She thinks Claudia . . . never mind . . . I'm not sure what she thinks. Just make sure that she waits there with you."

"What's she driving?"

"A fuel truck. It says 'Texaco' on it."

"An actual tank truck?"

"From the airport. Don't ask."

Whistler peered up the road. He saw nothing coming. "We'll wait. I'll get back to you, Molly."

"Leave Aubrey and those others for some other day. There's no way to take six men quietly."

"Walk away and leave Leslie?"

"Leave that to the police. If it's true that Carla knows where they are, find out and call the police."

He bit his lip. "Would you?"

"Yes, I would," she answered firmly. "I'm asking you to

back away from this, Adam. And you'd better brief Claudia
on Carla."

Poole's assistant, Robert, had returned to the house by way
of some woodlands and the neighbors' backyards. Felix
Aubrey had waited for him in the kitchen, unlocking the rear
door to let him in. Briggs had remained in the living room
out front to give warning when Kaplan's car appeared.

Aubrey had given Briggs and Robert their instructions.
He had spoken to each of them separately. Such a method,
he realized, was not ideally efficient, but it did serve to make
corroboration more difficult if this episode should go badly
and if charges were filed and if one or both should try to cop
a plea. Micromanaging again, but as they say, the Devil is in
the details.

Aubrey had agreed that it seemed only fair to let Mr. Briggs
shoot Mr. Lockwood. No talking, however, until Lockwood
was down. If Briggs then felt the need to discuss his motivation,
he could do so while Lockwood was writhing. Robert was, si-
multaneously, to shoot Mr. Crow. He would do so because, as
Aubrey had explained to him, Crow's actions were destructive
of all the good works to which Mr. Poole had devoted his life.
He told Robert that Poole had asked God for guidance and that
God had told Poole to send Crow to hell. And this, too, was to
be done without prior discussion. The quicker, the better, because then, if he wished, he'd have time to give Lockwood's
face a good slap before Lockwood was too dead to notice.

"Mr. Aubrey?" It was Briggs. "They're just pulling in."

Aubrey asked, "They're together? All three?"

"All three. Their car's in the driveway," Briggs answered
as he backed away from the window.

Aubrey touched Robert's arm. "Are you up to your task?"

"Yes, sir." Robert straightened. "I would die for Mr.
Poole."

"Not your turn. It's theirs. Get out there. Be ready. I'll be
waiting here in the kitchen."

"You'll be watching?"

"No need. I have faith in you, Robert."

Will I be watching? thought Aubrey. Of course not, you dimwit. I had no idea what you two intended. Must have been some private grudge. I was horrified, shocked, when I realized that you'd shot them. Unless, of course, all this goes without a hitch. In that case, I'm with you one hundred percent.

The first sign that there might be a hitch came from Briggs. He hissed, "There's Lockwood. He's getting out now. He's walking up to open the garage door. There it goes."

Aubrey heard the muted grind of the door on its tracks and the thunk that it made when it stopped.

Briggs had dropped to a squat, the better to see, "Guy driving, striped jacket, that's Kaplan, right? So that has to be Crow in the back."

Aubrey said, "No doubt," as he closed the kitchen door. Briggs stopped him by exclaiming, "What the hell—"

Briggs leaned forward. "There's a fight. Crow's jumping on Kaplan. He's smacking the shit out of Kaplan. Hey, wait."

Briggs moved closer to the window.

He said, "Damn. There's some women. She's jumping on Crow. Now Kaplan's got Crow; he pulled him over the seat; and the woman is helping. She's pushing Crow forward. No, wait. No, she isn't. She's trying to get past him. She's got the door open. She's trying to run."

Aubrey stood frozen. "What woman? Whistler's woman? Please tell me they didn't . . ."

"I'm not sure," Briggs told him. "I can't get a clear look. There goes Lockwood. He got her. He grabbed her."

"The Geller girl? Is it? You've met her. You'd know."

Briggs said, "Still can't see. He threw her back in the car. He reached in and punched her. No, he didn't. He punched Crow. Now he slammed the door shut; he's telling Kaplan to drive. He's telling him to get into the garage. Kaplan's arguing. Lockwood's saying, 'Shut up and get in there.' There he goes. He's driving into the garage."

There followed a violent crunching sound. Its vibration was felt through the house.

"What was that?" asked Aubrey.

"I don't know," replied Briggs. Then he added, "Oh, shit. You know what that was? Kaplan drove the car over that trailer that's in there. The trailer with the Jet Ski. That's why Kaplan was arguing. Kaplan knew the car wouldn't fit."

"Well, why didn't . . ." Aubrey grimaced. He stopped himself. He was about to ask why they didn't move the trailer, pull it out by hand, get it out of the way. But the question was pointless. The damage had been done. Aubrey crossed the kitchen and looked out its side window. From there he could see why the whole house had shaken. The trailered Jet Ski had smashed through the rear wall. It had taken a workbench and some garden tools with it. Old paint cans were rolling across the backyard.

Aubrey said, "Get back here. Into the kitchen."

Briggs told him, "The car's not in all the way. They can't close the garage door. They left the whole rear end sticking out."

Aubrey groaned within himself. He said, "Both of you. Get back here." He wanted all three of them well out of sight until he understood what was happening.

Robert asked, "Who is that woman? Why do they have a woman?"

"I don't know, Robert. Please go into the kitchen. Mr. Briggs, have they attracted an audience?"

Briggs asked, "Who, the neighbors? I don't know; I don't think so. I don't see anybody looking out."

"No traffic? No passing cars?"

"I don't see any . . . wait . . . there's an oil truck out there."

"Stopping?"

"No, passing. It kept going. We're good."

Robert said, "Those men have kidnapped an innocent woman. They intend to assault her. We can't allow that."

"They're not likely to have time. Get in the kitchen."

"Unless she's a harlot. But she isn't. She can't be. If she were a harlot, would she try to escape them? She must be a virtuous woman."

"Robert . . . in the kitchen. I'm sure that all will be revealed. Mr. Briggs, on second thought, stay where you are, but duck out of sight before they enter."

Robert muttered, "This is wrong."

"We will attend to it, Robert."

"This must be prevented. It cannot be allowed."

"Robert, try to keep in mind that they'll be dead in two minutes. You are making a pest of yourself."

Damned Lockwood, thought Aubrey. It must be the Geller woman. Lockwood had said that he wanted a crack at her first, so that Whistler would know what he'd done to her. And Lockwood had more than rape on his mind. He meant to cut her up before killing her.

Oh, the damned fool. So he's gone out and snatched her. That must mean, one would think, that he's already killed Whistler. Either way, he has started a war.

35

Whistler had chosen to say little about Carla. There was no quick way to explain her. He said only that Carla was experienced, but . . . well, different and needed to be handled with care. Claudia, in any case, hadn't paid much attention. All she cared about now was finding Leslie.

Within moments, a fuel truck had appeared in the distance. As it neared, it almost seemed as if no one was driving. All that showed above the dash was a crescent of red hair and perhaps an inch or two of Carla's forehead.

As Carla approached, she downshifted and slowed, nearly stripping the unfamiliar gears of the truck. She drove it past them to an opening in the center divider, made a U-turn, and pulled in behind them. She climbed out of its cab as Whistler stepped from the Taurus. Carla looked even smaller than he remembered her. He saw that her left eye was reddened and swollen. She was missing one of her shoes.

She said, "Hello, Adam. You've filled out. You're very handsome." She stepped around him and walked to the passenger's-side window. She said, "And this is Claudia? Hello, Claudia. I'm Carla."

Whistler asked her, "Carla, do you know where they are?"

She answered, "Uh-huh," without looking at him. She said to Claudia, while extending her hand, "I'm so glad to meet you. I've been hearing good things. I hope we can talk later on."

Claudia took her hand and she returned Carla's smile, but she didn't seem to know what to make of this woman. Neither, for that matter, did Whistler. First we have Molly sounding nothing like Molly. Now here's Carla sounding nothing like Carla.

Carla gestured toward the tote at Claudia's feet. "What's bulging? Weapons? What did you bring?"

Claudia lifted the sail bag to show the canvas tote's contents. She said, "Just these. From the boat."

"So you do work with guns? Not just knives? So do I."

Whistler said, "She does not work with anything, Carla. You've got the wrong idea about Claudia."

Carla gave him a glance, an if-you-say-so sort of glance, and returned her attention to the weapons. She said, "The sweeper will be good. What's that other one, an Ingram?"

"Um . . . yes, that's an Ingram MAC-10."

Carla made a face. She seemed critical of the choice. She said, "You know what's much better? You should try the new Calico. It's the one with the top-mounted helical feed. Fifty-round magazine. Never jams."

"I . . . really only know about these."

"These are okay for Adam. Too much kick for a woman. But I hear you're like me. You prefer to work close."

"Carla," said Whistler, "I'll say it again—"

"Who taught you how to throw? I hear you're real good."

"She knows how to throw a baseball, Carla. That's all."

Again, she ignored him. She gestured toward the fuel truck. "My weapon's in the truck. Come back and I'll show you. A helical feed is sort of a pod. The advantage . . ."

Oh, for Pete's sake, thought Whistler. "Carla, stop it," he said.

"Stop what? And say 'please' to your elders."

"Please stop with the guns, and please answer my question."

She replied, "I did. I said I know where they are."

"Where they are exactly? This minute? How could you?"

"A little bird told me."

He said, "Carla, cut the games."

At this, she winked at Claudia. "Is he always this rude?"

"Carla, I'd appreciate an answer myself."

She said, "Both of you, relax. They're not going anywhere. They're having a problem with their cars. We've got time."

She turned back to Claudia and she gave her a wink. She said, "You see? Birds talk to me, too. Except my bird was only Felix Aubrey's co-pilot. Is it true that you can talk to the other kind? Gotta see that. My boyfriend, Viktor, met the white light once himself, but you made out better than he did."

The bird thing, thought Whistler. His father must have told Bannerman. So much for his trying to squelch it. And he now understood how Carla's eye became swollen and how she'd lost one of her shoes. Aubrey's co-pilot. She'd waylaid him somehow. Whistler moved a few steps away to let these two have their one-sided chat. Let them kill a few more minutes getting acquainted until Billy or John Waldo can get up here.

It struck Whistler that he'd heard Carla speak, in two minutes, more words than he'd ever heard her utter all told. And she'd smiled. He had rarely seen a smile on Carla's face. And he had certainly never seen any sign that she grasped the concept of a good first impression. This must be a new Carla, reinvented for Claudia. She was trying to get Claudia to like her.

Claudia's mind, however, wasn't on making friends. She asked Carla, "Have you actually seen them?"

"I saw the three who you two are hunting. They were in an old heap of a Pontiac?"

"That's them."

"Well, right now their car's even more of a heap because they tried to get it into a two-car garage without making room for it first. It's still sitting ass-out with its exhaust pipe ripped off and it's jammed against a van that was already in there."

Whistler asked, "A white Dodge with Ohio plates?"

She nodded. "That's the one. How did you know?"

"A little bird told me. Carla, where is this house?"

She gestured with her thumb. "Twenty-two Lagoon Road. Blue house, black shutters, can't miss it with those cars. Are you ready to go back there and take them?"

"What about Aubrey? Did you see Felix Aubrey?"

She said, "No, but he's around. They came in a black Lincoln. They don't know it yet, but I totaled the Lincoln. They're running real low on transportation." As she said this, she gestured toward the fuel truck's front bumper. Whistler saw that the bumper was twisted and gauged. It was streaked with smears of black paint.

Claudia had stepped out of the Taurus. She asked Carla, "Did you see a woman with them?"

"In the Pontiac? What woman?"

"Her name is Leslie. She's a friend. They dragged her into their car. The big one, Lockwood, hit her with his gun."

Carla said to Whistler, "Lockwood's way overdue." She said to Claudia, "All I saw were the heads of three men, but if he hit her she would have been down on the floor."

"You didn't see them pull her out when they got to that garage?"

"I had to stay back. I didn't see them unload. Their car was already hung up when I drove past." She said to Whistler, "So this Leslie's in the house?"

"They had no time to dump her. She must be."

Carla seemed annoyed. Whistler thought he knew why. She would have preferred to go back there and blast anything that moves. Now she'd have to pick her shots. Avoid hitting Leslie. It would be harder for her to get chummy with Claudia if she were to blow Leslie's head off.

She said, "Claudia, get your sweeper. You're riding with me."

Whistler said, "Not a chance. We wait here."

"Wait for what?" asked Carla. "Her friend is in trouble. We take care of our friends, am I right?"

Carla, as she said this, reached in for the shotgun. She checked its action as she walked to the fuel truck. She said to Whistler, "You can have the Ingram." She said to Claudia, "He'll come with us. Hop in."

Whistler reached to take Claudia's arm. He said, "You're not going anywhere with Carla. You're staying."

"Adam, I can't. And you can't either. Let's go."

Carla said, "Adam, you and I will hit the house. Claudia stays in the truck. She just covers. How's that?"

"No one hits the house, damn it. Call Molly. Right now."

"Waste of time, Adam. What for?"

"Because for one thing, this area is crawling with police. Molly's right. We should let them handle this."

"What, a hostage situation? That'll take them a week. Adam, we can do it. Sixty seconds in and out."

Whistler pulled out his cell phone. "We wait."

"Then okay, but not here. You want to call them? Go ahead. In the meantime, someone has to watch the house. Let's get over there."

Claudia said, "Adam, she's right. We should be there."

"He knows we should," said Carla. "Hop in and let's roll."

Whistler muttered a curse. "We just cover. Agreed? And Claudia stays in the truck."

"Agreed."

"I'll scout out the house. You stay with her. Agreed?"

"We'll work out the details when we get there."

While Carla had gone looking for Whistler's beige Taurus, Arnold Kaplan was sitting in the green Pontiac thinking this is how people get heart attacks. He could hardly believe what just happened.

In front of him, he was looking at daylight because half of the garage's rear wall was now gone and that Jet Ski was in the backyard. And Lockwood just stands there. He's staring at the hole and he's cursing. Behind Kaplan, he was also looking at daylight because the car was part out and part in. He tried backing up. The car was hung up on the trailer. It was at an angle, almost touching the van. Both cars were now visible from the street.

The only good news was that Crow was out cold. Lockwood had clipped him some good ones. The girl was crying a little; she was scared half to death. And she was still struggling, but she couldn't get up because Crow had gone flaccid on top of her. He climbed out of the car and almost fell as he did so. He had tangled one foot in a blue plastic tarp that had probably covered the Jet Ski.

He said, "Vern . . . this tarp. Let's hang up this tarp."

Lockwood snarled, "Who taught you how to drive?"

You did, you schmuck. You screamed at me to get in here while I'm still busy fighting off Crow. But Kaplan didn't say that. He said, "I'm very remorseful. Now we need to hang up this fucking tarp."

"Over where? Oh, the door? Yeah, we should. Good idea."

"Look around where you're standing. You see any tools? Look for a hammer and nails."

He said, "The tools are mostly all over the lawn. No, wait. There's a staple gun. I'll get it."

Kaplan watched as Lockwood stepped out through the hole. He retrieved the stapler and returned with it. Kaplan gathered the tarp. It seemed almost big enough. It could mostly cover the whole garage door. From the street it would look like repair work.

He said to Lockwood, "You hang it. I can't reach high enough. Meanwhile, I'll get these two inside."

"You sure you can handle them?"

"Crow's asleep. And fuck you."

"Wait a minute," said Lockwood. "Let's see how asleep."

At this, Lockwood squeezed between the Pontiac and the

van. He opened the right rear door about a foot, which was all the space the van gave it. He reached in with the stapler and found Crow's ass. He snapped a staple in each of Crow's cheeks.

Crow never moved. Lockwood said, "He's still gone. Drag him out on your side. You got room?"

"I got room. I'll take the girl inside first."

"Drag him out. I can watch him while I hang."

"You'll bring him in?"

"I'll bring him. Two minutes. Go ahead."

Now and then, thought Kaplan, Lockwood does a good thing. That move with the stapler was one of them. Kaplan opened the rear left door of the Pontiac. He reached in and seized Crow by one arm. He started pulling.

He said, "Leslie? Push with me. Give me a hand."

He heard her swallow. She stammered, "Wh-what?"

"The guy's stuck. Help me here. You like him being on you?"

"He's drooling on me. Get him off me."

"So push."

"Did you mean what you said about not hurting me?"

Kaplan leaned closer. He kept his voice low. "Take my word. Here's the thing, though. You gotta behave. You gotta do exactly what I tell you."

"Like . . . what?"

He reached for a towel that was clipped to Crow's golf bag. A big one, orange, from the Bengals again. Kaplan yanked it free of its hook and he jammed it between Crow's mouth and her head.

He said, "I need you to cover your face with that towel. Then I'll wrap it with some of Crow's duct tape. Also I have to tape up your hands. After that, I'll take you inside."

"Why do you have to cover my face?"

"Because the less you see of me, the better for me. Fair enough? Shut up and indulge me."

". . . Okay."

"I'll steer you into a bedroom, but it's just to the closet. I'm not going to touch you in any bad way. That's a promise. Are you with me so far?"

"I . . . I guess."

Okay, thought Kaplan. So far, this is progress. Now we try to establish some reasonable doubt in case she's ever called as a witness, God forbid.

He said, "I'm going to leave you because I have to go. After that, you might hear things. This is after I'm gone. What you'll hear won't be me because I'm gone by that time. Is that clear in your head? It won't be me."

A little klutzy, thought Kaplan, but maybe she'll buy it. Leslie, however, had concerns of her own. She asked, "You mean you're leaving me with these two?"

"They'll be otherwise occupied. They won't hurt you, believe me. In maybe two hours, I'll call your cop friend and tell him where he can find you. Before that, however, you must not make a sound. That's no matter what you hear going on."

"Arnie . . . your name's Arnie?"

"I got lots of names."

"Can't you tell me what's going to happen?"

"Some people are coming. They're not very nice. You don't want them to know that you're here, so be quiet. Myself, I don't wish to be here when they come."

"Well, I don't either, damn it. Take me with you."

"Leslie . . . this is my neck I'm trying to save. I'll help you, but I can't have you fingering me. This is the best I can offer."

"And you swear that you didn't hurt Adam or Claudia?"

"Would I be talking like this if I did?"

"I . . . guess not."

"So push. Keep your eyes shut and push."

Felix Aubrey, taking care not to move the sheer curtains, had been watching through the kitchen's side window. He'd seen Lockwood step through what was once the garage wall and retrieve some chrome-plated tool from the yard. He called to Briggs in a whisper, "What on earth are they doing?"

Briggs answered, "I don't know. They're in there talking. I can't hear." A few seconds later, Briggs said in a hush, "I see Lockwood out front. He's got this big tarp. I think he's hanging it over the garage."

"To what purpose?"

"Hide the cars, I guess. It figures they're hot."

And therefore a sensible measure, thought Aubrey, so it must have been Kaplan's idea. And yet Kaplan, we fear, had allowed Vernon Lockwood to make good his threat against Whistler and the girl. Perhaps he wasn't able to stop him.

Aubrey asked Briggs, "Any sign of the girl?"

Briggs shrugged with his hands and shook his head.

"Or of Kaplan and Crow?"

Briggs whispered, "Still in the garage. I hear grunting. I heard Lockwood say he's going to bring Crow."

"Make no move until all four are inside. Once they are, do not dawdle, Mr. Briggs. Do your work."

"I hear them. They're coming. Get back."

36

Whistler, in the Taurus, had followed the tank truck as it wound through North Forest Beach. He had thumbed Molly's number on his cell phone. She answered. He told her that they were on their way to the house. He was in no mood to explain how it happened that Claudia was now riding with Carla. Nor did Molly bother asking. Her response was a sigh. She asked him, "What's that address?"

Having taken it, she said, "And you say they have no vehicles?"

"They're stranded, according to Carla."

"Adam, stay well back. I'm going to call the police."

"Don't do that just yet. Let us get in place first. We can block off both ends of the street."

"Are you sure you have Carla under control?"

"Carla's the least of my worries right now. I need to see that Claudia's kept out of this."

"Well, I worry about Carla. I know how she is. Carla tries to be nonlethal these days. Did you know that?"

"Nonlethal? With a Calico? How does one manage that?"

"She might try not to kill them, but she will shoot to maim. That Calico is better than a chain saw. You have no idea of the mess she can make. Let me call the police and be done with it."

"Hold off until I can scout out that house. I'd like to get Leslie out first if I can. Let me see how close I can get."

"Adam—you are *not* to put yourself at risk either. There's more at stake here than you know."

"You'll explain that to me, won't you? One of these days?"

"Your father will explain it when he gets here this evening."

An exasperated growl. "We're almost there, Molly."

"Then you're close enough. I'm calling the police."

"No, don't. I need ten minutes."

"I'm calling right now. Good-bye, Adam."

Whistler put the phone aside and stepped on the gas. He was already on Lagoon Road. He pulled around and in front of the Texaco truck and signaled for it to pull over. He got out and told Carla what Molly had said. He repeated that Carla was to cover, nothing more. She was to stop this truck a full hundred yards short of the house they were in.

She pointed. "That's it. Two blocks up on your left. The one just this side of that privacy fence."

He looked and nodded. He said, "I'll take that end. The fence is good cover. It might let me get close enough to look in some windows. I'll try to see where they're holding Leslie."

Carla said, "Say you spot her. Then what? You go in?"

"No, I don't. You don't either. We both wait for the police."

"Adam—"

"No, Carla. Look into my eyes. Do I look like I'm playing games with you now?"

"I'm not either."

"That's good because if you should get Claudia hurt, you'll never hurt anyone else."

"Adam," said Claudia, "there was no need to say that."

Whistler ignored her. His eyes bored into Carla's. He said, "The same goes for Leslie if you get her killed. Do you hear what I'm telling you, Carla?"

Carla smiled at him. "I hear you. Now will you lighten up? Not that I wouldn't like to see what you've got, but you won't have to fight me on this one."

"That's a promise?"

"It's a promise. Now get down there."

Aubrey opened the kitchen door just a crack as two figures came into view. The first thing he saw was the gaudily striped jacket and the flat straw hat worn askew. No mistaking that one; it was Kaplan. And he saw that Kaplan was leading the girl. The girl could only be Whistler's friend, Claudia.

Her hands appeared to be bound behind her back. Her head was covered by what looked to be a towel held in place by a wrapping of tape. She was bound and blindfolded, but apparently not gagged. He heard Kaplan telling her to be quiet.

It was only the lack of a gag across her mouth that kept Aubrey from opening the door. He wanted to let Kaplan know that they'd arrived, but his sudden appearance might cause her to cry out. The last thing he needed was for Lockwood to hear a shout of "Who's that?" from outside.

"Mr. Aubrey," Robert whispered, his breath at Aubrey's ear, "where is he going with her?"

Aubrey pushed him away. He mouthed, *"Shush."*

But Robert persisted. "Mr. Aubrey, he's taking her to a bedroom. All those rooms where he's going are bedrooms."

"He's got to put her somewhere. Be still."

"If he means to take his pleasure with her, we cannot allow it, Mr. Aubrey."

"Robert, you were told not to speak or to think. He has no such intention. Be quiet."

Aubrey chanced a better look. He opened the door slightly. He saw that they indeed had gone into a bedroom. He heard sounds coming from it. They were rustling, scraping sounds. It seemed the sort of noise that one makes in a closet, sliding hangers of clothing out of the way. Robert was beginning to breathe heavily.

Robert said, "That's a bed. The springs of a bed."

"No, it isn't. All you're hearing is clothing."

"Clothing? Do you mean he's removing her clothing?"

"He is not. And for the last time, shut up."

"He's assaulting that woman," Robert said through his teeth. "You said that you wouldn't permit it."

"Must I shoot you?"

"I will stop it," hissed Robert. "I'll be quick. I'll snap his neck."

Before Aubrey could stop him, he had pushed through the door. Aubrey reached to snatch Robert's collar. He missed. Briggs took a step from his place of concealment, frantically waving his arms and then pointing. He mouthed the words, *"Lockwood. He's coming."*

In that instant, the door from the garage was thrown open. Aubrey heard a deep-throated grunt from outside. The cause of the grunt was immediately apparent. Lockwood was pulling a body behind him, backing his way through the door. But the body was a live one. It had started to squirm. Aubrey saw that it was Joshua Crow.

Lockwood called, "Hey, Arnie. Come give me a hand."

Crow became more aware of what was happening to him. He felt for the hands that were dragging him. Flailing, he raked Lockwood's wrists with his fingernails. Lockwood cursed and called, "Forget it. I got him."

He snaked his left forearm under Joshua Crow's jaw, seizing him in its crook. He stood up, lifting Crow. Crow was choking and kicking. Lockwood's arm had formed a vise. He squeezed harder. He said to Crow, "I'm really sick of you, pal. You're dying now. You feel yourself dying?"

Aubrey saw that Robert had been frozen in place a few feet from the door to the bedroom. Lockwood still hadn't

seen him. His back was turned to him. Now Robert was low-
ering himself to a crouch, the better to reach the ankle holster that he wore. He seemed to be descending an inch at a
time. Aubrey could no longer stand it. He heard himself
shouting, "Well, shoot him, you dolt."

Robert unsnapped his pistol. Lockwood spun at both
sounds. Crow's dangling, kicking body shielded his own as
Lockwood groped for the gun in his belt.

Lockwood recognized Robert. "Where the fuck did you
come from? Did I just hear Aubrey? Was that Aubrey?"

Arnold Kaplan, in the bedroom, was as startled as Lockwood. He had seated Leslie on the floor of the closet. He had
quickly covered her mouth with his hand. He whispered,
"Like I told you. Bad people. Sit tight." But damn it, he
thought, now she's heard Aubrey's name. He might not be
able to save her.

Robert hadn't fired. He had no clear shot. Aubrey called,
"Robert? Do it now. Shoot them both," to which Briggs responded, "No, he's mine."

Briggs had emerged, his gun aimed at Lockwood's head,
his free hand touching his paperlike face. He said, "See this?
You did this to me. They got me because you left me, you
shit."

Lockwood had yet to tear his own weapon free. The big
silencer was stuck in his belt. Briggs said, "What's that? You
got a problem there, Vern? Let me give you a hand. I'll shoot
it loose."

And Briggs did. He lowered his sights and he fired. Lockwood, in that instant, had hurled himself backward. The
muzzle blast was deafening, but the bullet missed its mark.
Instead, it struck Crow in the buttocks. Crow squealed and
bucked. Lockwood struggled to hold him. Lockwood managed to back up into the garage, where at last he got the
Glock free. He could no longer see Briggs, but he could hear
Briggs moving toward him. He had a clear view of Robert,
who was bobbing and weaving, still trying to get a clear

shot. He heard Aubrey again shouting, "Shoot them both. Shoot."

Lockwood's best shot was at Robert, couldn't miss him at this range. But enraged by Felix Aubrey's betrayal, he swung the silenced barrel toward the door to the kitchen. He snarled, "You little faggot, you're dead," and squeezed the trigger. He added the word "Fuck" when nothing happened.

Suddenly there was Briggs. Briggs was filling the doorway, his pistol squarely aimed at the part of Lockwood's face that was visible behind that of Crow. Briggs asked, "What did you do? Forget to chamber a round? Go ahead. Slap one in there. I'll wait."

Aubrey gasped, "Are you out of your mind? Get this done." He had stayed out of sight in the kitchen.

Briggs called back, "No, you see—he needs two hands to do that. This prick's got himself in a quandary here. He's got to let go of Crow or he can't work the slide. That's unless he can work it with his teeth."

"Then please end it," called Aubrey. "Do it now."

"In a minute," answered Briggs. "Don't forget I'm entitled. Let's all take a little time to smell the roses."

Aubrey called, "Robert? You do it. Do it now."

Briggs raised a hand to Robert without turning his head. He said, "No, you don't. You stay back."

Aubrey called, "Mr. Kaplan, why are you not out here?"

Briggs said, "Hear that, Vern? A good question, don't you think? You've been standing here waiting for your guy to save your ass. I got news. He's with us. He's not your guy."

Robert said, "I'll go see what he's doing with that woman."

Aubrey hissed, "Don't you move. Don't you lower your weapon."

Briggs agreed. He said, "Yeah, stay. It doesn't matter what he's doing. We can't leave her either. Even Vernon knows that." He added, "Mr. Aubrey? Why don't you come out here? It's worth it to see the look on Vern's face. Besides, you got questions to ask, am I right?"

"You say he's under control?"

"No, he's thoroughly pissed."

"Under *your* control, you idiot."

"Yeah, come look. I got him cold. Right now, old Vern is trying to think. You can tell because he's pushing at his lips with his tongue. Right now, he's deciding what to do with the loony. Drop him, try to run, try to throw him, or what? Except he knows that if he twitches, he gets my whole clip, the first half of which goes through Mr. Crow here."

Aubrey called, "Then ask him what he'd done to Adam Whistler. Ask the damned fool—never mind—I'll ask Kaplan. Shoot him, Mr. Briggs. Shoot him now."

Briggs fired, but he shot to hurt, not to kill. He aimed to the right of Crow's swollen face. He aimed at Lockwood's left elbow. Lockwood twisted away; he tried to swing Crow between them. The bullet missed the elbow, but it creased Lockwood's arm. The muzzle blast caused another ringing in the ears of everyone there except Aubrey. The kitchen door had shielded Aubrey's ears.

It was only Aubrey, therefore, who heard the sound that was coming from the street and was building. He heard the roar of an engine, a powerful engine, and he heard the grinding sound of gears trying to mesh. He heard the groaning thump that large vehicles make when their wheels go over a curb. Aubrey pushed the door open to see what it was. He saw nothing because the front room's drapes had been drawn, but the sound almost seemed right on top of him.

He did see Briggs with his pistol still extended toward the door that led out to the garage. He caught a glimpse of Lockwood, Lockwood backing away, still desperately clinging to Crow. He was conscious of Robert, standing frozen in place, his face turned toward the front of the house. Robert was only then becoming aware of the sound that was building from outside the house. The house itself was starting to vibrate. In that instant, the wall of the front room exploded. The whole row of draperies and the windows behind them seemed to rise up and surge toward where Robert was standing. They enveloped him. They swathed him in fabric and glass. He seemed to melt under their weight.

But it wasn't the weight of the draperies alone. The draperies were followed by a great silver mass that thundered through the front wall behind them. It had a rounded top, a red star on its side. Aubrey realized, of course, that he was looking at a truck, but his brain had not yet allowed him to believe that a truck could be driving through the house. He saw something else red in the cab of the truck. It was hair. On the driver. Red hair.

He saw a burst of flame come from the driver's-side window and he heard a jackhammer's roar. He saw that Briggs had spun to confront this hellish thing, but his reaction had been far too late. For an instant, Briggs rose up. He seemed to be floating. He'd been standing on his feet, but they'd been pulled out from under him. His legs, in that instant, were as high as his head. Briggs settled to the floor, it seemed, in slow motion. He had dropped his gun. He was grasping his knees. He was trying to hold them together. He was screaming.

Felix Aubrey felt himself go light-headed. One part of his brain was telling him to run and another was telling him that this couldn't be real. It had begun to seem dreamlike; it was all in slow motion. As the truck rumbled toward him, there were other fleeting images. One was of Lockwood. He saw Lockwood again. Lockwood was now unencumbered by Crow. He was working the slide of his pistol. He was looking at the truck and he was looking at Briggs. He seemed undecided as to what he should do. Suddenly, he was shouting at Briggs. He wanted Briggs to look up at him, to stop writhing and look. Lockwood seemed intent on shooting Briggs in the face. He wanted Briggs to see the bullets coming.

But another burst of flame came out of the truck. Another jackhammer's roar. The door where Lockwood stood erupted in splinters down at the level of his legs. The eruption made him jump; he did a jig in the doorway, but he didn't seem as badly hurt as Briggs. He staggered out, stepping over still another pair of legs. These other legs were bare except for socks and they were moving. They belonged to Joshua Crow. He was crawling. Lockwood, in a blink, had vanished from sight. Crow was trying to get to his feet.

The truck had paused, but it was moving again. Aubrey thought he heard another engine starting. Yes, he did. In the garage. Lockwood must have reached a car. Next he heard the tearing and the snapping of metal as the car pushed another car aside. He only heard these sounds; he wasn't able to look because he couldn't take his eyes off this mass moving toward him. It was grinding over furniture, splintering the floor. A woman had jumped from the passenger side. In her hands she held a weapon, some sort of a shotgun. She had it at her shoulder. She was calling a name.

She called, Letty . . . Leslie . . . something like that. It seemed to Aubrey that she should have been calling something else. She was looking for the girl that Kaplan had brought here. Whistler's girl's name was Claudia, but she didn't call that name. She was calling for someone named Leslie.

She looked his way. She saw him. But she paid him no mind. He found himself staring at her. She was lovely. This was hardly a time to make that observation, but for some reason he couldn't help it. Shotgun or no, there was a gentleness about her. She seemed perfectly calm and unafraid. It was strange, but he found himself wanting to help her. He started to say, "Over there. In that bedroom." But he could no longer see where she was, where she'd gone, because the big silver truck had kept coming.

He tried to back up, to get out of its way. He managed a few steps back into the kitchen. Beyond those, his legs, like his brain, would not function. He stood as if frozen in the middle of the kitchen. There were cabinets on the walls to his left and to his right. They began to tilt toward him, spilling out all their contents. The walls, the counter, bulged toward him as well. Dishes and glassware fell and shattered around him. He raised his hands to his face and he covered his eyes because he knew that the truck would be coming through next. It would crush him if he looked. So he tried not to look. A part of his brain thought that seemed to make sense. He had no recourse but to trust it.

From what seemed a great distance, he heard spoken voices. A man's voice called a name, that name Leslie again. A woman's voice answered, "I can't find her. She's not here."

The man answered, "Then let's go. She must be in that van. They had to have stashed her in the van."

Suddenly, there was a great flash of light. It was blinding. And hot. Yet Aubrey heard no explosion. The sound it made was more of a *thump* and a *whoosh*.

The man's voice said, "This house is going up. Get out now."

Aubrey's legs must have started working again. He found himself moving toward the rear kitchen door that opened on a patio outside. It was the door at which he had waited for Robert while Robert was parking their car. Had Robert come back yet? He was no longer sure. He seemed to remember Robert going under that truck, but that, too, now seemed only a dream.

The car, thought Aubrey. Where did Robert put the car? He would have to wait for Robert to come back. Then he'd ask him. In the meantime, he might as well sit. There were no chairs on the patio, but there were wooden planters. Aubrey sat down on the edge of a planter. He kept his hands over his face.

He heard a woman's voice, this one very near. This one was calling his name. He thought at first that it must be that same lovely woman. He giggled. He had no idea why.

The woman spoke again. She was nearer than before. From the sound she stood only a few feet away. She said, "Felix . . . the girl. Where did they take her?"

He parted his hands. He saw the woman who had spoken. It was not the one who had jumped from the truck. This one was much smaller, even smaller than he was. And she had red hair. And her eyes were very strange. This was the one who had driven that truck. Her face and her hands were blackened with soot and the sweater she was wearing was scorched. One eye had been injured. She did not seem to mind. Her eyes were like the eyes of a cat.

She asked again, "Felix? Where is she?"

A man's voice called out from inside the house. He said, "Carla? Let's get out of here. *Now!*"

Aubrey saw that this woman had only one shoe. In one hand she was holding an oddly shaped firearm. She held a long thin knife in the other. She said, "Felix . . . last chance. Where'd they take her?"

He must have asked who she was talking about. It did seem that he spoke the word, *"Who?"*

This one, the small one, peered at him very closely. She asked, "Are you still with us, Felix?"

He heard himself answer, "Yes, I think so. I'm here."

He then paused to listen to the sound of his voice. Aubrey knew that he had just spoken those words and yet they'd almost seemed to come from some other place.

The woman said, "Felix, snap out of it."

"Yes."

"Where is she? Five seconds. I'm counting."

He said, "She's with Kaplan. She came here with Kaplan. She hasn't gone anywhere. She's there." He raised a hand and pointed. He was gesturing toward that bedroom. It was over there someplace. Or it was a while ago. "She's there," he repeated. "No one took her."

She held up her knife. She touched it lightly to his face. She said, "You don't remember me, do you?"

He didn't.

She said, "See this knife? Take a look at this knife. Will it help if I show you where you've felt it before? Is it starting to come back to you, Felix?"

He felt himself beginning to weep. Again, he wasn't sure why. It was as if some sad and distant memory had returned, but he couldn't think what it might be.

"Look at me, Felix. Don't say nobody took her. Two seconds, Felix. Last chance."

He heard himself say, "Kaplan. She was only with Kaplan. Ask Kaplan. He was with her. Where is Kaplan?"

She was peering again. She said, "Shit. You're not acting." And that man's voice was calling again.

She said, "Well, I have to go. I can't miss my ride. I guess it's time to say good-bye to you, Felix."

He didn't respond. He wanted to, but he couldn't. All his thoughts, all the sounds drifted farther away. He was vaguely aware that she had touched him with her knife. He felt nothing. No pain. He wanted only to sleep.

Very soon, this dream faded. Then nothing.

37

Whistler had driven the Taurus half a block past the house. He had doubled back on foot to the privacy fence with the Ingram carried low against his hip. He had listened for a moment and was ready to scale it when he heard a shot fired from inside the house.

In almost that same instant, he heard the truck coming. He looked over the fence in time to see it swing wide to the right and then make a hard left as it took dead aim at the house. To his horror, he saw Claudia. She was bracing herself and she was covering her eyes as the fuel truck plowed through the front wall. He was over the fence in one bound, gun in hand.

He had entered through the hole that the fuel truck had left. He saw none of the men whom he'd expected to be there. All he could see was the truck, still moving forward. He heard a burst from the Calico. Carla had fired. Because she was on the far side of the truck, he couldn't see who she was shooting at. He heard a second short burst. A male voice gave a yelp. He assumed that at least two were down. He saw Claudia as she jumped from the cab, scanning the wreckage with the shotgun at her shoulder, calling out, "Leslie, where are you?"

There was no answer.

He said to her, "Don't turn. I'm covering your back. You check those two rooms on your right." He did cover her back, but he was looking for Lockwood. He would have killed any of the six men on sight, but he wanted Lockwood especially.

Suddenly he heard a tearing of metal and what sounded like the squeal of car tires. He looked toward the hole that the fuel truck had left and he caught a glimpse of the van. It was careening, in reverse, back out over the curb. He hadn't heard the engine of the Dodge van start up because of all the noise from the truck.

He heard Claudia say, "She's not here. I can't find her."

"Check the closets. Under beds. She must be here."

"I did. I saw where I think they taped her up. She's not there anymore. No one's back here."

"Then they have her in the van. Let's get out of here now."

These words were barely out of his mouth when he heard a dull *whoomp* and saw a blinding white flash. It came from the far side of the truck. Flames spread over the ceiling and were searing the truck, but the truck kept on moving through the house. It was pushing through what looked like the wall to the kitchen. He heard more ripping and tearing, but not all from the kitchen. Some of the din seemed to come from the garage. He glanced out toward the street. He saw a second car leaving.

This one, the green Pontiac, had its bumper hanging off it. The driver's side door had been bent back almost double. Its muffler and exhaust pipe had been torn away. The Pontiac was dragging them behind it. He could see the driver clearly. It could only be Crow. Whistler wheeled and aimed, but he had no shot. All that he would have hit was dangling siding. The Pontiac was gone, but he could still hear Crow. Crow seemed to be screaming as he drove.

He said, "Claudia, get out. That fuel truck can blow." He called Carla's name. There was no answer. The house was filling with rolling black smoke. He called again. He shouted, "Carla, where are you?"

She answered, "I'm busy. Go ahead. I'll catch up."

From the sound of her voice, she was outside the house. He said, "Carla—*now*. This place is going."

He took Claudia by the arm. She said, "Not without Carla."

He said, "Trust me. Bad penny. She'll turn up."

Claudia, reluctantly, had let him lead her out. They hurried down the street to retrieve the Ford Taurus. Whistler drove it back to the front of the house, where he called Carla's name once again.

"I see her," said Claudia. "Here she comes."

Carla had appeared from behind the garage. She seemed in no particular hurry. She was walking with the Calico cradled in one arm as she sheathed her knife up her sleeve. Her free hand held what looked like two wallets. She'd apparently collected souvenirs.

"Adam, she's been burned," said Claudia, watching her.

Whistler could see that she'd been blackened by the smoke. Her hair, on one side, had been singed to its roots and the sleeve that held her knife was still smoldering. He wanted to say, "Serves her right," but he didn't. The damage, in any case, seemed more cosmetic than painful. She did not walk as if she were hurting.

Whistler heard police sirens. He called to Carla, "Now or never."

She broke into a jog and climbed into the Taurus. Whistler stepped on the gas before she'd closed the rear door, ignoring the smattering of staring faces that had emerged from the neighboring houses. Several were even approaching on bikes, attracted by the rising column of smoke.

Carla's first words were, "That could have gone better."

Whistler didn't trust himself to speak or to look at her. He very badly wanted to strangle her. But what he needed for the moment was to find a side road by which they might avoid the police.

Carla said, "Take a right. You'll come to some woods. It's just pines. You can probably get through them."

She must have checked it out earlier. He took her advice. He swallowed and asked her, "Did you see Leslie Stewart?"

"Uh-uh, but she got out. That's what Aubrey thought, anyway."

"You found Aubrey?"

"Uh-huh."

She had chosen not to say how she'd left Felix Aubrey, probably in deference to Claudia. Whistler needed to know, but that discussion could wait. He asked her, "Got out how? With Lockwood? With Crow?"

"Neither one. A man named Kaplan. She might be okay."

"Might be?"

"According to Aubrey, Kaplan's not like those other two. The way to bet is she's okay."

"Yes, but how did they get out? And if they did, they're on foot."

"Through the window," said Claudia. "That window was open. It's the room where I told you I thought they had put her. There was duct tape—used duct tape—and a towel with more duct tape. It was all on the floor. It had been cut with a knife. Kaplan must have cut her loose and let her go."

Out the window, thought Whistler. He supposed that was right. He had come over the fence on that side of the house. There was no open window at that time. He'd rounded the house and he'd gone in behind the fuel truck. That was when they could have climbed out. And if she'd been cut loose, she could have run; she might be hiding. More than likely, though, this Kaplan still had her.

Carla said, "That big flash back there was a bomb. Not a good one, but hot. Almost melted my sweater. Someone tossed it in the house from the garage."

"That would have been Crow. He got away."

"And Lockwood, too?" She mouthed the word *shit*. She said, "This really could have gone better."

Whistler had tried to bite his tongue long enough. He said, "Damn you, Carla . . ."

She said, "Adam, that'll keep. For now, see those woods? See those tire tracks going through them? That's our way out. Move this thing."

He was still going to strangle her. But she was right. It would keep. Those sirens were getting much closer.

Carla said, "Hey, those tracks. They look funny to you?"

They did. Most were old. But something had gouged a fresh furrow between them. "I would bet that's the Pontiac," said Whistler with a nod. "It was dragging some hardware when it left."

"He's also dragging something else. Someone shot him in the ass. He was down, so I didn't waste time on him."

"Then where could he go? Not far, I would think."

"Well, if this guy, Crow, is as nuts as they say, the way to bet is he'll head for the hospital."

"In his condition? He'll try for Ragland again?"

"How would I know? I'm a rational thinker."

"Yeah, right."

She said, "Okay, Adam, get it out of your system. Ask me why we plowed into that house."

"We?"

"Yes, *we*. As it happens, it was Claudia's idea. She heard the first gunshot, thought they might have shot your friend. Except Claudia was ready to bust in there on foot. You said don't let her get hurt. I respected your wishes. That was why we went in armor-plated."

He was silent for a moment. Then he said, "That's not the truth."

"It isn't? You saw it. What's not true?"

"You went in with that truck no more than two seconds after I heard that shot from my side. You never heard a shot while you were still down the street."

"That's right. I didn't. But Claudia did. She heard a shot and a squeal and a man's voice yelling 'Fuck.' That's either ESP or a good pair of ears. I wasn't going to argue with an angel."

He asked Claudia, "Is that right? Did it happen that way?"

She said, "That's exactly what happened."

"And you . . . do have a good pair of ears. Yes, I know that."

"So? I'm waiting," said Carla.

"For what?"

"An apology."

He said, "Carla, you do push your luck."

Whistler picked up his cell phone. He hit redial. Molly answered on the first ring. He said, "It's Adam."

She asked, "Adam, are you staying away from that house?"

"Um . . . yes. In fact, we're leaving. Listen, Crow got away. I don't see how he can get very far, but Carla thinks he might try for Ragland again. If he does, he might try it with a bomb this time. He seems to have a supply."

She asked, "That's one of Crow's bombs on your boat?"

"If there is one. We don't know that."

"Yes, we do. John Waldo found it. It was under your bed."

"Aft cabin?"

"Uh-huh. Let me guess. You sleep forward?"

"We do, but what kind of a bomb?"

"Poorly made, mostly thermite, more heat than bang. But it was over the fuel tank; you would have been toast. Adam, have you seen Billy McHugh?"

Whistler glanced at Carla. "No, we missed him."

"He hasn't checked in. He was not at that house?"

"If he was, we didn't see him. We'll keep an eye open. Listen, Molly, you should keep yours open as well. We'll look around for Crow on this end."

She said, "No, don't. That's why we have police."

"Very well. We'll try to stay out of trouble."

"Check in with me again when you get back to your boat. I need you to do more than try."

Whistler promised that he would. He broke the connection. As he did, they all heard a distant explosion. Like Crow's bomb, it made a *whoomp,* but a much larger *whoomp.* It was probably the tank truck, but it couldn't have been full. From the sound, the tank had either already ruptured, or it had been nearly empty to begin with. They looked back and they saw a fresh billow of black smoke, but nothing resembling a fireball. Small favors, thought

Whistler. It meant that, with luck, no neighboring house had gone with it. With luck no police and no bystanders had been hurt. But Aubrey . . . and Briggs . . . and Poole's assistant must have cooked. He wondered which wallets Carla kept.

Carla leaned forward. She touched Claudia's shoulder. She said, "You don't rattle, do you."

"Don't be fooled. I was frightened. It's just hitting me now."

"You don't show it now and you didn't back there. I'd go in with you any time."

Whistler said, "Carla—for now and forever—don't even let that thought cross your mind." He reached to touch Claudia. He asked "How are you feeling?"

"I'd feel better if we could find Leslie."

"Well, right now I'm taking you back to the boat. The minute we learn anything, we'll call."

"Where will you be?"

"Carla and I . . . have to get somewhere quickly. There is still some unfinished business."

"It's not Crow. You would have said so. Is it Lockwood?"

"Yes, it is."

"Do you know where he'll be?"

"Yes, I might. If I hurry."

Carla told her, "He'll be at the airport. You coming?"

"Damn it, Carla," said Whistler.

"Yes, I'm coming," said Claudia.

He said, "Claudia, you won't be protecting me this time. This is killing. This is not what you do. You're not coming."

Carla nudged Claudia. She said, "Maybe he's right.

"I'm supposed to be with Adam. I'm coming."

For Arnold Kaplan, however, it was time to go solo. The last thing he wanted was a traveling companion. He had pleaded with Leslie to go her own way. He said, "Goodbye and God bless. You don't owe me."

"Owe you? For what? For not leaving me there? You dragged me to that house in the first place."

"Like I said, now we're square. No hard feelings? Good-bye."

As he said this to her, he was pushing a bike. She was pushing a bike alongside him. The front wheel of Leslie's was bent. It wobbled badly. They were two streets away from the ocean.

She was limping as well. She had banged up her knee. It had happened when he threw her out of the window. There was no time to try to be gallant.

Kaplan had pulled her back out of the closet as soon as he heard all the bullshit going on by people who should have known better. You want to talk, talk; but when you go to shoot, shoot. You don't have a goddamned town meeting about it. By the time the shooting started and Lockwood still wasn't down, and everyone was shouting, all at the same time, the window began to look good.

But, luckily, he looked out of it first. And who does he see? Who's out there? It's Whistler. He sees Whistler sneaking up to the fence. Right then there's a second shot fired by Briggs. So here's two shots, close range, but Lockwood's still standing. Crow is not exactly standing; what he's doing is dangling and he's bleeding all over Lockwood's crotch. This can't get much worse, but it does.

Shit hitting the fan doesn't start to describe the events of the next thirty seconds. Someone drives this big truck through the living room wall. A damned gasoline truck, no less. Whistler's over the fence and he runs around to the front. This was a gift that Kaplan couldn't pass up. He was going out through that side window.

He hadn't intended to take Leslie along, but the least he could do was cut her loose. He cut off the towel that he'd wrapped around her eyes and he cut the duct tape from her wrists. He got it all off except for one piece that she couldn't pull out of her hair. So of course she not only gets her first good look at him, but she insists on bailing out with him.

He should have just freed her hands and left her to do her head while he was already out the window. He also should have told her that Whistler was there. If he had, she might have stayed put. On the other hand, she might have got herself shot by running out of that bedroom. As it was, she took too damned long climbing out. One leg at a time, hold my hand, help me down. That was when he lost patience and threw her.

Kaplan had even less time to waste once he was out the window himself. He would obviously go the opposite way from where Whistler and the truck came in the house. He would sneak around the back and find someplace to hide. The nearest place he could think of was on the far side. Over there was this jungle of solid bamboo that was thick enough to get lost in. So, okay, that's the plan. He takes off at a run. And what does Leslie do? She takes off along with him. She thinks he must know what he's doing.

They reached the bamboo and they both hunkered down. By this time, someone's blasting with an automatic weapon and the demolition derby is continuing. While the gasoline truck is still plowing through the house, the two cars in the garage are plowing out. First the van rips loose and soon the Pontiac follows, both leaving parts all over the street. Next comes a flash, not much noise, just a flash, and it figures to be one of Crow's amateur bombs. Kaplan's exit had been very timely.

He could see, although not well, some activity in the kitchen, aside from the kitchen caving in on itself. He could see a small man, it could have been only Aubrey, and he seemed to be maybe in shock. Kaplan watched as this figure came to the door. It was Aubrey, no question; and no question, he was out of it. He sits down on the edge of a patio planter with both his hands covering his face.

Then, out of the house comes this other little figure. Red hair, black face, like a Dennis Rodman dwarf. From her build, though, this dwarf is a female. She's talking to Aubrey; she's nose to nose with him. This redhead has a Star Wars gun in one hand and a scary-looking knife in the other.

Just then, there's a screech of brakes from the street. It's Whistler out there with his Taurus. With him is his woman, the one who took out Crow's partner. She didn't look the type then; she doesn't look the type now, but here she is right in the middle of this and she's holding a shotgun in her hands.

Whistler's yelling, it looks like, for the redhead to come. Kaplan looks back and the redhead is coming but she isn't in any big hurry. And there's Aubrey, slumped over like he's taking a nap. Kaplan doubted that Aubrey was sleeping.

He asked Leslie, "What just happened? Did that little guy get whacked?"

She said, "Hey, that's Adam and Claudia."

"Did I tell you? They're fine. But I'm asking what just happened back here on the patio."

She gave Aubrey a glance. "I wasn't watching," she said. While she's saying it, she starts to climb out of the jungle. She wants to run after Whistler's Taurus. By now, there are so many sirens in the air that it could have been a bagpipe parade. He grabbed Leslie's arm. "Would you mind? Get back down."

"I have to tell them I'm all right. Let me go."

"Yeah, but *I'm* not all right. I would like to live through this. Stay down or I'll smack you. I mean it."

The issue is moot because by now it's too late. The redhead gets to the car, she hops in and Whistler goes. He's gone, but other citizens are just showing up and a few of them are on bikes. Bikes, he thought. Good idea. That could work. The bikes off that van should still be there.

He said to Leslie, "It's been fun, but I'm outta here. You stay." He stepped out of the bamboo and walked toward the street, past the house that was now making some serious smoke. He made himself walk at a halting pace that matched those of the other concerned neighbors. Of course, none of them were dressed quite like him, but he'd remedy that very shortly. He got to the garage. There was one bike in good shape. He knew that him helping himself to a bike might look a little funny to the neighbors. So, okay, he's a looter. They should live with it. He took the bike, climbed on, and started pedaling. There was only one direction the cops wouldn't be coming from and that was the beach, maybe four blocks away.

He hears Leslie say, "Wait up. My wheel's bent."

He says, "Shit. This cannot be happening."

Kaplan knew that women do ridiculous things, but for this there could be no excuse. He asked, "Is there something that I didn't make clear? Try this. You're a citizen. You like the police. Me, being a felon, I avoid them."

"Yeah, but why?"

Kaplan thought, See this? He has to explain. "Leslie, pay attention. Avoiding them means I don't get arrested. Think of my mother, how embarrassed she'll be, when her friends find out her son's in the slam."

She said, "I'm not trying to get you arrested."

"Then, thank you. You're a dream. You're a wonderful person. The thing is, the cops might have other ideas. Now shut your eyes and count to a thousand. I've got some disappearing to do."

She asked, "And what's this about shutting my eyes?"

As she speaks, she's pulling at that one strip of duct tape that's still ensnarled in her hair. She asked, "What was the point in blindfolding me? I must have seen you six times at Jump and Phil's."

"There's a look and there's a good look. Big difference," he told her.

"Well, don't worry. I won't turn you in."

This is that syndrome he'd heard about, thought Kaplan. It's named for someplace in Sweden, maybe Denmark. It's when hostage victims and kidnap victims end up feeling sympathetic toward their captors.

He told her, "Like I said, I appreciate that. The thing is, though, I have a plan of escape. A key feature of any good plan of escape is not having people watch you while you're doing it."

All he needed was ten minutes to get out of these clothes and throw these damned glasses in a bush. Ditch the whole outfit except for the shoes. Underneath these pants is a pair of tan Bermudas, long enough to allow for a gun in his crotch. Underneath this shirt and jacket is a dumb tourist T-shirt from a bar down the road called The

Salty Dog Café. Underneath the hat is a bald head with freckles. Poof. In two minutes, he's unrecognizable. All that's left is to boost another car.

She asked, "You need a ride? I can give you a ride."

That was it. The Stockholm Syndrome. He remembered. He said, "No."

She said, "That means you have a car. How far is it?"

"No car."

"You know what I'd do first? I'd get out of those clothes."

"Good idea. I'll consider it. Now start counting."

"Wait a minute," she said. "The red Cadillac, right? And it wouldn't be far from here, would it."

"No Cadillac. I dumped it. Start counting."

"That's good because the Cadillac's as bad as that coat. You never thought about a Toyota?"

He said, "Leslie . . . I like you. I really do. But I think we could use some time apart."

They both heard the *whoomp*. They knew the tank truck had blown.

She said, "Arnie, I know these back streets. Do you?"

"I know how to follow a beach."

"You don't think you'd stand out on a beach dressed like that? Follow me. I'll get you to your car."

38

Lockwood found the pilot in the air crew lounge. The pilot was alone; he was watching TV. Lockwood said, "On your feet. We're taking off."

The pilot sat upright, surprised to see Lockwood. He was also surprised to see how Lockwood was dressed. He said, "What's with the poncho? It's raining?"

"It might."

"Jesus," said the pilot. "What happened to you?"

Lockwood had scrounged through the clothing in the van. Every piece was at least four sizes too small. But he found an orange poncho like they wear to football games. He could have done without it saying "Go Bengals" on the back. It would serve, however, to hide his left arm and the sleeve that was blood-soaked where Briggs winged him. It would almost hide the blood on the front of his pants where Crow's ass had leaked all over his fly. It did nothing, however, to hide his lower legs where wood splinters from that doorway had ripped up his trousers and embedded themselves in his shins. He'd been plucking them out ever since.

But Lockwood didn't care to explain. He said, "Move it."

"We can't. My partner, my co-pilot's missing. He went out for a smoke. I haven't heard from him since."

"Short hop. You don't need him. Let's go."

"What about Mr. Aubrey, Mr. Briggs, and that new guy?"

"Mr. Aubrey's made other arrangements," Lockwood told him. "That must be where your co-pilot went."

"Hey, man, I don't know about this. Can I call him?"

"Go ahead. Except do it when we get in the plane."

Carla knew a shortcut to the side of the airport where cargo planes unloaded and where private planes were parked. She'd had cause to scout it earlier that day.

"There's the van," she said to Whistler as they approached. Lockwood had left it in a tow-away zone with two wheels up on the curb. She said, "Aubrey's plane is a Hawker twin engine. It says 'XA-GA4' on the tail."

"I know the plane," said Whistler. "I don't see it, do you?"

"No, I . . . yes. There it is. Already taxiing."

Whistler saw it. It had almost reached the foot of the runway. He asked Carla, "How close can we get?"

"We can drive right down there."

"In full view of the tower?"

"There's no tower, Adam. This is not JFK. But you're right, there are bound to be other eyes watching. I know; we'll drive down there in the ambulance."

"What ambulance?"

She pointed to an emergency vehicle that was probably on standby for sick passengers and crashes. She said, "I have an in. We can use it."

Whistler asked nothing further. He took Carla at her word. He steered the Taurus through a gate that led to storage facilities. In seconds, he'd pulled up to the ambulance.

Claudia hadn't spoken. She asked, "How will we stop him? Are we going to block the runway with a car?"

"No, we're not," Whistler answered.

"Well, then how can you stop him?"

Whistler didn't respond. His eyes were locked on the jet.

Carla was already out of the Taurus. Whistler climbed out and went back and popped his trunk. But he waited until he saw that Carla had been right. She was able to get into the ambulance and start it. She gave him a thumbs-up sign from the wheel. She revved the engine. "Let's do it. Let's roll." Only then did Whistler reach into the trunk. He drew out the M-87.

Carla saw it and said, "Neat. I heard about those. And I heard about you in Iraq. Good plan, Adam."

Claudia frowned. She asked, "What plan is that?"

He said, "We gave you the chance not to see this, not to come."

Carla didn't give Claudia the chance to say more. She said, "Claudia, hop in the back. Don't mind Benny."

Claudia blinked as if to ask, *"Who is Benny?"* She followed the toss of Carla's singed head and she looked in the back of the ambulance. A man was lying inside. He was strapped to the gurney. His face was largely covered by an oxygen mask. Both his eyes were swollen shut. She wasn't sure that he was breathing.

"Co-pilot," said Carla.

Claudia asked, "Is he dead?"

"He's medicated, mostly. He's sleeping it off. Emergency crews use this thing to sack out. I guess that's why nobody bothered him."

Whistler checked the breech of the M-87. He handed it to

Carla through the driver's-side window. He said, "Claudia, climb in or stay."

Carla said, "Get in, Claudia. Don't feel sorry for Benny. The creep's a drug courier and a grade-A lump of shit. The pilot's even worse. I'll fill you in."

Whistler said to her, "Claudia, make up your mind."

"It was made up a year ago, Adam."

Aubrey's pilot had tried to reach Aubrey from the cockpit. Seven rings and he got a recording. "Says the phone's not in service," he said to Lockwood. "How could Aubrey's phone not be in service?"

"Who knows?"

"Maybe I better try Briggs."

"Suit yourself," Lockwood told him, "but don't waste any time." Lockwood then lit a cigar.

The pilot said, "Hey, Vernon, douse the rope until we're airborne."

"I'll try not to burn a hole in the upholstery."

The pilot tried Briggs's number. No recording, but no answer. He might understand Aubrey not wanting to be available, but Briggs should always be on call.

The pilot said, "I'll tell you; this doesn't feel right. I remember the last time we left Briggs behind. He ended up with no face."

"He's with Aubrey."

The pilot, doing preflight, saw the crash car coming toward them. He said, "That wouldn't be Briggs in that ambulance, would it?"

"No, it wouldn't. Let's go. Get this thing off the ground."

"Ten grand," said the pilot. "This'll cost you ten grand."

Lockwood puffed. He said, "You sure you want to fuck with me?"

"If this is straight," said the pilot, "there's no charge; we stay friends. If it's any other way, it's ten grand. We agreed?"

"Okay, deal. What's that ambulance doing?"

Carla had stopped two hundred feet from the jet. Whistler stepped out. He showed himself. He could see Lockwood's face in the co-pilot's seat. Whistler ignored him. He pointed his finger at the cockpit's left seat. He made eye contact with the pilot. He held out his arms, palms down, and he crossed them.

Carla said, "That's baseball, Adam. You're telling him he's safe."

"I'm telling him to abort and he knows it."

"You're giving them a chance?"

"I shouldn't, but yes."

"So, show him the scope on the M-87. Let him know he's not going to outrun you."

"Not yet."

The jet started to roll. It began to pick up speed. "Now I'll show it," he said. "Hand it out to me, please."

She passed him the rifle. The plane was almost abreast of them. Whistler let the pilot see the .50-caliber weapon. Whistler saw that Lockwood had his own gun in his hand and he saw a look of rage on Lockwood's face. Lockwood twisted in his seat to try to aim the silenced Glock through one of the cockpit's side windows.

Carla said, "Well, this ought to be interesting."

Lockwood had to throw off his seatbelt. The space he had was too cramped; the silenced Glock was too long. He tried to line up his sights, but his cigar got in the way. He had to spit it out and start over. Whistler watched in near disbelief as Lockwood forced the muzzle against the Plexiglas window. Lockwood fired. He blew a hole through the window. Now he could shoot through the hole.

The pilot, his face livid, was screaming at Lockwood.

"So much for its pressurization," said Carla.

"It's not pressurized yet."

"But it will be."

"No, it won't."

"Look at him," said Carla. "He's still trying to draw a bead."

Whistler kept his eyes on the cockpit while calling out, "Claudia? Where are you?"

"She's right behind you," said Carla.

She was, and then she wasn't. She came up and stepped in front of him. He hissed, "Claudia—get away. Behind the ambulance. Stay down."

"Use my shoulder," she said calmly. "Rest your rifle on my shoulder."

Carla said, "Honey. That's a good way to break it. That thing is no twenty-two."

Whistler told Claudia, "You're not in this. Get back."

Lockwood did fire. Whistler saw the Glock spitting. But he also saw that Lockwood couldn't line up the barrel for more than an instant for each shot. He saw that one bullet kicked up a wad of Tarmac a good sixty feet from the ambulance. But another created a second black geyser within inches of Claudia's feet. She never moved. By the time it spat again, the jet was well past them, its engines now roaring to full throttle.

Carla said, "Um . . . Adam, now would be a good time. Let's see you blow that cockpit apart."

He said, "We'll wait." He walked back toward the ambulance.

Carla said, "Wait for what? They'll be airborne in five seconds. And we shouldn't hang around here all day."

"We'll wait until it's high enough and far enough, Carla. There are homes between here and the ocean."

"You can do this?" Carla asked him "You can hit him at that range?"

Whistler flipped the rifle's bipod to its forward locked position. He adjusted two knobs on the rifle's scope. He laid it across the roof of the ambulance and slowly, deliberately, took aim.

"We have liftoff," said Carla. "About now would be good."

He told her, "Be patient. Let it clear."

In seconds, the big Hawker looked more like a distant toy. Whistler squeezed the trigger. The rifle jumped six inches. Carla watched the plane. She said, "Nothing. You missed."

Claudia stood, rock still, staring at it as it climbed. She almost seemed to be in a trance.

Whistler opened the bolt and ejected the cartridge. He drew a second cartridge from a leather pouch that was strapped behind the trigger assembly. He inserted the cartridge, fully nine inches long, into the chamber and slammed home the bolt. He took aim again and he fired.

Carla watched. She said, "Damn it. Still nothing. You missed."

"I don't think so," said Whistler. "Let's pack up. Time to go." Claudia still hadn't moved.

Carla said, "Adam, that plane's leveling off. You never scratched the paint. He got away."

"No, he didn't," said Claudia. "He won't get away."

Carla asked them both, "Have I missed something here? I'm looking at a plane that's still flying."

Claudia took a breath. She said, "He didn't get away. He'll never hurt anyone again."

39

The car that Crow drove had no muffler, no exhaust pipe, and it left a trailing cloud of blue smoke. It had a left front wheel that wobbled. It had lost its front bumper. Somewhere along the way, its right front door had fallen off. Yet he'd managed to drive it, unimpeded, all the way to the Medical Center. No side roads, no detours, no attempts at evasion. He had driven straight down the island's main parkway, watching for the signs with the big blue H that would show him the location of the hospital.

The only reason, later given, as to how this was achieved, was that virtually every police car on the island was, by then, converging on North Forest Beach. At least five, plus two fire trucks, must have passed him.

Crow himself had seen nothing remarkable in the fact that he'd reached his objective. He knew whose hand had

cleared a path for him. And he was the instrument of that
hand.

The journey, however, was not without further trials. He
hummed loudly as he drove to keep his mind off the pain
that he felt with every bump and every touch of the brakes.
His jaw had been broken and probably his cheek. The worst
of it, however, was the pain from his buttocks. His buttocks
felt as if they were on fire.

He had almost reached the hospital grounds before he
thought to reach under him and try to relieve whatever was
hurting him so badly. He knew that he'd been shot, and
where he'd been shot, but the soreness seemed to have
spread well beyond where the bullet and entered and exited.
He found those wounds with his fingers, but he found something else. Thin slivers of metal were imbedded in his flesh.
He used his thumbnail to pry one of them loose. He examined it. A staple. And then he found another. He could not
imagine how he'd been stapled.

The signs, and the aid of that guiding hand, led him to the
Emergency ward entrance. He pulled in and parked behind
an ambulance. He got out, still humming, for the pain hadn't
lessened, and reached into the Pontiac's backseat. He pulled
out the golf bag and reached into the pocket where he'd kept
the third and last of his bombs. His fingers were trembling
almost out of control, but he managed to press the right buttons on the timer. Next, he drew most of the clubs from the
bag and these he left on the backseat. They had made his
shotgun too hard to retrieve. But for that, he would surely
have killed those two men who had said they'd come to help
him, then betrayed him.

He would find them again. He would heal, and then he'd
find them. Especially that Jew who was the first one to hurt
him and who, before that, had done nothing but mock him.
Well, God is not mocked. Nor is his instrument.

The Jew, however, might already be dead. He might
have burned in the fire of the bomb that Crow had thrown
before he'd made his escape. Crow tried to remember; was
there also a truck? Yes, there was. A tank truck. Where

could it have come from? No matter. More fuel for the fire.

The Jew might be dead, but the big one was alive. That one had escaped before he did. The big one, Lockwood, had taken the van that Crow had borrowed from that family from Ohio. But he would find Lockwood, wherever he'd gone. It was that one, the bully, who had broken his jaw. He could feel the bones grind when he moved it. It was that one who'd attempted to choke the life out of him. It was that one who'd held him, using him as a shield, causing him to be shot in the buttocks.

But who were all these others? He'd seen two, perhaps three. And he'd heard the voices of still more. And now that he thought of it, he felt quite sure that one of them had been Felix Aubrey. He hadn't actually seen Aubrey. But he'd heard his name called. Yes, he had. Lockwood called it. Lockwood had cursed him. Therefore, Aubrey was no friend of Lockwood's.

He would visit Delbert Poole. Poole would sort all this out. He would offer Mr. Poole a chance to explain why these men Poole sent to help him had betrayed him. He would ask Delbert Poole, "Was it you who betrayed me? Was I to be punished for Leonard's mistake in failing to send Philip Ragland to hell? Well, I've remedied that failure myself, Mr. Poole. But you must still answer, nonetheless."

Crow found his golf shoes in the backseat's well where the Jew had forced him to take them off. He jammed his feet into them, but he left them unlaced. He threw the lightened golf bag over his shoulder and limped to the Emergency Room entrance. A young doctor and a nurse saw him coming. They did not rush to his aid. They stood blinking, rather stupidly. Crow was fully aware that he must be a sight. His cheek was swollen, his jaw hung crooked, and he still had those Band-Aids all over his face and all over the backs of his hands. His powder-blue golf shorts had a big wet spot in front. He feared that he had soiled himself while he was dangling. And the seat of his shorts was covered with blood, as were the backs of his legs. His golf shoes flopped loosely and loudly.

The nurse finally hurried toward him. She tried to take his golf bag. He told her, "No, I'll need it. I haven't finished my game."

She blinked in disbelief. She asked, "What happened to you?"

He said, "Bees. Perhaps wasps. Bees, more likely."

She cocked her head toward his buttocks. "How big were those bees?"

Then she said, "Come with me. We'll have you looked at."

He said, "I know. It's like a bullet wound, isn't it? But it isn't. A broken branch did it."

"If you say so."

"But if a bullet had done that, where would you put me? Is there a particular section or floor where people with bullet wounds are kept?"

She said, "Three floors up. And I suspect that's where you're going."

"And knife wounds to the head? Same location?"

"Same location."

"Thank you. I'll go up there now."

"No, you won't. You're going to lie down right here until we have you examined."

"May I first use your rest room? I'm in very great need."

"Third door on the right. Leave the golf bag."

"No, thank you."

She turned to another nurse. She said, "Security, stat."

"I'll be with you very shortly," he said.

Molly Farrell had been patrolling the corridor while Olivia tried to keep Kate Geller occupied. Molly had been on the phone almost constantly for most of the past forty minutes. She kept a smile on her face and she chose her words carefully, but her mind was in utter turmoil. She kept that smile for the benefit of Kate Geller in case Kate should step out of Ragland's room.

John Waldo had been the first to report. Adam had not shown up at the marina. Next came a report from Billy

McHugh. He'd missed Adam and Claudia and Carla in her fuel truck. They had probably gone in after all.

She'd told Billy, "Don't you go. Keep your station."

He asked her, "You called the cops yet?"

She said, "Olivia has. She called Sergeant Moore. He's the one who's been helpful to Adam."

"Sounds like this sergeant called everyone else. I'm starting to hear all kinds of sirens."

"Stay and watch."

She had tried to reach Adam on his cellular phone. No answer from him. She tried Carla. Same result. Billy McHugh called again to report that he could see smoke from a fire.

"Big-time," he said. "I guarantee it ain't leaves."

He couldn't be certain, but according to his street map, that fire was at or near Lagoon Road. He said that by then he saw Mars lights all over. "Sheriff's cars, state troopers, fire trucks, EMS trucks—all of them heading toward that smoke."

She had asked, "Have you seen any cars coming out?"

"A few. And a garbage truck. And a van just now. Not anyone we know, though. I oughtta go in."

"No, you stay," she repeated. "My map shows two, maybe three ways out. From where you are you can see all three. If you go in, you're likely to get blocked by those police cars. I need to know that you're mobile."

Billy had said, "Whoa. I think something just blew. I'm looking at a whole lot more smoke."

She closed her eyes and rubbed them. "Okay, keep me advised."

She'd spent the next twenty minutes torturing herself with thoughts of what she might have done differently. Her instructions had been to avoid all contact with Aubrey or with any of his people. Protect Adam and Claudia. Get them both off the island. Get Claudia's mother off with them. Leave Aubrey for another day. Leave him for the twins. She appeared to have failed in almost every respect and, what's more, she should not—repeat *not*—have brought Carla. No one's better to have at your side in a fight. No one's worse when you're trying to avoid one.

Molly saw a nurse go and speak to the guard who'd been posted outside Ragland's room. The guard nodded, then left. He took the stairs. Molly asked her, "Why did he leave his post?"

"He's needed in ER. There's some sort of disturbance."

"Disturbance? What sort?"

"You needn't worry yourself."

Molly pulled a large-caliber pistol from her purse. "Do you see this? I worry. Please answer."

The nurse stared at the gun. "There's . . . a man, a golfer; he's apparently deranged. He's on the loose somewhere in the building."

"A golfer?"

"Miss, you can't have a gun here. I must ask you—"

"Describe him."

"He's . . . dressed like a golfer. He came in with his clubs. Small injuries all over his face and hands. He claimed that he'd been attacked by bees, but he also had a trauma to his buttocks. He wouldn't let them take away his golf bag."

The nurse said, "Just a minute. They're ringing me again. I'm afraid I'm going to have to report you."

She walked back to her station, picked up the phone and listened. Molly saw a look of new concern on her face. She cradled the phone without mentioning Molly. She said, "They think he might be coming up here. He asked them where bullet wounds are treated."

Molly's eyes narrowed. "Now, listen to me. This golfer, very likely, is one of the men who tried to kill Mr. Ragland last night. If he is, he is probably carrying a bomb and he's certainly armed with a shotgun. Tell that to Security. Tell them not to fool with him. Tell them to shoot him on sight."

"They won't do that. Not here. Not in a hospital. I mean—what would happen if you're wrong?"

"Tell them anyway."

Molly turned away and walked back to Ragland's room.

Philip Ragland was still in a drug-induced sleep. She told
Olivia and Kate Geller to stay in the room and to barricade
the door with the room's second bed. She told Olivia to have
her gun cocked and ready and to shoot through the door at
anyone who tried to force it. "Don't ask who it is. Simply
shoot. Can you do that?"

"Yes, I can. Where will you be?"

Before Molly could answer, they heard a dull boom. It
seemed to come up through the floor. Another boom followed. Were they bombs? Molly doubted it. The bomb that
John Waldo had disarmed and had described would not have
made such a sound. More likely, she had just heard a shotgun.

Crow had bypassed the elevator bank in favor of the fire
stairs nearby. Elevators were not good. They left one with
too few options. The stairs, however, had the twin disadvan-
tages of being steep and being made of concrete. Steep was
bad because he was tired; he'd been weakened. Concrete
was bad because the spikes made too much noise. Stocking
feet would be better. Stealth was called for.

That business about needing to use the rest room was a
ploy, but now he wished he'd taken the time. All the excitement had put pressure on his bladder and he hadn't relieved
it for hours. He would do so at the first opportunity. For the
moment, however, he would pull out his shotgun and make
sure that it held a full load.

It was good that he'd decided to kick off his shoes because a guard had appeared on the second-floor landing. The
guard didn't see him or hear him at first. When he did, at
last, the guard ordered him to halt and to put his hands in the
air. Crow obliged him because his hands held the shotgun.
He fired. Too high. He fired again. The guard yelped and
then dropped out of sight. Crow could hear him scrambling
through the landing's fire door and slamming the door shut
behind him. Crow didn't know whether he'd hit him or not.
It didn't matter, perhaps. The point had been made. The
guard would think twice before confronting him again.

Crow crept up to the third-floor landing, where he slipped the golf bag from his shoulder. He leaned it against the cement wall, very quietly. His bottles of Snapple clinked together, but not loudly. They reminded him that he hadn't had his lunch.

He reached into the largest compartment of the bag and carefully removed the device. He had set the timer so that it would go off within seconds of being released. All he had to do now was to press one more button. That button would start the ten-second count the instant he removed his thumb from it. He pulled the door partway open and held it with his foot. He picked up his shotgun. He was ready.

A woman's voice shocked him. "If you move, I will kill you."

He turned his head slightly. The voice had come from behind him. He swung his shotgun back toward the stairs he'd just climbed. The flight of stairs was empty. He saw no one.

"Up here," the voice said. "Very slowly, put those down."

He saw her at the top of the next flight of stairs. Another woman, he thought. Why so many women? This one was a new one. Long dark hair, dressed for business, a purse at her feet. He'd have thought that she would be hidden or crouching. She was neither; she was standing up straight, quite erect. She held a pistol in both hands, but she held it pointed downward. She seemed rather unready. He felt sure that he knew why. The hand that had led him here would not let him be impeded. Not this close to the fulfillment of his task.

He said, "You're too late. Do you see what I have here?"

He wanted her to look at the bomb that he held. He wanted her to take her eyes from the shotgun. In that instant, he would bring it to bear and he would shoot her.

She said, "Put them down slowly or die. Up to you."

"Oh, I'll never die. You will, but I won't." As he said this, he lifted his thumb from the button. "You see, it makes little difference what becomes of my body—"

"In that case, you won't mind," Molly said, and she fired. She fired at the thing in his hand.

*   *   *

Olivia Ragland had heard the shot and she heard the great
whoomp that came after it. She had promised to stay, but she
couldn't bear not knowing. She pulled the bed away from
the door and peered out. She had Adam's Beretta in her
hand, the safety off. She saw nothing at first, only smoke
near the fire door. But she heard a muffled shriek, then another.

The door pulled open, inward, and a mass of flame
lurched through it. The fire was so hot that it had no shades
of red; it seemed whiter than a high summer sun. The figure
at their center was already charred black and almost totally
naked. A few last strands of clothing were peeling from his
flesh and becoming little wisps that floated up and away. It
was probably Crow, but it was difficult to tell. It could have
been the security guard.

She saw that the figure's right hand was gone. What was
left of his forearm flapped loosely. But his left hand still
gripped what appeared to be a weapon. The figure was still
shrieking. So very high-pitched. It sounded like an animal.
Or a woman.

Olivia gasped. Oh, my God. Where is Molly?

She felt Kate at her side. Kate had had the same fear.
Kate shouted Molly's name and began to run forward. As
she did, the overhead sprinklers kicked in. Their hiss combined with the hiss from the fire, creating a popping and
crackling sound. Through all this, Olivia heard a muffled
female voice. The voice called, "Stay back. Don't come
down here."

She saw that the fire door remaind partially open. They
both saw that Molly was trying to get through, but the
sprinklers had not yet cooled the door's metal surface and
more fire could be seen where Molly stood on the landing.

Molly called again. "I'm all right here. Stay back."

Olivia was in no mood to obey. She shouted, "Who is
that? Is that Joshua Crow?"

"It is, and there are shotgun shells in that fire. Stay away
until the sprinklers cool it down."

Crow was still standing with the help of the wall, still gripping the shotgun; it seemed welded to his hand. An odd bleating sound was coming from his mouth. He sucked in a breath of flame and he roared Leonard's name. He roared it again until he choked on it. It didn't seem possible that he could still speak or that he still remained on his feet. His flesh bubbled and spat from his scalp to his knees. But Olivia saw that below his knees he seemed almost untouched by the fire. His shins were pinkish white, the only part that still looked human. She saw that he was wearing orange socks.

Olivia felt herself raising the Beretta. She took a step forward through the smoke and drenching spray.

Molly called, "Do not shoot him. I don't want a bullet in him."

"But he's still—"

"There's no need. Don't shoot. Let him burn."

In an earlier time, Olivia might have argued that to shoot him was a mercy. But Olivia had no thought of mercy in her mind now.

Kate Geller said, "Don't. You're not like him, Olivia. You'll never feel right about doing this."

"The hell I won't. He came here to kill my husband."

Gently, Kate Geller put her hand on Adam's gun and eased it down toward the floor. She said, "Molly's right. There's no point. Let it go. Let's both get in out of the rain."

40

There was still a glow in the western sky when Harry Whistler's plane prepared to land. While airborne, he'd been briefed on the afternoon's events through a series of phone calls from Molly Farrell and another call from Paul Bannerman.

As his plane approached from five miles out to sea, his pilot had buzzed him to look out the starboard window. He said, "Down on the water. Two o'clock."

Donald Beasley looked first. He said, "Rescue ships. Coast Guard."

Harry saw them. And their lights. They were picking up debris, what debris they could find, from the aircraft that had plunged in hours earlier.

Donald asked, "Just two aboard?"

"Only Lockwood and the pilot, from what I've been told. Almost everyone else has been accounted for."

As Harry's plane circled for its final approach, he peered down toward the southern end of the island, where the house that he'd been told about had burned. He knew that the fire had only lately been extinguished, but he'd thought that he might see where it had been from the lights. There should have been police cars, their lights strobing around it, keeping the curious at bay. But he saw little.

"Too much tree cover down there," said Donald. "We'll take a look later if you want."

Harry shrugged. "Look at what? There's nothing there anymore."

"Little prick was lucky."

"Well, his luck has run out. He was warned. There won't be another truce."

The reference, of course, was to Felix Aubrey. First Harry had heard that Carla had finished him. Next he heard that she hadn't, according to her, but that he'd probably died in the explosion. That wasn't true either. The firemen had found Aubrey wandering dazed, in a stupor, with no ID on his person. The police had taken him to the Emergency ward. Molly saw him after he was brought in.

Carla said that she'd thought about finishing Aubrey to save Harry Whistler the trouble. But her heart wasn't in it. He would not have known what was happening. His mind had apparently shut down.

Harry doubted that Aubrey had gone insane on more than a temporary basis. Deep shock, however, wasn't hard to imagine. All that shooting. The fire. Carla ripping through the house in a fuel truck. And if those were not enough to numb the man's senses, at the end he found himself face-to-face with the woman who'd cut him so badly before and, as then, she had a knife in her hand.

Carla says that isn't it. She says, for one thing, he never saw her face that other time. He seemed to have had no idea who she was. Even so, she must have looked like some creature from hell, all sooty and smoldering, walking out of the flames. Come to think of it, thought Harry, if creatures were to come up from hell, a fuel truck seemed a suitable conveyance.

The other one she'd cut had also survived. Lockwood's partner, Briggs, was still alive, but not by much. The first police car to arrive had found Mr. Briggs. He was trying to drag himself out of the garage while it was almost totally engulfed. Briggs would probably lose at least one of his legs. Carla again. She'd shot to maim, not to kill. Briggs had no ID on him either.

Donald said, "You know, she really ought to rethink that. I mean her thing about being nonlethal for a change. I mean, you got to remember she goes up against people who might have a different philosophical bent."

Or maybe it was Dennis who said that, thought Harry. Philosophical bent? That did sound more like Dennis. Either way, Harry found himself inclined to agree.

The only fatality, not counting Crow and Breen, seems to have been someone named Robert. Poole's man. Carla wasn't absolutely sure about that. She says she never saw him when she plowed into the house, but Robert had been with them, no question. She says she and Claudia checked out every room, all except for under the wheels of the truck. If that's where he was, and that seemed the way to bet, they probably won't even find his teeth.

The other one, named Kaplan, had also confirmed who was in the house at the time. Kaplan had been grabbed by Billy McHugh. It seems that Billy had been posted to watch several streets by which any of the Aubrey crowd might escape from this beachside community they were in. He saw a man and a young woman come out pushing bikes. They were pushing them because the young woman's bike was bent. He recognized Kaplan the moment he saw him because Billy had heard a detailed description of the way this Kaplan was dressed. Billy says he could hardly believe his own eyes. He says Kaplan might as well have been carrying a sign that said, "In case you didn't notice, this is me."

Billy says he recognized the girl, the kidnap victim, because they had a description of her as well. Blond hair, black pants, maroon blouse, one sleeve missing. But the girl wasn't acting like a kidnap victim. Not only did she have every chance to get away; this Kaplan was trying to get rid of her. But she stayed with him; they crossed the main road, and they pushed their bikes to a big parking lot that had a sign saying BEACH PARKING ONLY.

The car they went to was a red Cadillac. It was an old El Dorado with fins. Billy heard Kaplan saying, "Now will you go away?" The girl said, "Arnie, you can't use this car. Let's catch a bus, go down to mine and I'll drive you." But it seems that driving a red Cadillac was not quite as dumb as Billy thought. It seems that Kaplan had another, less conspicuous car stashed and all he wanted to do was get to that one. And Kaplan had been trying to get rid of the girl so that he could strip down to less conspicuous clothing that he had been wearing underneath all this time.

To make a long story short, McHugh proceeded to detain him. McHugh paralyzed Kaplan with a punch to his kidney while telling the girl, "You're okay now. Don't scream." She almost screamed anyway. Billy has that effect. She threw herself over Kaplan and said, "Don't hurt him again. This man saved me."

Billy wasn't going to hurt him. At any rate, not yet. All Billy intended was to take him to the boat and hold him until he could be questioned. Billy told the girl that she could go, but she wouldn't. She wanted to stick close to protect her protector. Billy drove them both to the boat.

"You know what that sounds like?" said Donald. "That syndrome."

"Stockholm Syndrome?"

"Yeah, that one."

"Well, you go have a talk with them. You sort it out. I'll be busy with Adam and Kate."

Harry's Gulfstream jet was on its final approach. That approach took it past the hospital complex. At that point, the plane was at four hundred feet. Harry saw that there were police cars and fire trucks still ringing the hospital building. Olivia and her husband were still there, no doubt, although probably on a less smoky floor. Aubrey and Briggs were there as well, under guard. Molly and Kate had gone back to the boat to meet up with Adam and Claudia. Carla had gone there as well to take a shower and to borrow some of Claudia's clothing.

He'd have thought that Molly would have been detained after helping that lunatic burn himself up. If she'd shot him, she would have been. She was smart not to do it. And Adam and Claudia seemed to have some clout with a deputy sheriff named Moore. Moore had merely told her not to leave the island until she was told that she could go.

Speaking of bombs . . . Harry turned to Donald Beasley. "Molly says that boat's clean now. Are we sure?"

"If John Waldo cleaned it, it's clean."

Donald pointed out the window as the Gulfstream touched down. "See that ambulance?" he asked. "That must be the one. Back door's open. They found the co-pilot."

Harry knew that. He knew that they'd found him alive. Another of Carla's half-measures. On seeing the ambulance, on seeing this runway, he was able to envision a good deal more clearly what had seemed incomprehensible when Molly reported it. Not so much that Adam took out both that jet's engines at a range of almost a mile and a half. That's what an M-87 was for, but it's still one hell of a shot. Adam, of course, had done things like that before. Well, not a jet, maybe, but choppers, same range. What had been hardest to imagine was Claudia offering to let him rest that rifle on her shoulder. That and seeing with no scope, just her naked eye, that Adam had made two killing shots.

Boggles the mind. That sweet girl from the ski slope. Add to that what she did at that house, busting in there with Carla, no hesitation, after hearing things that Carla couldn't hear. And of course that knife. The throw that saved Ragland's life.

Donald had said, "A plain knife? Like what comes with forks and spoons?"

"That's the story. You doubt it?"

"Yeah, I do," said Donald. "That one, I'd have to see."

"Well, I wouldn't count on her giving demonstrations. But look into it and tell me what you think."

The Gulfstream was down. It had taxied to a stop. Two rental cars were waiting near the terminal building. A man with a clipboard stood near them.

Donald asked, "Why two cars? We're not all going to the boat?"

"You two get down there. Check in with Molly. I'm going to that restaurant where the shooting took place. I need to have a private meeting with Adam."

"The place called Jump and Phil's? Molly said it's boarded up."

"That's what makes it a private meeting, Donald."

41

The two owners, Jump and Phil, were there to let them in. They had long since been told that Leslie was safe and that they'd be seeing her shortly. Whistler introduced both men to his father. He introduced Jump by his true name, John Griffin, and Phil by his full name, Phil Henry.

Harry said to them, "I hear you've both been good friends."

Jump said, "We try to please our valued customers."

"Well, I very much appreciate what you didn't say."

"We don't know what you mean. You guys hungry?"

"No, we're fine."

"You're sure? We're long on the mustard-crusted grouper. It was last night's special until we had to close early."

"No, thanks. We're fine. A couple of Scotches?"

"Coming up," said Phil. "Nothing else? You guys sure?"

"No, we just need to talk."

"Try not to bust the place up."

Harry and Adam took seats at the bar. Harry asked, "Is this where you were sitting?"

"Claudia was sitting where you are."

"She was here; you were there. The shooter was where?"

"He came in that front door, walked straight through to that fireplace."

"All that time he was moving?"

Whistler nodded. "Uh-huh."

"Glad I saw this. Donald's right. A throw like that can't be done. No wonder people say she didn't do it."

Whistler took a breath. He said, "Speaking of shooters, let's talk about you. You were shot yourself. Everyone seems to know that but me. Is it true, and why didn't you tell me?"

"Why would I?"

"You're going to make me say it? Because I'm your son."

"Adam, you were in basic training at the time. You were much better off where you were."

"Because whoever shot you was also looking for me?"

He said, "Adam, let's stop dancing. The man who shot me was hired; I think you know by whom. The twins settled up, but it took them two months. By that time, I was pretty much back on my feet. The story's old news. It's done with. Forget it."

"Those Hollywood people? Alicia?"

"It's done with."

"Except they left you with a souvenir. Am I right?"

"One fragment," said his father. He pointed. "Down here. Never gave me a problem for a good ten years afterward. Then it moved. And it lodged. It's now in a bad place. I'm going to need some repair work."

Whistler looked into his eyes. "It could cripple you, correct?"

"I'm not winning many dance contests anyway."

"Is paralysis possible?"

"Worst case, yeah," said Harry, "but let's be optimistic. Either way, Adam, I'll be down for a while. I'm going to need you to come home."

"I'll be there."

"That's it?"

Whistler said, "I'm your son. I'll be there."

"Well, I might need you to take care of things. I might need you to help run the business."

"I will do whatever needs doing."

"No, Adam, I mean run it. First learn it, then run it. A lot of people count on me, Adam. They trust me; they'll learn to trust you."

"I said I'll be there." Adam leaned closer. "I'll be there as long as you try to remember that I'm not a kid anymore."

A grimace. "I know that. So does everyone else. I'll try harder to show it. I promise."

"I'll remind you."

"Will you give me two years? You and Claudia both?"

Whistler said, "I don't know about Claudia."

"You're a package, Adam. You're a hell of a package. And don't say you'll have to ask her. She's with you; you're with her. I'll try to get Kate to come, too."

"I'm sure she'll be thrilled to push your wheelchair around."

"If I have to, I'll ask her to marry me."

"You're a shit."

His father winced. He said, "I didn't mean to say it like that. The last time we spoke, the woman wanted no part of me. This episode of yours on this island did nothing to enhance her already slim interest in becoming part of the family. She just watched a guy turn into charcoal with socks."

"Well . . ." said Whistler. "She's here. Go mend your fences."

"Yeah, I will. You and I can talk details later. For tonight, I have a number of people to see. Oh, and by the way, I brought Aubrey's ledger with me. Do you care if I give it to Olivia?"

"I wish we'd known to do that a year ago. Sure."

"All those names in the ledger . . . let the Raglands bring them down. But not Poole and Aubrey. I'll deal with them myself. I assume you understand why."

Whistler nodded. He did understand. It had nothing to do with personal vengeance. His father had made an agreement with them. A deal had been struck and they broke it. For the sake of his father's reputation, credibility, he could not allow that to go unpunished. Having those two sent to prison was never an option. His response would be swift and very final.

His father added, "I'll tell you, though, Adam. There are parts of this I still don't understand. I assume you've figured out what Recon-JC means. That notation that appears in Aubrey's ledger?"

"It only hit me a few hours ago. Reconstructionists— Crow. I finally got it."

"Well, I understand Poole and why he'd tie in with those people. I understand Poole siccing Crow on Philip Ragland. What I don't understand, not me, not Molly, is why Felix Aubrey would go near the damned thing. Or why he'd break the deal by coming down here after you. Or why he'd come down here at all, for that matter."

"I had the same problem with that," Whistler answered.

"If Aubrey thought that you had tied in with Ragland, what's the first thing that he should have done?"

"Call you. Remind you that you have an agreement."

"Would he have tried to kill you before calling me?"

"That would have been much too direct for Felix Aubrey. That man has more twists than a snake."

His father smiled. "Yeah, he does."

"Why's that funny?"

A shrug. "I guess I kind of enjoy the little bastard. He

might have the single most devious mind that I've run across in my lifetime."

"Are you thinking of giving him a pass?"

"No, I'm not."

This conversation, although basically finished, was interrupted by Jump. He entered the bar grinning. He said, "Leslie's outside and there are two men with her. Is it okay with you if they come in?"

Whistler matched Jump's smile. He said, "Absolutely." He'd be pleased to introduce Leslie to his father. The two men, he assumed, must be the twins, although they seldom showed up anywhere together. More than likely, one of them would come in while the other one watched from outside.

Leslie Stewart entered through the plywood-covered door. At her elbow was Donald. He was half right, so far. But behind them, hanging back, looking very ill at ease, was the man in the ugly striped jacket, Arnold Kaplan.

Donald said to Kaplan, "Go and sit in the corner. Me and Leslie need to talk to our friends here."

Kaplan spread his hands in a supplicating gesture. He said, "Mr. Whistler . . ."

"These are *both* Mr. Whistler. Now sit down and shut up."

"I just want them to know . . ."

"Wait your turn."

Whistler introduced Leslie. They chatted for a few minutes. His father, as usual, turned on the charm in the presence of a young woman. In response to his performance, Leslie smiled and told his father, "Well, now I can see where Adam gets it."

"Gets what?" asked his father.

"His looks. His twinkle."

His father made a show of being confused. He said, "Adam . . . has a twinkle? This Adam? Right here?"

Donald cleared his thoat, Whistler thought, to defend him. He said, "I agree. He's as cute as a button. But could we get some business off the table here first?"

Donald said to Leslie, "Give us maybe ten minutes. We

got just a couple of things to discuss. Then I'll call you and we'll talk about Kaplan. That okay?"

"Okay," she answered. "Can I bring him a drink?"

"Bring him the whole bottle. He could need it."

Donald waited for Leslie to get out of earshot. He huddled between the two men. He said to Harry, "We were right about Aubrey. He had nothing to do with the hit on Ragland. He had nothing to do with those two meatballs who did it. He did send Lockwood down here to keep an eye on Adam after Kaplan told Lockwood—are you following this?— about what happened last night in this bar here."

"Which Kaplan saw," said Whistler. "He'd been watching us for days."

"For a whole lot of days, but we'll get to that later. This morning, Aubrey hears who the two loonies were. He knows that Poole was funding this weird church they belong to and also some murders these guys did. Long story about that. It'll keep. Aubrey sees a chance to squeeze some money out of Poole, but for that he needs to make Crow disappear. He sends Lockwood down here to deep-six him. Lockwood, however, has ideas of his own and decides he'll use Crow to kill Adam. Net-net is that Aubrey is more or less innocent. He came down here to stop both Lockwood and Crow because he knows how this was gonna look to you guys. It was Kaplan who blew the whistle on Lockwood when Lockwood decided that he'd do his own thing. He was ready to pop Crow and Lockwood himself, but he had to go along and try to keep them both busy until Aubrey could show up with some heat."

He added, "Oh, and by the way, Kaplan doctored Crow's bombs. He couldn't get to the one Lockwood put on the boat, but he wet the other two down with some Snapple."

"Snapple?"

"Iced tea," said Donald. "Which is why they mostly fizzed. Not that they were that good in the first place."

"Uh-huh," said Harry. "And Kaplan's role in snatching Leslie?"

"Which reminds me," said Donald, "Aubrey thought she

was Claudia. This made him crazy. It's the last thing he wanted. He really did try to contain this."

"Get back to Kaplan. His role in the snatch."

"Couldn't help it, couldn't stop it. He looked out for her, though. Lockwood intended to kill her."

"And Leslie knows that? Now she wants to help Kaplan?"

"That would be the bottom line. It's not that syndrome thing either. She says he doesn't deserve to get hurt."

Harry shrugged. "Then she's called it. Tell him he can walk. Adam? You have any objections?"

"Not so fast," said Donald. "This guy's full of information. This guy knows of at least two attempts to kill Adam, both set up by Lockwood and without Aubrey's knowledge."

"Did he try to stop them?"

"Who, Kaplan? Why should he? Anyway, he didn't know until later. You want to know who queered those two tries on Adam's life?"

"I'm breathless," said Harry.

"Well, you should be. It was Claudia."

Whistler listened as Donald detailed the two attempts. The yacht that needed ice. That restaurant on Grand Cayman. Claudia, he realized, had been right in both cases.

Donald went on. He said, "Then there's the tracker. It was Kaplan here who arranged for that and again it was Claudia who—I don't know—sensed it somehow and almost crowned the kid who installed it."

Donald saw that Whistler was staring at him. Donald said, "You feel dumb? That's progress. You should. Next time listen when that lady tells you something."

Whistler sat slowly shaking his head. All the other instances came flowing back. Instances in which he had doubted her. Just today, on the boat, her saying that she knew that Vernon Lockwood had been on it. Her telling him that she could smell him. Her saying, before that, how all this was tied together. She'd said, "I just feel it," and he had dismissed her. Her saying, before that, that Sergeant Moore could be trusted. That Sergeant Moore was a friend.

Moving that bullet. Maybe she really did that. Making

Ragland more comfortable. She definitely did. Knowing that Lockwood intended to kill Leslie. Well, maybe not that one. Too easy.

But the knife—that throw—could she do that every time? Perhaps he shouldn't have doubted that either.

Donald was chuckling. This was also new to Whistler. He could not recall Donald ever chuckling.

He asked Donald, "What is it?"

"Random musings. Nothing much."

Whistler had also never imagined that Donald ever had random musings. He asked, "Like what? Is this more about Claudia?"

"Yeah, a couple of things," he said, "but first Kaplan. You know what I think we should do with him?"

"What?"

"Probationary, mind you, but I'd give him a job. This guy is pretty straight in his way."

Whistler blinked. "You've got to be kidding."

"It was Kaplan's suggestion. You can't say he don't have balls."

"And you're saying you would actually consider it?"

Donald rocked a hand. Then he said, "Yeah, I would. Let's remember that he tried to save some lives down here, Adam. Let's remember that he would have popped Lockwood and Crow before anymore damage was done. All he had to do to get rid of Leslie was whack her once in the mouth. If he did that, he could have been gone."

"Yeah, but still . . ."

"And besides, he took a bath on the deal he had with Aubrey. Guy could use the work. Why not try him?"

Harry said, "Adam? You'll have to call this one."

Whistler grunted. He asked Donald, "Will you check him out?"

"Yeah, of course. I'm feeling generous, not stupid."

"Let's talk again after you've done that."

Whistler made a mental note on the subject of hiring. He wondered how Sergeant Ed Moore might feel about working out of Geneva.

Donald said, "Where was I? Oh, Claudia and Carla. What three words would you never expect Carla to say?"

"I love you?"

"No, I'm serious. Try again. This is good."

"I forgive you?" asked Whistler.

"Who, Carla? Get real. Try again, but think social. Think women."

"Let's do lunch?" asked Harry.

"You got it," said Donald. "She wants to take Claudia to lunch."

As the shock from that revelation receded, Whistler noticed that Donald wasn't smiling anymore. His expression had become pensive.

Whistler asked him, "Something else about Carla?"

"About Claudia."

"Well?" Whistler asked.

"It's too dumb. Never mind."

"Come on, give," said Harry. "What about her? What is it?"

Donald grimaced. He asked Whistler, "Are you sure you hit that plane?"

"Yes, I'm sure. Two clean hits on the engines, killed them both. It had no place to go from there but down."

"Hell of a shot. But as long as you're sure. I just wondered about Claudia being with you, is all."

"Donald . . ." said Whistler, "tell us what's on your mind."

"I hear she talks to birds. Is that true? She talks to birds?"

"What could that have to do with Lockwood's plane?"

Donald hesitated. He said, "I don't know. I guess nothing. It's just that back on your boat, they had the radio on. The news guy was talking about that plane and why it splashed. He was talking about what they think downed it."

"Well?"

"He was saying they think it was birds."

42

Three days after the attempt on Philip Ragland's life, Poole's death made the six-o'clock news. It was not a major story. It appeared in fourth position. It was only three sentences long.

The director of the Center for Policy Analysis had thrown himself through the eighth-floor window of his office building in Washington. Poole was alone in his office at the time. No suicide note had been found. Some who knew him reported that in recent days Delbert Poole had seemed profoundly depressed.

Whistler asked his father, "Was that really a suicide?"

His father said, "It's over. What's the difference?"

Poole might, in fact, have taken his own life. He might have received a telephone call telling him that he would soon be indicted and disgraced. The caller might have described in detail the public ordeal that would follow.

Whistler knew, however, that the Beasley twins had not been seen on the island that day. He knew that Carla Benedict had also departed on her way back to Westport, Connecticut. He knew that soon he would probably begin to hear rumors that the three of them had paid Poole a visit. The story would go something like this:

The Beasley twins would have found a way into the building where Poole had his office. They would have brought Carla Benedict with them. While one twin stood guard to ensure a private meeting, the other would have introduced her to Poole. The twin who remained would have told Delbert Poole that she was the one who, a year before that, had restructured the face of his man, Briggs. He would have asked her to show him her knife. He would have told him that Carla was also the one who had shot off Briggs's leg at the knee.

Carla would have sat quietly during this recitation. She would have kept her eyes locked on those of Delbert Poole. Her cheek would have shown a disturbing twitch of the kind one associates with madness. She would have caressed her long and thin knife as she sat.

The twin doing the talking—Donald, most likely—would have described next what she'd done to Felix Aubrey. Poole had seen for himself the extent of Aubrey's injuries and was aware of how badly he'd been crippled. But he hadn't been told how slowly, and precisely, and painfully, the incisions had been made. Donald might have asked Carla to demonstrate by showing him where she would begin. Or Carla might have laid out a few other tools. A corkscrew. A saw. A pair of pliers.

Donald Beasley might have told him that he had two choices. The slow way or the quick way: the window. He might have told Poole that they would much prefer the knife. Poole would now have ten seconds to decide.

It may or may not have happened that way. They might have had to throw him out the window and been done with it. Whatever the story, it would spread over time. It might vary in a number of details. But Carla would be a constant. And her knife would be a constant. One other constant would have been that Poole had died because he'd broken his word to Harry Whistler.

There might be those who would challenge the story, citing the fact that the building was secure. Coded cards were needed at every entrance. Coded cars were needed in the elevators as well. Without the proper card, the elevator would not have stopped on the floor where the Center had its offices. Those cards were said to be impossible to duplicate. No uninvited visitor could possibly have gained access without having been issued a card. But Whistler remembered what was in Carla's hand as she emerged from that house in North Forest Beach. She was carrying two wallets in her hand.

So, no matter what the truth might have been, no matter whether Poole was with them or alone when he threw himself from that window, the story would be some version of the former. If the story was doubted, either Donald or Carla would probably produce one of those coded cars and lay it on a table. Enough said.

Whistler's father had always known the value of such stories. He knew how to use reputations.

Felix Aubrey, with treatment, had largely recovered from a state that had been near catatonic. Still hospitalized and under close guard; he was in FBI custody.

Whistler's father had decided to go easier on Aubrey. This turned out to be at Kate Geller's urging. He'd been persuaded that Aubrey was more or less innocent of much that had happened on the island. More than that, Felix Aubrey had been genuinely horrified when he thought that Whistler had already been killed and that Claudia had been kidnapped by Lockwood. True enough, he might have seen to it that Adam Whistler's photo would appear in the media, worldwide if he'd had time, but otherwise he'd kept the agreement.

The agreement, in any case, was now null and void. Aubrey knew that his ledger would soon be made public. He'd already agreed to cooperate fully with the various legal authorities. Aubrey, as far as Harry Whistler was concerned, was welcome to make whatever bargain he could in order to avoid a term in prison. He was welcome to avail himself of Witness Protection whether he served time or not. Harry's friend, Roger Clew, the State Department official, had flown down and visited Felix Aubrey to make sure that Aubrey understood his options.

Once he was relocated—and Harry Whistler would know where—Felix Aubrey would be told that he must never again step beyond the city limits of that place. While there, he would spend nearly all his free time performing community service. Specifically, for three nights a week, he would serve as a cook in a shelter for the homeless. He would join a church, never failing to attend. He would volunteer as a Sunday school instructor and he'd work with the Scout troop if it had one. If no troop, he'd volunteer to be a crossing guard at the nearest elementary school.

Kate Geller, on hearing this, said to Adam's father, "You have a weird sense of humor, Harry Whistler."

It had also caused Whistler to shake his head. He had said to his father, "You don't really expect him to do all that, do you?"

"At the start? Sure, he will. He's pretty snakebit by what happened to Poole."

Whistler asked, "Is it true that you'll know where he is?"

"Oh, yes."

"And that you'll have someone watching him?"

"No, but he'll think so."

"And you know that this Sunday school, crossing-guard business isn't likely to become his life's work."

"Hell, no. But, as I've said, he's such a devious little bastard that it ought to be fun to see how he schemes out of it."

"You almost sound as if you like him."

"Not like him. Enjoy him. He has an interesting mind."

"I'm . . . never going to hear that you've hired him, am I?"

His father said, "Hey, you know? That's a thought."

"It's a terrible thought. Tell me you're not serious."

He said, "Adam, as you know, we use all kinds of people. As you've seen, they're not all seminarians."

Kate Geller had agreed to move to Geneva, especially since Claudia would be based there for a while. And Kate, by the way, knew perfectly well that his father had bought her garden center. She had told him, "You got ripped on the price."

"Yeah, but look at the company it bought me."

She said, "It bought you two years. Or till you're back on your feet."

"But you will move in, won't you? I mean, no separate rooms?"

"I think we're beyond the separate-rooms stage."

"Want to marry me, Kate?"

"Ask again in two years. That's if I haven't murdered you first."

"Fair enough."

"Will you let me redecorate? Add some touches of my own?"

"Ask me again in two years."

He had taken Claudia for a predawn sail. The sail would be their last, or one of their last. They'd be leaving for Geneva in a couple of days. They'd be flying back with his father. Her mother would follow in a week to ten days. First she needed to go back to Silver Ridge, Colorado, to pack and to settle her affairs.

He'd asked Claudia, "Do you think your mother will stay?"

"Yes, I do. She's very fond of your father."

"Will she try to change him?"

"Not the way you mean. She knows who he is. I guess we're all who we are."

That last remark seemed to invite a discussion, but Whistler chose to leave it alone. They drifted for a while, enjoying the quiet, and watched the glow building in the eastern sky, as they'd done so many times in the Caribbean.

She asked him, "What will we do with the boat?"

"I'll arrange to have it brought over."

"You've told me that it's mine. Is that true?"

"You've seen the papers."

She said, "It doesn't really feel like mine anymore. It was taken from Felix Aubrey, correct?"

"I wouldn't exactly say it was taken. It was part of a settlement that those people agreed to for putting that hole in your neck."

"Where did he get it?"

"He had it seized. He stole it."

She asked, "From whom?"

"It was taken from a crooked Florida lawyer. Or maybe a

crooked banker; I forget. Don't tell me you're thinking of
giving it back."

"Oh, no. Not to them. But Leslie might like it."

"A half-million-dollar yacht? I guess she would."

"It would be a nice thing to do, don't you think? After all,
we'll be living on land over there. And we'll have all that
travel. How much could we use it?"

The travel that she was referring to was a sort of a training program. His father had asked him to spend a few
weeks in Westport being tutored in the business by Paul
Bannerman. From there, they'd go to Washington, spend
some time with Roger Clew, whom he hadn't seen since
his mother's funeral. It was Clew, incidentally, who'd used
his State Department juice to see that none of them were
detained.

After that, he and Claudia would go on to Moscow, where
they'd be under Leo Belkin's wing for a month, learning
about Leo's operation. Actually, "training" and "tutoring"
were not the right words. He'd spend much of that time
meeting powerful people, or rather seeing to it that they
knew who he was. Harry Whistler's heir apparent, Paul Bannerman's friend, and Leo Belkin's respected associate. And
those people would hear stories, some true, some legend.
They would surely hear about Lockwood's plane.

Whistler had told Claudia that she needn't go with him.
And, of course, she had answered, "Don't be silly." His father had said pretty much the same thing. He said, "They'll
all be dying to meet her."

"Dad, what have you told them?"

"I only know what I hear. She already has quite a reputation."

"Claudia, listen, on the subject of the boat . . ."

"I really think Leslie should have it."

"Tell you what. Let's ask her if she'd like to sail it over.
An Atlantic crossing. A cruise up the Rhône. A week or two
sailing on Lake Geneva. And we'll show her the lodge in
Chamonix."

"You expect her to bring this boat over by herself?"

"No, of course not. I can hire a crew. But I bet she'd have no trouble finding her own. I bet Phil would come over. And maybe Jump. Maybe even Sergeant Moore. Would you like that?"

She smiled. "Yes, I would. That would be very nice."

"Then, if you like, you can tell her it's hers. On the other hand, we'll have it on Lake Geneva. If you keep the boat there, they'll come over again. That's one big advantage of not giving it away."

She nodded. "That's something to think about."

It was possible, thought Whistler, that there, right then, he might have won an argument with Claudia. It was possible that they just might keep the boat.

The sun was rising. More birds were aloft.

He said, "Listen, Claudia . . . that time with Lockwood's plane . . ."

"Let's not talk about that sort of thing now. Hold my hand."

"Well, we'll need to talk sometime. It's about reputations. There's going to be an awful lot of talk about you. Even I am not sure I know what's true and what isn't."

"Do you want to know something?" she asked. "I'm not sure either."

"You're not?"

"Well, I know what I am. And I know what's been done. I'm just not sure who's actually been doing it."

"It's you."

"Am I crazy, Adam? Be honest. Do you think so?"

"If you are, I hope you never get well. The whole world should be your kind of crazy."

"Thank you, Adam."

"I'm going to quit trying to understand how you do it. I mean, whether it's you or your friend, the white light. It's time that I learned to . . ."

"Count your blessings? Me, too."

"I love having you as my guardian angel. I'd love you just as much if you weren't."

"That's good."

"But I do have to ask . . . about those birds . . . about that plane . . ."

She raised his hand to her lips. She said, "Hush."

"Claudia, I'm sorry, but I'd really like to know."

"Hush, Adam. Watch the sunrise. Let it warm you."

**THE FIRST OFFICIAL BANNERMAN
NOVEL IN MORE THAN A DECADE!**

Coming in January 2003

BANNERMAN'S GHOSTS

*They are called Bannerman's People. They come
and go like a breeze in the night, visiting any
who would break the peace or do harm to any
neighbor or friend. They've learned to blend
invisibly into Westport, Connecticut—the town
they've chosen as home, and will defend. Retired
operatives, they could be the bartender, the gar-
dener, the librarian...*

*But some of them, like Elizabeth Stride, are
among Bannerman's Ghosts. Believed to be dead
and no longer feared. Still others, like Martin
Kessler, are known to be dead.*

Except sometimes the dead don't stay dead...

Artemus Bourne drew an envelope from his pocket. "I need to find someone. I think you can help me. You won't do so out of the goodness of your heart, so I'm offering an exchange of information."

"I'm listening."

"This envelope holds details of an illegal arms shipment that is now on its way to Sierra Leone in defiance of a U.N. embargo. The intended recipient is a rebel commander, a notorious butcher named Colonel Mobote. The name is not unknown to you, I'm sure."

Clew nodded.

"The shipment contains hundreds of Claymore mines with which he intends to mount a terror offensive against any and all residents of Freetown. It also includes thirty shoulder-launched missiles with which he intends to destroy any aircraft that try to use Freetown's Lungi Airport. If you've ever seen that airport, you know how easily he can do it. The arms, as we speak, are aboard a cargo ship that is making its way up the African Coast. They will be off-loaded twenty miles at sea and taken ashore under cover of night."

"Explain to me why you would care," said Clew.

"I don't. I'm simply offering a trade."

"And why the sudden interest in Sierra Leone? You haven't finished looting Angola."

"I have interests in a great many places, Mr. Clew. Can we stick to the subject at hand?"

"You have the name of the ship?"

"I have everything, Mr. Clew, including the coordinates of the rendezvous point. You might suggest to the Navy that they hit fast and hard. The crew won't resist, but Mobote's men will because they know what Mobote will do to them if they should come home empty-handed. You'd be wise to blow them out of the water, but tell them to try not to hit the ship. It will have some twenty children on board."

"What children?"

"Slaves. Mostly female, none over twelve. They were

taken on in Gambia for sale in Cameroon. That trade is still in full vigor, I fear."

Clew made no move toward the envelope Bourne was holding. "What is it that you want in return?"

"Do you know, or know of, Elizabeth Stride?"

"The one they called The Black Angel? I've heard of her."

"I want only the answer to two simple questions. First, is Elizabeth Stride still alive? If she is, where can she be found? And I hasten to assure you that I mean her no harm. All I want is a meeting, nothing more."

"Jut a meeting?"

"Only that. A few hours of her time."

Clew curled his lip. "Stride was an assassin. No one has 'just a meeting' with assassins."

"Even assassins have personal lives and this is a personal matter. I have no wish to hire her, if that's what you're thinking."

"Then, why?"

"I'll say it again. It's a personal matter. It is none of your affair, but this envelope is. I won't offer it twice, Mr. Clew."

On the matter of hiring her. Clew tended to believe him, but only because Stride was never in it for the money. Her motive was strictly retribution at first, and later to discourage those who hunted her. Clew couldn't imagine her working for Bourne, but he surely hopes to use her in some way.

As for the envelope Bourne was offering in trade, embargoed arms were being shipped all the time and this would be a drop in the bucket. On the other hand, he didn't want to learn next week that a plane full of Red Cross relief personnel had plunged into the ocean off Freetown. He didn't want to know that he could have prevented it. Just as much, he wanted those children. And Bourne knew it.

But the last he'd heard of Elizabeth Stride was that she'd died perhaps three or four years ago. And her death, as he recalled, was more or less natural. He'd never laid eyes on the woman himself. He knew her by reputation only. He was never quite sure how much of it had been earned and how much of it had been folklore. Whatever the mix, she was certainly deadly. And as for Bourne's claim of no sinister intent . . .

"I'm not sure I can help you, Mr. Bourne."

"That sounds like you can, but you won't."

Clew decided to let out a little more line. "I don't know where she is at this moment."

Bourne brightened. "And *that* sounds as if you know she's alive. Is she? Do you know that for a fact?"

"She was alive last I heard. But it's been more than a year." This was a deliberate lie.

"And she was . . . and is . . . in this country, correct?"

"I had no reason to ask. I don't know."

"Would Paul Bannerman know? You still control him, do you not?"

"I worked with Paul Bannerman. No one's ever controlled him. And he's out of the game, so forget him."

"But he seems to know every world-class cutthroat on the planet. He surrounds himself with the most murderous of the lot. Is that what one does when one is out of the game?"

"He surrounds himself with friends. They look out for each other."

"Within the happy confines of Westport, Connecticut. So he's just a simple suburbanite now, doing violence only to crabgrass?"

Clew shrugged.

"And these *friends* of his have all bought charcoal grills and have taken up golf, I imagine."

"I imagine."

Bourne snorted. "I'm told by my own friend, the secretary of state, that no one seems to know how many they are. But you must know. Do you?"

"No, I do not."

"I think that's a fib. I'd bet that you know exactly."

Clew looked at his watch. "You've run out of time."

"I've heard them referred to as 'Bannerman's Ghosts.' Is that why? It is because they're especially elusive or is it because no one knows?"

Both, thought Clew, but that still isn't why, and, believe me, you don't want to find out. He said, "Now *you're* getting off the subject, Mr. Bourne."

"Or are they called his 'ghosts' because some of them, at least, are people who are widely believed to be dead?"

Clew smiled. "I can see where you're going with this."

"Then I'll ask it straight out. Might one of his ghosts . . ."

"Be Elizabeth Stride? I doubt it. Stride worked alone."

"Will you ask him?"

"Waste of time. He'd want to know why I'm asking. I'd say, 'Because Artemus Bourne wants to find her.' It would be a very short conversation."

Bourne started to reply. Instead, he held up the envelope. "You'd be asking because you want to save lives. These arms will maim and kill a great many people if they are allowed to go ashore. You can keep that from happening. All I want is an address."

"So that you can kill and maim them with your own mines and missiles? This shipment is from one of your competitors, correct?"

"There are always mines and missiles. Their source is irrelevant. As for Stride, you have my word that I mean her no harm. And, of course, I will make it worth her while."

Clew gestured toward the envelope. He held out his hand. "I'll need to see whether your information checks out. If it does, I'll go into our database at State. If it shows a current location for this woman, I will ask her if she's willing to see you."

Bourne exhaled slowly. "Please don't take me for a fool. I know that there's nothing of use in those files. But those files are less than complete, are they not? Your own are said to be so much better."

Clew, with effort, concealed his annoyance. He had just been informed that a member of his staff had been doing some digging for Bourne. It would not have been Bourne's "friend," the new secretary of state because he wouldn't know where to look. He had also been informed that Bourne was aware that Clew kept a set of files of his own.

Bourne said, "Oh, don't pout. Yes, I've tried by other

means. You are hardly the first person I'd have asked, Mr. Clew. I am perfectly aware of your feelings toward me."

"Does the FBI like you any better?" he asked.

"They don't have a file either. One is moved to wonder why. Even dead, she should still have a file."

"CIA?"

"They have files on several Elizabeth Strides, all of whom have claimed to be the Black Angel and none are the genuine article. And those people need me. They wouldn't have lied. So I'm reduced to coming to you, not hat in hand, but offering a generous quid pro quo, Mr. Clew. Do you want this envelope or not?"

"And if she can't be found? Or if she's really dead?"

"You would have to convince me of that."

"If I do find her . . . and that's still a big if, why would she agree to see you?"

"You can give her this message. 'He isn't dead either.' Say those words and she'll know what you mean."

"Who is 'he'?"

"It's a personal matter, Mr. Clew."

She was running late. It was almost seven. Her three dinner guests were due very shortly and Elizabeth still hadn't showered and changed. The meal that she'd prepared was almost ready, however. All that remained was to light her gas grill. After that, she could be dressed in twenty minutes.

She'd stepped onto her patio to fire the grill when she heard police sirens in the distance. She paused to listen, as most people would, to determine where the sirens seemed to be headed and to wonder what might have happened. She then went about her task, as most people would. She had felt no sense of alarm.

That in itself was remarkable, she supposed. She stood for a moment looking at her reflection in the sliding glass door to her patio. Look at you, she thought. Relaxed and at peace. Still young, still healthy and living a life that you never would have believed to be possible. Having friends who know who you are, what you've been, and it simply doesn't matter to them. Who'd have thought that your best friends would be Muslims.

It was not so long ago that the sound of sirens would have triggered a less passive response. She realized that if they were coming for her they would not be likely to announce their approach. Even so, she would have erred on the side of caution. She would have moved calmly but quickly.

Elizabeth Stride would have gone to a closet where she kept a blue duffel, packed and ready, well hidden. It contained cash and weapons and two changes of clothing. One change consisted of tennis attire. Tennis whites tend to make their wearer invisible because they're so common in this part of the country. What the mind categorizes, it tends to dismiss. The other change of clothing was all black, head to toe. The inner garment was a snug-fitting jumpsuit. The several outer layers were all shapeless by design. It was an outfit that she'd worn many times in broad daylight. Later on, it was better for night work.

The duffel held a pair of dark wigs and a pair of theatrical contact lenses that would mask the distinctive amber color of her eyes. It also contained two sets of false documents and about a million dollars worth of diamonds.

Within seconds she would have been out of her house. She would have been walking, not running, toward a spot she'd selected from which she could watch unobserved. If the sirens passed her by, nothing lost; she'd go back home. If they'd converged at her address, she would have vanished.

But on Hilton Head Island where she had made her new life, and especially in Sea Pines, her gated community, all that a siren usually meant was that some older resident had fallen ill and that someone had called 911. Less often, it meant that some inattentive tourist had driven off the road and hit a tree or a deer. Police sirens seldom meant that a crime had been committed. There was crime on the island, but not much and mostly petty, almost all of it nonviolent in nature. Almost none of it took place within the gated communities. They were wealthy, therefore tempting, but not worth the risk. Most had only one exit, easily blocked, and all were well guarded and patrolled.

An exception, of course, was that episode two years ago when the bounty hunters came to the island. But to her great surprise, they had not come for her. They had come for the women who were now her closest friends. She saw them first and they died here.

It was far from over. The men who had sent the bounty hunters turned out to have a great deal at stake. They sent some others, three Algerian fanatics. The Algerians came by boat, across the Atlantic, to do what the bounty hunters had failed to do. The Algerians, however, were out of control. All they cared about was killing on the greatest scale possible. They intended to wipe out every person on this island. They intended to turn it into a desert for a thousand years into the future.

It had almost happened. It was a very near thing. There were sirens, many sirens, on that day as well. But few knew how close to death they had come. The federal authorities had gone to great lengths to keep the attack out of the media. It might have caused panic along the whole eastern seaboard if those living there knew just how vulnerable they were. At the very least, it would have caused millions of tourists to re-think their vacation destinations. That alone would bring economic ruin.

A dozen or so suffered radiation poisoning, but they were lied to as to its cause. They were told that they'd contracted scarlet fever. An isolated outbreak. They symptoms were similar if the exposure was light enough. None of them died. The toll could have been twenty thousand. They would never know that they were alive because Martin had given his own life to save them.

They would not have known anyway because part of the cover-up involved Martin not even being here. He couldn't have been. He was already dead. The authorities had con-trived a romantic fiction that Martin, the year before, had put a gun to his head because he could no longer live without her. And if she, Elizabeth, had pre-deceased Martin, she could not have been part of this either. The problem, there, however, was that she was indeed here. Her name was in the phone book. E, period, Stride. Her last name was even on her mailbox.

"Very dumb, Elizabeth," Martin said more than once. "God forbid that those who hunt you should be inconvenienced. This way they can send you a bomb through the mail and save a fortune in travel expenses."

He would not have understood. She wanted to be real again. She wanted to live like everyone else and to try to find the person she'd been before all the pain and the blood. But, of course, he was right. That was pushing it. That was dumb.

The authorities solved that problem through a simple device. They created a file on the Elizabeth Stride whose name was in the Hilton Head phonebook. The photo in that file was of her next door neighbor, a woman almost eighty years old. That file showed that she was a widow who'd moved here from Warren, Ohio. Clearly not the Black Angel. Look elsewhere, not here. There was no Martin Kessler here either.

She lit the gas grill. She felt her eyes growing moist. It was not from the gas. It was from Martin again. "Don't keep doing this yourself," she muttered softly.

Damn him.

He didn't die to save all these people. That's another romantic fiction right there. He died because to him, this was just one more adventure. He died because it probably never occurred to him that one day his lunatic luck might run out. He died because he didn't have the sense that God gave him. He should never have come to this island.

She'd told him not to come. She'd told him not to try to find her. She'd told him, "No, Martin. I don't love you. I don't."

She'd told him, "What's more, you bring nothing but trouble. If it doesn't find you, you find it, and I'm tired. I'm tired of living with a price on my head. You're as hunted as I am, but with you it's a game. You don't avoid them; you entice them. You revel in outwitting them. And when we've outdistanced them, at least for a while, you'll get bored and go looking for some dive of a saloon that has two or three Harleys parked out front. You with your damned Swisher Sweets.

She'd told him, "I've had it. I want a life, Martin. I want to have friends. Normal people. Women friends."

She'd said, "I want to do the things that normal people do. I want to go shopping, play tennis, perhaps take up golf. I want, for a change, to walk into a restaurant, not having to check out the exits in advance and not having to scan every face in the room."

She'd said, "I don't love you. You don't love me either. What we are is a habit and a bad one at that."

She'd said all these things to him. And other things just as hurtful. She'd thought most of it was true when she said it.

Did she love him? Well, yes. But she didn't know it then. Was she grateful to him? Sure. He'd saved her life more than once. He'd stayed at her bedside for almost six months after she had been shot in Romania. And later, much later, he'd gone back to Europe and spread the word that she'd died in the States. She should have thanked him for that. She never did.

She was grateful, above all, that he had saved the life of the girl who had become like a daughter to her. Young Aisha was the one the bounty hunters were after. Aisha was the heir to considerable property in and around Cairo, Egypt. She had an uncle who was desperate to gain control of that property. The uncle, and the people with whom he did business were willing to kill anyone who stood in their way. But under the law, it couldn't be touched unless Aisha could be found and brought back to Egypt where her uncle would become her legal guardian. Or unless it could be proven that she's dead.

The bounty hunters found her, they took her, they hid her, until they could arrange to have her flown out. It was Martin who found them. She and Martin got her back. The bounty hunters died where they stood. Then her uncle's associates sent in the Algerians with instructions to kill her and be done with it. Instead, every one of them died on this island or in the waters around it. Even the uncle and the uncle's associates. They all died, but Martin died with them.

Aisha was fourteen years old when this happened. Very brave, but still very young. She'd been living here, in hiding, sent here with false papers by her parents who had reason to fear for her life and who, themselves, were soon to be murdered. How well she had accepted that terrible loss. Aisha's strong Muslim faith had sustained her. It was a faith that Elizabeth had at one time despised. Then, it was a faith that she almost wished that she shared when she saw how it had comforted Aisha. It was Aisha, in fact, who had comforted her in the weeks after Martin Kessler died.

Damn him.

Damn you, Martin.

You could have survived.

All you had to do, if you hadn't been so . . . you . . . was to let them at least try to save you.

Elizabeth forced herself to shake off the memory. She did not want to think about this any more. She did not want to think about Martin. She went into her bathroom and turned on the shower, stripping out of her clothing as it ran. She avoided looking at herself in the mirror. She did not want to see her scars either. She stepped under the spray and lathered herself thoroughly before rinsing hot and then cold. She patted herself dry and returned to her bedroom where she'd laid out the dress and the shoes she had chosen. The dress was oriental, full length, a soft yellow, with an embroidered ivy vine at one shoulder. Very soft, very cool, very feminine, she thought. She had just the right bracelets to go with it.

She still heard the sirens. Perhaps more than before. And they did seem to sound more urgent than usual. She could hear the whooping sounds that police cruisers make when they want other vehicles to get out of their way. And now the harsh bleat of a fire truck. They were nevertheless headed in the opposite direction. They grew farther and farther away.

Her three dinner guests were now a few minutes late. They were probably held up by that activity. Just as well. She could use the time to touch up her hair and to do a final check in the kitchen. She'd set a table for four on her

screened-in porch that looked out on a tidal lagoon. She saw
that there were just enough clouds in the sky to promise a
colorful sunset. She had prepared a nice salad of fresh fruit,
mostly citrus. The main course, from the grill, would be a
butterflied lamb that had been marinating most of the day.
Dessert would be a blueberry cobbler that she'd made. She'd
never tried one before and she'd burned it just a bit, but a
sprinkling of brown sugar would hide the charred edges. In
any case, the sun would have set by that time. They'd be eating it by candlelight. Perhaps no one would notice.

She had chosen a wine, a good cabernet, even though her
guests would probably decline it in favor of iced tea or
Pepsi. All three were Muslims, but not equally devout. There
was Jasmine who'd converted to Islam while in prison, but
had yet to fully embrace those teachings that related to di-
etary laws. Jasmine saw little harm in an occasional Jack
Daniels and even less harm in a pork chop.

Elizabeth had never asked why she'd been in prison. But
she knew that Jasmine, who was black and had grown up in
Brooklyn, had once been a drug addict and probably a dealer
and possibly a prostitute as well. Not that it mattered. Nor
did her real name. The person she was before she became
Jasmine was a person who no longer existed.

Well, perhaps not entirely. She had not lost her street
smarts; the hard edge was still there, and she could still, in
her thirties, have done well as a hooker. Good body, chiseled
features and a big easy laugh. She would still have no trouble stopping traffic.

Nadia Halaby, the second of her guests, had been a Muslim from birth. She was born in Algeria to a well-to-do family, but educated in France. Nadia was a graduate of the
Sorbonne and still kept an apartment in Paris. She'd grown
up playing tennis, stayed with it through school, and eventually won several amateur titles before briefly turning professional. She was now an instructor at a tennis academy
where talented young hopefuls came to train.

Nadia, however, was much more than that. And her tennis academy was much more than that. While in France, she

had set up a safe house of sorts for Muslim women who had
fled from the homelands. That first one was attacked and
under constant threat. Nadia fled to this country, flew those
women here with her, and set up a much larger one on this
island. These were women who had fled the oppression of
their sex in their various Islamic homelands. Some wanted
education that had been denied them. Some ran from mar-
riages that had been arranged for them. A few had talents,
artistic or otherwise, that they had been forbidden to pursue.
They were, in the eyes of those Algerian terrorists, no better
than whores and already lost to God. Such women, if found,
were to be stoned or burned and so should those who'd given
them shelter.

Young Aisha was no runaway. Aisha's mother had known
Nadia and was one of her supporters. When it became clear
that Aisha's life was in danger, Aisha's mother knew where
to send her because she knew that Nadia would protect her
with her life. But the bounty hunters tracked her and, later,
the fanatics. When the Algerians realized that it wasn't just
Aisha, when they were told that all those runaways were living here as well, not to mention the notorious Nadia Halaby,
it seemed that Allah himself must have led them to this island. The Koran, according to their reading of that book, en-
joined them to "make wide slaughter of the enemies of
God." Those words are in there, but they refer to invaders.
Nazi armies, for example. Not children.

Elizabeth, again, tried to push this from her mind. This
was not a time to indulge in old sorrows. This was a bright
and lovely occasion. Aisha had turned sweet sixteen. Elizabeth dearly wished that her parents could have lived to see
the splendid young lady that their daughter had become. But
they would not have been surprised. They had raised her
after all. And, according to Aisha, they're still around anyway, so make that five guests instead of three.

Nadia says that Aisha is the image of her mother and she
says that Aisha's mother was gorgeous. The same enormous
dark eyes, the same raven's wing hair except that Aisha wore
a much shorter cut now. The same skin coloring under her

tan; it was somewhere between olive and gold. The same ultra-wide smile, the same perfect complexion and, according to Nadia, the same heart.

Aisha's only fault, thought Elizabeth, was her tennis game. She was getting frustratingly good. Elizabeth had played her two or three times a week and she hadn't beaten Aisha in months. Not legitimately, anyway. Sometimes Aisha would have the final set in her pocket and she'd suddenly start double faulting and such to let Elizabeth back in the match. And of course she denied that she was just being kind, but she does that with other opponents as well. No killer instinct. She should work on that. Save the kindness for after the match.

Perhaps the new racquet she'd bought Aisha for her birthday would encourage her to go for the jugular more often. It had a good name for it. The Wilson Sledge Hammer. She'd seen Aisha admiring it in the pro shop.

Suddenly, Elizabeth felt an unwelcome chill. What if Aisha and Nadia and Jasmine were late because they were the cause of those sirens? Someone after them again? No, don't even think it. Those sirens had seemed headed more toward the main gate than toward the tennis academy. Even so, Elizabeth stepped out onto her driveway. She waited and worried for another ten minutes until at last she saw Nadia's car coming.

Elizabeth didn't turn because her eyes were on the boat. She saw a woman's figure climbing up through the hatch. The woman was dressed in a dark business suit and she was holding a cell phone to her ear. She stood with one hand cupped over her eyes as if to shade them from the glare of the shore lights. She was looking directly at Elizabeth. Now a young man, or a boy, came through the hatch and joined her. Elizabeth took a breath. No, it wasn't a boy. It was a small, slender woman with red hair.

She said, "Aisha, turn now and walk back to the car."

"What's happening?"

"I'll be two steps behind you," said Elizabeth. "Just do it."

"Oh, boy. I'll try. But I think we're too late. Those two men came over. They're blocking the ramp."

Elizabeth turned. She saw that they had. And that they weren't so old after all. Now she saw that the woman with the cell phone was coming. She'd gestured to the smaller one, telling her to stay. The smaller one argued, but obeyed. She seemed angry. The one with the cell phone was approaching the ramp. Her eyes had yet to leave Elizabeth's.

Aisha took her hand. *"How much trouble are we in?"*

"I want you to leave. They won't stop you. Go now."

"Leave you here? I won't do that. Who are they, Elizabeth?"

The two men at the top of the ramp heard her name. The big one said, *"Hey, I told you. Did I tell you?"* The other said, *"I'll be damned."*

Elizabeth sighed. *"Hello, Billy. Hello, John."* Then she cursed herself under her breath.

Bannerman's people. She supposed she should have known.